⟨✓ W9-BLR-157

Also by David L. Golemon

Event

Legend

Ancients

Leviathan

Primeval

Legacy

"The Roswell Incident—whether legend, fact, or some combination of both—has inspired countless novels and movies over the years, but David L. Golemon's *Event* peels back the layers of Roswell with refreshing originality. The action is spectacularly cinematic, the characters compelling, and the story is a flat-out adrenaline rush that pits real-world, cutting-edge military technology against a literally out-of-this-world threat. Even better, the Event Group itself is one of the best fictional agencies to arise in the literature of government conspiracies."

> —*New York Times* bestselling authors
> Judith & Garfield Reeves-Stevens

"Fans of UFO fiction will find this a great read, and fans of military fiction won't be disappointed."

> —SFsignal.com on *Event*

"Imagine mixing in a blender a Tom Clancy novel with the movie *Predator* and the television series *The X-Files*. . . . [R]eaders who enjoy nonstop action and lots of flying bullets will enjoy Golemon's series." —*Library Journal*

"Golemon puts his military experience to good use in this promising [series] . . . evokes some of the early work of Preston and Child." —*Publishers Weekly*

Praise for David L. Golemon and the Event Group series

"A tale worthy of the giants of the genre like Clive Cussler, James Rollins, and Matthew Reilly, *Legend* is a definite must-read for action and adventure fans. Don't miss it."
—Megalith.com on *Legend*

"The author . . . draws the reader in with an intriguing prologue . . . satisfying adventure."
—*Publishers Weekly* on *Legend*

"Golemon can write action sequences with the best of them, and he lands a solid uppercut with this book. The depth of science fiction . . . is surprising and ingenious."
—SFSignal.com on *Legend*

"Golemon combines his typical action-adventure fare with more thriller elements this time, and he focuses more on the personal stakes of his characters. . . . Golemon knows how to make readers turn the pages, and *Primeval* will only further enhance his reputation."
—*Booklist*

"Fans of *Twenty Thousand Leagues Under the Sea* will enjoy Golemon's recasting of the Jules Verne novel."
—*Publishers Weekly* on *Leviathan*

"Golemon's third novel in the Event Group series proves to be his best yet. . . . a mix of the James Rollins action-heavy adventure, the military gadgetry of Tom Clancy, the pacing of the television series *24*, and the conspiracy theories devoured by fans of the radio show *Coast to Coast AM*."
—*Booklist* on *Ancients*

MORE...

RIPPER

DAVID L. GOLEMON

St. Martin's Paperbacks

NOTE: If you purchased this book without a cover you should be aware that this book is stolen property. It was reported as "unsold and destroyed" to the publisher, and neither the author nor the publisher has received any payment for this "stripped book."

This is a work of fiction. All of the characters, organizations, and events portrayed in this novel are either products of the author's imagination or are used fictitiously.

RIPPER

Copyright © 2012 by David L. Golemon.
Excerpt from *Carpathian* copyright © 2013 by David L. Golemon.

All rights reserved.

For information address St. Martin's Press, 175 Fifth Avenue, New York, NY 10010.

Library of Congress Catalog Card Number: 2012010066

ISBN: 978-1-250-02540-1

Printed in the United States of America

St. Martin's Press hardcover edition / July 2012
St. Martin's Paperbacks edition / April 2013

St. Martin's Paperbacks are published by St. Martin's Press, 175 Fifth Avenue, New York, NY 10010.

10 9 8 7 6 5 4 3 2 1

For my granddaughter, Kiera—
the most beautiful flower in the world

. . . within the empty streets of London
upon the witching hour, a specter of the past awakens,
its purpose, to devour . . .

. . . So remember my friends
you can close your eyes to reality,
but never to a memory . . .

**—Unknown author,
from the poem "From Hell"**

PROLOGUE

November 8, 1888
Whitechapel, London

Mary Jane Kelly stood silent and still as the man watched her from a rickety chair in the darkened corner of her shabby two-bed flat. The oil lamp had been dimmed on that side of the small room so the only thing Mary could clearly discern were the shiny white spats that covered the tops of the man's expensive shoes. The ornate cane the invisible visitor used was propped between those shoes and would move only when the man spoke in his accented English.

Mary tried her best to control her breathing as she felt the man's eyes roll over her in that infernal darkness. But it was the well-dressed man's voice that unnerved her like no other she had ever heard—it was as though she were hearing the voice of the Big Bad Wolf from the nursery rhymes she heard when she was but a child. She could feel the rage boiling just beneath the surface of her visitor as the hate emanated from the dark recesses of the room.

"You're so lovely my dear. Perhaps you could sing me a little song, something sweet—a song from your childhood. It will help cool my blood."

For the first time the man blinked and she saw the glow

of the eyes. At first she thought it was a trick of her imagination, but then the eyes flashed again, and this time Mary knew she had seen a ring of yellow and one of red surrounding the black abyss of his pupils, which were the largest she had ever seen.

Mary closed her eyes as she stood before the man. In her fear she tugged on the white linen apron she always wore over that same moth-eaten skirt and blouse she wore at least four days of the week. She opened her mouth to comply with the visitor's request, but any memory of a happy childhood song had fled her terrified mind. She tried to open her mouth once more and the first words of a song came pouring out.

"London . . . bridge . . . is falling . . . ," her cracked and halting words stopped as Mary sobbed, and then her right hand shot upward and covered her mouth to stop the scream that threatened to escape her constricting throat.

In the far corner the glint of metal in the dim light and then a gold coin appeared as if by magic. Its glimmer shown in the weak light from the lamp. She could see that the coin was one she had seen before on more than one occasion in the drinking establishments that lined the streets of Whitechapel. It was a twenty-dollar American-minted gold double eagle.

"Perhaps this will persuade you to help soothe the animal that is awakening inside of me. Sing well and there will be two more of these at the end of our . . . session."

The word *session* sent chills up and down the fine skin of Mary's neck and back. She knew who this man was. The entire city of London had been terrified of what and who this man was in the months leading up to this night. Her eyes went from the sparkling coin to the door. The slide lock was in place, and Mary knew she would never be able to open the door in time before the man would be upon her. She opened her mouth to start the song again, but the only sound to exit her mouth was an even louder sob than the one a moment before.

The coin disappeared and the man made a sound that made Mary Kelly cringe. It was so animalistic that she came near to swooning. It was a low growl that came from the deepest recesses of the faceless man's throat. She kept her eyes closed.

"Very well," the words were far harsher than the ones uttered before them. "Perhaps we should conclude our business." The cane moved between the man's feet and then the tip was tapped three times in succession. "You may remove your clothes my dear." At the end of the request, the word *dear* was sounded through a growl, as if a wolf were speaking to her from the darkness of a long-ago dead forest.

Mary removed her apron first and let it fall to the floor. She heard the man remove something from his breast pocket and then realized he was holding a piece of paper.

"No, no. Fold your clothes as you remove them. Neatness is a virtue my dear—a virtue!"

The shouting of the last two words drowned out Mary's involuntary cry as she reached down and hurriedly picked up the apron.

"You have a physician that treats you and your . . . colleagues for the harsher social diseases and problems that may arise with unwanted conception?"

"Yes, Doctor Freemantle," Mary said through whispered words that actually made her feel weaker than she was.

"You are with child?"

"Oh," she moaned through her tears.

"You are with child?" he asked once again with the low-based growl sounding once more with a steadily increasing crescendo.

"Yes," Mary answered as she closed her eyes tightly.

The man suddenly stood in the darkness and emerged into the dim light. This time there was not the glimmer of gold that shown in the dim lighting, but the chromed blade of a large knife that froze Mary Kelly's heart.

The next twenty minutes were the most violent of all the attacks that took place in Whitechapel that summer and fall.

Jack the Ripper was not the man the newspapers described as meticulous. It was an attack that symbolized the violence of the times that were coming and would lead to a legend being born that would haunt mankind for a century to come.

Blood flew as the flesh of Mary Kelly, the attractive brunette that had no enemy outside of her landlord, was cut and hacked until the young woman was unrecognizable as anything resembling a human being.

Outside the rundown flat in Whitechapel, the fog started to roll in from the river.

The man's eyes watched as the policemen came and went from the small room that had quickly become the most vicious crime scene London had ever been witness to. He saw the familiar form of the chief inspector for the municipal police force as he stepped from the small flat. The tall man and his constant companion pushed through the crowd of curious onlookers who had gathered after the body of Mary Kelly had been discovered at eleven that morning. As the two men approached the chief inspector they could both see he was not feeling that well after seeing the body. The chief inspector gathered his wits and then noticed the man in the tweed suit with his companion close beside.

"You two again," the inspector said as he angrily eyed the two men. "I am obliged to ask what you gentlemen are doing here at my crime scene."

"Chief Inspector Abberline," the taller of the two men said as he removed his bowler hat. "What have we here?" he asked as he first eyed the gathered residents of the area and then the house itself.

Frederick George Abberline looked the man over and then his anger rose even more than a moment before. He took the man by the arm and pulled him away from onlookers who took no notice of the three men as the body was finally being removed from the shabby flat. Abberline glanced at the covered remains and cringed as an exposed arm of the victim fell free of the sheet that covered her.

"My cooperation with Her Majesty's armed forces has come to an end until I get some explanation of your interest in this and the other murders, do you understand Colonel?"

Colonel Albert Stanley stopped and pulled his arm free

of the chief inspector's tight grasp. He gave the smaller detective a look that broached the subject of him being manhandled. The colonel looked around and then reached into his tweed jacket and pulled out a sealed envelope and handed it over to the inspector. "Perhaps this will be explanation enough."

The chief inspector, a man who had handled the Ripper case from the beginning, turned the white envelope over and looked at the wax seal that held the document secure. The image in wax of twin facing lions made Abberline close his eyes. He then opened them and quickly broke the wax seal. He pulled the single sheet of paper free and read the letter. It was brief and to the point.

> *Chief Inspector Frederick Abberline,*
> *Upon reading this order you will give full cooperation to Colonel Albert Stanley of my loyal Black Watch concerning the matters taking place in Whitechapel. Cooperation I may add to the point that you will supply the colonel with any and all information related to the two cases you are involved in. His voice may be considered my voice, and the voice of Her Majesty's government.*
> *HRM*
> *Victoria*

After reading the words on the fine paper, the chief inspector folded the note and replaced it in the envelope. He started to place the document in his coat pocket, but the small man standing next to the colonel reached out and took the order from the inspector's hand. He replaced the order in his own coat pocket.

"Apologies, Chief Inspector, but the letter was for your eyes only. As far as your colleagues are concerned, Her Majesty's request for your cooperation with her armed forces was never given. You never read nor ever saw the letter. Is that clear?"

Abberline didn't respond. He glared at the taller man before him.

"Now, the circumstances surrounding this latest victim, what can you tell me to this point?"

Abberline finally came to the conclusion that he was in a corner. The two men standing before him had been seen by him at every crime scene generated by the Ripper case since the start. They would show up, look, listen, and then vanish into the day or the night.

"Quid pro quo, Colonel—or tit for tat as they say, why don't you tell me just what Her Majesty's army has done here in Whitechapel? Don't bother to deny it—I can see it in your eyes. I have been a policeman for far too long not to know. And now my suspicions have been confirmed by the queen herself. Just what is it that you have unleashed in my city?"

The colonel stood his ground and then looked from the corpse being loaded onto a rickety wagon to those of the chief inspector. His dark eyes bored into Abberline's. "The army has nothing to do with this mess Inspector. The queen has nothing to do with it. Perhaps you can keep that in mind if you like . . . well, if you like living. This thing may be well over your head, both professionally and politically—now, the crime scene please. More importantly, was the poor girl . . . how should I put this . . . was she missing something that the newspaper boys will never hear about?"

Abberline heard the harshness of the last words and then made his choice—one made in the name of self-preservation. He pulled his small notebook from his pocket and then looked at the last five pages he had written.

"Mary Jane Kelly, prostitute. Her body was discovered this morning by the landlord's assistant. Age, twenty-five years. Last seen, or I should say last heard from, at one a.m. last night. A neighbor heard the snippets of a song coming from the room at that time. Nothing after."

"A song?" The colonel looked from Abberline to the shanty standing before him. "That doesn't seem to fit our man's profile at all, does it Chief Inspector?"

Abberline was in no mood to expand on his written notes. "For the first time we will have crime scene photographs of the victim."

"Good, I expect copies to be forwarded to my office as soon as they are ready."

Again, Abberline didn't comment or respond to the colonel. "The woman's clothing was folded neatly and placed on a chair next to the bed." Abberline swallowed and then continued reading from his notes. "Her carotid artery was severed. This was the main cause of death."

"A little less than the others, perhaps this was an isolated murder," the small man standing next to the colonel said as if he were bored to death.

"Allow the chief inspector to continue Sergeant Meyer. I believe he has more to add."

"Her attacker had hacked off her nose and ears, slashed her, and removed much of her face, leaving her with no features that would tell if she were a man or a woman. Her body had been sliced and split open like a melon. I believe from my viewing that some, or even all, of her organs had been removed and left upon the table top. You could never tell that the woman had been pregnant at all—that is what you are worried about, isn't it Colonel? That is the one item that warns that this is the man you have been tracking . . . or is it watching?"

Only the sergeant reacted to the last bit of information and the innuendo from the inspector. He turned away and swallowed heavily as the chief inspector had done moments earlier as he realized what had been done to the whore inside her rundown flat.

Abberline lowered his small notebook and looked Stanley in the eyes. "This was not a murder, Colonel. This was a butchering. Something akin to a monstrous rage took place in that room. Violence was done to her just as the other victims. You see, I did a little investigation you didn't know about, sir. Every one of the victims was with child, no more than three months, but pregnant nonetheless. And this fact is verifiable through their doctor."

"Ah yes, the physician who usually treats the whores in this district for various social diseases—Doctor Jonathan Freemantle, a rather despicable sort who just happened to have a severe heart attack this very morning. Pity he cannot verify what you have learned." The man's eyes gave credence to the warning he had just delivered. "Thank you, Chief Inspector Abberline. Your cooperation will be reported to the very highest authority. Now please remember to send me the pictures of the crime scene, that's a good chap."

With those words, Abberline watched as the colonel and sergeant turned and left, looking around casually as if they were just on a morning stroll.

"I think I would have better luck finding the Ripper by following you my dear colonel, than by chasing my own tail in Whitechapel."

Frederick George Abberline, chief inspector for the London Metropolitan Police, sat at the small table where he normally found himself at such a late hour. He had to come here to wind down and relax before heading home to a restless night's sleep after the events of the past year. The Mary Kelly case five months before had been the last of the killings, but that didn't stop the nightmares Abberline faced every night when he went home to his darkened flat.

The restaurant was small and owned in part by a former colleague of his from the London police force. The small eatery was kept open late for policemen changing shifts from all areas of the city. Even at 1:20 a.m. the restaurant was filled.

The area of the establishment with the most boisterous patrons was the separate barroom where men of the law hoisted pints of bitters and other liquids designed to numb the senses of a dark and lonely city that was reeling from the nightmare of their times.

Chief Inspector Abberline sat and read a report from one of his detectives regarding a recent kidnapping. Abberline shook his head and then reached for his cup of tea. He grimaced at the weakness of the drink as he placed the cup back onto the saucer. During the times of the Ripper case the inspector had become used to drinking strong coffee, of which he was trying to wean himself. Still, the weak tea did nothing for his palate. Abberline placed the report on the table and closed his eyes as he remembered the tiredness he felt for the past year's hard work and knew long before this moment that he was no longer meant to be a police inspector. The horrors he had seen in the recent past had successfully driven his desire to help people straight from his heart. The world was mad and he knew if he didn't leave the service he would end up just as insane as the men and women he chased.

Abberline leaned back as a waiter brought him his kidney pie. Once the waiter had left the inspector placed his napkin in his lap. He stopped short of his fork digging into the crust of the meat pie. He tapped the cooked dough several times with the tip of his fork and then glanced outside and into the thickening fog beyond the large window that looked out onto the street. Its white veil had moved into the city not long after his extended shift had ended. He turned away and looked at his meal one more time and tossed the fork onto the table and then waved the waiter over and handed him his cup and saucer.

"Bring me coffee, please," he said, and the waiter turned away. Abberline thought quickly and then called out. "Apologies old boy, but would you make that a double scotch?"

"Double scotch, sir," the waiter said and then moved off.

The inspector grimaced as he took in the hot kidney pie and then slid it as far away from him as his arm could reach.

"Inspector Abberline?" the voice said from his shoulder.

Abberline closed his eyes, angry at the interruption. He knew if he opened his eyes and saw a newspaper man, who was not allowed inside this particular building, he would be tempted to use the butter knife in front of him to stab the man in the heart.

Instead of following through with his imagined murder scenario, he said, "Yes?" as he opened his eyes and saw a rather tall, thin man standing next to him. The well-dressed gentleman was twisting his hat with anxious hands.

"Sir, my name is Robert Louis Balfour Stevenson, perhaps my name is not unfamiliar to you? I wrote you a letter three months ago?"

Abberline looked over the tall man with the brimming moustache. He saw that the man didn't look well at all as he nervously twisted his hat into ungodly disarray. The words were spoken with a barely disguised Scottish accent. As he saw the man looking down with worry etched into his dark eyes, Abberline gestured to the empty chair across from him.

"Who wouldn't recognize the great Mr. Robert Louis Stevenson? Sir, please, have a seat."

Abberline watched as the man hesitated. Stevenson walked the short distance to the chair, but then looked lost as to what to do with his hat.

"We lack the formality of one of the nicer establishments Mr. Stevenson. Just place your hat on the table, it looks as if it could use a rest."

Stevenson looked flustered as he glanced at the crumpled hat. He grimaced and then placed it on the white table cloth. He half smiled as he pulled the chair out and sat.

"May I offer you some refreshment? I know it's a little late, but I just ordered scotch for myself."

Stevenson swallowed and then nodded his head meekly. The chief inspector waved at the waiter standing at the bar and signaled for two drinks instead of the one.

Abberline turned and watched the man sitting before him. He was silent and waited for the famous author to state his piece.

Stevenson looked at the men around him as if he had stepped into a lion's den.

"If you wrote me a post in advance of this date, I can tell you I have received none." Abberline then fixed the man with a hard stare. "So, if your lost post was to attempt to get information on . . . well, on one of my cases, I'm afraid that is quite out of the question."

"Excuse me?" Stevenson asked, looking bewildered for a moment. "Oh, oh, you think I'm here to ask you about the Ripper case for a possible book? That was not the intent of my letter to you Chief Inspector. And, I not only sent two letters from the States where I was on holiday, I sent three more upon my arrival in London."

"Isn't that why a famous author such as you would visit such an establishment as this at one o'clock in the morning, to get a good yarn to write yet another lurid and morbid novel?"

"No, Chief Inspector, I am not here for that. In case you hadn't noticed I have already done my horror novel and have no intention of ever writing something like that again."

Abberline raised his brows at the man's statement. He knew that Stevenson's foray into the horror genre came with his novella the *Strange Case of Dr. Jekyll and Mr. Hyde*, published two years before to far-above-average sales. He was surprised at the author's venomous reply to his reference to that particular story.

"So, Mr. Stevenson, what you're saying is that your letter had nothing to do with the Ripper case? If you weren't seeking information, then what pray tell prompted the notes?"

Once more Robert Louis Stevenson turned and watched the men of London's finest as they talked in loud voice and laughed with even more zest. He finally looked satisfied that no one was listening. As he leaned back to face the chief inspector, the waiter returned and placed the two drinks on the table. Stevenson immediately took a sip and then grimaced. He placed the glass back down and then looked at Abberline who ignored his own double scotch as he waited for the writer to answer his question. He himself was aware that he shouldn't be discussing the Ripper case with anyone from outside his offices.

"I am not here to ask questions of you Mr. Abberline. I wouldn't do that," he said as he once more nervously looked around. "I am being followed, have been ever since docking three days ago in East Hampton. I suspected even in San Francisco I had company following my every move."

"Mysterious indeed, worthy of a novel in and of itself, wouldn't you say?" Abberline waited for a reaction; he didn't have to wait long.

"I believe I stated sir that I would never attempt such a literary farce again," he said with his eyes bulging. "Dr. Jekyll and Mr. Hyde may have contributed to—"

Abberline watched as the words froze in the throat of one of the most articulate men in the history of literature. After a brief flare of emotion, Stevenson closed his eyes and then shook his head.

"I know who your Jack the Ripper is."

Abberline froze. His eyes never left those of Stevenson. "I believe you have to explain that rather remarkable statement, Mr. Stevenson."

"I met him in California during my research for Dr. Jekyll and Mr. Hyde. He is an American, a professor of chemistry, and . . . and . . . something to do with flowers. I'm sorry, but my notes for the book have been misplaced, or stolen, I am not sure which. But I'm sure it had something to do with flowers, which was part of his work he wouldn't discuss."

Abberline looked at the man sitting before him and knew that the odds of his notes being misplaced was the better of the two scenarios. He could smell the paranoia coming from the frightened man before him.

"Who is this gentleman?"

With one last look around the crowded eatery, Robert Louis Stevenson related how he had met Professor Lawrence Ambrose and researched material for his upcoming novel, the *Strange Case of Dr. Jekyll and Mr. Hyde*, due to the good professor's work with aggression and metabolism changes that could possibly occur in the human body. Stevenson spoke for close to an hour.

Abberline listened politely, refraining from making faces or leaning one way or the other in his uncomfortable silence at the fantastic tale being related to him from one of the most influential people in all of the Empire.

Silence hung over the table and the two double scotches sat untouched in front of the two men.

"Mr. Stevenson, you are an educated man, probably far more than myself, so I will be careful when I use the words *too fantastic to believe*, sir."

"Which . . ."

"Everything, Mr. Stevenson, from the science you claim

this man has developed to Her Majesty's government trying to silence you. Take your pick, sir, it all sounds rather far-fetched." Abberline checked his anger at this obvious waste of time. He reached out, took hold of his glass, and raised it to his lips; with one last shake of his head he downed the double dose of fire without a grimace.

"Chief Inspector, I saw this man actually change into something he is not. Not just changes in his demeanor and attitude, but physical changes to his body as well."

Abberline placed his glass on the table in front of him and then reached for Stevenson's untouched glass. He pulled the glass forward but hesitated before he drank.

"And this, this . . . Dr. Jekyll, and your Mr. Hyde, how did you come about meeting him in America?" He finally lifted the second glass and downed that also, all the while holding his gaze on the famous author.

"Inspector, this needs to be resolved now, and not wait for—"

The angry gaze stopped Stevenson from continuing. He realized that policemen do things at their own pace and are even slower sometimes when confronted with an obvious truth. Robert Louis Stevenson could see it in the chief inspector's eyes—he believed his story.

"I met the gentleman in San Francisco three years ago through a friend who works with Corvallis Lens Company of London. He was there to deliver the most unique set of lenses ever created by his company. These lenses were specially ground, beveled, and buffed for the man who ordered them to use in his laboratory work. These lenses are so well constructed that Ambrose is now seeing things that were once only seen in the realm of the imagination. This man is actually discovering the origins of thought, the use of the human brain, and the power that is hidden in us all. The reason my friend thought I would get along with this professor was due to the fact that this man was slowly piecing together the most unique and advanced microscopic viewing system ever. Intrigued, I went to meet this man for my research."

"And this Professor Ambrose was accommodating?"

"As accommodating as anyone I have ever dealt with in the business world. He couldn't stop talking about his work into the naturally occurring aggression that occurs in all living animals. He scared me to the point I had to slow down the real science or my readers would have never understood it. He has the ability to change into something other than he is, and that was three years ago Chief Inspector."

"And you think your Jekyll and Hyde is my Ripper? Is that what you are saying, sir?"

"One and the same."

Abberline watched the man closely. He was as experienced as anyone in spotting someone not telling him the truth. But he could see from the demeanor of Stevenson that he was telling nothing but the truth—at least as far as he was concerned.

"As I said, my letters have been intercepted. I have written to you on many occasions, only to have my inquiries go unanswered. Finally, I had to come after hearing the news of this last victim of the Ripper."

"And why was that?" Abberline said as he continued to look at Stevenson for the lie that would soon surface.

"Because I finally have proof, Chief Inspector," Stevenson said actually smiling for the first time, and for the first time Abberline could see the exhaustion in the man's eyes and face. Stevenson reached into his pocket and brought out a folded daily. He swallowed and actually shivered as he opened the newspaper. "This is the *London Times*, but the picture I am about to show you was picked up by hundreds of newspapers around the world, and this one, the *San Francisco Chronicle* was no exception. This is why I came as fast as I could." He pushed the paper toward Abberline who looked from Stevenson down to the paper.

The picture was a rather famous one now. It was taken on the morning of Mary Kelly's murder. Abberline saw the picture of himself at the crime scene. He looked up at Stevenson without saying a word.

"Chief Inspector, that man standing next to you in the photograph?"

Abberline didn't have to look at the grainy photo again; he knew who Stevenson was talking about. It was Colonel Stanley of Her Majesty's Black Watch. Stevenson was pointing out the man who had dogged this Ripper case since the beginning.

"He's the man that was tailing me three years ago in the United States, and this very same man ransacked my room this very night."

"And you believe the Ripper case, your Jekyll and Hyde, and this gentleman are all wound together in a nice little ball? And that this Professor Ambrose is making monsters for whatever reason there may be for doing so."

Stevenson looked confounded. He closed his eyes, thinking he had failed to convince the chief inspector.

"When I met him, Ambrose was working closely with the military aspect of his medicinal application, that's all I know. The only evidence left from my research is this," Stevenson said as he pulled a small kerchief from his coat pocket and then looking around suspiciously once again, slowly slid the folded kerchief toward Abberline who made no move to touch the small bundle. Stevenson flipped the kerchief open and Abberline was left looking at a small square of what looked like dried clay.

"Interesting," Abberline said, still not even giving Stevenson the courtesy of leaning forward to look at the item.

Robert Louis Stevenson looked exasperated as he reached out and picked up the object and then slid over closer to the chief inspector.

"Do you know what this is?"

"I haven't the faintest."

"Chief Inspector, this is what is called a relief." Stevenson looked frustrated for a brief moment when he didn't see recognition in Abberline's face. "It's a proclamation. Or a warning . . . or maybe just a take. See this hole here at the top? Well, it used to be a hole, it's broken now after two thousand three hundred years. This was a warning placed on the line of retreat taken by the Greeks from Northern India. It's in Ancient Greek."

"Again, Mr. Stevenson, very interesting."

"See this here," Stevenson turned the tablet over, carefully exposing the inscription on the back. It was hard to read for Abberline, but Stevenson easily ran his finger across the ancient script. He made sure the chief inspector could see the inscription as he read. "It warns all Greeks to follow the line south and stay out of the jungle and beware the jhinn. It's like a genie from the *Arabian Nights*, only of course it's an ancient Indian legend that originates in the Delhi area and is virtually unknown throughout the world, and this tablet is the only historical reference to that legend. This placard was given to me by Ambrose with a tale that froze my blood."

"You have my interest piqued, sir," Abberline said as his eyes were locked on the strange-looking clay tablet.

"This tablet tells the tale of magic . . . magic that was used against an invading enemy. Truly the power of nature. Beasts that attack alone, in packs, they kill without remorse and follow their orders to the death. The Greeks were attacked from the North of India all the way through the heart of that country. They were running scared from something let loose upon them by a magician."

Abberline refused to say a word as Stevenson spoke. He thought he would let the man run his course.

"Do you even know what Greeks I am speaking of Chief Inspector? It was this retreat and the legend of the magic used against them that set Lawrence Ambrose on a trail of invention that has become murderous beyond measure. The professor researched the ancient legends of magic from all over the world, and in the deep valleys and vast area of India, he found it. And the legend was believed by one very important man in world history, and it was this man that sent Ambrose off in the right direction." Stevenson then turned the tablet over and showed Abberline the bust. When the policeman showed no sign of recognition, Stevenson almost angrily pointed to the word just below the relief of the ancient Greek. "Μέγας Ἀλέξανδρος, or in its more familiar tongue, Mégas Aléxandros," the writer said, smiling.

Chief Inspector Abberline looked from the clay tablet into the eyes of Stevenson.

"That signature on the warning is Alexander the Great of Macedonia."

"Now I have heard of him."

Robert Louis Stevenson rolled his eyes. "When he found he couldn't defeat the many armies of India, Alexander started heading south, looking for an escape route off the subcontinent. He left a rear guard of one thousand of his best men. For six hundred miles these men fought a running battle with a force of men that could not be killed. One would attack many. Tales of men in the attacks taking seven, eight arrows and still fighting. This tale is straight from the mouth and signature of Alexander the Great. You see, Ambrose discovered the facts behind the legend and the truth behind not just the magic of what happened to the Greeks, but the real chemical science behind the slaughter. There are many more tales of these . . . these Berserkers. It happened several more times, far more recently in India against the Raj, the uprisings, the slaughters of British soldiers by inferior forces of the Sikh and others. There always seems to be magic coming to the aid of the lesser armies inside of India. Why I . . . I—"

"I believe your tale, Mr. Stevenson," Abberline said directly.

"But, I thought—"

"The man in the picture is named Colonel Albert Stanley. He is Black Watch, the Queen's own. If this man Ambrose is who you say he is, he has powerful friends in the highest of places, Mr. Stevenson, far more influential men and women than I'm sure your address book could help but fall short of. This Colonel Stanley is in the Ripper case up to his eyes, and I smelled a rat long before you stepped into this room tonight. He's protecting someone, and this someone is possibly this Professor Lawrence Ambrose you met in America." Abberline quickly brought out his notepad and scribbled the names down.

"It had to be more than just that picture that convinced

you Chief Inspector. What was it?" Stevenson asked as he finally relaxed for the first time since entering the restaurant.

"It's not the evidence you brought Mr. Stevenson, but the terror in your eyes. For a man who wrote the most popular horror story since Frankenstein, you show an immense amount of fear when you mention this man's name, this Ambrose. I see and feel the fear coming off of you. That is why I believe you Mr. Stevenson."

The chief inspector turned away from Robert Louis Stevenson just as one of his men, Harold Washington, a veteran of the Ripper horrors, walked toward the table at a brisk pace, fast enough that Abberline's heart sank. He quickly raised his hand at the waiter for more drinks.

Washington was a young man who looked as though he had also lost his zeal for police work since the murders had begun in Whitechapel. If only the lad knew the real truth as he himself had just learned, he would have gone running into the night on his way to resign. Even with not knowing the truth of Mr. Stevenson's story, Abberline could see the young man's anger and his feelings of helplessness in his written reports on other crimes in the area. The boy was like him, he just couldn't do it any longer. With the Ripper investigation officially ended for at least Abberline and his department, he knew his career would end on that failure. The Ripper had escaped justice and the inspector knew it was because of interference from the palace. And now here was an independent witness, one that not even the queen could silence if he chose to go to the newspapers.

"Washington old boy, may I introduce Mr. Robert Louis Stevenson, I believe you may know of his work?"

"No, Chief Inspector, I do not know of him, and if you don't mind I'll also have what you just ordered from the bar."

Abberline tried not to show his surprise at the boy's request as he knew the young man was not a drinker. Washington drowned his worry and sorrow every night with the help of a young wife, not like the chief inspector, with libation.

"By all means, Washington, please have a seat and explain why a young man such as you would need a drink at this late hour, and whilst he is on duty."

Washington tossed his hat on the table and then sat, practically ignoring Abberline's disapproval and the way Stevenson looked at him. "I have just come from Whitechapel."

Abberline closed his eyes, fearing what the boy was about to say.

"That is over with. It's been five months since Mary Kelly departed this world for a better one," Abberline said as he raised his napkin and covered his lower face so the patrons couldn't see the mask he had become adept at placing over his emotions when it came to Whitechapel.

"I have closed and secured the scene. Only our people know about it, sir. I don't know how long we can keep others out of it." He leaned in closer to Abberline, trying to talk below a whisper so the stranger sitting at the table couldn't hear. "Two victims, a shavetail prostitute and one of our own boys in blue. The heads were completely removed, unlike the other murders, but the proximity to the hunting grounds of . . . ," he looked around to make sure no one was listening. His eyes locked on Robert Louis Stevenson and then back to Abberline, "you know who? I thought it best—"

The waiter brought their drinks and placed one each before the three men. Abberline ignored his while Washington and also Stevenson took the double scotch and drained the two glasses. "Chief Inspector, I do not know how long we can keep the area secured. You must come now."

Abberline opened his eyes and took in his young colleague. It seemed he was having a hard time swallowing, but he stood nonetheless. He braced himself against the table for the briefest of moments and then waved the waiter over and asked that the drinks and the untouched meal be placed on his account.

"Mr. Stevenson, I think you better come with us. I don't think the government is too happy about you having certain information."

"I'm not brave enough to take on the queen herself," the

writer said as he stood along with Washington and Abberline.

"Don't worry about that, sir, because after tonight the
queen may have to do some explaining herself . . . if that's
what she chooses to do after we stop this Ambrose . . .
tonight is the last night of the Ripper," Abberline said as he
slammed his hand down on the white tablecloth. "It ends
here, tonight."

More than just a few of the off-duty policemen saw the
famous chief inspector Frederick Abberline stumble as they
moved past their tables, and most nodded as they understood the man's possible drunkenness after what he had
been through with the Ripper case. After all, who more deserved to hoist a few now and again than the chief inspector? Most understood that Abberline had been witness to
one of the most horrific murder sprees in modern times.
What most didn't know however was the small fact that not
only had the murders started again, they were about to
spread across the seas to a place where few were afraid
of the dark—the Ripper was returning home.

The carriage and the twin black horses pulling it raced
through the streets of London cutting dangerously close to
the fog-shrouded corners where the gas lamps could not
penetrate. Abberline sat beside Robert Louis Stevenson with
Washington sitting across from them. The chief inspector
held on to the right-hand strap and swayed with the carriage
without saying a word. Stevenson tried his best to still his
shaking hands.

"Perhaps I better tell the driver to slow a bit in this
wretched fog, Inspector," Washington said through clenched
teeth as the carriage took another corner on its two right-
side wheels.

"Sergeant Anderson knows what he's doing," Abberline
said as he stared at nothing. Suddenly he pulled the window
down and leaned his head out into the humid night, not noticing as his bowler hat nearly went flying from the carriage
and into the white night. He held on to his hat and then

shouted out, "Sergeant, faster man!" As Abberline sat back into his seat he looked into the younger Washington's surprised face. Then he took a quick glance at Stevenson who seemed to be deep in either thought or prayer, Abberline didn't know which.

Suddenly the horses screamed and the carriage slid to a halt, throwing Abberline forward and forcing Washington to catch the chief inspector as the carriage wheels finally came to a sliding stop. Stevenson was still holding his strap and seemed to be muttering to himself.

They heard Sergeant Anderson cursing at someone unseen at the same time they heard footsteps approaching the carriage door. As Abberline straightened and then nodded his thanks to Washington for saving him a nasty headache, the door opened. As the inspector sat back into his seat he saw a familiar face, only this time the man was dressed in his scarlet army uniform complete with gold braid. Abberline's jaw set and then he angrily stepped from the carriage, pushing the man out of his way.

"You bloody bastard, you told me this nightmare was ended," he hissed as he leaned into the face of the tall but strong Colonel Albert Stanley of Her Majesty's Black Watch. "Now we have not just one, but two. One of my men was butchered tonight alongside another woman by the man you said was no more of a threat!"

For the first time in five meetings with Stanley the man's face was not one of arrogant disassociation, but one of fear. The colonel looked around and then said, "My apologies Chief Inspector for the intercept. Whitechapel will have to wait."

"Hey, what the bloody hell is going on here," Inspector Washington said as he exited the coach and angrily approached the colonel and Abberline. Suddenly the small but impressive Sergeant Anderson stepped swiftly in front of the younger inspector and just shook his head. The black cap was lowered toward the eyes, but Washington was still able to see the man meant business. Abberline held up his right hand to stay his man.

"Inspector Washington, this is Colonel Stanley of Her Majesty's Black Watch. I believe he has something to add to the night's doings."

Washington stopped but kept staring at the Sergeant, who stood his ground in between the young policeman and the colonel.

"We have business elsewhere Chief Inspector, and you of all men deserve to be a part of what has to be done."

"Then I can expect your cooperation in protecting a material witness who may be able to identify the man known as the Ripper?"

"I am not following you Chief Inspector," Stanley said in frustration at the delay.

"Mr. Stevenson?" Abberline called out.

At that moment, Robert Louis Stevenson leaned out of the carriage and then locked eyes with Colonel Stanley.

"That's the man who has followed me for three years, off and on through Europe and America."

"I see you have finally caught up on your homework Chief Inspector?" Stanley looked from Stevenson and to Abberline as the fog swirled. "You may do with him as you wish. I have my orders, and nothing in them mentions Mr. Stevenson here."

"Then I have your word as a gentleman that no harm will befall my witness by you or any member of your unit?"

"Damn you sir, we must go, and go now!" Stanley said as he turned away.

At that moment a wagon with twenty armed soldiers came around the corner and stopped mere feet from the three men.

"May we use your coach?" Stanley said as he stopped and then gestured to the men to step in. "This official nightmare ends tonight."

"Against Her Majesty's orders, Colonel?" Abberline asked, not moving toward the open coach door and the worried-looking Stevenson inside.

"On the contrary, Chief Inspector, the queen has signed this man's death warrant and has authorized his elimination. That means that this man, this writer, is witness to nothing.

How could he be if the Ripper, or Jekyll and Hyde if you prefer, never existed. Now, do you want to assist in the Ripper's destruction, or do you wish to stay here and listen to more children's stories by the great Robert Louis Stevenson?" Stanley asked as he held the coach door open, not even sparing a glance at the famous writer.

Abberline turned and entered, followed by Washington and then the sergeant major.

The colonel looked at Sergeant Anderson on the coach's bench who was trying hard not to look upon the strange scene. "The east end docks, Sergeant, and speed is the order of the day." He raised a hand at the wagon of soldiers for them to follow. "And personally, Chief Inspector, I would have chosen to remain in the dark," Stanley mumbled as he too entered the coach. "You should have known that if Mr. Stevenson has relayed his tale correctly, because the man we are going after has perfected the art of killing."

The cobblestone roadways leading into the East End of London were the worst in the old city. The roads surrounded the rundown and mostly abandoned warehouses and docking facilities lining the Thames River. The trip across the city had nearly cost them the wagon full of soldiers and it was that thought alone that sent chills down Colonel Stanley's backside, even on the moist and hot night. If they didn't have the squad of soldiers at their disposal Stanley knew he would be nowhere near the docks on this July night.

"Can I presume you gentleman to be armed?" Stanley asked loudly above the sound of the horses' hooves on cobblestone as the black coach streaked through the foggy streets.

"Inspector Washington is armed. I am not so equipped at the moment," Abberline said eyeing the Colonel.

"Sergeant Anderson, will you remedy that please?"

The sergeant major produced a loaded Webley pistol and handed it over to Abberline butt first. The chief inspector looked from Stanley to the offered weapon and then reached for it. "I would prefer to take this man alive," he said looking back at the uniformed colonel.

"That will not be happening. Her Majesty has ordered

this thing to end tonight." Stanley looked from Abberline to his young detective and then saved his most threatening look for Robert Louis Stevenson. "And it will end here, now."

"What is going on here, Chief?" Washington said as he pulled his own pistol out and checked the loads. "What if we find the Ripper and he accedes to surrender himself?"

Stanley smirked and then looked out of the open window. "He will not acquiesce to giving himself up. And any attempt to apprehend him will have dire consequences, young inspector. My men have been instructed to shoot on sight. You have the same orders. And yes, you may presume that order came directly from the queen. If you do not understand the order, we will stop and let you out of the coach this moment. As a matter of fact, I think we should leave Mr. Stevenson here with a couple of my men for safety reasons."

Abberline saw the look that was afforded Stevenson and then he knew exactly what else was to happen tonight other than the stopping of the Ripper. Not only was Robert Louis Stevenson to be silenced, but also Washington and him. They would never make it out of this alive. All traces of the Ripper and his financial backers would be covered.

At that moment the coach came to a bumping halt and Stanley never hesitated as he opened the door and stepped into the fog.

"Chief Inspector?" Washington said as he looked at his boss.

"I'm sorry Washington, but I have to be in on this ending. I have to."

Washington watched stunned as Abberline with pistol in hand stepped from the coach. His eyes then went to the sergeant major that sat across from him and held the door open. "Do as he says laddie. Show no quarter, because the Ripper will show none to you. Shoot anyone you come across that isn't the chief inspector or a man wearing the red uniform," he said, and then added, "And then after this night you can say you did God's work."

A shocked and frightened Washington finally moved out

of the coach and joined the gathering men. As for Robert Louis Stevenson, he sat motionless in the coach. Before Colonel Stanley knew what was happening Chief Inspector Abberline quickly turned and closed the coach door and then looked into the eyes of the writer. "This is over for you. I thank you for your assistance. I understand you are a very wealthy man Mr. Stevenson. May I make a suggestion that you spend that wealth and leave the country. Leave immediately and never come back. Sergeant, take Mr. Stevenson back to his hotel, and then take him to the train station." He looked back at Stevenson. "Take the train to Scotland, leave the country from there. Do you understand, Mr. Stevenson?"

Robert Louis Stevenson nodded his head in understanding. "Good luck, Chief Inspector."

"I doubt if luck will have anything to do with this night's work." Abberline slapped the side of the coach and the sergeant whipped the horses away from the warehouse.

"I wanted that man to remain here," Colonel Stanley said as he stopped and turned to face Abberline.

"I know you did, but Her Majesty's letter said nothing about eliminating material witnesses."

"You judge me too harshly, Chief Inspector."

"I don't judge at all, Colonel. I investigate, I discover who the rat is, and I suspect that the rats are not only inside the warehouse, but out here in this damnable fog also."

Stanley smiled and then bowed his head and removed his black cap at the same moment. "Shall we see this business concluded?"

Abberline watched Stanley and his approach to the large, rundown building. He took Inspector Washington by the coat sleeve and stopped him.

"Stay close to me old boy. I don't want any accidents to befall us."

"You mean like a well-intentioned but stray bullet reaching out and finding us?"

"I knew there was a reason they made you inspector, Washington old boy. Now, as the colonel said, let's finish this business."

The warehouse was large and they could see lights streaming from several of the windows that looked out onto the street.

"You men have your orders. Shoot anyone on sight. He has a large man in his employ working as his assistant—he will not be allowed to live. He may have several more men inside, but we cannot be sure. Have no mercy upon these people. They are enemies of the Empire." Stanley pulled out his own revolver that was attached by a cord to his polished holster. "Gentlemen, his workshop is located on the river side, but be careful as we move through the building; we don't know what to expect. Now, let's move."

As the men started to move off, Abberline realized that Colonel Stanley had been to this particular warehouse before.

Two of the soldiers of the Black Watch approached the double sliding doors of the warehouse and used a large pry bar to tear off the hasp and lock that secured the building.

"Colonel, you have been here before," Abberline said as the lock and hasp clattered to the roadway, making all of the twenty-three men cringe as the fog failed to cover the noise.

Stanley noticed that the statement from the chief inspector was not put into the form of a question.

"Yes, Chief inspector, I was here for the first time five months ago."

"The day we found Mary Kelly in her room?" Abberline asked, his anger growing. "You knew who the Ripper was then?"

"Yes," came the curt answer. "And I suspect I will burn in hell along with a lot of other people for knowing just that, sir." He finally turned and faced Abberline as the twin doors opened to the foggy night. "And I will be happy for it just to get a chance at killing this monster. No matter what you think of me, know that I was never in favor of what you are about to see." Colonel Stanley followed his men inside the massive warehouse.

"Inspector Washington?" Abberline called out.

"Sir?"

"Keep your pistol at the ready to defend yourself. If I fall, return to headquarters and start screaming your bloody head off about Colonel Stanley and the Black Watch's involvement in this. The notoriety may protect you to some degree."

"I will do just that Chief Inspector."

Both men held their gaze a little longer, and then with Colonel Stanley waiting at the door, Abberline and Washington entered the lair of the man that had become the inspiration for one of the most horrific fictional characters ever—Dr. Jekyll, and his alter ego Mr. Hyde, who it seems became the very real—Jack the Ripper.

Abberline immediately felt the heat inside of the building and knew it not to be all natural. He was stunned to realize that the building was actually being heated, or better still, he thought, humidified. He looked at the men as they spread out on the lower floors of the warehouse with their Lee-Metford ten-shot repeating rifles at the ready. He saw that several of the men carried heavy fire, American-made Winchester Model 1887 single-barrel shotguns. He saw that Colonel Stanley and a few of his men were standing near several tables that stretched a hundred feet in length. As he and Washington approached he saw that the ridged tops of these tables were filled with dirt.

"They're gone," Stanley said as he grabbed a handful of the dirt and then let it sift through his fingers. Then he angrily slapped at the thick, rich soil. "They've all been removed. They cannot have acted so quickly after the murder . . . unless they knew they were leaving tonight!"

Abberline watched Stanley as he moved off to join the rest of his men. As Washington started to follow, the chief inspector reached out and took him by the arm.

"Look at this," he said, reaching for something he had spied in the dark earth inside the table Stanley had been standing at.

"What is it?" Washington asked.

Abberline held up the long, thin stalk of a plant that had

been partially hidden in the soil. He held it to his nose and sniffed. "I don't know, but it does have a familiar smell to it." He held the stalk out so the inspector could also smell the strange, yet familiar aroma of the plant.

"Yes, but like you I cannot place it."

Abberline let the stalk fall back into the moist earth and then turned and examined the immediate area around them. There were bags of pig and cow dung and fifty barrels of fresh water. There were gardening tools and other instruments he did recognize upon an adjoining table. Then he looked up into the high rafters of the warehouse and saw the massive skylights that came nowhere near the age of the building itself. The answer dawned on him.

"A greenhouse."

"Sir?" Washington asked.

"This whole building is nothing but a massive greenhouse."

Suddenly a shout and then several curses were heard from a far corner of the warehouse. Both men turned and ran in the direction of the frightened and angry voices. When they arrived at the scene they were stunned, as were the red-clad soldiers at the sight they were witnessing.

"Oh, God," Washington said when he saw what stopped the soldiers dead in their tracks.

As Colonel Stanley hurried over he saw two of his men, soldiers that had seen more than their share of military action, bent over double as they vomited up their evening meals.

"Why have you stopped searching, what is—?"

The question died in the colonel's mouth as he saw the two severed heads sitting on either side of the staircase banister. They had been viciously jammed onto the twin railings with such brute force that the wood had been shoved through the top of their heads. One was a bearded man in his early twenties and the other a woman, complete with tattered hat still on her head with the wooden post sticking through its top.

"Colonel," the sergeant major said holding out a piece of paper. "This was nailed into the head of the man."

Abberline was shocked to see a nail still protruding from the forehead of the bearded victim. Without investigation he knew the young man to be one of his men. He had to turn away as the colonel took the note.

"What does it say?" Abberline asked, finally feeling that the heavy-caliber Webley was not such a burden after all.

Colonel Stanley, instead of answering the question, gestured for ten men to move to the far side of the building and use the wooden staircase at that end. He then handed the note over to the chief inspector and then quickly started taking the stairs two at a time.

"Chief Inspector?" Washington said as he watched the blood drain from Abberline's face. Instead of answering, he too handed over the note, not wanting to utter the written words aloud. Washington read the note as his boss followed the soldiers up the stairs. The words were scrawled as if they were written by an untrained, brutish hand.

Colonel Stanley, if I may presume this is who the ministry of defense has chosen to terminate my contract, please join me in the laboratory at the head of the stairs. I am available for a demonstration of the work I was so well compensated for. It is shameful that I am not allowed to complete my assignment, but tonight you can have the results as promised.

—A

Washington was as confused as ever as he allowed the note to fall from his hand. He went up the stairs, but not as enthusiastically as the rest.

Abberline heard the men on the upper floor as they moved about. He gained the uppermost floors and then looked out onto the warehouse. Half the building had a second floor; the other half was a high roof with the new skylighting used for the greenhouse. Abberline aimed his pistol ahead of him. The building lacked the gas lighting of the more modern warehouses that lined the river, so in every corner and underneath every table, chair, and barrel, he saw moving shadows. He finally spied Stanley as he kicked over a small table that held beakers and glass tubes of every shape and size. He seized the colonel's arm.

"We must leave the building and surround it with more men. This is a trap and we're walking right into it."

"My orders are to kill this maniac, and that is exactly what we are going to do. If you have doubts as to our abilities, perhaps it is a good time to leave." Stanley shook Abberline's hand free of his arm. "But you can also expect a visit from the palace as to why you refused to assist Her Majesty in this apprehension."

Abberline was about to explode. Now Stanley was even veiling his threat with word games—it was real; they would kill him and Washington and think nothing less of themselves. He opened his mouth to speak, but a thickened, rich, booming voice froze every man on the second floor.

"Your men seem to need some of the fire I could have provided them and the Defense Ministry paid for if I had not been betrayed by those very same men, Colonel Stanley."

The voice echoed in the almost-empty building. Abberline was sure that it emanated from a megaphone at the very least. It swirled and then settled upon the twenty-three men as the fog had done outside.

"This was supposed to end many months ago; you gave your word to the ministry. Now come Professor Ambrose, let's finish this business."

"Very well, but allow me my medicinal interlude."

Abberline jumped when the sound of breaking glass broke the silence after the words were spoken. As he looked he saw the vial in pieces on the floor at the colonel's booted feet. He watched as Stanley went to a knee to examine the broken glass. He reached out and retrieved a small piece of the shattered vial. He sniffed and then he stood so suddenly that his men jumped.

"Professor, you did not drink the whole of this did you?"

Silence.

"It will not avail you, tonight you die."

It seemed every man saw the shadow as it fell from the

rafters above their heads. The darkened mass hit the floor and then vanished into the blackness at the far end of the warehouse. Three shots rang out from the nervous soldiers to Abberline's left. Washington stepped forward and stood by the chief inspector.

Suddenly the sergeant major and two men skirted the colonel and ran forward on the right at Stanley's direction. Then he motioned again and another two ran forward on the right. Again there were more gunshots. A loud explosion announced that one of the American shotguns had discharged. Then something flew out of the darkness and struck the wooden floor. It was one of Stanley's men. His torso had been torn in two with the upper half missing. Then several shouts were heard and men started moving quickly.

"There!" Stanley shouted and fired his Webley at a large shadow that moved quickly through the darkened end of the large room.

Abberline heard the heaving grunting and the horrifying chuckle that announced that the Ripper was no longer in hiding. The sound made the experienced inspector freeze in terror. Then he saw the enormous shadow rise up in between two large tables with test tubes, beakers, and jars on its top. The shadow grabbed the first table and held it before it just as several large-caliber rounds struck the wood. The shield allowed none of the bullets to pass through. Several men rushed the large and quickly advancing shadow. The first was knocked across the room as something large and club-like struck him, sending him through a large window. The second was stomped upon with brutal force as more bullets struck the thick, wooden table. Then the sound came that froze every one of the professional soldiers and also the two policemen in their tracks—a roar, not like the sound of a wild animal, but more of a purposeful act to scare everyone who heard it. More screams, more shots, and then the sound of breaking, tearing, and the horrid screams of men as the Ripper waded into them.

Abberline grabbed Washington and the two men skirted to the left as gunfire erupted from all over the second floor.

The large table was finally thrown and that afforded Abberline his first look at the man Robert Louis Stevenson had dubbed Mr. Hyde, but he and his men knew as Jack the Ripper.

"My God!" Washington said as his feet froze at the sight.

The clothing had been ripped and shredded. Tatters of a once-white shirt hung along the beast's long arms as they swung at two men who charged him. The soldiers were immediately broken and lifeless as they slammed into the far wall. Abberline saw the face of the man he had chased for nearly two years. The face was crevassed and lined. Dark fissures were deep and dingy where there wasn't muscle supporting the skin. The beard was thick and an inch long. The eyes were wild and the forehead massive. The teeth were large and misshapen and the man was clearly ten sizes too large for the clothing that covered his body. The beast standing before the remaining men was no less than seven feet tall.

Several bullets hit the man before he could move, but they seemed to have no effect.

"The head—shoot for the head!" Stanley shouted as he tried to get to a better location in the darkness for a clear shot. Before he reached his spot he tripped and fell, and that was when he looked over and saw that the club that had been used against his men had been the remains of the sergeant major. He lay headless and lifeless beside him. Colonel Stanley scowled and then with a shout he stood and charged the creature that could not possibly exist. He started firing the Webley as he ran toward the large beast. Then just as the bullets struck in the shoulder and chest, the Ripper moved. It was like a large cat that maneuvered for the kill. It quickly seized the colonel by the neck and pulled him up and in front of it. The Ripper was now using Stanley as a shield.

More bullets hit the beast from behind, but still the Ripper elicited no sound other than the loud grunting and snarling of a large predator. It was as though the thing standing before Abberline and Washington had lost the ability of speech. There was no scream of pain and no words. Stanley tried to raise the pistol, but the hand was taken and the fingers slowly crushed until the large weapon fell free. Abberline charged, firing his own weapon. Two bullets hit the Ripper in the side and one actually clipped Colonel Stanley as he was dangled and shaken like a small doll before a cruel child. Suddenly a fist struck out and hit Abberline in the chest and he flew five feet backward. As Washington ran to the chief inspector's side he saw Stanley released. The Ripper lifted a large and bare foot over the prone and stunned Stanley and then raised its misshapen head to the rafters. This time it was indeed an animalistic roar of triumph that shook the very building.

Inspector Washington slid to the floor to assist Abberline. The chief inspector had been slammed into a table and then to the floor, knocking free an oil lamp that had burst open, and its now freed flame had engulfed Abberline's left leg. Washington quickly slapped at the burning material until the yellow flames were snuffed out. He kicked away the tin container that held the oil so it wouldn't again engulf Abberline. As Washington raised his head he saw the large foot come down as even more bullets struck the Ripper from the front, back, and rear. One of the bullets struck the beast above the left eye and the thickened bone produced a ping as if the large round had struck thick plate. The Ripper then turned toward the two prone men. It charged.

"Oh," was all Washington could utter as he tried in vain to pull Abberline free of the Ripper's speedy attack. Young Washington knew it was too late, but instead of waiting for the death that came at them, he quickly reached out and took the shattered oil lamp's base and threw it at the altered man that came at them. The oil hit and then spread on the once-formal shirt of the Ripper. As Abberline started to awaken he saw the young inspector reach his sleeved hand into the burning fuel that was still blazing brightly in front of them. As his hand and arms caught fire, he stood and actually ran at the beast. He struck and the world erupted before the chief inspector's eyes like a lightning bolt. Washington rebounded and then fell to the floor as the flames coursing up his arm spread.

The Ripper roared as the flames erupted over its entire body. He slashed and spun, knocking over tables and chairs, breaking laboratory equipment as it tried in vain to extinguish the burning fuel.

"Open fire, damn you!" Abberline shouted at the remaining soldiers.

Ten, fifteen, twenty shots were heard as the beast spun in circles, sending pieces of flaming clothing in every direction. Then it suddenly stopped and ran for the windows fronting the river. With the massive body still flaming, the Ripper smashed the many paned window and vanished into the night's fog.

Abberline slid quickly across the floor and started slapping and cursing at the flames that were now covering the body of young Washington. His whole left side was ablaze as he tried desperately to roll on the flaming floor. Abberline reached up and pulled a large barrel marked *water* over onto the inspector that had saved his own life just a moment before. The water and barrel hit Washington and the flames quickly vanished. Abberline reached the inspector and turned him over. He was still alive but in much pain.

"Easy boy, we'll get you out of here," he shouted as he stood and ran for the smashed window. As he looked into the thick fog all he could see was the swirling whiteness that was just now starting to thin.

As he turned away from the window he prayed that the Ripper had been too badly hurt to survive his burns, much less the fall to the river below.

As he faced the destruction that had been reaped in less than two minutes from beginning to end, he saw the body of Colonel Stanley lying next to that of the sergeant major. His head was no longer there. The large foot had smashed it into pulp. Abberline turned and looked down at his feet while bracing himself against the sill of the large window. Everywhere men lay dead and broken.

Chief Inspector Abberline ordered four of the surviving soldiers to get young Washington down to the remaining wagon, and then he turned to stare out into the lifting fog.

He heard the river far below, but that was the only sound in this night of horrors.

The large coal-fired scamp eased to shore along the Thames River. A tall and very thin man stepped from the small wheelhouse as the river pilot held the little boat steady. The man with the blue turban waited at the railing. He turned and noted the secured barrels holding the seedlings and the ten thousand dried plants grown in the warehouse and nodded his head, satisfied they were safe.

After a few minutes he heard the noise emanating from the fast-flowing river. He saw the shaking, burned hand reach out of the water and take hold of the thick, wooden rail. The turbaned man gestured for several of the small boat's deckhands to assist the man out of the Thames River a full mile from the East End docks.

A few minutes later the boat turned back south toward the sea where a large cutter waited offshore, its destination—America.

The Jack the Ripper case would be closed the following day and the death of the Black Watch soldiers and their colonel would go unread in any newspaper.

Young inspector Washington survived his severe burns and led a productive life in the Metropolitan Police force. He would be killed in the Battle of the Somme twenty-seven years later during the Great War, and would go to his grave never uttering a single thing about that night in the East End of London. And if the world knew the truth, he was all the happier for being as quiet as he had been for seventeen nightmare-filled years, and taking that night with him in death.

Frederick Abberline would eventually leave the London constabulary and head the office of the American-owned Pinkerton Detective Agency. And for years after that night in 1889 he would check the newspapers from around the world only to see if Dr. Jekyll had released his Mr. Hyde and Jack the Ripper had once more reared his ugly head in another country, for his nightmares always told the chief inspector that Jack was still out there somewhere.

Frederick George Abberline died in 1929, age eighty-six, at his home without muttering a single word about that long-ago night by the River Thames. He allowed speculation to flourish that Queen Victoria had been in on a cover-up of massive proportions to protect one of her relatives. Abberline didn't have any sympathy for the monarchy—after all, it was on her orders that Jack the Ripper came to the shores of the British Empire. They deserved the dark rumor and innuendo that would hound her to her own death in January 1901.

Chief Inspector Abberline received one last letter that had not been intercepted by the government. It was a coded letter from a Mr. Steve Hanson and he had written it from, of all places, India. Abberline knew it was the last he would ever hear from the man as the only words written inside the envelope were these: "Our mutual friend owns quite a lot of property in South Texas and across the border in Mexico—if that should interest you." It was signed Steve Hanson, but Abberline didn't have to be much of an inspector to know it was from Stevenson. Robert Louis Stevenson. Abberline could only pray that if the Ripper was alive, he would be nothing more than a burnt-out hulk of a man. Robert Louis Stevenson died in September of 1894 at the age of forty-four years. He went to his grave never telling anyone the truth about his fictional characters being copied from the most brutal mass murderer in British history—Jack the Ripper.

It would take over 114 years for the world to receive the answer that Frederick Abberline feared most of all in his long life after the case had been shunted aside—that indeed, Jack is back.

Laredo, Texas
August 23, 1916

A thick and rolling sea of fog came off the Rio Grande and partially hid the ninety-six men of B Company of the 8th

United States Cavalry regiment. Sound was confusing inside the white gauze of mist as horses and men awaited the order to cross into Mexico. Bird songs and insect noises became one cacophony of blended night elements that added to nervousness among the troopers.

On a small rise above the northern side of the Rio Grande River an armored car sat motionless as men and horses awaited the command to move across the river. The large detailed map was stretched out on the hood of the car and was held in place by an old oil lantern as a medium-sized man placed an index finger on a small rectangular mark south of the border.

"Your target area, Lieutenant, is this compound."

The taller and far-younger first lieutenant stood confused as he studied the map in the light of the small lamp. "General, have we received intelligence other than our earlier reports that say Villa is two hundred miles to the south and nowhere near this hacienda?"

General John Joseph "Black Jack" Pershing kept his eyes on the map and didn't look up at the man standing to his left. He nodded his head and then took a breath.

"Pancho Villa is not our task here this morning, Lieutenant." Pershing finally looked up and into the cold eyes of the blonde-haired First Lieutenant George S. Patton. The aide held his ground as the general waited for the inevitable question.

"We're using the president's official mandate to cross into Mexico, and the capture of Pancho Villa is not in the directive? May I ask the general what the objective is?"

Pershing finally reached out his hand, and one of his aides that had been standing off to the side filled it with a large manila envelope. The general held the envelope with both hands a moment and then as if he had drifted away in thought and body looked around him slowly as if he were looking at something deep inside the fog bank.

"Reminds me of the morning just before the fight at San Juan Hill in Cuba," Pershing said as he glanced skyward.

Patton could see the general not only looking at the fog

surrounding them but also looking back at his days as a young lieutenant in the 10th all-Negro cavalry, thus his moniker—Black Jack.

Pershing slowly looked down at Patton and then his eyes went to the sealed envelope he held. He placed it on the map and slid it across. "Sorry for drifting. Your orders Lieutenant, precise and clear-cut. You are to cross the Rio Grande River and enter Mexico and destroy the hacienda indicated on the map at the aforementioned coordinates. You will treat all persons you come in contact with as hostile. After the property's population is . . . ," the general looked away for the briefest of moments before finishing. He touched his graying moustache and then caught himself once more . . . "eliminated, the hacienda and outbuildings are to be burned. No structure is to be left standing."

Patton looked at the envelope. He knew he didn't need to read the orders inside. The general's demeanor told him what he needed to know. He had just been given orders for a murder raid across the border into a sovereign nation.

"Your main target is an American citizen. He owns the property and is responsible for all that has happened there." Pershing looked at Patton and his visage became stern. "The American's name is Professor Lawrence Jackson Ambrose. You are to confirm the death of this professor personally, Patton. This order comes directly from the president of the United States. You are to eliminate everyone in the compound and burn any papers, laboratory equipment, or specimens you may come across."

"Villa being in this neck of the woods was only a ruse to send in the troops?" Patton finally asked.

"Yes, Lieutenant, a ruse, lie, use whatever word you want," came a voice from out of the fog.

Patton turned to see a small man in dungarees and a blue denim work shirt. The man actually wore a kerchief around his neck and a black cowboy hat cocked jauntily to the right side of his head.

"This is Lt. Colonel John Henry Thomas, a personal representative of President Wilson. He is present this morning to assure the president that the mission parameters have been fulfilled."

Patton looked the man over. "What is your unit, sir?"

"Lieutenant!" Pershing said in anger at the presumption of a first lieutenant questioning not only a lieutenant colonel but also a representative of the president of the United States. "I am attached to the National Archives, Lieutenant. And while my answer creates more questions as to my affiliation, that will have to be enough, okay Lieutenant?"

"I have my men to watch out for, sir, that is my only concern."

"You not only have them to watch out for young lieutenant, you have me. And as you now know, I have at least one powerful friend in office. So don't let me down, son."

"Yes, sir, but these orders are ambiguous at best."

"Exactly, because we don't know what it is we will find across that river," said the small man as he removed his hat and wiped the brim with another handkerchief he produced from a pocket.

"Just follow your orders, Lieutenant." Pershing once more looked up and into the thickening fog. He placed his hands behind his back, turned away, and slowly moved a distance from the armored car. "Good luck Lieutenant, Colonel Thomas . . . God's speed."

George Patton watched as Black Jack Pershing melted into the thick veil of fog. He looked at the envelope in his hand and then quickly unbuttoned his tunic and slid the orders inside. Patton turned and made his way forward toward his waiting company.

Ten minutes later elements of the 8th United States Cavalry crossed the Rio Grande into Mexico.

The two Apache scouts from C Troop, only recently released from their imprisonment in St. Augustine, Florida, returned from the small valley that hid the hacienda. One of the men shook his head and removed his campaign hat, allowing his long black hair to shake free of its confinement. Lieutenant Patton waited for the report as patiently as he could, knowing that the lt. colonel from the National Archives was listening intently.

"Nothing but women and children as far as we can see. They seem to be doing their chores and nothing else," the larger of the two Apache scouts said as he replaced his hat. "The fog has almost completely lifted near the hacienda, so we will have no cover in the charge."

Patton looked down at his pocket watch, which was almost impossible to see in the night. He looked up and saw that every minute they delayed the attack allowed the fog to lift that much more.

"Five fifteen in the morning and women are already doing their daily tasks." Patton looked at the two scouts and then over at the mysterious man sent here by the president. "Doesn't seem too damn threatening to me." The young first lieutenant shook his head. "I sure hope Washington knows just what in the hell they are doing." Patton looked away from Lt. Colonel Thomas, clicked the cover of his pocket watch closed, and then turned and mounted the large roan, which pawed the ground anxiously.

"The orders regarding the women and children, Lieutenant, do they still stand?"

Patton looked down at Second Lieutenant Roland McAfee, a recent graduate of West Point on his very first field assignment, then again at the man from National Archives. Patton then scowled at the colonel and angrily shook his head. "No. If hostilities are evident, only then are the men to fire on anyone. If you can, I want the women and children scattered. Our main target is this Professor Ambrose and any other men of *fighting age* in the compound. I am not firing on women and children. Now, report to your troop and let's get this over with." Patton looked once more at the colonel. "Report it if you want to, Colonel. I will not kill women and children without more of an explanation from Washington as to the why of it."

Thomas looked taken back. "Lieutenant, you are in operational command of this mission," he started and then smiled. "Hell, son, I would have refused that order myself."

"Yes, sir," McAfee said looking from Thomas and back at Patton, not understanding the back and forth between the two officers.

"Colonel Thomas, just who in the hell are you, really?" Patton asked, knowing this man wasn't just an ordinary U.S. Army officer.

"Just a soldier on detached duty to the National Archives, young lieutenant, that's all. I'm no one really."

With a dubious look at the now smiling Thomas, Patton spurred his mount forward and joined the long line of cavalry with Thomas turning toward the rear of the mounted line. Patton rode to the front of the skirmish line and absentmindedly reached for his saber, actually forgetting he had ordered the useless weapons to be left behind for noise reasons. Instead he raised his gauntleted right hand and waved the line forward just as the last of the fog lifted and the first rays of sunshine eased over the rise to the east.

"Company, forward at the cantor," he ordered in a not-too-loud voice.

The 8th United States Cavalry started forward at the trot. Ninety-eight men pulled their British-made Lee-Enfield rifles from their scabbards and Patton withdrew an old Colt .45 Peacemaker from its holster. He then thought better of it and replaced the old six-shooter with a model 1900 Colt .45 automatic. The line moved steadily forward, and the hacienda was now seen in all its large glory. The men now knew the task at hand was a large one.

"Bugler, sound the charge!"

The early morning bugle call was heard throughout the small valley south of the Rio Grande as men of the 8th charged the ten-acre hacienda known as Perdition's Gate.

Professor Lawrence Jackson Ambrose stood in front of one of the subject cells buried far beneath the hacienda and watched test subject 197 as he squatted in the darkened corner of his cell. The young man was one of a slew of dregs from the barroom alleys of Laredo, just across the Rio Grande, as were another four of the ten subjects he had under medical observation. The professor had not moved since administering the final dose in the series of injections that would complete the full script of medicinal delivery.

Ambrose was dressed in a filthy white lab coat and the tie he wore underneath was askew. His gray hair was tumbled and his beard still held food from the day's evening meal. The deep scars from that long-ago night on London's East End held firmly to the left side of his face, creating a permanent scowl. His clothing covered the rest of the burns he had received, several of which still broke open and bled on occasion. Ambrose hardly noticed when he heard the footsteps descending the stairwell from the hacienda two floors above. The door opened and the professor spared a glance at the object of the interruption.

His East Indian servant, RaJan Singh, a Sikh that stood six feet six inches in height and was well over three hundred pounds, was his ever resplendent self. His blue turban was covering hair that when loose would travel downward to his hips. His black beard had two luminescent streaks of white coursing down either side of his whiskers. His long white jacket covered bright-blue pants that made the Sikh the complete opposite of Ambrose in size, demeanor, cleanliness, and dress.

"I gave orders not to be disturbed until the final doses of the drug had been administered. I have nine more injections to give to complete the series on these subjects."

"Excuse me, Sahib. I have held my tongue for far too long. You need rest. You are not seeing things as you once did. While at one time your direction was merely reckless, it has now turned onto a road which will not only be your destruction, but many others on this plantation as well."

Ambrose smiled and turned with a fresh syringe in his thick fingers. "Do I include you as one of those others, old friend?"

"My life has always been yours to either end or prolong. But was it not I that gave you the rare poppy which in turn gave you your life's work? I would like to see the potential of the experiments proven. Still, we must realize that our actions have attracted attention from north of the river, Sahib."

"I am too close to finishing this. With soldiers such as these that I have created, foolish governments could never afford war mongering. If I had gone uninterrupted in London, the problems in Europe would have ceased before they started. Men such as these in the holding cells would make moot the art of warfare—men that will kill and die without a second's hesitation."

Singh stepped up to cell number nine and looked at the man-animal crouching in the dark corner. The man was staring at him with eyes wide and his drooling mouth agape. The look of sheer murder that coursed through his rough features was enough to make the giant Sikh want to turn away. For as large as he knew himself to be, he also knew the man in the cell could take him apart, piece by piece.

"For years I have watched you make men into something that was never meant to be. We have gone too far, Sahib. The taunting of the British authorities almost twenty-seven years ago nearly brought the world down upon us. Your decision making was flawed then, and it is now becoming more so." He watched the eyes of the professor as they remained neutral as he spoke. He decided to press further. "I was willing to allow this to go on as long as there were no more killings of the innocent. But it is now starting all over again. I assume you are planning to test these . . . soldiers on living subjects?"

Ambrose finally turned to fully face his manservant. The syringe he held dripped amber fluid from the needle and struck the professor's filthy boot.

"You *were* willing?" Ambrose chuckled as he ignored the stated question. His laugh was a cold, harsh sound in the darkness of the subbasement. "Wasn't it you who carried me to Whitechapel in the old days in the coach? Was it not you who assisted in luring women to that coach?" Ambrose took a step toward the very much larger Singh, who to his credit stood ramrod straight. "Old friend, was it not you who originally saw the potential of the splicing of the flower and its new seed? Maybe you were once just a willing participant, but now I believe you may be considered one of the architects of Perdition's Fire." This time the smile did reach his eyes just before he turned to unlock cell number two. "After tonight there will be no more need for test subjects. Outside of training these men to not attack their own people, the process is perfected. Can you imagine a whole division of Berserkers? The earth would tremble."

"And what nation would be willing to pay your price?"

Again, the laugh. "Just as soon as one side or the other starts losing the war in Europe, we will have plenty of takers."

The manservant watched as the cell door was opened and Ambrose stepped into the darkness. He heard the sharp rattle of chain as the test subject, a young Texan he himself had found sleeping off a drunk by the river, charged Ambrose. With every inch of thick chain around the subject's neck stretched to its limit, the boy growled and hissed at Ambrose who calmly kept his ground just inside the cell door. After a moment the subject settled and started sniffing. The test subject's drool coursed down his chin and neck as he took in Ambrose. Only five previous injections had brought the test subject to this point of barbarity. The last injection would make him into what Ambrose dreamed—a lethal, brilliant killing machine—just as he had proven with himself as a test subject in London. This man would soon be a soldier that was able to plan and carry out the most animalistic attacks ever seen. A soldier never seen before. The strength of a bull and the intelligence of the very man who made him into what he had become. He was now a beast that would send any civilized enemy running through sheer terror. And all of this was because of two small, little-known poppy flowers that grew only in the remotest northern regions of India. That coupled with the stem serum would open up that which God may never had intended to be used—the opposite side of the brain. Full brain function coupled with animalistic fury.

As Singh watched, the professor slowly lifted his free hand and allowed the subject to smell the oils and sweat emanating from the pores of Ambrose. The smell seemed to calm the boy down and the chain slackened somewhat as the man knew one of his own. Someone who released this scent told the Berserker he was amongst one who had also taken the formula. Ambrose had absorbed enough of Perdition's Fire into his system over the years that anything that had also been injected with the script would know the other as an ally, one not to be feared or attacked. It was a system of protection the professor had worked out years before through trial and error.

"Is it not amazing to you my old friend how the brain of the subject, even though it is ravaged with cancerous growth caused by the long-term injections, is still able to use its higher brain functions? This subject tested out at over a 165 IQ. Amazing, Singh, just amazing. This opens up not just one avenue for the eventual benefits of Perdition's Fire, but so many more."

"It is not the benefits of higher brain functions that is the concern here, Sahib. It is the murderous abilities coupled with that intelligence that is the true danger." Singh stepped toward the open cell, and that was when the test subject lunged at the manservant, almost knocking Ambrose over.

"That is not wise my friend," Ambrose said as he quickly reached out and jabbed the needle home into the arm of the boy. The test subject was so absorbed in his want, his very need to get at Singh, that he never felt the sharp jab. Ambrose quickly stepped from the cell and closed the door. "There, eight subjects more to go."

"Sahib, we must—"

Suddenly, and before Singh could finish, the basement door flew open and a man came through. He was armed with an old Winchester and wore the white clothing of one of the field workers.

"We have soldiers approaching, Jefe. They crossed the river an hour ago."

Ambrose reached for another of the syringes and then turned to look at one of the many guards he had posted around the hacienda. "Federalies?" he asked.

"No, señor, Americanos," the man said as his eyes saw the boy inside the cell for the first time. The peasant saw the way the beast inside had the restraining chain stretched to its limit as it growled, sending the guard back a step. "There must be over a hundred of them," he said, in a hurry to finish his report.

Ambrose slammed the syringe onto the table's top, denting the barrel of the tube, and then grabbed the guard by the shirt. It was that quick motion that not only sent the two men who had the final series of injections into a frenzy of movement and anger, but the other test subjects as well. Animal sounds started filtering through the darkness of all ten cells, sending chills down the spines of both the guard and Singh.

"You and the other guards will delay them as long as you can, dying in the effort if you have to."

The guard looked shocked. He knew he and his men could never take on an experienced charge of light cavalry. Ambrose angrily shook the man, sending the test subjects into a fresh round of growling and other sounds that could never have emanated from the throats of mere men.

"If I do not receive the time I need, I will release these men into your village after they have finished with the soldiers. Your wives, your children, they will all die a horrible death. Now go and delay this force of men while we get ready to abandon the hacienda." Ambrose shoved the shocked and stunned guard away.

Singh half turned and watched the man leave the laboratory. He then faced his employer. "You would release these creatures into the villages around the hacienda?"

Ambrose grinned and then took another syringe from the table. "I would release them into heaven or hell to get the time I need. Now you go and retrieve the Perdition journals in my office. The up-to-date series of formula is in notebook number thirty along with the antidote. That is most important. As for the viles of powdered solution in the secondary laboratory, dump them into the sand. The powdered form is far too strong. With the liquid solution we have more control. Now go my friend and do as I—"

He stopped talking when the pistol appeared in the Indian manservant's hand. Ambrose raised his thick brows at the sudden appearance of the weapon. It seemed as though the professor wasn't surprised in the least by this latest development.

"This ends here, tonight, just as I should have allowed it to end in Whitechapel."

"You brought the soldiers here, didn't you Singh?" Ambrose asked as his eyes roamed to the still-unlocked cell door of test subject number two.

"Yes, I knew the American soldiers that are searching for Pancho Villa were within a hundred miles of here. I have arranged your demise through forces working with the president of the United States, Sahib. Forgive me, but I have been communicating with your government for over three years now. I have been reporting on your progress—progress that has now gone too far with the new series of script you have begun. These men will never be controlled as you believe, and the Americans want this stopped."

Ambrose couldn't speak or move at first. He had never suspected his manservant could be capable of total betrayal until the deed had showed itself. Instead he turned from Singh and then quickly slid the needle expertly into his own arm. As he did he moved to the left. The sudden motion made Singh adjust his position and he stepped in front of the still-open number-two cell.

"Please, Professor, place the syringe on the table top."

Ambrose chuckled, a sound that sent chills down the neck and arms of the large manservant. Then to Singh's horror, he saw the syringe fall from where Ambrose had hidden it in his hand. It clattered on the flagstone floor—empty.

"What have you done?" Singh asked as he involuntarily took a step backward toward the open cell door.

"I do what always needs to be done old friend," Ambrose said as saliva slowly ran from the left side of the older man's mouth and traveled slowly through his thin beard. The distinctive facial tick, indicating that the muscles under his skin were receiving information from the extreme frontal lobe of the brain, started on the right side of the face and seemed to spread into the upper reaches of the facial muscles, most notably just above the eyes, making the brow pulse and grow. The professor took another step to the right and then one quick step forward, forcing Singh to step closer to the cell door. Ambrose smiled again—the once-straight teeth were now jumbled and separated. The professor's blue eyes were now ringed with a red circle where the subsurface blood vessels had exploded from the massive rise in heart rate. He reached into his lab coat pocket and pulled out a small shiny object.

"An object lesson old friend—a bit of problem solving for the ultimate soldier." He held up the small key that maintained test subject number two securely bound to his chains.

"I'll kill you before I allow the release of that beast from its cell. The test subjects must be destroyed," Singh said as he cocked the British-made Webley pistol.

"Release them?" Ambrose said with a laugh.

The gesture allowed Singh to see the blood that had forced its way through the now widening gaps between the teeth of the professor. The lab coat was now drawstring tight around the professor's arms. The material was starting to give way as the now thriving right side of the brain started to activate and send out new signals to the nerves controlling muscle movement, growth and strength. Singh knew that Ambrose's body was starting to take defensive measures toward its survival as ordered by the expanding brain and the already overdosed and dying medulla oblongata.

"I said this was your object lesson. Problem-solving capacity amongst the strongest, most ruthless creature in the world has been obtained. They need no key old friend. The last journal explains it all. They have been opening and closing the locks on their chains since the third series of injections. So I had to change the locks to a more advanced model. Now they have the reasoning to avoid capture, just like I had in London twenty years ago. It works, Singh, the formula works!"

Singh felt his heart jump in his chest as he absorbed the

words from Ambrose. Then his heart stopped when he heard the cell door behind him open. He closed his eyes and then he suddenly realized what he had to do before his own life became forfeit. He pulled the trigger.

Ambrose was hit in the chest and thrown back just as test subject number two jumped onto the back of the manservant. As the professor absorbed the large-caliber bullet and as he hit the table with the remaining syringes on its top, he heard the beast as it tore its teeth into the neck of Singh. He reached down and started to gather the remaining doses of Perdition's Fire from the floor. He looked down at the wound he had sustained and saw the blood pumping out of his chest from the bullet hole. He laughed as he watched the flow of life-sustaining blood dwindling to a trickle.

While the quickly dying Ambrose started giving the final injections to the last eight patients, he ignored the sounds of test subject number two as it did what it was created to do as its brain functions started to die—it was dismembering, tearing apart, killing, and worst of all something else that had not been programmed into its cycle of violence during the professor's long-winded readings to his test subjects, something the professor could never figure out—it would feed on the corpse of what it had just killed—a basic throwback to the primitive days of beast against beast. The total brain function brought on more than just advanced IQ; in some ways the formula reverted it also.

For the world as a whole, the genie was now out of the bottle, and a new form of warfare was about to explode onto the landscape of the Mexican chaparral.

The living versus the dead—and the dead had the advantage.

Perdition's Fire was now perfected.

Ambrose laughed as blood spilled onto the wooden flooring. As he stared at the last test subject he felt his knees weaken and his mouth go dry. His head started to spin and he quickly gave the last dosage. Then without realizing what was happening he turned and stumbled out of the cell and crashed into the dosage table, knocking it over.

Ambrose knew he had injected himself too late to stem the flow of blood from the bullet wound and now he would die before he could prove to the outside world that his theory of chemical balancing of the entire brain and the releasing of controlled violence would never be achieved. His eyes started to flutter closed. Suddenly he felt the sharp jab of something through the lab coat and into his arm. He opened his eyes as he felt the rush of the drug as it coursed up his arm. His strength was returning fast. He was pulled to his feet, and that was when he realized it was test subject number two. The beast had finished his work with Singh and had actually refilled one of the used syringes and had injected him again.

"That is too much, the dosage will kill me."

"As you have us?" came the slow, deep voice from test subject number two. The beast let him go and then smiled. His mouth was wide and filled with large carnivorous teeth. "Now your only option is to fight . . . fight alongside of those you have condemned to hell with your God-like man building. Now FIGHT!"

Ambrose felt his mind let go as the section of his brain he had only barely touched on in London came to full life. Instantly memories came to him of those nights in Whitechapel and the pleasure he took from testing his serum.

"Yes, YES!" Ambrose shouted as the physical change went far beyond anything he had ever experienced.

Jack the Ripper and Mr. Hyde combined was now loose upon the world.

As First Lieutenant George Patton led the 8th Cavalry over the last rise, the early morning sun burned off the last of the fog and illuminated a strange scene below. Women and children, peasant farmers, and their animals were streaming out of the hacienda and the outbuildings that surrounded it. Patton galloped toward the front gates of the main building. Each troop in the unit did as previously ordered. They split into four separate companies for each side of the massive hacienda.

As Patton rode past the first of the terrified farm workers, he could sense they were not only running from the danger posed by the raid, but from the way they turned their heads back, also from something inside the hacienda. They braved the charging horses of the 8th to distance themselves from their employer—or something even more terrifying.

The main troop with the lieutenant in the lead never hesitated as they charged two abreast through the wide double gate at the front of the hacienda. Patton was the first to discharge a weapon that morning as a man with an old Winchester rifle was downed in the center of the wide courtyard. Then other loud reports were heard as the troopers behind Patton opened up on several men, both armed and unarmed.

The first six men reigned in their mounts and came to a sliding stop on the flagstones of the courtyard. Patton held up his hand and then gestured for them to split up to cover the eighteen possible entranceways into the main building. More gunfire erupted on the other side of the house. The other troops opposite Patton's men were coming across the same sort of weak defense. The man beside the lieutenant raised a boot and then smashed in the French style doors before him. He held a sawed-off double-barrel shotgun before him as he stepped into a large room. A man in a darkened far corner came from the shadows with his hands held high in the air. The sergeant turned quickly and fired both barrels into the man who flew backward until a whitewashed wall stopped him.

"Jesus Christ, Sergeant!" Patton said angrily as he shook his head to clear his hearing after the loud report from the shotgun.

"Sorry, sir," said the small but stocky sergeant as he broke the weapon he was holding and pulled free the two smoking and expended shells. As he did this he looked up in time to see a darker shape lunge from another room. He quickly shoved Patton out of the way and swung the empty shotgun at the man's head. It connected solidly but seemed to have little or no effect on the strangely shaped man in front of him.

Patton kept his balance after being pushed out of the way

of the charging man. He turned in time to see the twin barrels of the sergeant's shotgun strike the attacker in the side
of the head. He could have sworn he heard the sound of
cracking bone, therefore he was surprised to see the man
just turn his head slowly back toward the sergeant. Patton
hurriedly raised his Colt. The crazed-looking man actually
growled in the split second that he jumped on the sergeant.
Patton couldn't believe the speed at which the man moved. It
was like watching a large predatory cat lunge at an unwit-
ting victim. Each blow rained down upon the sergeant was
something that was so shocking to see that Patton was frozen. This time he knew for sure he was hearing bones break.
The sergeant never had time to scream before his skull was
crushed. The attacking beast was crazed. His dark hair looked
ragged and wet. The exposed muscles bulged with each
movement of arms or legs. The nails on its fingers were long,
dirty, and as lethal looking as small knives.

Finally the shock of what he had just seen slid from him
as if he had just awoken from a momentary nightmare. Now
Patton became angry that whatever this thing was had
caught him by surprise. He quickly aimed and fired two
times into the right side of the man-beast as it finally straightened from the dead body of the sergeant. The two bullets hit
almost simultaneously. The first struck the sergeant's attacker in the armpit, the second just below the ribcage. The
man only staggered. It screeched something and then jab-
bered something else as it looked toward the man that had
caused it the pain it was feeling. The malformed man then
turned its horribly misaligned features up toward Patton. It
tilted its head and then screamed a murderous roar as it
started forward.

Patton took a step back and fired again. This time the
bullet hit the oncoming beast squarely on the right side of its
head. The skull jerked backward at the impact, but to the
lieutenant's amazement the hunched-over man still came
forward. Even with part of the man's brain hanging like a
gray piece of meat from the side of his head, the crazed attacker came on.

Patton took a quick glance down at the smoking .45 in his right hand. Then he raised it again and fired. That was when he saw that the slide on the automatic was locked open. Patton braced himself as the man charged when suddenly a fusillade of bullets struck the charging man at the last second before he slammed into the waiting Patton. The beast-like man flew to the side just as several of Patton's men fired again before the maniac stopped rolling. Just as the lieutenant was about to say something a shout was heard, and then before he could turn toward the commotion more shots rang out in the large room. When he finally managed to turn he saw that his men had fired again when they saw their attacker was trying to get to his feet. Patton could see the large bullet holes in the man's filthy white shirt. He saw that the portion of brain matter that had clung onto the shattered skull had finally fallen free. Then to his horror the badly wounded man started to push himself upward from the floor.

"What in the hell is this?" Patton said, but no one heard as even more shots rang out. One blast was from another shotgun. This time the large pellets struck the front of the face, taking off the upper half of the crazed man's head. The body finally slumped and fell over onto the floor.

Without saying another word, Patton started reloading his Colt. His hands were shaking, but he knew no one noticed because theirs were shaking just as badly. He knew that if he concentrated on reloading he wouldn't have to think about the impossibility of what just happened. When another loud report sounded Patton dropped the full clip he was trying to insert into the Colt. When he looked up he saw that Colonel Thomas had entered the building and had fired both barrels of a shotgun down into what remained of the beast's head, totally removing it.

"Now listen, it was as we suspected. You have to remove the head, damage the brain completely, and even remove the top of the brain stem. Any part of the brain still functioning can outthink you, and outfight you," Thomas said as he broke open the double-barreled shotgun and inserted two more shells. That was when Patton saw that the shot he

loaded was solid lead and not buckshot. The colonel was using an elephant gun.

Suddenly screams, roars, and gunfire erupted from all
sides of the hacienda. The loud reports were from the American weapons—the screams were emanating from something else.

As Patton and his men turned to leave the large room,
two of the French style doors smashed inward sending glass
and wood flying. As he aimed and fired his pistol, Patton
saw it was two more of the same white-clad, insane-looking
men as the one a moment before. They never hesitated once
they rolled after smashing through the doors. The first one
pounced on a private who had reacted too slowly to the attack. The man was up and into the poor boy's throat before
he knew what was happening. Blood flowed as one of the
private's buddies shook off his fear and fired an Enfield into
the side of the attacker's head. The beast jerked away, taking
a large amount of skin and muscle of the private with it. The
soldier fired again, not waiting to be stunned once more by
the lunatic before him. The third bullet hit the beastly looking creature on the lower chin, blowing most of the jaw
away. Another bullet hit it before it could recover from the
first of the devastating blows.

Patton saw the second of the crazed men rise still wrapped
in the large curtain that had covered the glass doors. He
aimed and fired quickly. The bullets punched holes into the
white lace curtains. Blood exploded, soaking the material as
the man underneath lost his balance and crashed to the floor.
Men fired point-blank at the still-moving lace curtains. Bullet after bullet hit the struggling man. Colonel Thomas
stepped forward and emptied both barrels of his shotgun
into the curtains. Blood misted in a small cloud, but still the
beast fought to free itself. Patton finally placed the reloaded
.45 automatic a few inches away from the outline of the
man's head and fired. The shot reverberated in the room as
the large-caliber bullet slammed into the side of the man's
head. Brain matter and a red spray of blood splattered over
the lace curtain and the men beyond. Then Thomas quickly

reloaded and added another two rounds of solid shot to the area where the beast's head was approximated to be. The body ceased moving.

Outside, the screams of the 8th were now mingling with the roars and animalistic yells of the attacking force of crazed killers.

Patton slid another clip of ammunition into his Colt and then stepped hurriedly out onto the veranda that looked onto the courtyard. He saw two troopers ride in through the open gates, and before they could react, he saw one of the strangely dressed men jump in front of one of the charging horses. The rider and horse reared up as the insanity-driven man hit the front breast of the huge animal. The beast bounced off as the horse reared over it. Then to the rider's astonishment the man sprang to his feet as if he were a gazelle. Patton took another two steps out onto the porch when the most amazing sight he had ever been witness to presented itself. The beast actually caught the forelegs of the horse before the animal could bring the sharp hooves and steel shoes down upon it. The man-beast twisted the legs of the horse until the body had to follow. Horse and rider hit the flagstone surface of the courtyard. Patton quickly aimed and fired as did the rider's companion. Bullets hit the killer, but they didn't stop him from leaping over the fallen horse to take the man before he could fight his way out from under his own horse.

Above the din of the strangest fight the young lieutenant had ever been witness to, he heard the soldier start screaming as the attacker started to use his teeth on the fallen man. Thirty, forty shots rang out in the course of a minute as more of the man-animals broke free from somewhere inside the hacienda.

"What in the devil are we up against here, Lieutenant?" the heavyset sergeant major asked as he tore his neckerchief free of his neck and started wiping blood from his bearded face.

Patton didn't answer as he took aim and fired two rounds into one of the filthy, muscled men that ran after another of the galloping horses.

"We have at least fifteen men down, sir." The sergeant major aimed the shotgun and fired both barrels at another of the men as he actually lifted a dead horse off of its rider just so he could sink his long, filthy teeth into his neck. "This is all wrong, Lieutenant."

Patton thought about the orders he had received. That after the hacienda had been taken, he was to burn everything. He remembered the general specifically mentioning the laboratory equipment. Screams entered his mind, pushing thoughts of his orders away to a more suitable place for the moment.

"One of those men, those things, took eight rounds to bring it down and then it still tried to get up. It took two of these to its head to put it down!" Colonel Thomas raised the shotgun he had just reloaded. "We didn't know that maniac had gone this far."

"Who in the hell are you?" Patton shouted as he started to feel his grip sliding free of the situation.

"My group is here to stop this nut; now follow orders Lieutenant and let's get this job done!" Thomas shouted at Patton, and for the first time he realized that this Colonel Thomas on detached duty to the National Archives was a stone killer. A man experienced in the art of death.

"Come, we have to finish taking the house. What we're looking for is in the basement. Get me ten men, tell your men to secure this courtyard, and then get a troop of men out to round up those civilians—we may need to find out what they know."

"Yes, sir," Patton said as he frowned and then pulled his old six-shot revolver from its holster. He went back through the same broken window he had exited from. Sunlight was now streaming into the main house and Patton could see much better. He saw the two men they had dispatched earlier. One was lying next to the dead sergeant, and to his shock and amazement, that one was even now still moving. Hands, jaws, and eyeless sockets where bullets and pellets had taken out the eyeballs were moving, twitching, and shaking. The two beasts' movements were uncoordinated and slow. The damage to their brains was so severe that their higher functions weren't cooperating. Patton for the first time in his adult life wanted to vomit from something he had witnessed.

"I am not going to deal with this!" Patton shouted over the gunfire. "Sergeant Major, tell Alexander to get in here with the explosives!"

The sergeant major turned and once more ran from the hacienda. Patton gestured for four troopers to start searching for the way into the basement, but before they could move a large door opened at the far end of the main room. Patton turned to see nothing but darkness at first, and then he saw the dim outline of a giant of a man. It stood there framed just beyond the door. Patton was shocked as he could swear he could see the glowing eyes looking right at him. Then just as suddenly the dark shape was gone. Before Patton could move he heard something that would cause him years of nightmares afterward—the laugh trailed out behind whatever had been standing in that doorway.

"This way," Patton shouted to his four men.

The lieutenant hit the open doorway and slid to a stop. He looked down into a black abyss that seemed to go on forever. He waited and gathered his courage and then started down. It was only thirty feet down to a dimly lit basement that smelled of dampness and mildew, and then he felt the coldness of the area beneath the first floor. He held both of his heavy weapons out before him as the other men pounded down the stairs. Patton looked around, hoping his eyes would adjust to the dimness of the basement faster than normal. Despite his bravado in all things, the blonde-haired lieutenant held his ground at the base of the steps.

"Come now, you have invaded my home. You have killed my test subjects just to get to me, and now you hesitate when the time draws near to meet your adversary?"

The voice was booming and had a growl hidden just beneath the words. Patton felt the chills slide up his backside as the meaning of the invite hit home. He knew then that they weren't dealing with a man at all, but some abnormality created artificially in this lonesome place south of the border.

"That's Ambrose himself," said Colonel Thomas as he reloaded his shotgun yet again. "Whatever happens Lieutenant, go through the remains of this place and get samples of whatever you find. Our government needs to find a way to fight this. An antidote, maybe, because if this thing gets onto the open market, there will be hell to pay. If I'm not there, get the samples to the president—only the president," he said, waiting for the young lieutenant to nod his head. "Now, may I suggest Lieutenant Patton that we kill the son of a bitch?"

George Patton quickly gestured for two of his men to go left; the other two he placed behind him and Thomas, and the attack element advanced through the dimness toward the spot they thought the voice had come from.

"I have been waiting for a test such as this."

Another laugh after the words.

"Jesus Christ, Lieutenant, what is this place," the private immediately behind Patton and the colonel hissed.

"Take hold of yourself private and get ready to—"

Several loud reports and shotgun blasts sounded in the dark basement as something in front of the advancing men moved. Then before Patton could see what was happening, more boots pounded down the stairs. He turned and saw the sergeant major and immediately behind him was Lieutenant Alexander with a set of saddlebags over one shoulder and two Colt .45s at the ready.

"I have the dynamite, Lieutenant."

Patton was tempted to just place the charges in the basement, ignite the fuse, and get out of the hell he now found himself in, but he remembered the orders that Pershing had given him. He was forced to confirm the death of this Ambrose. He shook his head and then cursed his luck. He noticed that the gunfire from above had dwindled to almost nothing as the troopers started taking full control of the hacienda. Remembering his dead men up on the main floor, Patton swallowed the fear he was feeling and then waved his men forward.

"I'm waiting for you—come, get what you came for!"

"We're coming, Ambrose, we're coming. This isn't London and you sure as hell aren't in Whitechapel. We know all about your deals, we're here to stop you!" Thomas shouted around Patton.

The lieutenant knew the name Whitechapel, but that statement by the colonel offered nothing of an explanation to him whatsoever.

"Ah, Whitechapel, the good days, the fun days, the turning of the tide as they say . . . now come and get me and see what awaits you!"

This time the words were barely understandable as they came from the darkness ahead. As Patton stepped forward he looked down and saw light streaming up through the cracks in the floorboards. There was another level below this one and he knew then that he and his men were being led in that direction. He swallowed, and for the first time in his entire arrogance-filled life, George S. Patton was terrified. He shook himself to bring his terror under control and then advanced farther into the basement.

"It's alright to be frightened, Patton. There are things in the world that are truly terrifying, and this is but one of those nightmares . . . I know, I've seen it, and—"

They heard the creaking of a door ahead of them, quieting Thomas. Then a far-thicker wave of mustiness hit their noses.

"There, a trapdoor!" Lieutenant Alexander said as he squeezed by Patton and Thomas and then ran forward.

"Goddamn it, no!"

Alexander was already three steps down through the door in the flooring before Patton could stop the young West Point graduate. He hurriedly followed. He and the others descended the stairs as fast as the darkness around them would allow when suddenly the entire wooden staircase was wrenched out from under them. They were thrown to the left, the right, and then they all felt the bottom of their stomachs fall free of their bodies as they became airborne.

Patton hit the dirt-lined floor and two of his men fell across him. They were all lucky it hadn't been but ten feet from top to bottom. As he tried to kick free he saw that the staircase had fallen directly on two of his men, crushing them to death. The lieutenant cursed and then gained his feet. He had lost the automatic somewhere in the fall, so he pulled out his second six-shot Peacemaker. He cocked both pistols, and that was when he heard the laugh coming from his front. He and the remaining men aimed their weapons into the blackness ahead. But before he could move, he heard the voice from behind. It was Colonel Thomas. He was trapped underneath the staircase and it was obvious that his legs were crushed, and the large wooden splinter coming through his lower abdomen made the leg problem that much less of a burden. The colonel was a dead man, he just didn't know it yet.

"Kill the bastard for me, and get the samples to Washington, code 5656," Thomas said as his eyes slowly closed. Patton would never get any answers from the brave lieutenant colonel as to who he really was and who he really worked for.

Patton heard moaning at his feet and then he realized that young Alexander was hurt as well. The saddlebag containing the dynamite was still clutched in his hand. Just as Patton reached down to help Alexander to his feet something shot out of the darkness, grabbed the boy, and disappeared before Patton could react. In the brief flash of movement, Patton could not believe what he had just seen. Alexander was not only gone, pulled into the blackness ahead, but in that briefest of moments he had seen something that could not have existed. The man, or whatever it had been, was a giant. The clothing was in tatters and the smell was atrocious. The hair was long and the teeth flashed for the few seconds it took to drag Alexander away. They were hideously long, canine in appearance, and sharp. It was as if whatever it was had reverted back to a time when men were nothing more than the monkeys Darwin said they had sprung from. He couldn't help it—his hands once again started shaking.

The screaming started almost as soon as the attack had

happened. They all heard Alexander screeching, a sound that couldn't possibly come from the throat of a human being. The pain was etched in every decibel of that scream.

The sergeant major reacted without orders. He charged forward with one of the shotguns and then he just disappeared, vanishing through the dirt-covered subbasement. Patton ran to the spot as did his remaining troopers. There was bright light streaming through a hole that had opened up beneath the sergeant major's feet. As Patton looked through that hole he could see the sergeant major below, just coming to his senses.

"Are you alright?" Patton called down into the hell pit beneath their feet.

The sergeant major rolled over onto his back, but just before he could answer something grabbed his left-booted foot and pulled him off the ground. The man vanished just as Alexander had a moment before. Patton could not believe what was happening—a hacienda that had not one or two but three sublevels. He grimaced as he saw through the bright lights below that he was looking at a completely new portion of the old building. Barrels and lab equipment lined the walls far below. Modern equipment was everywhere. Then he jumped when a large figure appeared below and looked up through the gaping hole in the floor. The smile was apparent, but what really made Patton shudder was the fact that the beast still had the sergeant major by one leg.

"Come, come down and see the miracle I have created!" the beast shouted up as he raised the screaming sergeant up by his one leg and then spun him around so quickly that the sergeant major never felt his own death as his body was slammed into the stone flooring below.

One of his privates tried to push by Patton to get into the hole, but the lieutenant held him back.

"No, not one more man!" he screamed as the beast below laughed, a maniacal-sounding noise that reverberated throughout the dirt-lined false basement. He looked around in a panic as he failed to think of how he could handle this. That was when his foot kicked something on the floor near the

hole in the ground. It was the double saddlebags containing
the explosives. There was a twin lying next to it. He quickly
made a decision. He reached down and then started pulling
out the wrapped dynamite. There were six bundles of five
along with enough fuses to do the job. He started tossing the
wrapped bundles to his men.

"Spread these out all along the basement."

"You hesitate to see my miracle; come now and join your
men in my workshop!"

"Go to hell, you son of a bitch," Patton screamed as he
started pulling fuse line and stretching it across the dirt
flooring. He didn't notice that he accidentally kicked the
second set of leather saddlebags into the abyss below. There
was a laugh as the beast kicked the bags out of the way as it
continued to stare upward, daring the men there to do something.

Once the fuses were connected Patton chanced a look
into the wide hole. The beast was there, smiling as it looked
up. The sergeant major was lying broken at the creature's
feet. The mouth opened and closed and then it saw what Patton was holding.

"This is for my men, you bastard!" Patton screamed and
then lit the short fuse. The creature roared and then tried in
vain to leap upward toward the hole. Patton angrily emptied
both Peacemakers into the upturned face with three of the
rounds slicing through the cheeks and entering the left-side
forehead. The creature stumbled, fell to the floor, and then
slowly started to rise. Patton cursed again and then was
pulled away from the hole. One of the privates screamed
something he did not understand. Then he found himself
standing where the staircase used to be. He had forgotten
that they had fallen into the second level and thus had no
escape route.

"Jesus, that was well thought out!" he yelled.

Suddenly four ropes appeared from nowhere as the animalistic roar from below actually made the dirt flooring
beneath their feet shake. The men above started pulling
them free of the second level. As Patton waited for the last

private to be pulled up, he chanced a last look at the hole. A hand reached through, tried in vain to gain purchase, and then fell free. The creature was actually jumping the twenty feet and almost making it. Patton's eyes widened as he grabbed the last rope. The men above yanked up and through the hole, leaving his dead men behind him.

"Go, go, go!" he shouted at the men as they started streaming from the building. With one last look down, and in his mind's eye and wild imagination he knew the beast had indeed gained the top of the hole, Patton slammed the door closed and ran for his life just as the explosives below detonated.

The hacienda shook and shuttered, but the old adobe held firm as the first level of basement collapsed onto the second, burying the third for all time, at least he hoped.

Patton bent at the waist inside of the main room of the hacienda and allowed his stomach to relieve itself of its contents.

"Sir, we have Mexican troops approaching from the south. I suggest we retreat across the border. We're down to twenty-seven men, and we have thirty-two wounded," a corporal said as he helped Patton straighten.

"Spread the word to all the men to assist the wounded. Get them mounted so we can leave this place."

The corporal vanished. Patton looked around and then, feeling he had accomplished his mission to a certain degree, he too left the interior of the hacienda.

As the remaining men of the 8th United States Cavalry limped back across the border, Lieutenant George S. Patton knew he had disobeyed his orders in not confirming the death of their target, Lawrence Ambrose. He assumed that whatever horrible force was at play in Mexico had killed the professor prior to their attack no matter what Colonel Thomas had stated. He knew this man could be no man of science. The beast was sent from hell, and Patton would never believe that it had been the man they called Ambrose.

Patton was shocked a year later when he was introduced

to the president of the United States just after the war was over in Europe. The president was sick even then, but he managed to pull Patton aside and ask him a pointed question.

"Tell me that Colonel Thomas died doing his duty."

Patton had not thought of Thomas since the dark night he dropped off the small package of serum he had recovered and hidden from the army. He had again disobeyed orders from Pershing and delivered Colonel Thomas' last request to the president.

"He was a particular friend of mine, and someone I thought was indestructible."

Patton told the president his firsthand account of that night and the battle of Perdition's Gate. The president never said a word. When his tale was complete, Patton saw the president of the United States swipe a tear from his tired face and then smile.

"He was quite an officer, I can tell you."

"Sir," Patton braved, "code 5656, what is that?" Patton leaned in closer to Wilson. "And that officer could not be working for the archives; I don't think the army would waste him there."

Wilson continued to smile as he nodded his head. "There is no such thing as a code 5656, nor do we have any army staff officer on detached duty to the National Archives. Why on earth would we need soldiers doing file clerk work . . . as you said Lieutenant, why would the army waste a man there?" The president patted the silent Patton on the back and then moved off. That was all the information the future general ever learned about the strange lieutenant colonel on detached service from the National Archives.

For the rest of his military life, Patton would never be the same. He would overcompensate for every moment of fear he would ever encounter. Men would know the crazed general in later years and never know why he acted the way he did. They would never understand that the famous man had entered hell and saw the darkest side of men.

In that time long ago Patton assumed that the professor and his miracle drug had succumbed to his attack, but he would never know that Perdition's Fire would only ferment and become stronger until it would be released among his countrymen one last time.

Hell on earth was buried and forgotten along with Dr. Jekyll, Mr. Hyde, and the infamous Jack the Ripper.

PART ONE

Día de los Muertos
(Day of the Dead)

What is death? It is the glass of life broken into a
thousand pieces, where the soul disperses like
perfume from a flask, into the silence of the eternal night.
—Unknown Author

1

State of Tamaulipas, Mexico,
Thirty-five Miles South of Nuevo Laredo
(Present Day)

Geologist Sarah McIntire studied the cave's lower passages but could see little in the klieg lighting that had been placed by the students from Baylor University. She was accompanied by three undergraduate kids that knew nothing of Sarah's real employer, and that was the way it would be kept. Not even the professor, or even the doctor from the University of Mexico and his twenty students, had any idea just who Sarah really was and who she was employed by.

The Event Group had placed Sarah on the field expedition not long after the joint venture was announced by the two universities to explore and document one of the many excavated caves that had been used as small armories and hideouts at the turn of the century by none other than Pancho Villa, the Mexican revolutionary. The stash of weapons, food, and horses were placed inside the natural cave formations by the bandit before raiding into the Texas border towns across the Rio Grande River. Sarah and her two-man security team were there to document not the bandit's secret hideaways, but the ancient cave paintings that everyone outside of the higher fields of learning seemed to ignore. If she found them to be authentic, and she could tell this by the geological makeup that the paintings were depicted upon, she would then authorize further study by the Event Group and their anthropological division.

The small man stepped up to Sarah and whispered as he squeezed past her in the narrow cave passage.

"Not exactly Carlsbad Caverns is it?"

Sarah smiled at Jason Ryan who was part of her two-man security team. She half turned and shined the small flashlight into his face.

"We can't have everything, Mr. Excitement. And as a matter of fact I'm beginning to think this could be quite a find for the Southwest. I think these were made by Southern Cheyenne Indians, and not the Apache people like the good professors believe. We do need to get a team down here from the Group; it looks like some of the theories that have been floating around by the Anthropology Department may be true about the Southern Cheyenne having led raids against the Apache this far south. This may be the proof they need."

Jason kept his face expressionless and then yawned as wide as he could.

"Asshole," she said as her light went from him to a space that was void of pictograms. The spot was hollowed out, as if a piece of the granite had been sliced out by a power tool.

"Yeah, well this asshole could have been playing football today, but Director Compton thinks you need a babysitter on this gig. Why am I—"

"This is wrong; some idiot has cut into this wall and taken . . . ," she stopped speaking and shined the flashlight farther down the cave wall. "Damn it! Someone's stealing this stuff." She moved the light back to Jason who had his own light out and was looking at the ground.

"Yeah, well whoever they were wore U.S. Army–issue combat boots, and one," he pointed to a smaller set next to the larger, "ladies, or midget male, designer Timberland work boots," he said as his light picked up several more footprints in the loose soil of the cave floor. "You know, for the past two days, starting across the border in Laredo, I've had the feeling we were being followed. I wrote it off as just being paranoid about everything lately."

"This is criminal. Hell, no one's supposed to know about this place. You think someone knew we were coming here and followed us?"

"I don't know, but Sarah, Mexico is a convenience store for antiquity theft, you know that. Hell, I bet when we head back through the border you can pick up a piece of this wall at the flea market in Nuevo Laredo."

"It's sickening. Come on, let's get these kids back to the cave opening," she said as she shined the light on her wristwatch. "I promised to meet Jack and his mother for dinner in Laredo at seven."

"And I better get you there on time for the big meeting—scared?" Jason asked with a smirk.

Sarah didn't answer as she moved the light over at least six areas where the cave paintings had been removed by modern power tools.

"I asked if you're scared meeting the colonel's mom."

Sarah finally looked over at her friend. "Absolutely terrified, now shut the hell up about it."

Jason smiled and started to follow Sarah out of the lower passages of the natural cave system, shouting at the students in English and Spanish for them to head back to the surface.

"I wouldn't worry too much about his mother. I mean the colonel's a nice guy, isn't he? Someone had to have taught him right. I'm sure they are just like one another. Hell, you may even find out that he cried when he was a kid when he saw Bambi's mother got killed."

"That isn't helping, Ryan!"

In the bright sunlight Sarah placed her sunglasses on as the first of the two buses of students pulled out, heading north to the border. The second bus filled with university students from Mexico City would head south to a cheap hotel that was rented for them. Sarah waved at the bus as it passed by. She then glanced over at her security escort of two men.

Ryan was bent at the knees and was examining something in the dirt. Jason straightened and moved to follow the academic team toward where Sarah was standing.

"I would like to thank you for your excellent evaluation of the geological deposits surrounding the pictographs, Miss McIntire. I must send a letter of appreciation to your employer."

Professor Salvador Espinoza, dean of anthropological studies at the University of Mexico, was smiling and holding out his hand. Next to him were three professors from that department, and bringing up the rear was the lone professor from Baylor University, Dr. Barbara Stansfield. Jason Ryan brought up the rear, and that was when Sarah noticed Jason raise his sunglasses and then point to the ground next to the American professor's boots. He then lowered the sunglasses when he saw Sarah had indeed noticed her footwear.

"Yes, I agree," the American professor added, "excellent job. Where should we send that letter, Miss McIntire, was it the National Geographic Society?"

Sarah slowly released Professor Espinoza's hand after shaking it and then looked the American woman in her sunglass-covered eyes. She held out her hand and the two shook as Sarah sized the woman up, even though young Sarah was far shorter than her counterpart.

"No, I was sent by the Texaco Corporation. They've had dealings here before and they knew I was an expert on the formations that make up the surface area of most of Tamaulipas, and the vice president of the company is a graduate of Baylor," she said as she removed her gloved hand from Stansfield's own. Sarah had stuck to her cover story, with her bosses at the Event Group supplying the information about her fictitious employment history, so she knew the part about the Texaco VP was true.

"My mistake, Texaco it is," Stansfield said as she removed her sunglasses and looked closely into Sarah's. McIntire then removed her own sunglasses so the professor could get a better look. "I was just wondering because I overheard your two men over there call you lieutenant."

Sarah smiled as she looked at Ryan and Marine Lance Corporal Kyle Udall. It was Ryan who rolled his eyes and looked away first.

"Yes, well I used to be in the army, that's where I received my degree, and my military title stuck after it became known throughout my department at Texaco."

"I see," Stansfield said and was going to ask another question when three vehicles came into view over the crest of the small hill that fronted the cave system.

Ryan and Udall moved to separate. Udall moved toward the cars that were waiting for the academic teams, while Ryan moved toward one of the lean-tos where he had a large backpack.

Sarah saw their movement and immediately became alert to danger herself. She spied the three vehicles. One was a new Cadillac Escalade; the other two were fairly new Range Rovers. They looked to be full of men.

"Who is this?" Stansfield asked as she raised a hand to shield her eyes.

"Professor Espinoza, were you aware that more than just a few of the pictographs were removed from the cave system prior to our arrival here?"

"No, I was not," the Mexican professor said as his eyes went from the three SUVs to those of Sarah McIntire. "What do you mean *removed*?"

"Cut straight from the stone by mechanical means. Several hundred thousand dollars worth if I know the black market well enough." Sarah chanced a glance down once more to the boots worn by Professor Stansfield. She confirmed they were women's Timberlands, approximately size five. "Maybe these late arrivals can explain what happened. They seem to be driving fast enough toward us and they do look like men with a purpose." Sarah looked at the American anthropologist. "Doctor Stansfield, you claimed that you had never been in the lower galleries of the cave system before, so can you explain why your boot prints were there?" Sarah said as she smiled, not looking at the American professor but keeping her eyes on the three cars as they came to

a sliding halt, creating a dust cloud that covered Jason
Ryan as he removed a nine-millimeter Berretta from his
backpack.

"I assure you this is the first day that I have had an opportunity to study the system, I—"

Sarah turned from watching the three cars dislodge their
passengers of fifteen salty-looking characters.

"There may be one or two pairs of designer Timberlands
in the whole of Mexico Doctor, and you seem to be wearing
a pair, and the footprints we found in the lower galleries
were Timberland size five, and I'm only guessing here, but
you seem to fit the shoe."

Sarah saw that the men were armed. Some held hand-
guns and others had very lethal-looking mini AK-47s. She
also noticed they were pointed at them.

Professor Espinoza, with wide eyes, moved his two assistants to his rear as the men approached.

"May we help you?" Espinoza asked in Spanish.

The man leading the fourteen others never hesitated—
he raised his automatic weapon and shot Espinoza in the
forehead.

Sarah couldn't believe what she had just witnessed. The
man had been talking to her just a second before.

"This wasn't in the deal, what are you doing?" Stansfield
cried as she took two involuntary steps back.

The same man who had just murdered Professor Espinoza aimed and quickly fired a round into one of the male
anthropology assistants. The young man crumpled and fell
dead into the dust. The murderous man then walked over to
Stansfield and looked the forty-six-year-old over. He suddenly raised the automatic and brought it down onto the top
of her head, sending the blonde professor crashing to the
ground. He then waved his companions forward. Three men
came toward Sarah, but five steps were as close as they got.
Two bullets apiece slammed into their heads and chests.

Sarah dove for cover as Jason Ryan came forward in an
assault squat as he took in more of the men. He aimed at the
man who had killed Professor Espinoza and fired once, but

one of the assassin's men who had come forward stepped in his line of fire and took the round to his chest.

Suddenly an automatic weapon opened up and Sarah ducked her head down as two of the fifty bullets fired from the other ruthless men in the group hit Ryan and he fell backward. He lay there unmoving. Sarah started to stand, but the leader of the group kicked her in the stomach and sent her rolling on the ground. Then she heard the female anthropology assistant that had been pushed aside by Espinoza scream before being silenced. Sarah, as she held her stomach in pain and shame, heard another AK-47 open fire. She remained on the ground and never saw Lance Corporal Udall die as he came out of one of the vehicles where he had been rummaging for his weapon.

The leader of the group of men sneered as he used his boot to roll Sarah over onto her back. He pointed at her and then at the younger woman he had just silenced with a punch to the face, and then he used the barrel of the automatic to point one last time at the bleeding and unconscious blonde professor from Baylor. He smiled and wiped the sweat from his dripping face and beard.

"Jefe will be pleased with his new guests—two gringo women and one young seniorita from Mexico City." He reached down and pulled Sarah up by the hair and looked her in the eyes. "Pleased indeed."

Sarah was let go and she fell back into the dust. She immediately rolled over and tried to look at the spot where Jason had fallen, but she couldn't see him. She managed to look up, and that was when she saw the sprawled body of Corporal Udall. He was lying face down in the dirt. Sarah shook her head, but she remained silent as the leader of the group pulled Professor Stansfield up, also by the hair. He shook her hard.

"Our arrangement is at an end. You were supposed to delay these fools from examining the cave until we had all of the artifacts out, you stupid gringo bitch," he shouted at the woman who was just coming around. "Señor Guzman will be very angry, so you better hope he will be happy with two new women for his stable, or you may learn why he has earned his nickname."

Sarah saw the American woman shake her head, still unable to find her voice after the blow to the top of her head. Sarah slowly started to rise and then stopped suddenly as she heard the nickname of the man they were to be brought to. Her heart froze as she recognized the name of one of the most ruthless men in the world.

They were to be taken to Nuevo Laredo and Sarah knew they would come face to face with the most ruthless drug lord in all of Mexico—Juan Guzman—the Anaconda.

The man with the binoculars lowered them and ducked behind the small rise as the women from the colleges were ruthlessly pushed and shoved and beaten until they were all inside the three vehicles. The man rolled onto his back and felt to make sure he still had his small .38 caliber handgun in his waistband. He then pulled a cell phone from his pants pocket and with shaking hands raised it to his face. He opened the cover, still shaking from witnessing the ruthless murder of four men in front of the caves, and then to his disappointment he saw that the cell phone's signal strength was only at two bars. That had to be enough.

"Good God," he mumbled as he pushed a selected number from his address book and hit it. He had to do it twice as he lay with his face to the sun. He couldn't stop the shakes from making the simplest of tasks so daunting. Finally the call went through and a phone on the other end was answered.

"Yes?" answered a firm voice.

"Señor, I did as our contract asked for and tailed the subject from her hotel in Laredo. She crossed the border just as you said she would."

"And the main target?"

"He was not among the two men that accompanied her."

"That is not very good news," came the reply.

"Señor, they are all dead," said the man as he removed the small gun from his pants, fumbled it, and then finally caught it and held it to his chest.

"Explain that. The woman you followed is dead?" asked the voice, this time without some of its confident manner.

"Señor, the three women are alive, but all of the men are dead. They were killed by other men who arrived in cars."

"Who are these men?"

"There is only one man in all of Mexico that kills with such abandon, señor. It had to be the work of Juan Guzman; no one else would dare such an attack in his territory."

"I know this name, yes I know it well. I have done business with this rather unstable gentleman in the past. He has some silly nickname down there if I remember right."

"Señor, the man you wanted me to find was not among the dead, but the woman I was asked to follow hoping she would lead me to him has been taken by the most brutal man in all of Mexico. What am I to do now?"

There was silence on the other end of the phone. It lasted for a full thirty seconds until the shaking man thought he had finally lost the signal. He tried to press the gun into his chest to assist in stopping the shakes.

"You still have my business card?" the voice finally asked.

"Si," the man answered as he rose partially to his knees and looked around to make sure he wasn't to be the next target of the murdering men from below.

"Good, I now want you to wait for two hours and then go to see this Guzman and tell him an old acquaintance would like to discuss some business. Relay to him that I am most particularly interested in hearing about his Anasazi Indian collection. Tell him my opening offer is twenty-five million dollars, which should at least get you in the door. Once there explain that I am on my way to meet with him. Is that clear?"

"Are you insane señor, I will be killed!"

"Do this and I will wire transfer one million dollars into your San Antonio bank account. Now do this or do not come back to the States, or you will discover that the truly ruthless men do not only reside in Mexico." The phone connection ended.

"Madre di dios," the man said as the cell phone fell to his chest where he allowed it to lay. He looked at the business card he had pulled from his pocket.

The man moaned at the thought of traveling thirty miles north to Nuevo Laredo and presenting himself to Juan Guzman, the Anaconda, just like a lamb to slaughter. First he was contracted out of his agency's offices in San Antonio to follow this small American woman. He was then told that this McIntire woman would eventually lead him to the man that his employer sought—a Colonel Jack Collins. Now he was to be sacrificed to Juan Guzman for a reason he knew nothing of.

The man slammed the business card to his chest and cursed the one-million-dollar bribe the man had offered. He sniveled and then looked at the card once more. It was one of the expensively printed business cards you can only pick up at the best stationery stores—Mr. Hanover Jones, Antiquities Acquisition and Auction House, New York City—London—Paris.

The man placed the card back into his pocket and knew he would follow orders as he sat up and took a deep breath. After all, a million dollars could buy a very nice funeral.

Two thousand miles away Colonel Henri Farbeaux, the man known as Hanover Jones to the legitimate world, calmly hung up the rented office phone and then slowly stood and furiously tipped the desk he was sitting behind upside down. Not only was he not to kill Jack Collins, he now learned that the only woman he admired outside of his dead wife was being held by a murderous scum.

Farbeaux stood and looked at the phone on the floor with the broken desk tipped beside it. He took a deep breath and then forced calmness into his body. Nothing could infuriate him more than the thought of Collins, the man responsible for his beloved wife's death, still breathing, but nothing could ever match that feeling more than the thought of little Sarah being hurt. He reached into his expensive coat and brought out his cell phone. While he hit the number he wanted, he kicked absentmindedly at the broken phone upon the floor. His eyes were blazing in anger.

"Have my plane ready with a flight plan to Laredo, Texas."

Event Group Complex
Nellis AFB, Nevada

The director of Department 5656, Niles Compton, sat on the small set of bleachers and watched the flag football game that was being played between the nuclear sciences division and the security department. The second in command of security, who was quarterbacking the muscular and far more physical team of security personnel, Captain Carl Everett, was starting to look frustrated as the larger men and women could not seem to shake the much smaller but far more agile scientists of Assistant Director Virginia Pollock's nuclear sciences department. The former SEAL kept looking at the clock and was seeing that time was running out on their three-point lead.

The underground complex was built to house the greatest historical treasures, objects that had a defining moment in either the history of the United States or, more importantly, the world. Department 5656, known to a select few in the federal government as the Event Group, was tasked to find parallels in world history with the events unfolding in modern times to avoid the same pitfalls of our shared past. The artifacts stored in the Event Group's ten thousand steel vaults represented spectacular finds in archeological history. Most would eventually find their way into the public domain after study, while others would be forever kept secret from the people of the world, due to either political, religious, or military sensitivities. The judge as to what constituted a top secret find is the president of the United States.

The massive complex was an underground labyrinth of naturally formed caves far beneath Nellis Air Force Base. The complex was built by President Roosevelt during World

War II after the original site had been moved from Arlington, Virginia. Department 5656 is the darkest department of the American federal system and is solely answerable to the president of the Unites States. It had been that way since its inception in 1863 through to its official charter in 1917 by Woodrow Wilson, who brought the Event Group into legitimate being.

Director Niles Compton smiled as he was nudged by the computer sciences director, Pete Golding, who nodded at the clock as it continued to run down. The intramural games played by the sixteen separate departments were a needed relief used by the six hundred personnel inside the massive complex that ran eighty-nine levels beneath the desert sands of Nevada.

"Looks like the security force dominance may be finally coming to an end if Virginia's people can get the ball back," Pete said as he watched Everett and the rest of his offense take their time lining up for the snap in an attempt to take as many seconds off the clock as possible.

"Can you imagine the look on Jack's face when he hears his department's unblemished record could possibly be in jeopardy? God, I wish he were here," Niles said as he watched Everett pointing to his favorite wide receiver, Lieutenant Will Mendenhall, who had thus far caught everything thrown his way.

"Well it's really hurt security not having Jack at running back today," Pete countered.

"Thank God he's visiting his mom in Texas, and thank goodness he's meeting Sarah there when she's finished with the dig in Tamaulipas. Still, I think I'll call him if security loses; I can't pass that chance up." Niles Compton eyed the clock and then frowned.

Everett called out the signals and the ball was snapped. Instead of running the ball, and thus running the clock out, the captain had decided to go for the nuclear science department's jugular and win by ten. Mendenhall shot off the line and then sprinted past the science department's defender. Everett heaved the ball as far as he could. The female defender, a nuclear regulatory specialist on detached service from Los Alamos, tripped as Will flew by her. In the bleachers those rooting for the sciences moaned as they saw the end coming right before their eyes. Niles frowned as he felt his wallet getting lighter due to the bet he had placed with Colonel Collins before he left on leave to see his mother.

Will smiled broadly as he saw the ball fall from the sky. His feet firmly planted on the athletic turf of the underground recreation arena, and only a foot from the out-of-bounds line, the ball was only inches from being laid into his hands. He was merely twenty yards from the goal line for a chance to keep the security department's winning streak alive at ten in a row.

Unbeknownst to Everett, Mendenhall, and the rest of the security department team, they had been outthought. Virginia Pollock, the least likely of suspects, had placed herself at the goal line knowing that the captain would not be satisfied with a mere three-point victory. The tall lithe woman with the dark-brown hair sprinted in her sweatpants and shirt to the spot where Will Mendenhall thought he was alone, and just before the ball touched his fingertips she stepped in front of him and intercepted the pass. Her body nudged him just enough that Will lost his balance and went crashing onto the fake grass of the field, shocked because he had had no idea Virginia was in the area.

The security team, the people running laps on the track, and even the weightlifters working out on the side of the field were all stunned as Virginia sprinted down the field in the opposite direction. Carl went from jumping up and down as the vision of a fifty-yard pass play went flying from his thoughts to attempting to gain momentum to head Virginia off at the pass. He saw the MIT grad and former nuclear engineer from General Dynamics Corporation running free. Everett started his pursuit.

The spectators watching were on their feet as the older woman saw Everett approaching at an angle. She decided that, flag football or not, she could not allow Everett to catch her. She switched the ball to the protected right side of her body, and as Carl came into reach for her flag dangling behind her, she shot out her left hand and arm, catching him squarely in the jaw and face. It was a straight-arm the pros would have been proud of. Everett grunted and then fell face first onto the turf as Virginia sprinted by. As she crossed the goal line with the rest of the security department chasing her, Virginia raised the ball into the air and then spiked it to the cheers of all watching.

"I'll be damned," Everett said as he looked up from his prone position. He swiped at the blood that had come from the split lip he now had thanks to the assistant director.

Mendenhall came up out of breath and helped his boss to his feet, and as they both looked around they saw Pete Golding and Director Compton jumping up and down in the bleachers, high-fiving each other, enjoying the celebration as Virginia's nuclear sciences division hoisted her on their shoulders. The 0–9 sciences had just pulled off the upset of the intramural season. Both men suspected the word would spread throughout the complex as fast as a lightning strike.

"The colonel is going to be pissed," Mendenhall said as he tried to catch his breath.

Everett again swiped at the blood that was now not only coursing from his split lip but also the rug burn on his chin.

"And I'm going to tell him over the phone," Everett said. "I'll wait until he gets back from his leave; by then the humiliation may have calmed down a little."

"Good idea," Mendenhall said as he saw the victors winding their way toward the vanquished. "Oh, this is going to suck!"

As Virginia was placed on the ground she smiled in a purely female way and batted her eyes at Carl.

"That split lip looks bad. Did I do that?" she said as she placed her hand over her mouth in an "oh God, what have I done" falsity.

"I didn't think you had it in you, madam A.D.," Everett said as he straightened and then took Virginia in his arms and hugged her. "I have to admit, you got us."

She smiled and pulled away and then someone handed

her a cell phone and she punched in her security code for the supercomputer Europa so she could get an outside line.

"And just who are you calling?" Everett asked near panic.

"Why, Jack, of course. I want to be the one to tell him."

"Ah, Virginia, can we talk about this?" Everett said as he started following her as she tried to make the connection.

Across the field Niles Compton was still smiling as he watched the two teams meet. He smiled even wider when he saw Everett and Mendenhall running after Virginia Pollock. He was about to go down onto the field and take some fun time for a change when he was approached by a blue-clad marine PFC.

"Excuse me, Dr. Compton, you have an emergency call from the security duty officer. He says he has our contact at the FBI in Washington on the line. It seems we've had trouble in Mexico—" the marine looked from Niles to Pete and then leaned in toward the director—"sir, we have people down."

Niles immediately lost his smile. "Pete, run and catch Captain Everett and Virginia and get them to my office, ASAP. Tell him we may have gone Code One in Mexico."

Pete immediately started running to head off Everett. He knew what a Code One was, as did all Event Group personnel—people in the field had come into harm's way and may be down, or even lost.

Niles turned and left the athletic complex wondering how a university-sponsored field team in Mexico could have an emergency when Sarah was there only to validate the geological formation in which some old pictographs had been painted on a cave wall.

With Ryan and another security man with her, that was three Event Group staff that may be hurt, or even killed. Director Niles Compton knew at the very least there was big trouble in Mexico.

Laredo, Texas
Four hours later

The man sat at the table at the Alamosa Chop and Steak House in downtown Laredo. He was well dressed in civilian attire, a charcoal gray suit highlighted by a bright red tie. His hair was cut short, but not as short as it had been throughout his eighteen years in the Unites States Army. His smile came easier to him since he had been reassigned after testifying against the army and the White House back in 2006 about interference of command in Afghanistan. At the time, Major Jack Collins had thought his career was finished as he was sent to the high desert of Nevada and literally buried underneath Nellis Air Force Base. That was where his tour of detached service had begun for Department 5656, the Event Group, as its head of security operations. Tonight Jack Collins was on leave. He was to meet the woman he had fallen in love with when she returned from across the border where she was involved in an archeological find in northern Mexico.

Jack smiled as he eased the cover of his cell phone closed and then looked across the table at his mother, Cally, who returned the smile as she placed her drink on the table before her. The woman would never be placed in the age category she claimed. She was young looking to be Jack's mother. Her face and body belonged to that of a woman of thirty-four years and not the fifty-four years of age her birth certificate said she was. The brown-haired Cally looked from Jack to her youngest child, Lynn, who had come back into Jack's life after many years of being estranged. Their careers had kept them far removed from the normal brother-sister relationships that most families share, Lynn's with the CIA, Jack's with the army.

"Well, Sarah's not answering her cell phone, as usual," Jack said as he reached for his glass of beer.

"She may be having a hard time getting through that damn border crossing. You know how rough it is since the border's been exploding with the drug war over in Nuevo

Laredo—she'll be fine, you said she was quite a distance away from the trouble zone," Lynn said. "From our reports at the agency, and also from the FBI and Texas Rangers, the drug thing seems to have sorted itself out. The border alert level has been downgraded significantly."

Jack's little sister watched him as he sipped at his beer. She had noticed a large change in Jack since he had become involved with Sarah. He smiled far more than she could ever remember her serious-faced brother ever smiling. His gait had a spring to it, and when she had seen him with Sarah the few times they had been together she could see Jack's face light up. For the first time in straight-as-an-arrow Jack Collins's life he was actually slowing down to smell the roses, and it was all because of the woman he called "small stuff," Sarah McIntire. Lynn could see Jack was dying inside in his nervousness at Sarah meeting their mother for the first time.

"Yeah, you're probably right," he said and tried to push all thought of Sarah being late aside for the time being.

Cally Collins watched her son closely. She was happy for Jack. He had become a new man since his time on detached service, wherever that was. Her son had always been quiet about things in his personal as well as his professional life. After losing so many men in the field during his time in special operations, he had become detached, even secretive of his emotions and personal feelings. Now came along this woman she was here to meet. Sarah, that's all Jack could talk about in his e-mails and his phone calls home.

She smiled as Jack talked with his little sister. He reminded her so much of his father, John, lost when Jack was only eleven in some far-off place that was never really described to her by the U.S. Army. He had been a colonel at the time, the very same rank and age of his son now. Cally suspected that in his position and rank he may have found out many more details about his father's fate—far more than Cally herself knew, but if he had, her oldest child had never shared that information with her.

Cally realized many years before that she didn't need to know anything other than what she had been told. If her

husband's death had been by any other means or circumstance than what the army had said, Jack would find a way
to tell her. And she also knew her son well enough that if
anything about his father's death was darker than the army
had told her, Jack would also fix it. It was enough to know
that he was just like his father, honest to the point of pain,
and that was good enough to tell Cally that their son turned
out the way his father would have liked.

"Jack, with everything you've told me about her I feel
like I already know Sarah. And if I'm right in my assessment of her she's probably as scared as I am in anticipation
of meeting each other. Believe me, anyone who won over
your stubborn heart scares me with her womanly powers,"
Cally said, smiling wide as she raised her martini glass.

Jack shook his head as his face turned red. He never
thought of himself as a guy that was stubborn at all, but if
his mom and Sarah, along with Lynn, Everett, Mendenhall,
Ryan, and the director, say it's so, it must be true. Jack raised
his glass of beer and toasted his mother. Lynn laughed and
joined her glass with theirs.

Cally excused herself from the table and Lynn waited
until she had disappeared into the semidarkness of the restaurant before she smiled at her brother.

"So, what's happening in spooksville these days little
sister?"

"And why should I tell you? I still don't know what you
are doing and who you're doing it with."

"I am not doing anything and especially not doing anything with anyone of importance. You haven't been prying
have you? I would hate to have to sic Mr. Ryan on you—you
know he had a thing for you."

"Jason Ryan has a thing for anything that wears a skirt."

"There you have it. How good an outfit can I be running
if Ryan is a supervisor in my unit?"

"Touché," Lynn said as she sipped her drink. She smiled
as she lowered it and then her face became serious. "Since
you asked, and since it's no big secret at the agency, I have
been handed something at the North American desk that's

strange to say the least. It seems we have a rumor of a rogue element inside the U.S. government, possibly inside either the FBI or at Langley."

"Should you be telling me this?"

"Well, the information handed down to me from my boss in intelligence thinks this group was busted up by the FBI several years ago . . ." Lynn actually chuckled. "Believe it or not one of this group's monikers was the Men in Black. Can you believe that?"

"Sis, why are you telling me this?" Jack said as he picked up his beer after spying his mother returning from the rest-room.

"My report says that this group is comprised of ex-military. Since you seem to know any and all Special Forces operatives inside and out of our armed services, you may have heard something that could help me."

Jack paused before drinking his beer. He knew every detail of what it was she was talking about. He knew the Men in Black—the Black teams of the Centaurs Corporation, broken up by the Event Group after the incident in the Arizona desert six years before.

"I never heard of the Men in Black outside of the usual running jokes about them. And despite the rumors about me, I don't know every mission specialist in the world," he smiled, "just the Western world."

"Ass!" Lynn whispered as their mother returned. Jack stood and pulled her chair out for her.

Collins looked at his little sister, wondering if she was heading into trouble. Because if the Men in Black, or the corporate Black teams, were being reformed, that meant that they just may have a rogue element inside either the Bureau or the Agency. He made a mental note to bring the subject up with Director Compton.

Jack sat back down and then sipped his beer while looking at his wristwatch. Sarah was now over an hour late, and unlike what he had told his sister and his mom, Sarah was never, ever late for anything. She had an inner clock and she prepared for everything ahead of time. And a meeting of this magnitude was not something she would have taken lightly as she had been asking to meet his mother for the past two years. Finally Lynn reached out and placed a hand over his watch.

Jack sat his beer back onto the white tablecloth. "I know she'll be here, I just—"

"Jack," Lynn said as she held his wrist while her eyes were on something beyond her brother's vision, "Carl and Will are here."

Jack's heart froze when Lynn mentioned the two names. He turned around in his chair, and for the first time in his life after seeing the countenance of both of his men, his legs felt as if they were made of jelly. He swallowed and stood, absentmindedly allowing the napkin in his lap to fall to the floor as Everett hurried through the crowded restaurant toward their table.

"Well, what are you two doing here?" Jack said with a confidence and false levity he wasn't feeling at that moment.

Everett was dressed in Levis and a white Polo shirt and Will basically the same. Everett nodded a greeting to Cally and Lynn. They all noticed the split lip and the Band-Aid on his chin.

"Mrs. Collins, Lynn, sorry to intrude," was all Everett said as he pulled Jack away from the table by the elbow.

"Things have gone to hell across the border, Jack," he whispered. "A Mexican professor, his male assistant, and Lance Corporal Udall are dead." He looked around and Jack could see the anger in his face. "And Ryan is hurt real bad and is now at a hospital in Nuevo Laredo."

Jack clenched his jaw and was staring at Everett, waiting for the rest.

"Whoever did it took Sarah, another girl, and the professor from Baylor that was on the dig list Sarah sent us from the site a day ago."

Jack was thinking, but none of his thoughts were making it to the surface through the fear that suddenly gripped his mind. He wasn't used to the feeling, as it had become sec-

ond nature for him to think during the stress of command
that called for quick and precise reactions. He didn't notice
Lynn as she joined the three men. She already had her cell
phone out waiting to assist Jack in any way she could after
hearing the last part of the conversation.

"Is that all we know?" Collins finally asked.

"We have a plane at the airport we're using as a command post at the moment. Pete Golding is there along with
an eight-man security and assault team. Pete is doing what
he can with Europa. He has a list of suspects, but there is
only one name that keeps coming across the boards, and the
computer says it's—"

"It has to be Juan Guzman," Lynn said before Carl could
finish.

Jack turned to his sister. Her job as the assistant director
at the North American Operations desk at the CIA would
give Lynn the expertise on everything that goes on within
that continent.

"Explain," Jack ordered hastily.

"Nothing happens in northern Mexico without his ex-
pressed say-so. He's the undeclared winner of the drug war
across the border. He has money and his own private army.
He has never hesitated about going to war on this side of the
border with anyone that crosses him," Lynn explained as
she opened her cell phone and made a call, stepping away as
she did so. Looking back she said, "And that small regiment
on his payroll is better equipped than the Mexican army."

"The FBI and Homeland Security is on this, and Niles is
talking to the president as we speak, trying to get us juris-
dictional operating room. But everyone in Washington is
throwing a fit. The stuffed shirts want the Mexican authorities to handle it. And us being secret, we're the last in line
when decisions are handed down."

"No, I'm not leaving Ryan and Sarah over there while we
wait to go through channels." Jack looked at a worried Mendenhall and then at Everett. "Look, I need Pete and the intelligence he and Europa can come up with. However, you two
won't need the grief that would come down if the president

orders us to stand down; you need to stay with the plane at the airport."

Everett looked from Collins and then over to Will Mendenhall. He shook his head as he once more locked eyes with the colonel.

"You know damn good and well that isn't going to work, Jack. Now we have to go."

Lynn joined them after closing up her cell phone.

"Look, my desk at Langley agrees, Jack. It has to be the Anaconda—that's the slick bastard's nickname. Listen to me, Guzman is not only the largest drug dealer south of the border, he deals in women also. Let's hope that's why he took Sarah and the others; that will buy you some time. Whoever in the hell you people work for."

"It won't buy us time, Sis, you get Mom out of here and to a safe place. This town may not be safe for very much longer."

"Jack, you can't go to war with Guzman; he's got an army over there. As I said before, he has never hesitated at crossing the border to take the fight to us before."

Jack raised his left eyebrow in that irritating way he had and then went to kiss his mother goodbye.

"Mom, I have work I've gotta do," he said as he kissed her on the cheek.

"You be careful, Jack."

Collins winked at Cally, and then he turned and walked past Everett, Lynn, and Mendenhall as he made a beeline to the front door of the restaurant.

"You have to stop Jack and make him think, Carl. If he goes barging over there with some hastily drawn-up plan he'll get Sarah and everyone else killed. The Anaconda is ruthless as hell, but he's also smart, and what's more, he is a businessman. Tell Jack to use that if he can. Tell whoever your boss is that Jack wouldn't stand a chance in hell over there. This has to be done through channels, so let the FBI handle it," Lynn implored.

Everett watched as Mendenhall hurried to catch up with Collins, but stayed a moment to look Jack's sister in the eye.

"I would rather go with a hastily drawn-up plan by Jack than someone else's well-thought-out scheme. My money is always on your brother."

Lynn knew Carl was right. She clenched her cell phone tightly and then placed a hand on Everett's shoulder. "I'll do what I can from the intelligence end of things. You go on now, I have more calls to make."

Captain Carl Everett turned away and hurried to follow Jack and Will. Lynn watched a moment, hoping that Jack listened to her warnings. She turned and stood next to her mother.

"Don't be scared, Mom. Jack knows what he's doing," Lynn said as she watched Cally drain her martini glass.

"That won't stop me from worrying, dear," she said as she placed her empty glass on the table and then stood. "His father knew what he was doing also."

Lynn could only nod her head as she saw her mom lower hers.

Laredo International Airport
Laredo, Texas

By the time Collins, Everett, and Will Mendenhall made it through to the charter flight area, there was another Event Group aircraft parked next to the first. On either side of that were two UH-60 Blackhawk helicopters. The first aircraft was a small Lear Jet; the second was an old Boeing 707 conversion used as a mobile command unit. The trio had been notified that the director himself, Niles Compton, was now on station and had transferred Pete Golding to the command post to use the far-more-sophisticated equipment aboard the venerable old 707.

Jack, instead of running up the portable staircase, forced himself to walk only at a quickened gait, removing his coat and tie as he went. Everett and Mendenhall followed him into the aircraft where Director Compton met them just inside the door and took Jack by the elbow, steering him toward the communications center of the extensively modified Boeing aircraft.

"What have we learned so far?" Collins asked as he leaned into communications.

The navy signalman covering the radio removed his headset and looked first at Niles and then Jack. "So far the FBI has placed their field office on alert for a possible hostage rescue across the border. The State Department has already been in touch with Mexican President Juarez, but he's hesitant about allowing an American rescue unit to cross the border. Our president is currently on the phone with him now."

Niles pulled Jack away from the communications area and waited for Will and Carl to join him.

"The situation in Nuevo Laredo is still unstable. The armed men this Guzman has running around his hacienda number in the hundreds. The FBI has intelligence that says this warped bastard collects women for these mercenaries to use—part of their benefits package." He saw Jack's jaw clench. "Sorry, Colonel, I could have worded that far better."

Collins just nodded his head.

"Niles, what is this Guzman into?" Everett asked as a way to steer the conversation toward something more constructive.

"Drugs of course are the number-one factor in his makeup. The FBI reports that he is responsible for the elimination of all of his rivals in the area, and that includes men that dealt directly for the Colombian factions. In other words, he's one powerful son of a bitch. He has no problems sending hit teams into Texas or anywhere else he sees a problem."

"Why would he have raided an archaeological site?" Jack asked as he started walking toward the computer center forty feet aft.

"Simple. Number one, he considers anything in a thousand-mile radius his personal territory. Number two, he does collect anything and everything concerning his Mexican heritage. He actually conducted an interview last year on

Mexican television where he extolled the need to keep Mexico's history and heritage in Mexico. I think Sarah and the field team were a convenient target of opportunity, nothing more."

Jack listened and then pulled back the curtain to the computer center. There, revealed like the Wizard of Oz, was Pete Golding and his expanded computer team. Pete turned away from a large 55-inch monitor and rolled his chair back to face the colonel.

"Jack, you have my—"

"Later, Doc. What have you come up with?"

"Yes, of course," Pete said as he turned to face the large monitor. "Well, thanks to the director and the U.S. Air Force, we have a Predator drone up and flying high over the Guzman hacienda. Thus far Europa has pinpointed seventeen guards on the outside of the immediate hacienda, but it has picked up numerous heat sources coming from the buildings outlying the main house, which as you can see is expansive as hell. There could be another hundred inside of those buildings, and according to the FBI and the Mexican national police, that estimate could be on the low side."

Collins looked at the monitor and the large hacienda that belonged to Juan Guzman. He saw a large swimming pool, a tennis court, and riding stables. It had a private airstrip and hangars for at least five or six aircraft. A helicopter sat upon a helipad at the center of the compound.

"I see the drug trade is still paying high dividends," Everett commented as he saw the same thing Jack was seeing.

"Pete, is there any intel on where this son of a bitch would keep . . . ," Jack swallowed, "would keep the women he has taken?"

"No, but I can ask Europa for her best guess just as soon as she steals the hacienda's specs from the Mexican government."

Jack and the rest knew the supercomputer's job was "backdooring" other systems, and she was damn good at it. She had even broken into her sister Cray's systems at Langley, the FBI, and the Pentagon in the past.

"Why would the Mexican government have his house plans? Wouldn't that be under the state's purview?" Niles asked ahead of Collins.

"Normally, yes it would be, but it seems Europa has dug up a title of deed that says this property and house used to belong to the federal government of Mexico at the turn of the century. And here's another little bit of interesting history. In March of 1916, none other than General John "Black Jack" Pershing himself, with Lieutenant George S. Patton at his side, raided into Mexico." At this point Pete turned to the large screen, punched a few buttons on his keyboard, and the screen changed to some very old photographs of the same Guzman hacienda, but in far-earlier times. The pictures were scratched and were stamped "Property of U.S. National Archives."

"Europa got these from our own database?" Niles asked.

"Just now uncovered them," Pete answered with a little bit of pride at what his supercomputer turned up. "It seems our own department, in one of the first missions ever assigned to it, had business in 1916, and Europa says that we have a vault full of information, but since it was one of the first missions of Department 5656 the material was never catalogued." Pete looked up with a bit of sadness etched into his features, "Things may have been a little different for the Event Group in the early days."

"No excuse. Find the vault number and get our archivists into it."

"Europa already tracked the vault down. It's in Arlington, the old complex site. Get this, President Franklin Roosevelt ordered the vault sealed and left behind when the department moved operations to Nevada."

"Good information, Dr. Golding, but what does this have to do with what's happening now?" Mendenhall asked, frustrated at the slowness of the intelligence.

"Possibly nothing, but maybe everything," Pete said as he tapped the screen. "The official reason for the raid into Mexico by the 8th United States Cavalry regiment was to capture or kill the Mexican bandit, Pancho Villa. Now ac-

cording to history and U.S. Army reports, Villa was nowhere near the border town of Nuevo Laredo at the time of
the raid, yet the regiment spent two days in Laredo and at
this very same hacienda, named Perdition's Gate. Three of
its outer buildings were burned to the ground and several
people were killed by American troops. It caused quite a stir
in the Mexico City newspapers. Thus far we have found no
justification for Pershing's raid on that particular hacienda
or the Event Group's involvement in the attack. But if we
can get into that vault, number 0011 inside the old complex,
we may find a way inside that hacienda."

"Maybe it was a safe harbor for Pancho Villa," Everett
said.

"Not likely. Now here is the most interesting part. This
very same land two years before was owned by none other
than Ramon Carbajal, a very close ally and friend to Villa. It
is documented that Pancho Villa never went there, and he
gave orders to his men never to frequent that particular part
of Mexico. That is documented from former members of his
revolutionary council. And here is something far stranger
gentlemen. The land and hacienda were not owned by a Mexican national; they were sold to an American citizen, a
Professor Lawrence Ambrose. We're currently running a
check on him as we speak. However, I get off the point. This
Professor Ambrose is the reason we have the hacienda floor
plans, a detailed drawing by an Army Corp of Engineers
captain during the time of the Pershing raid. According to
the grids on this property map, they were very systematic,
like they were searching for something. This is how Europa will base her best guess as to the location of any hos-
tages."

"Damn good, Pete," Everett said. "Can we get a printout
of those drawings?"

"Does the FBI have access to this?" Jack asked.

"No, I haven't forwarded any of our information through
the president as of yet."

"Don't. This stays in-house for the time being," Collins
said as he looked over at Niles, who reluctantly nodded.

"I'm with you, Jack—for now. But we have to wait for the president's word on when to go in."

"What is Mr. Ryan's condition?" Jack asked, ashamed that his lieutenant had been his second thought in all of his worries.

"The American consul in Nuevo Laredo got to him before he was wheeled into surgery. He was then secured by a field team from the FBI and he's now on his way to Las Vegas. It's serious, but our docs say he'll make it. He hasn't given us a statement as of yet."

"Colonel, what if we're rushing this on Ryan? If he needs surgery, why didn't we leave him in place and allow the surgeons to take care of him there?" Mendenhall asked, worried about his close friend.

"What do you think this Guzman is going to do when he learns he may have left an eyewitness to the murder of two Mexican nationals and the kidnapping of two American women?" Without another word Collins turned and left the computer center to make his way into the tactical room where he would pore over every bit of intelligence Pete had come up with.

Will nodded his head and then followed the colonel.

Carl Everett hesitated a moment before following Jack and faced the director.

"Niles, you know Jack's going to that hacienda with or without the president's order."

"I know that, but we need to give him the time to plan it out right," Compton explained and then took the printout of the hacienda plans from Pete. "Use these and find a way in there. I need to find out exactly why our Group was there almost a hundred years before we even heard of Perdition's Gate, and exactly why the mission wasn't catalogued in our archives. Now, please find a way in there and get Sarah the hell out."

Everett smiled as he took the offered floor plans.

"That, Mr. Director, you can count on."

Nuevo Laredo
10 Miles South of the Border

The brand-new Sikorsky S-76C++ executive helicopter, painted in magnificent maroon and gold colors, circled the hacienda twice before the pilot saw a man step out onto the heliport at the center of the compound and with two brightly painted paddles, start to wave him down next to the helicopter already there. It had taken three minutes of radio communication with a man who had claimed no English before they were allowed in. The whole time the passenger in the rear compartment knew instinctually they were being tracked by not only one but several heat-seeking missiles.

As the garish executive Sikorsky slowly sat down upon the well-maintained heliport pad, it was immediately surrounded by ten men with menacing-looking automatic weapons. The pilot chanced a look into the back compartment and shook his head.

"It seems we have a welcoming committee, sir," he said into his microphone.

The tall man in the back didn't respond; he just removed his headset and then ran his fingers through his blonde hair. As the helicopter sat down gently he leaned into the pilot's cabin.

"Stay inside and be ready to exit this place on a moment's notice."

The pilot didn't like the sound of the order but nodded his head nonetheless.

A man in a white business suit stepped from the shadows of the hacienda and came out to meet the tall man stepping from the helicopter. The suit he wore was silk, and the blonde man could see he was sweating through it. The white shirt was stained with something at the collar and his face was unshaven.

"Mr. Jones, my employer was surprised to hear from your representative. After the failure of our last negotiation, we thought we would not hear from you again."

The man going by the name of Hanover Jones was loath

to take the man's offered handshake. His nails were filthy and he had an odor that while not disgusting, was at the very least unpleasant. The helicopter's rotors wound down and Henri Farbeaux took the man's hand and shook.

"Speaking of my associate, he was to meet me in Laredo, but he didn't show up. I just had a text message telling me to come here," Henri said as he released the man's hand and fought against the urge to wipe it on his own black trousers.

"Ah, Mr. Guzman insisted that your man accept his hospitality and remain at the compound. Do not fear señor, the man is being well treated."

Farbeaux saw the lie in the man's eyes immediately, just a second before he placed a pair of expensive sunglasses on.

"Please, Señor Jones, Jefe is waiting to see you," the heavyset man said as he gestured toward the hacienda.

Farbeaux buttoned his suit jacket and without turning his head had counted the men in the hacienda's enclosed court that surrounded the helipad. There were ten men with five more hidden in the shadows. He moved his eyes behind his sunglasses and saw four more tucked away at windows on the upper veranda. He showed no emotion as he ducked his head to enter the villa itself.

Henri removed his sunglasses right away so his eyes could adjust to the darkness inside. He immediately saw an older woman, perhaps in her early fifties. She came forward, wiping her hands on a white apron. She sneered at the man escorting Farbeaux and he backed away.

"Welcome to our home, Señor—?"

"Hanover Jones, Mama," said a small well-dressed man with a moustache as he stepped out from behind his ample mother. He said something in Spanish, words Farbeaux knew almost as well as the people in the room. He explained that she needed to go to her room and not the kitchen and ignore anything she may hear in the next hour. Henri Farbeaux thought the man before him was either sloppy in his memory, knowing he spoke Spanish, or he had done it intentionally. If it was the latter, he knew he would have to approach his business very carefully.

"Mr. Jones, it is good to see you once again. The last time was in Colombia if memory serves. I was the intelligence liaison for Pablo Escobar at the time. Back then my antiquities trade was purely a hobby with my . . . rather limited income."

Henri smiled. "Yes, I believe you were, and yes, it was Colombia. I'm glad to see you moved on after Señor Escobar's . . . er, mishap."

Juan Guzman had not offered his hand to Farbeaux. He did smile at the memory of betraying the world's largest drug dealer and allowing Colombian and American Special Forces to kill him in December of 1993.

"His time was over, señor. It was time for men with vision to take the lead in affairs that concern the southern regions of the hemisphere."

Farbeaux knew what that vision was and how it had been put into practice. In eliminating all of his competition in the distribution end in Mexico, along with his takeover of the manufacturing cartels in the south, the Anaconda had murdered no less than eighty of the top drug people in Mexico and South America, but it had been the little people who had suffered the most in this drug civil war with a very conservative estimate of over thirty thousand lower-end hoods and civilians losing their lives before the dust settled just across the border in northern Mexico. Now Juan Guzman was in charge of the largest drug operation in the entire world, and he was now known as the Anaconda for his powerful, suffocating, squeezing grip on anything south of the U.S. border.

"But that is history." He finally smiled and held out his manicured hand for Henri to shake, which he did. "According to your man you are interested in my Anasazi collection?"

"Yes, my collection is lacking where yours is overflowing. And since the Anasazi lived north of the border, I figured it was something you could part with." Henri released the man's small hand and then looked around the well-appointed living room. He saw three men standing close by and their eyes never left him. "I am particularly interested in the piece you purchased in San Diego, a very nice artifact of silver."

The Anaconda smiled and then looked Farbeaux in his blue eyes. "Ah, yes, the silver serpent. That is a very rare piece, señor. The only Anasazi artifact found that depicted a serpent of such splendor. But I must correct you, that particular piece was not purchased, it was . . . how do I say? Oh, yes, willed to me by its late owner."

Henri knew well what that meant. Guzman had murdered the former collector and relieved him of the piece.

"Well, since your investment is minimal, perhaps we can come to an accommodation?" Farbeaux said smiling.

"Perhaps, señor, perhaps," Guzman said as he gestured with his right hand for Farbeaux to precede him. "Why don't we examine the piece so you can appreciate its beauty and thus make me an educated offer that would not be too insulting?"

The former French colonel stepped by the smaller Mexican drug lord, noticing that the man's smile never reached as far as his dark eyes. The nickname Anaconda was well deserved in the Frenchman's opinion as his eyes were like that of a large predatory snake. He knew the look well, because he was capable of the same thing.

The men in the room fell in behind their boss and followed them toward a large door. As Guzman stepped past Henri, he opened a huge oak door and then used a set of keys to open a steel gate behind that. He clicked on a light switch and Henri could see the descending stairs as they curved deeply into the ground.

"I have yet to have the piece cleaned by my artisans, so if you will follow me, Señor Jones, we can view my wares in a far more comfortable setting."

Henri turned from the stairs and looked at the small man before him. His hackles rose as he knew he was stepping into a trap. His makeshift plan had fooled no one and in his haste to find little Sarah, he had made a large mistake by thinking the drug lord would be greedy enough not to have had him checked out thoroughly. Farbeaux nodded his head and then out of the corner of his eye saw the trailing men watching him. He had no choice but to smile and enter the dark abyss beyond the gate.

The eyes of the Anaconda never left the back of the man his intelligence people said was not Hanover Jones from New York, but one Henri Farbeaux. The Anaconda knew that collecting, while being his main profession, was not the reason he was in Nuevo Laredo. He also knew the real reason and had decided to have fun on an otherwise boring day. He smiled as he started down the stairs after his guest.

The Anaconda would soon tire of the game.

2

Laredo International Airport,
Laredo, Texas

The entire private sector of Laredo International Airport was now closed off to regular traffic. A Chevrolet Tahoe pulled alongside twenty other Chevys of the same model. Jack now knew the Feds had arrived in force. He looked over at Everett and Mendenhall and saw Carl nod his head toward a large sealed-off hangar that was visible through the aircraft's window. Inside he saw a Laredo Police Department SWAT van and pulling up next to that was a large step van Jack knew to be the FBI HRT unit. The Hostage Rescue Unit gave Jack the cold chills. He shook his head, knowing now that the president of the United States had made his decision—the rescue, if there was to be one, would be conducted under federal auspices, not the Army's, and certainly not the president's most protected and black agency, Department 5656. Jack normally understood that secrecy was paramount, but at the moment he couldn't care less about the black aspects of their department. He knew as he looked at the gathering federal authorities that the rescue would be strictly a law enforcement operation.

Jack and Everett shook their heads when a news van was stopped by the FBI agents and questioned. They both knew the news was spreading about the incident across the border, which in turn meant the operation was fast becoming too visual for the Event Group to participate.

"Will Director Compton and Colonel Collins please report to communications; the president is on video link through Europa," the communications room said over the loudspeaker.

Jack was joined by the director and they slowly made their way to the communications area of the 707.

Jack stopped in front of the director and watched as he took a deep breath. The director spoke and listened for three minutes as Collins anxiously awaited word on if they would get the chance at the rescue attempt.

The news delivered by the president wasn't good.

"Yes, Mr. President, not until you get definitive word," Niles said as he felt the heat of Jack's anger behind him. "But sir, may I recommend that this be turned over to DELTA? We've already had a breakthrough by the media into the secure zone of the airport, which means Guzman will know of any rescue attempt before it even leaves here." Niles handed Jack a small slip of paper and the colonel cursed under his breath as he read the words, "No Go." "Yes, sir," Niles said and then placed the phone down and nodded at the signals officer on detached service from the navy and assigned to the Event Group. "The president wants a word, Jack," Niles said standing and pacing a few steps away.

"Colonel, are you there?" asked the stern voice.

"Mr. President," Collins answered.

"You are hereby warned as I just warned Niles: you are not to exceed your authority, Colonel. Our dealings with President Juarez have been shaky since his election. We cannot go charging across the border with a group of men whose presence I would never be able to explain. Your department's secrecy is paramount, even above your personnel. Is that clear, Colonel?"

Niles could see Jack half turn and almost walk away, but he stepped up to him and gestured toward the speakerphone where the president was still speaking.

"I give you and that little bald bastard under the desert a lot, and I mean *a lot,* of leeway, Colonel, and I expect my orders to be followed. This is an international incident for Christ's sake."

"Mr. President, you know for a fact that my security teams have a far better chance at getting our people out of there than anyone. We're tight, we know how each other reacts. I implore you to give us a shot at this."

"Do not interrupt, Colonel. Your boss explained things to me, after the goddamn fact. That's the only reason I don't have agents from the FBI storming that aircraft of yours right now. If I allow this, you could cost your Group your cover. You have to stop and think."

Collins remained silent and Niles closed his eyes and removed his thick glasses.

"I don't hear an 'I understand you, Mr. President'."

"Yes, sir. I understand."

"Now, all I am asking is that you give me time to coordinate with the Mexican authorities. We need that president down there. He knows what a threat this Guzman character is. However, he does not want a military incursion into his country. This has to be a law enforcement issue, not a military one. How is Mr. Ryan doing?"

Jack shook his head, stepped closer to the speaker, and took a seat, allowing his body a moment's respite. "Ryan's a strong kid. Now that he's in American hands I give him a far better chance than being possibly operated on by Guzman's surgeons."

"Now, give us time, Colonel. We will get those women back across the border. Baldy, you keep your people in check over there or I will fry your ass."

Niles stepped up to the microphone. "Keep us informed, Mr. President."

"Damn you bookworm, say it!"

"Yes, sir, we will stay put." The line disconnected and

Niles turned to face Jack, giving him a weak smile. "It seems I'm running out of favors."

Jack stood and took Niles by the shoulder. "I know the feeling, Mr. Director. What about my other man, Udall?"

"The Mexican police recovered his body and it's on the way back across the border."

Collins nodded and then looked at Pete Golding, who stood next to Niles. He had several items in his hand, which he handed to Compton while slowly looking away from Colonel Collins's gaze.

"What is it?" Everett asked.

"Our surveillance drone," Pete answered, "the Predator, well, it took these. They're grainy, but I think you'll be able to see what we and Europa saw." Niles, after studying the picture on top, then handed Jack the first blown-up photo. "These were taken just fifteen minutes ago," Pete said by way of explanation.

Collins looked the eight-by-ten proofs over and his heart froze.

"That's just great," Everett said looking over Collins's shoulder as he examined the first and the second picture Niles passed over. "What in the hell is with this guy?" Carl asked.

The first photo showed a large blonde man as he stepped from a luxurious helicopter. The second was taken only moments later, and the man had glanced skyward, as if he knew a Predator was flying overhead. The face was one no staff member on the Event Group aircraft would ever fail to recognize. It was Colonel Henri Farbeaux.

"I figured that son of a bitch for a lot of things, but not to be involved in this," Everett said as Jack gave the photos back to Niles.

Compton watched as Collins walked toward the open door of the 707. He quickly made a decision and gestured for Mendenhall and Everett to join him.

"Colonel, I suspect that the president's going to go with a joint operation, split between the Mexican HRT team and the FBI. Europa broke into the FBI mainframe and she says they will more than likely go in two hours. I forwarded the plans for the Perdition hacienda to the president who passed them through regular channels to the FBI HRT unit," Niles said, trying not to look into Jack's eyes as he did so. "I figured they needed all the advantage they could get."

Jack waited until the director met his eyes and then caught the curse before it could escape his mouth. Everett and Mendenhall knew that Niles had done the right thing. Jack just nodded his head, knowing that the odds of Sarah surviving this thing had just dropped by 75%. He knew the country hadn't learned anything after the failed rescue attempt in the desert of Iran in 1980. Operation Eagle Claw had been an unmitigated disaster because of a multiservice plan, one that was doomed to fail before it ever happened. And now this rescue wasn't just split by differing branches of the service, but by two different nations, and one of those nations may have divided loyalties as far as the Anaconda went. Jack knew if he didn't react to the fluidity of the situation he would never again see Sarah alive.

Niles bit his lip and then nodded at the two marines at the 707's door. They understood and then closed it.

"Jack," he said as he handed Everett the recon photos, "Pete and Europa have something to show you. It's something I didn't share with the president or the FBI."

Collins impatiently waited for the director to explain.

"Pete may have found a way into that compound."

Suddenly hope appeared in Collins's cold, blue eyes.

"And," Compton said as he turned away, "the border's still open to vehicular traffic, as it seems the local Mexican authorities are a little slow to catch on that there's a major problem in their own backyard."

"But you'll have to find a way past the FBI and do it before their HRT team lifts off in two hours," Pete said as he joined the group of four men once more.

Everett smiled.

"I never met a fed I couldn't ditch."

"Then, Colonel Collins, you and your men are dismissed. Take some time off while the president figures this out."

"Yes, sir, maybe Jack, our young lieutenant Mendenhall here, and I will try out the fishing in the Rio Grande," Everett said with a growing smile. "You know we love our fishing."

"I know," Niles answered. "Now I think you better get to tactical and put a plan together. And gentlemen, make it a good one, because we all may hang for it, even if it works."

Director Niles Compton was disobeying a direct order as told to him by the president of the United States, his best friend, once again.

Hacienda Perdition
Nuevo Laredo, Mexico

Henri Farbeaux, still in the guise of Hanover Jones, stood on the rickety floor of the massive basement. There were tunnels, some new, some very old, winding off the main corridor every fifteen feet. As far as he knew Sarah could be held in any one of the ten branches inside the basement. He felt the eyes of Juan Guzman and six of his henchmen as he waited for his host to take the lead. As he stood there several men and women in casual clothes strolled by on their way to one of the many tunnels. One of these workers held a scale and the others articles that Farbeaux didn't recognize. He did notice the fresh-air masks they wore around their necks. Henri looked at Guzman who only smiled.

"I have many employees whose function it is to test shipments of . . . well, let's just say they check the purity of certain items supplied to me by countries farther south of Mexico. Please, Señor Jones, what you are seeking is right over here," Guzman said as he gestured to a large steel door to the right.

Henri was having a hard time reading the man. One thing *was* clear to him: he didn't trust the man named Hanover Jones. Farbeaux had noticed that none of the mini AK-47s being used by his bodyguards had their weapons on *safe*. He watched Guzman as he entered a security code for the locking mechanism on the large door. It opened with a whoosh of escaping air.

"This is just part of my Anasazi collection; the rest I have donated as a peace offering to my brethren in Mexico City. But I believe I have some very interesting pieces for you to view." Guzman stepped aside and allowed Henri through the door.

Henri knew he could possibly take the six men escorting them, just as long as Guzman was close enough to be pulled into running as a shield for him. However, he suspected they were not only being watched by the many security cameras he had counted in just the short walk in the basement, but also by many more guards nearby.

"Here are two very nice pieces right here. They have been cleaned and expertly restored."

Farbeaux made a show of pulling a jeweler's loupe from his coat pocket and smiling as he bent low to examine a large eagle that resembled something the Aztecs would have sculpted. It was a beautiful piece, Farbeaux noted as his eyes scanned the ancient work. Then his eyes moved to the next piece that had been placed on a small table. It was a carved stone work taken from a cave wall in Colorado. It depicted a mother and child—the mother sitting on a throne of sorts and the child feeding at her breast.

"These are very nice." Henri straightened after a cursory examination.

"Yes, particularly so since the man I relieved them from was a greedy gringo from Los Angeles, one of those so-called brothers of mine who have sold out their heritage. I wouldn't mind so much if the gentleman had the least bit of knowledge, such as you, as to their real history. I'm sure you can appreciate that?"

"Yes," Henri half bowed, "I can, Señor Guzman." Henri smiled wider and then cleared his throat. "Since you relieved this person of his possessions so readily, you won't be asking exactly market value for these two pieces," Farbeaux asked with a small smile.

"Ah, just because I came into possession of them at minimal expense does not mean they are not far more valuable, Señor Jones."

"I estimate their value as a pair at just shy of two million."

"Close, señor, but even closer to five million."

Henri nodded his head. "I'll take them. Now, I know a good salesman always saves that *one* piece that would guarantee the buyer walks away happy."

"You are indeed a savvy collector," Guzman said as he gestured for Henri to follow him out of the small vault. They and Guzman's bodyguards stepped into the dim hallway and started moving farther down the long corridor. "Tell me something Señor Jones; does it bother you that I am more than just a collector of antiquities?"

"If you mean your relationship to the recent unpleasantness in Nuevo Laredo, or even your expansion into countries south of your border, no. Whatever a man does for a living never factors into my choices for business relationships."

Guzman laughed. It was a hollow sound that gave the ring of untruth to everything the drug kingpin had said thus far. Henri knew the two pieces of Anasazi carvings were absolutely fake, nothing but cheap knockoffs. After all, he had the second of the two pieces sitting in his house in the south of France. He knew he had to say something just in case his cover was still intact.

"Señor Guzman, I sincerely hope the pieces we are on our way to see are a little more authentic that the two we just examined?"

Guzman laughed and gently slapped Farbeaux on the back. "I hope I did not embarrass you with my little test, señor. In my line of work, on both fronts, I can never be too careful."

"I understand," Henri said as he chanced a look back at the bodyguards who kept pace with them down in the carved-out basement.

Guzman stepped ahead and paused by another door. This one had no electronic keypad, and it was far from being the same sort of steel door they had just come from. The hackles on Henri rose again.

"Señor Jones, behind this door I have exactly what you came here to see. Two marvelous pieces I have from north of the border, and many, many more domestic works of art I prize above even my product from the south." He smiled and opened the door, gesturing for Henri to step through first.

Henri did as suggested and was assailed by a horrid stench. While his eyes adjusted to the weak lighting inside this larger room, he heard the crying of a child. Then he saw the cells, or more to the point, the cages just to his front. He scanned the nightmare before him. Women of all ages were strewn about six cold and dank cells. Many more guards were inside this room, as if they had been waiting. Henri's dire suspicions were proven right.

"These are some of my lesser works, Señor Jones. There are two I am most proud of that I really have not had a chance to examine on a more base level yet, but I am sure you would appreciate their value." He gestured for a guard to shove two of the dirty, hurt women out of the way.

Guzman watched as Farbeaux's jaws clenched. Sitting on the flagstone floor were two women—one blonde, the other with short dark hair. The smaller of the two was tending to a wound the blonde had sustained on the top of her head. With a rag held firmly to the older woman's head, Sarah McIntire looked up and saw who was standing to her front, just outside of her cage. Her eyes widened, but she caught herself when Henri closed his eyes tightly shut and gave her an imperceptible shake of his head. He then noticed his pilot and the San Antonio private investigator lying headless on the floor inside the first of the cells.

"Are they not what I described, Señor Jones," Guzman said as he gestured behind Henri's back for his men to move forward. He also stepped back behind a small wall of those men. "Are these not the articles you came to examine, to take, to steal from me . . . Mr. Farbeaux?"

Henri never hesitated nor did he give any advance indication of what he was going to do. He lashed out before ever turning and caught the man he was hoping was Guzman himself with a palm to the throat, dropping him like a heavy sack of potatoes. Then he elbowed the next closest man to him, smashing his nose deep into his brainpan. The next man in line stepped forward with the steel stock of the AK-47 raised to strike the Frenchman, but Henri was too fast for the smaller man. He quickly lashed out with his foot and slammed it into the man's left knee. Just as the guard collapsed Henri caught the mini AK-47 and tried to swing it around. He heard Guzman somewhere far off as he laughed and started to clap his hands in admiration. That was when a gun barrel slammed into the back of Farbeaux's head, sending him to one knee and the purloined weapon skittering out of his reach.

"Your reputation and your prowess has been greatly undervalued, Señor Farbeaux," Guzman said as he advanced farther into the room, still clapping his hands. "I thought maybe you would get one, possibly two of my men, but three? Outstanding!"

Sarah lowered Professor Stansfield's head to the filthy floor and stood and ran to the bars. She didn't understand what was happening or how Henri Farbeaux had found his way into the fix he was in. She saw Henri on one knee, dazed from the blow to his head as the animal Guzman clapped behind him. She watched as the drug lord grabbed Farbeaux by his blonde hair.

"To think you thought me the fool, señor. I will show you the price many have paid for underestimating me." Guzman let go of the Frenchman's hair and then nodded to his men.

Sarah cried out when ten men went to work on the archenemy of the Event Group. Henri tried to defend himself as best he could, even managing to take down three of them before he succumbed to the brutal kicks and blows to his head and body.

Sarah looked up at the Anaconda as he smiled and leaned against the whitewashed wall of her prison. She was lost on how to feel as Henri had obviously done something very stupid—he had stepped right into hell's living room just to save her. How and why this came about she was now afraid she would never know.

"Stop it!" she called out.

Guzman looked over at the cell and directly at the small woman as she held on to the bars with her eyes wide and staring at Henri Farbeaux. His smile never wavered, but still he did not say anything. He did however get a curious look on his face as the grunts from the Frenchman diminished to almost nothing.

"Alto," he said as he stepped away from the wall. "This man means a lot to you?" he asked Sarah.

Sarah let go of the cell bars and stepped back away from the Anaconda.

"Well little woman, he will soon die with you." Guzman gave Farbeaux a final kick to his head and then gestured for his remaining men. "Place him in with those he came to see. Later we will have sport." He looked at his watch. "I have no more time for this," he said in Spanish, "Mama will be furious if I am late for dinner."

Sarah watched as the small well-dressed man smiled again and, with a last look back at Sarah, stepped from the room.

Sarah saw Henri pulled roughly to his feet. He was bleeding almost everywhere and he was out cold as he was pushed toward her cell.

"You stupid son of a bitch, Henri, what in the hell were you thinking?" she said as Farbeaux moaned his reply and his eyes fluttered open just as the cell was unlocked.

"I . . . think . . . now would be . . . a . . . good time . . . for your boy scout . . . to make an appearance." Colonel Henri Farbeaux passed out before he was unceremoniously thrown onto the cold floor at Sarah's feet.

Sarah went to her knees and pulled a lock of Henri's hair from his face. She shook her head as she saw how badly beaten he truly was.

"You and Jack piss me off more than any dozen men, you

stupid Frenchman." She looked up just as the cage door was locked behind the retreating guards. "And yes, I have no doubt Jack will be as dumb as you and try something just as foolish."

She placed Henri's head in her lap and smiled at him nonetheless. Farbeaux was still as she wiped some of the blood from his face and head. She was amazed at what he had done, not understanding the how or the why. Henri never gave a damn about anyone other than his dead wife, and now here he was giving up himself for her.

"What am I to make of you, Colonel?" Sarah touched Farbeaux's cheek as he fell deeper into his bloody stupor. "You are the strangest bogeyman I have ever seen."

Laredo International Airport
Laredo, Texas

Niles Compton stepped from the cockpit and nodded his head at Jack, Will, and Carl. "The pilot just received clearance from the tower to taxi. He filed a flight plan for San Antonio. We'll circle for a bit and then declare a small-enough emergency to turn back. That means we should be on the ground here in Laredo in," Niles looked at his watch, "exactly one hour. By that time either you're across the border or in FBI custody."

Jack nodded his head and then looked toward the rear of the aircraft where two of his men were quickly coming up the aisle with two large bags. Jack accepted the first and then looked at the army sergeant who had gathered their equipment.

"This everything?" he asked.

"Yes, sir. The only item on your list we didn't have is the satellite hookup. Dr. Golding said as long as you have a cell phone they should have no trouble with communications through our KH-11 Blackbird and Europa."

Jack patted the sergeant on his shoulder. "That will have to do," he said as he made one last check on the contents of the large black bag. The Blackbird he spoke of was the famous, but very old, KH-11 satellite that had come in handy on more than one occasion. All this meant that Niles was pulling in some assets that were meant for somewhere else. He looked at Everett who was checking the second bag. "Sergeant, you and the rest of the security team stay with the director. After the plane lands back here in Laredo, no one, and I do mean *no one*, gets near the aircraft until I return. Is that clear?"

The sergeant was soon joined by another army sergeant and the two marines.

"Sir, can we—"

"No," Jack said and then softened somewhat. "No, Sergeant. This is a job for a small regiment, or two or three men, and I'm afraid the FBI and the Mexican government have a chokehold on the small-regiment thing today. Stay here and protect this aircraft." The sergeant nodded his head. "Your volunteering is duly noted," Jack said while looking at the marines also, "all of you."

At that moment they heard the four engines of the old and venerable 707 start up. Everett closed the black bag and then gave Jack a thumbs-up.

"Boss, thanks for this," Jack said holding his hand out to the director.

"Get her back, Colonel, we'll hold off discussion of anything else until we get home to Nevada—if we have a home after this." He smiled and shook Jack's hand and then Mendenhall's and Everett's. "You better get below."

With those last words the army sergeant and the two marines tore away a section of the carpeting just outside of the cockpit and then opened a small trapdoor.

"I sure hope the pilot has it in him," Mendenhall said as he looked down into the blackness of the avionics compartment.

"Don't worry, Lieutenant, the pilot and Ryan are flying buddies," Everett said as he tossed the second black bag down to Collins far below in the belly of the plane.

Mendenhall watched Everett slip down the small ladder

and then looked at the director. "Is that crack about Ryan and this pilot supposed to make me feel better about all of this?"

Outside the aircraft the head of the Laredo FBI field office stepped from the hangar where the planning for the joint raid was being finalized. He saw the large 707 start to roll as one of his men handed him the phone. He was connected directly to his director in Washington, who in turn was relaying information to the president.

"Yes, sir, their aircraft is preparing for takeoff. They filed a flight plan for San Antonio," the special agent said into his secure cell phone. "No, sir, no one left the aircraft. The colonel and his men are still onboard, yes."

Suddenly the 707 started rolling and made a sharp turn in front of the hangar where the HRT unit and their Mexican counterpart were preparing for their raid across the border. The words of the FBI director and the president of the United States were drowned out by the piercing scream of the Boeing aircraft. With a smirking Niles Compton looking out of one of the passenger windows, the pilot applied his brakes when the 707 was directly in front of the agents and the hangar. He throttled all four of the large GE engines to near full power, making the wings shake and flutter. The special agent in charge was pushed back toward the open hangar door as a small hurricane of wind and noise buffeted everyone in the building. Men scrambled to close the hangar doors and the agents on the outside ducked behind the cover of the cars lining the front.

As the agents sought protection from the man-made gale force winds pummeling them, they failed to see three men scramble from the nose wheel compartment of the large plane where they had just torn away the insulation from the avionics room to enter. They ducked and ran for the cover of an idle Blackhawk.

The 707 pilot, a true friend of Jason Ryan, applied the last of his power to the four engines when one of the FBI agents braved a look over the hood of his Chevrolet. The wings were threatening to be ripped from the aircraft as they wagged up and down as if it were a giant bird. The brakes were overheating as the pilot saw three men scramble to a waiting car.

Inside the passenger compartment Niles Compton and a grinning Pete Golding watched as Jack, Carl, and Will Mendenhall pulled quickly out of the secure area just as the pilot pulled back on the aircraft's four throttles. He cracked his window and then waved at the agents as if in apology. Fifteen field men of the FBI's Laredo office finally stood after the man-made windstorm had stopped.

"Where did that bastard learn how to taxi an aircraft," the lead agent asked as he placed the cell phone back to his ear. "Yes sir, sorry. No, their aircraft is taxiing and no one left the plane."

Niles turned away from the small window and looked at Pete.

"Well, they're on their way."

Pete smiled as he took in his boss.

"Do you think I'll be able to have access to Europa from the jail cell we'll be sharing when the president finds out about this . . . again?"

"What makes you think the president will stop at throwing us in jail, Pete? It's more likely he'll line us up against the wall and shoot us."

Pete nodded his head and smiled.

"Now that's the way to go out."

Vauxhall, London, England
Office of MI6

The most successful counterintelligence operations in history are conducted out of a state-of-the-art building that, thanks to the James Bond films, is currently one of the largest tourist attractions in all of London. From the outside, American, European, and Asian visitors to London can take snapshots and wonder how such a marvelous building could house a brilliant intelligence service and not somehow be much darker because of its intent.

Housed deep in the subbasement of the giant concrete and glass structure was a small and little-known office that housed several supercomputers that had but one function and one function only—to spy on the best friend that the United Kingdom had today—the United States of America. Certain protocols have been handed down from minister to minister over the years that have remained secret for over a century, long before America and Britain were allied together in a mutual defense mode that was brought on through necessity since World War II. Although spying on each other has been a foregone conclusion since the beginning, no one in either government would ever say the words to confirm it—it just wasn't Cricket.

The code-breaker section of MI6, actually titled MI1, has a sub-branch that sits off in a far corner in the darkest recesses of the basement. This section had one specific reason for operations—spying on the cousins across the sea in their communications between law enforcement and intelligence services. It was here that three men were hustling about the room after several red-flag, coded communications from Langley, Virginia, the home of the Central Intelligence Agency, America's version of MI6, had come in. Two key words and one name had been deciphered from five different communications from a field operation being conducted by the American Federal Bureau of Investigation and relayed through the CIA command center. One of the three men shook his head and slapped the keyboard on his computer.

"We get a red flag on the two words and one name and there's nothing in the computer on it," the man said in exasperation. "And what's this bloody icon attached to the flag? I've never seen this before."

Another man walked over with a computer printout and looked over the operator's shoulder.

"You dolt, that flag means this whole thing gets bumped upstairs to ministry level." The man frowned and looked closer at the icon that was flashing next to the red flag beside the two words and one name in the American communiqué. "What's this?" he said as he reached for a book that listed all the department numbers and their corresponding computer terminals. "This is bloody strange," he said as he laid the large book on the desk, "it says it not only goes upstairs, but we are to copy Department 1106, that's SIS."

"You mean it's connected to not only internal security, but foreign as well—the Secret Intelligence Service?"

The man behind the operator straightened when he saw another icon start flashing beside the first two.

"This is far above our pay grade, mate. Look at this; it's also to be forward to the Ministry of Defense, some office called Bluebell."

"Why do I have the feeling we just uncorked a stinker here?" the operator said as the supervisor for the area just hung up his desk phone ten feet away from the two operators.

"Send it along to the three recipients," he said as he turned in his chair with a white face and worried look. "Just get the damn thing out of this office." The supervisor turned and ran a hand through his thinning hair and then removed his glasses. "Sometimes I hate this job."

The first to receive the communiqué deciphered from the Americans was the head of SIS, Sir John Kinlow. When he opened the computer package from downstairs he didn't exactly know what it was he was looking at. He knew because of the red flag, the special security numbers, and the key words that were passed along that this was information only available to certain members of British Intelligence. But he had never been briefed on anything such as this before in his five years on post. He knew only his computer terminal would have access to the material concerning the two key words and one name mentioned by the CIA and the FBI.

"Well, 'tis a boring night at any rate," he said as he entered his security code and pulled up the file. Little did the president of the United States know, he had inadvertently passed the info to the British when he forwarded the information

Niles Compton had passed to him. The code breakers received the information from the communiqués of the FBI and CIA when they informed the hostage rescue team of the history of the hacienda.

The head of the SIS read, and as he did his eyes widened. He whistled when he saw the original file date . . . September 3, 1900, the very turn of the century. He looked down at the key words that had set the security alarms off deep inside the code-breaking room downstairs. *Perdition*, *Mexico*, and finally the name mentioned, Lawrence Jackson Ambrose.

Sir John clicked on the heading for the file and started reading. By the time he was done it was near eight o'clock at night. While he had read the top-secret file, his secretary had buzzed several times without him answering the calls. Finally when she poked her head into his office he hastily waved her off without looking up from his computer screen. It wasn't until he read the file another two times that he finally looked away and shook his head.

"What in the hell were they thinking back then," he said to no one but himself. "What kind of bloody mess did we inherit?"

Another knock sounded at the door and this time the secretary came in without waiting. She saw Sir John looking as pale as she had ever seen him. The man had been practically euphoric for the past year since his office was instrumental in the American operation that killed the world's leading terrorist, Osama bin Laden, and he hadn't come down from that high for ten months—until tonight.

"Sir John, the minister of defense is on the line, and he is very adamant about speaking to you. He said it is of the highest priority."

Sir John acted as though he didn't hear his secretary. She came a few steps closer into the darkened office and then jumped when he suddenly straightened in his large chair and snatched up his phone, practically slamming his finger down on the flashing button.

"Kinlow," he said not too delicately into the phone. "Yes, I just read it, several times as a matter of fact. Just how in the hell are we to hush this up without exposing this massive shit cake?"

The secretary watched Sir John start to rub his left temple and then he looked up and waved her out of the office as if a sudden plague had erupted at Vauxhall.

"Look, Wes, we cannot allow ourselves to be brought down by something like this. If even a smattering of this dirty business leaks out, the media would eat us alive . . . not counting our friends across the ocean. Could this possibly be real? I mean, my faith in everything has just gone tits up, old boy."

Sir John listened to the minister of defense and was soon joined in conference by the head of external intelligence, who had just been on the phone to the prime minister's office.

"Do we have a consensus as to how we handle this mess?" the minister of MI5 asked his counterparts.

"Maybe it's just a coincidence?" Sir John said into the phone, not believing the tale he had just read.

"Maybe the key words in the communiqué were a coincidence, Mexico and Perdition, but the name? You read the file gentlemen the same as I. Can we afford to ignore the name of Lawrence Jackson Ambrose? I think not—at least not after the horrid facts of this sordid affair. Great Britain would never live this down."

"We cannot handle this mess ourselves as we cannot be connected to this if things blow up, and they always do. We need an outside source to deal with this," said Sir John as he stood from his chair and paced a few steps away from his desk. "May I suggest we bring in our source at Langley? Maybe he can utilize the new teams they are putting together," he said, not even wanting to mention the contact's name. "The operators, after being suspended from activities the last five years, are back in business again. They are now being run by our friend at Langley. Let him get a handle on this thing and close it out for good. We'll owe them something awful, but I see it as the only way."

"Excellent," answered the minister of defense. "Sir John, you are closest to our asset there. Can you get the ball rolling, as the Americans would say?"

"I think we best not use any American euphemisms for the time being; after all, if they find out what our good old government did back in the day, they may not be that pleased with us." Sir John finally sat back down in his chair and regained some of the composure he was known for. "I just can't believe they were capable of this kind of massive cover-up back then."

"Think what you want. We need to settle this thing," the head of foreign intelligence said.

Sir John nodded his head and absentmindedly hung up his phone without saying anything else and not even realizing the men on the other end of the phone couldn't see his nod. He reached over and unlocked his right-hand drawer and pulled out a small book. He quickly ran his finger down a list of code names and numbers and then took a deep breath and made the call.

CIA Headquarters,
Langley, Virginia

The special operations director for field incursions, or what amounted to the dirty-tricks department, a man that racked up favors from others in the intelligence community for cashing in at a later date, hung up his phone. He shook his head knowing that the Brits had screwed up royally on this one. He laughed. The whole thing was of minor concern to him.

The operations director flipped a switch on his computer and there appeared a coded e-mail from MI6 that he immediately opened and read. The details were all there; it was just missing the whys and what for's, and those he really didn't care about. He almost wanted to laugh. What kind of story were they trying to get him to believe? Oh, he would send the Black Team in alright. They'll even destroy the serum and lab equipment if it's all still there, but he will also learn the truth about what it is they were so afraid of across the water.

He finally reached for his phone and made the call to the Black Team that he and his superior had just reinstated as part of his small department. The team used to be a part of a corporate security department that worked for a defunct defense contractor, and they were known to be rather ruthless. He and his superior had seen a need in the future to bring this nightmare back into being, and now they would be sent on their first field assignment since they were brought back into the fold. What better way of testing these men than this little farce in Mexico? After all, his job was to be a sneaky, mean bastard and that meant everyone was fair game. He knew himself to be a true patriot.

The man who ran dirty tricks, Hiram Vickers, made the call to one of the most ruthless security teams in the history of the United States, now being run by a rogue element inside CIA at Langley and once thought destroyed—the Black Team, also known in American myth as—the Men in Black.

3

The Border Crossing
At Nuevo Laredo

A half hour after Jack, Carl, and Mendenhall had made good their escape from the international airport, they found themselves at the checkpoint, ready to start their second unofficial invasion of Mexico. The border guard eyed them, and then after all the nervousness in the preceding minutes, he just waved them through with an admonition to spend as many dollars as they could while in Mexico. Everett had nodded his head, smiled, and made a drinking gesture at the bored border guard.

"What are Pete's glossy eight-by-tens tellin' you, Jack?" Everett asked as he checked his rearview mirrors out of paranoia.

"Well," Collins said from the backseat of the stolen 2005 Chevy Blazer, "it looks like we're going to get a little wet, and our knees may get scraped up some, but Pete and his female computer counterpart actually pulled something out of the official geological survey of Mexico." Jack leaned forward as Everett drove and perched himself between Carl and Mendenhall and showed them what Pete Golding had found. "Here by the river, we have a culvert that runs from the Rio Grande ten miles inland almost directly into Perdition. The hacienda is damn near sitting right on it. Maybe it was used in the old days to feed river water to some sort of agriculture."

Will took the old map first and studied it, and then he looked over the Predator intelligence picture.

"Colonel, this survey map is dated 1927." Will half turned in his seat as Jack reached into the back and pulled out the bags they had packed back on the 707. "Do you think that old concrete culvert is still there?"

"The opening at the river is there, and I suspect it's still used by illegals crossing the border. It's watched by the U.S. Border Patrol, but not until after nightfall." Jack quickly looked at his watch. "That means we have about fifteen minutes to get inside that thing before we start hearing helicopters coming down on us."

"I take it our plan ends at that point?" Mendenhall asked, lowering the map and the photos.

"See Will, you hang around us long enough and you start figuring out how we work," Everett said smiling as he turned off the main road and tore down a large side street that ran along the Rio Grande.

As Jack started passing over to Mendenhall their night clothing, body armor, and night vision scopes, his cell phone rang. He opened it and answered. He closed his eyes for a moment and then thanked the person on the other end.

"Ryan just came out of surgery. The doctors say he'll make a full recovery. He's already awake and wondering where everyone is."

Mendenhall in the front seat looked out of the passenger window and sighed. His best friend was going to live, and he had a hard time not showing his commanding officers how close he and the navy aviator had become. Collins watched Will for a moment and then closed his large hand over Mendenhall's shoulder. He never did hide feelings that well.

"The culvert should be right around here somewhere," Everett said as he slowed the Blazer down to a crawl.

Collins looked back across the river and saw no traffic on the U.S. side of the border, but he knew that didn't mean there weren't eyes on them.

"Here we go," Carl said as he pulled to a stop.

The culvert's opening was hard to spot in the setting sun, but Everett was right, it was there half camouflaged by weeds and other river growth. As they started pulling on their body armor and other clothing, Will reached into their bag of tricks and pulled out his weapon of choice—a silenced, or suppressed equipped, German-made MP-5 submachine gun. Will called it his oldie but goody. He handed Collins and Everett their Berettas, and they equipped themselves with the weapon they had used most of their careers, the M-14 carbine, an M-16 variant that also came with suppressors. All three assault weapons were laser-sighting equipped. Everett had what Mendenhall called the captain's ballsy weapon with the M203 grenade launcher attached, what the captain called his big negotiator. They each placed their night vision scopes onto their heads and then darkened their faces with greasepaint.

Everett watched Collins as he handed him the extra magazines of 5.56 ammunition and tossed Mendenhall six extra clips of nine-millimeter rounds for his MP-5.

"She's still alive Jack," Carl said as Collins stopped what he was doing and then just nodded his head.

"Then let's get over there and make sure she stays that way."

With that Everett took the lead and started for the culvert's wide opening. He stopped short and quickly brought up his weapon. With his night vision scope raised up over his brow, he must have scared someone because there was a small yelp, and then Jack and Will heard a child start crying. Collins stepped forward and saw what had stopped Everett at the opening.

"I'll be damned," Mendenhall said as the last of the sun vanished.

Inside the culvert were about eight women, six children, and four very frightened men. They all had bundles of clothing and the men were wearing backpacks. Collins stepped forward, lowering his weapon.

"Hola," he said and tried his best to smile. "Se habla English?" he asked as he saw two of the children were barefoot.

"Si," the first man said as he stepped forward, "Inmigración?" the thin man asked as he removed his dirty and worn cowboy hat and half raised his hands. They all three noticed that he stepped in between the women and children and the heavily armed men he faced.

"No," Jack said as he took in the frightened men and women. As far as he could see they weren't being escorted by the slimy men that charged Mexicans their life's savings to get them across the border. Collins reached into his black nylon pants and produced a pair of large wire cutters.

Everett and Mendenhall exchanged looks of curiosity.

Jack handed the man the cutters. "Good luck. Try crossing a mile or so down river; this place is watched after dark."

The man hesitantly took the dykes from the strange and dark man in front of him, and then he nodded his head as Jack, followed by Everett and Mendenhall, squeezed past the family attempting to get across the border for new life in the United States.

"You never cease to amaze me, Colonel," Will said as he lowered his night vision goggles.

"I can't blame people for being poor and hungry and out of work, Lieutenant."

With that small confrontation behind them, the three men invaded Mexico.

Perdition's Gate
Nuevo Laredo, Mexico

Sarah McIntire looked up as the door to the cell room opened. Several of the teenage girls whimpered and tried to bury themselves into the rear wall of their prison. Sarah turned to face them and held her index finger to her lips, trying to quiet the young and very frightened women. She laid the head of Henri Farbeaux gently onto the concrete floor just as Guzman stepped through into the light. He was followed by three of his men. The Anaconda stepped up to the old and rusty bars.

"Señora, I have a question for you," he said as he smiled his best disarming smile. "Just who are you?"

"I'm a geologist," Sarah answered, not allowing her eyes to shy away from the small man before her.

The Anaconda put a hand to his mouth and then lowered it after he had thought something through. "I find that hard to believe. First we have a retired lieutenant colonel from the French Army trying to rescue you . . . or buy you as it may be, and now we have a joint operation between your government and mine to conduct the same action, only on a far more violent scale, all on yours, or Professor Stansfield's, behalf. Now I own the woman from Baylor, but I don't own you. So, I'm afraid the popularity is strictly yours."

Sarah stepped closer to the bars. "I really don't give a flying fuck what you think. Your men shot and killed two friends of mine and two other good men. So if you would just ask your men to sit this one out, and you allow me out of this cell, I'll kick your ass from here to the border." Sarah actually grabbed the cell's bars tight enough to make the skin on her fingers turn white with the pressure.

Juan Guzman laughed out loud and then looked back at his men. They didn't take Sarah's threat to their boss as well as he did. "If my madre heard you speak that way she would wash your mouth out with lye soap little woman." He stepped closer and the smile disappeared. "The raid across the border will not happen, so lower your hopes. El presidente has had a change of heart. He has canceled all plans to rescue you. He instead will send out the local police to investigate the incident at the archeological site this afternoon, of which I have guaranteed him personally that all attempts will be made to get to the bottom of that despicable crime."

"You slimy bastard," Sarah said staring a hole through the fierce Anaconda. "At least get the professor and my friend to a doctor."

"I have many questions to ask our French friend here, but," he gestured to one of his men, stepped forward, and unlocked the cell, making Sarah step back. "Professor Stansfield I can assist right now."

The cell door opened with a loud screech and Guzman stepped in, followed closely by his men. He easily reached out and removed the sawed-off shotgun from the first guard and then placed the barrel to the blonde professor's head. He looked up and smiled at Sarah.

Second Lieutenant Sarah McIntire couldn't believe the ruthlessness of what she was about to witness. Sarah started forward, trying desperately to get to Guzman, but she was grabbed by the ankle and stopped. She looked down and couldn't believe the man holding her back from attempting to save Stansfield was Henri Farbeaux. He was holding on with both arms as she tried to kick away from him. Sarah stopped struggling when the sound of both barrels of the shotgun reverberated in the closed space, sending Sarah down to the ground. Out of frustration she started crying and nearly vomited when she looked up and saw that the professor from Baylor University no longer had most of her head.

"You murdering son of a bitch!" she cried as she lowered her head, kicking Henri's grip free of her ankle.

"Now, Señora, remember this lesson when I come back

to ask you more pointedly just who you are. And this act of being a simple geologist, well, as you can see, I don't take disappointments well at all. This woman was an employee, as you are not, so I will be very straightforward with my questions to an outsider." He tossed the still-smoking shotgun to the guard and then stepped out of the cell and started up the stairs.

The guard looked at Sarah and then gave Farbeaux a hard kick to his stomach, making him curl up into a bloody ball. Sarah noticed he didn't even let out a grunt. He did however look up at the guard with murderous eyes. The fat man smiled and then followed his boss out of the cell and the basement.

Sarah lay on the floor a moment trying to regain some of her composure. Her ears were still ringing from the blast of the shotgun, but that ringing was also successfully drowning out the cries of the frightened young girls sitting on mattresses lining the walls.

"You . . . have a tendency . . . to drive men a little . . . mad, dear Sarah."

"Shut up, Henri, you stopped me. I could have—"

"Gotten yourself . . . killed," said Henri, stopping her complaint before it was fully voiced. He tried to sit up but fell over.

Sarah eased herself over to the Frenchman and pulled his head off the cold floor. She remained silent for a moment as she cradled his head in her lap once more.

"And what are you going to do when he comes for these girls?" she asked, giving Farbeaux a small test of her own. She looked straight ahead, knowing in advance what his answer was going to be.

"Nothing, dear Sarah." He opened his eyes and looked at her as she stared ahead. "They mean nothing to me."

"I really find you heartless and disgusting sometimes, Colonel."

"Thank . . . you, my dear . . . Sarah."

Sarah looked down and saw that the Frenchman had passed out once more from his pain.

* * *

The three men had passed several openings in the ancient culvert as they made their way south toward Perdition's Gate. Mendenhall used these large openings that were obviously used by the illegal immigrants for entering the concrete tube. As everyone passed he would hoist the small global positioning unit that was part of the equipment. Thus far they were on a straight line toward their final destination.

It was at one of these openings that Jack's cell phone vibrated. He held up a black gloved hand and Carl and Will stopped behind him, taking the opportunity to drink some vitamin water. Jack opened the phone as he drank energy drink from a small aluminum package.

"Colonel, we've landed back at the airport. Imagine our surprise to see that the hostage rescue team hasn't budged from the hangar. The Mexican element is no longer on station. Jack, their mission is on hold." Niles Compton became silent after delivering the bad news.

"There goes our cover," he said as he angrily tossed the energy drink into the moving water at his feet.

Everett glanced at Mendenhall and saw the young lieutenant just shake his head, knowing without being told that the diversion they had hoped for was no longer an option.

"Jack, I think I should come clean with the president. He could possibly get this Guzman's attention and give you some time to move in."

"That would end up costing you your job. No, I'm sending Will and Carl back now."

Everett smiled and shook his head. He set his jaw, a look Collins knew well. "Tell Dr. Compton that I quit."

"Me too," Will added as he tried to get comfortable in the curving tune of the culvert.

Collins shook his head. "Okay, we're going ahead; do what you can without letting the president know you were involved. This is my thing and I'll be the only one to hang for it." Jack closed the cell phone and looked at the other two men who waited for his angry rebuke at their failing to follow his orders. He opened his mouth to speak, but Everett stopped him by holding up his own gloved hand. No words needed to be exchanged after that.

Colonel Jack Collins nodded his thanks and then turned to finish the last three miles to Perdition.

Laredo International Airport
Laredo, Texas

Niles waited in front of the large-screen television for his call to be answered. It didn't take the president long.

"I answer my phone, but you don't answer yours. Is that the way things work now, Niles?"

"You have my apologies, we . . . ," Niles paused and removed his glasses, ". . . I was in the air as a diversion for Colonel Collins and his two men to leave the aircraft."

The president looked through the camera on top of the monitor on his small laptop inside the Oval Office and didn't say a word. He waited.

"My orders," Niles finally said. "I think it was wrong of you not to allow me to use the assets of my department to rescue one of my people. And now that this rescue mission has been suspended, delayed, I don't believe you ever had a handle on the situation, at least as well as you thought you did."

The president stared at the face of the best friend he ever had. The polar opposite of himself in most everything except politics, Niles usually knew just how far he could push his buddy from their college days. And as usual, his conscience, as he called Compton while by himself, was right.

"The president of Mexico is juggling too much. Hell, he's hanging on to power by the skin of his teeth. This Guzman has a long reach and the whole of the Mexican government is terrified of him."

"This is clearly an act of war if they are allowing this to continue unchecked," Compton said.

"Baldy, they don't believe young McIntire is even on his property any longer. They say she's already been moved."

"But we—"

The president held his hand up. "We know Guzman is lying, Baldy. That hacienda is now covered by more cameras than they had at last year's Super Bowl." The president closed his eyes while he thought a moment. He opened them and then looked at his friend two thousand miles away in Laredo. "This madman thinks he's immune, that we have our hands tied. And he's right to a point. With Department 5656 so black in nature, Congress would hang me in front of the Capitol for sending in an armed force over there for a purely law enforcement issue." The president shook his head angrily and held up his hand once more when he saw that Niles was about to explode.

Compton was joined by Pete Golding at the communications console. He sat out of picture range and placed his hand on the director's arm to calm him down.

"If this fails, of course you have my resignation."

"Resign? No, that won't happen. If you attempt it I will fire you and then whoever else I need to fire, and then order you back to the Group without some of your key people. Is sneaky little bastard Pete Golding there listening? I know he is, so he's witness to what I say. And if for one minute you don't think I have the power to do it, just try me Director Compton. Friends are damned. And I want to speak with Colonel Collins if he gets out of this mess without getting wacked in Mexico. Now, what can I do to assist the colonel and get my people back safely?"

Niles dipped his head in thanks.

"Remember, Baldy, they're also *my* people, not just yours."

Perdition Hacienda
Nuevo Laredo, Mexico

Collins, Mendenhall, and Everett stopped to take a breath. They were muddy and filthy and because at several points in the long-winding fresh-water culvert they had encountered age-old cave-ins and a narrowing of the pipe itself, their backs ached, and all three were feeling the cramps in their legs.

"They don't describe things like this in all those, 'Be All You Can Be' or 'Army of One' commercials, do they, Lieutenant?" Everett said smiling as he removed a small black box from Jack's backpack. He opened the box and then quickly removed a small flashlight-looking device attached to the box by a long cord.

"According to GPS we're about a half a mile from the hacienda. It's time to see just how much company we have waiting for us out there," Everett said as he spied the broken culvert a few feet ahead of them. Jack only nodded his agreement.

As Carl positioned himself near the break, he lowered his night vision goggles and slowly eased himself upward toward the now star-filled sky above them. As his head came free of the underground world, he brought the heat-sensing probe up and pointed it toward the spot he hoped the hacienda was located. Down below him Jack wiped sweat from his face and brought the small LCD monitor online. His heart sank when, one by one, each of the roving patrols of Guzman's guards appeared as a bright blob of red, yellow, and white heat. Collins hissed as Will looked over his shoulder.

"How are we looking?" Everett whispered from above them.

Jack could only lower the monitor back into the small black box and then in anger kick it away.

"What was I thinking?" he asked no one but himself.

Everett eased himself back down into the culvert and then looked from Mendenhall to the colonel.

"What's wrong now," he said as he coiled up the long cord and replaced the heat sensor back on its clip on the side of the black box.

"At least two hundred men, between us and the hacienda," Mendenhall answered for Jack. Will shook his head at Everett, not wanting the colonel to see the gesture—one of hopelessness. He then moved off farther down the culvert toward Perdition.

Jack was thinking furiously when Mendenhall returned. "More good news here—the culvert ends. We have a massive collapse of the concrete and it's pretty much filled in ahead."

Collins lowered his head and angrily slapped at his wool cap, and pulling it free of his head along with the night vision goggles. Everett was also lost for words. He knew they were trained to think on the fly, to improvise; that's how Special Forces operatives thought. But now they were all out of options. To make a run on the hacienda through all of that open space was suicide—especially against well-armed men that basically used the same night equipment as themselves.

"I'm all out of ideas," Collins said as he stared at the running water beneath his feet.

Everett thought as hard as he could, but he could see no way out of their dilemma. He thought the colonel was not going to say anything, when Jack suddenly removed his right-hand glove and then shoved it into the flowing water at his feet. The small stream from the Rio Grande was moving at a pretty good clip south, toward the hacienda.

"Will, if the culvert is collapsed ahead, where in the hell is this water disappearing to?" he asked as he replaced his cap and night vision goggles and then lowered them and moved off to the spot Mendenhall had been at earlier.

Everett gave Will a curious look and then followed Jack. Mendenhall, instead of going with his commanding officers, leaned once more against the old and cracked concrete of the culvert and pulled out another foil container of energy drink.

When Everett caught up with Jack twenty feet farther along the culvert, he saw the colonel was looking down at the water as it disappeared about a foot before the cave-in.

"Look at this," he said without looking up at Everett. "Where in the hell is this water draining off to?"

"It could be anything, Jack. Maybe there's a fault under the old culvert.

"But wouldn't it be—"

Before Jack could state his own opinion on the disappearing stream, they both heard a loud crack and then the vibration hit them and they felt the cave-in. Collins knew immediately what had happened and bending over ran past Everett. When he got to the spot they had just been he raised his goggles and then quickly turned on a small flashlight and panned it around through the swirling dust. Everett hurried in behind him, and Jack had to put his hand out to stop Carl before he fell into the large hole that had appeared at the very spot they had been just a moment before.

"Damn, Will, are you alive down there?" Collins asked as he leaned over the hole where the water was falling on a prone shape about ten feet below them. He saw movement.

"Yeah, I hit my goddamn tailbone though, and I bit my tongue. Other than that, I think I'm in one piece."

"What in the hell did you fall into?"

Jack saw a light come on far below and then he saw Mendenhall go to his knees in the gathering water as it fell into the hole from above.

"A tunnel," he called up through the swirling dust. He saw something dug into the side of the tunnel and then plucked it from the wall. "It's a reinforced tunnel, and it's an old one, Colonel," he said as he leaned back and heaved the object up and through the hole where Collins caught it.

"A lantern," Jack said as he looked it over and then handed it to Everett.

The lantern had an old reflection dish attached to its back. They all knew that the reflector was once used to add enhanced light to the otherwise weak oil-filled lantern.

"This is over a hundred years old," Everett said. "We have so many in our vaults at the Group that I would recognize them anywhere."

Down below Jack watched as Mendenhall limped off toward the south. He knew it wasn't prudent to start shouting in the enclosed space, so he would have to be patient while the lieutenant did his job—one that he was very good at. It only took a few minutes for Will to return—the longest few minutes of Jack's life. Mendenhall looked up at the two officers as they waited for his word.

"You're not going to believe this one, Colonel. We have a large door down here. It's half buried, but damn, it's a door to somewhere."

Jack shook his head and then without hesitation made the jump down to join Mendenhall. Everett quickly followed. When Collins examined the tunnel he saw that it was well worn and expertly constructed. Every few feet there were old timbers supporting the roof and walls of the excavation. Every ten feet or so there was another oil lantern half dug into the dirt wall. He used his flashlight to examine the door Mendenhall had found. It was buried almost to the top with a small cave-in that happened many years before their arrival on site. Jack tossed his light to Will and then started scraping dirt away. Everett joined him while Mendenhall kept the light on them both. Using the stock of his weapon, Carl made more headway than Jack and they soon had the old, wooden door uncovered.

"The lady or the tiger?" Everett quipped as he tried the old and rusty latch.

"I'm betting on the lady," Jack said hoping beyond hope it was a secret way into Perdition.

Carl tugged on the door, but it refused to budge. He gripped the old steel handle with both gloved hands and tried again. This time the door opened so suddenly that it caught Everett unawares. The cascade of sand and dirt almost covered him before Jack could pull him free of the avalanche of debris from the opposite side of the wooden door.

Mendenhall stepped forward and his eyes widened. In

the greenish hue of the ambient-light goggles a secret underground world opened up beyond the door. He raised his goggles and brought his flashlight up and shined it around. The dust was thick, but that didn't stop Will from seeing an amazing site. It looked like an ancient, underground laboratory. He recognized items used in the labs back at the Group and many more things that were just as unfamiliar to him. Jack and Everett added their light to the strange scene in front of them.

"What in the hell did we just open up?" Will asked as his light played over tables, glassware, and in one corner of the concrete-lined room, barrels upon barrels of something staked three high.

Collins stepped into the room over the large mound of dirt and sand that had buried the door on both sides. He quickly shut down his flashlight and then gestured for Everett and Mendenhall to do the same. He placed his hand with fingers curled inward as an order to cease all movement. He was looking up at the high ceiling above their heads. He looked back at the two men who had frozen just inside the door. Above them there was light filtering through small cracks in the wooden planks directly over their heads. Jack tapped his right ear and pointed, and that's when Carl and Will heard it. It was the sound of women weeping.

Before Jack could turn and say anything, he flipped on his light once more when his hackles rose. He played the light around the large laboratory, and then the beam slicing through the swirling dust struck upon an even more eerie sight. There a few feet farther into the room was another cave-in. And at the edges of the pile of dirt, sand, and concrete were the remains of khaki-colored leggings. They were old; possibly turn-of-the-century old. The boots were time worn and brown, and that made Collins aware that they had stumbled into something that the drug kingpin didn't know about his house south of the border: a secret and long-buried site that had once been a laboratory for an American scientist named Professor Lawrence Jackson Ambrose.

Above their heads they heard more cries and whimpers from many, many women.

"I have a feeling that we have both, the lady, or ladies," and as he heard the steps of heavy boots walk directly over their heads, Jack added, "and the tiger."

"Well," Everett said easing back the charging handle of his automatic weapon, "I didn't put on my best suit to stand here looking stupid."

Jack nodded his head and then started screwing a suppressor onto his nine millimeter.

"Let's see what kind of quality help the Anaconda has at his disposal."

After searching the collapsed areas, a space Everett had dubbed Mr. Wizard's laboratory, Jack became convinced there may be no way up through the flooring except to blow their way through, which wouldn't be too stealthy at all. He lowered his suppressed Beretta, raised the ambient-light goggles, and then wiped the sweat from his brow. He heard Will in the far corner digging at the area where the body lay covered by debris from the one-hundred-year-old collapse of the floor above them.

"Jack, whoever repaired the floor above this one never realized anything was down here. That's my best guess. They must have covered up any access to this area during their repairs. Look up there. Half the flooring is wood, and the half closest to the walls is concrete." Carl swiped at the sweat he had built up in the search.

"Jesus Christ!" Mendenhall hissed as he stumbled backward from where he had been digging out the body.

Jack flinched at the loudness of Mendenhall's frightened voice.

Will realized his mistake by crying out, but made no apologies as he straightened up and then placed his hands on his knees. Everett and Collins joined him and then looked around to make sure any extra lighting they put on the scene would not be seen through the cracks in the flooring over their heads. Satisfied, both men added their flashlights to the one Mendenhall had shining on the collapse.

"You tell me just what in the hell that is?" Will said shining his light on a large lump next to the skeletal remains of the uniformed soldier he had pulled free. He was taking deep breaths in an attempt to get his fear under control. The white coat was in tatters and through the swirling dust they could see a skull that was horribly malformed. The teeth in the grinning skull were long and crooked. But what had frightened Will so much were the thick, long, and beastly looking arm bones that were exposed through the torn and aged white coat. The eye sockets of the remains were overly large and the mouth that held the long, sharp teeth was the same.

"Whoa," Everett said, conscious of keeping his voice low. He held his light on the scene as Collins bent low to inspect Will's find.

Jack could make out the remains of a beard, the course hair of which was lying next to the skull. There were bits and pieces of it still clinging to the lower jaw line of the remains. All in all Collins had only seen something like this a few other times and that was because they had remains such as these in the vaults deep inside the Event Group compound in Nevada. They were nearly matching the skeletal remains of what is known as Neanderthal Man. Only this skeleton was much larger than the small specimens the Group had inside the vaults. He moved his light to the remains of the uniformed skeleton.

"Jack, are you seeing what I see?" Everett said as Will stepped up and joined them, adding his light to theirs.

Indeed Jack was seeing the large teeth marks on the remains of the much smaller skeleton. Through the ragged and aged blouse of the soldier, both arms had been snapped in two and the teeth marks upon the bone were evident.

"I don't think a cave-in can explain that," Collins said as he duckwalked forward and then pulled the upper torso of the remains free of the dirt and sand. He saw something shiny in the flashlight's beam. "Look at this," he said as he

raised the collar so Will and Carl could see. There was a
U.S. button on the left collar and on the epaulet was the em-
blem Jack recognized immediately. It was a shield with the
upper half of a rearing horse. The walking bear on top of the
shield gave the unit its identity: "The 8th Cavalry regiment."

"Then I guess the report from Pete was accurate enough,"
Everett said, his eyes not moving from the large bite indentations in the bone of the hundred-year-old remains.

Jack noticed something in the collapsed debris and reached
out and picked it up. It was a large chunk of old concrete. He
lifted it to his nose and smelled. He then tossed the small
piece to Everett who did the same.

"Dynamite, or something close to it," Carl said as he
found others near the two bodies. As he examined the piece
of concrete, he noticed a strap of some kind poking from the
remains of the rubble. He dropped the scorched remains of
old flooring and reached down and tugged on the strap. He
saw that the old piece of coarse material was starting to rip
away so he went to his knees and dug out not only the strap,
but a cracked and weathered saddlebag. He saw the *U.S.*
marking on the double bag and then opened it up, shining
his flashlight inside. His eyes widened as he saw the gleaming, glistening objects inside. Carl stepped away from Jack
and Mendenhall and toward the far wall of the old laboratory. He sat the bag down easily and then stepped away.

"What is it?" Collins asked as he noticed the careful way
Carl handled the old saddlebag.

"Oh, about twenty sticks of old dynamite, with enough
nitroglycerine sweating out of it to blow this room to bits."

"That's the nice thing about dynamite; it only gets better
with age."

"What do you make of these, Colonel?" Mendenhall said
as he stepped over to several of the undamaged wooden barrels. He bent over and with his gloved hand started to pick
up some of the fallen contents, but before he could Jack
reached out and stayed his hand. Collins just shook his head.
"They look like dried flowers," he said and then saw Jack's
eyes as he took in barrel upon barrel of the same foul-smelling

and fermenting dry goods. Mendenhall was suddenly glad
the colonel had stopped him from touching the contents.

"Jack, this stuff, it looks like poppies, but not anything I
have ever seen before," Everett said as he examined more of
the sealed barrels.

"Maybe Guzman is producing heroin down here," Will
offered.

"Not unless his great grandfather was down here making
it." Jack straightened and looked around the large room,
only half of which they could see due to the cave-in. His
light illuminated a hundred glass jars on shelves that had
survived the eruption. Then he moved the light to a small
table with many steel syringes upon its top. He was about to
comment when there was a loud noise that came through the
floorboards from above. Heavy boots of more than just a few
men had entered the basement above them.

"I will ask one last time. Who you work for? My contacts
at your front company, Texaco, say they have never heard
of you."

Jack tried to trace the voice but ran into the thickest part of
the cave-in. He tracked the sound with his Beretta aimed but
knew he could not blindly shoot up through the floorboards.

"Then you leave me no choice. I will leave my brother
Eduardo here to ask again. He will not be as polite."

All three men below the voices heard the men above turn
and again vanish up what must have been a set of stairs.

"I have looked forward to this since we took you this afternoon," the deeper voice said as the sound of keys was
heard through the cracks in the wood flooring.

"You're the son of a bitch that shot my friend at the excavation site."

Jack closed his eyes as he heard the female voice. Everett
patted Collins on the shoulder and nodded his head. Sarah
was alive. The smile immediately left Carl's face when they
heard the keys enter the lock.

"Sí, I shot your friends, just as I am going to start shooting everyone in this cell, starting with the girls you seemed
destined to protect." The creaking of the cell door opening

was heard, and Jack's face became a set piece of rage just as
the screams came from women they could not see.

Jack heard a slap and a grunt and he assumed Sarah had
just been struck. Then he heard, "Ah, ever the hero, señor."
They all heard a thud and then a loud grunt.

"Stop it!" came Sarah's voice.

"That's the bastard that killed Udall and shot Ryan,"
Mendenhall hissed.

"Quiet Lieutenant," Everett hissed.

Will stormed off to the far wall where the glass jars of
liquid and some of the powders were stored. He felt like
striking out and slapping all of them onto the floor.

Collins knew he had to chance it. He holstered his nine
millimeter, raised the M-14 carbine, and aimed it at the old
wood flooring above, ready to cut his way through. Everett
reached out and placed an old rickety stool beneath the spot
where Jack was about to make a brand-new doorway.

"No," Will said almost not loud enough to stop them.

Collins angrily lowered the weapon and then pointed to a
section of the flooring above the stored jars on the shelving
against the far wall. Somehow they had missed that area in
their recent search. As they looked, Mendenhall was pointing at a spot that had two missing planks in the flooring.
Jack closed his eyes, thankful that Will had found what he
had. He nodded. He and Everett went over to the spot and
looked up. They could see the ceiling on the floor above.
There were no obstacles blocking their sight. They had a
way in, and it was far enough away from the cell above to
give them the advantage.

"Okay, we move before this asshole's friends return. I
need a boost," Collins said looking at Everett, who looked
down, not wanting to meet Jack's eyes.

"Will is the better shot, Jack." Everett looked from the
colonel to the younger lieutenant.

"Besides, that pig shot my friend," Mendenhall said as he
reached out and took Jack's nine millimeter out of its holster. He handed over his MP-5 and then made sure he had
a round chambered in the Beretta. He also twisted on the

large suppressor at the barrel's tip to make sure it hadn't worked its way loose since they entered the culvert.

Collins nodded his head as he realized that in the past five years Mendenhall had surpassed him and Everett both at the gun range. The lieutenant was now the best shot he had ever trained.

"Don't you miss," Everett said before Jack could. "Or don't come back," said Jack, trying to get Will to relax.

Mendenhall dipped his head and then took a deep breath. "I've counted three hanging light fixtures through the cracks in the flooring. Do you think you old guys can take them out through an inch of wood?"

The two men didn't respond but did give Will a dirty look.

"Good. I'll wait until it's dark before I take that slimy prick out."

Everett bent to one knee and cupped his hands together. "If you fuck this up, I'll be the first to tell Ryan you missed the guy who shot him."

After Will nodded his head, he took a few more breaths and then stepped into the hands of the captain. Then he was up and through the empty space where the planks were missing. Everett quickly scrambled away after making sure Mendenhall didn't have to beat a hasty retreat.

"I figure you take out the light here. I'll get the one closest to the cell, and then we meet to take out the middle one. The darkness should give Will the time and advantage he needs."

"Right," Everett said as he raised his M-14 at the gap between the planks above. "Jack, what about the girls in the cell?"

"Everyone goes home tonight."

Carl nodded his head and then took up his station as Jack moved to the closest spot he could get, standing right over the hundred-year-old corpses. He looked down at the strange malformed shape of the white-coated man, and he too took his breaths and then aimed as best he could, knowing it would take more than one shot to douse the light above. Just as he aimed he heard more screams from above.

Collins gave Everett the nod he was waiting for, and a moment later all hell broke loose at Perdition Hacienda.

The brother of Juan Guzman kicked Farbeaux as hard as he could when the Frenchman had once more tried to trip him up. Sarah lashed out with her hand and that was when the man hit her across the bridge of the nose with his automatic, eliciting a round of screams from the teenage girls cowering against the wall inside the cell. The man smiled and then easily reached out and plucked a young Mexican girl up by her black hair. Sarah swiped blood away from her broken nose and tried to clear her eyes of the tears that had formed. Farbeaux was actually trying to stand and had made it to one knee when the dark eyes of his soon-to-be killer turned and smiled at his feeble attempt. He aimed the automatic at Henri as the struggling girl in his other hand kicked and screamed.

"Goodbye, señor," he said just as the flooring beneath their feet erupted in a loud splintering sound. Wood chips flew in all directions as six rounds penetrated the floor beneath them. The light only a few feet away exploded as the heavy rounds found their mark at just the same moment the light farther down the corridor was hit from below.

As the man's eyes widened, he saw Sarah out of the corner of his peripheral vision dive on top of Farbeaux, shielding him with her own body. The man quickly took aim as the third and middle light blew up as more than fifteen high-velocity rounds smashed through the wood. The cell area went completely black with the exception of the weak lighting farther down the long corridor.

As Guzman's brother aimed his weapon just as the lights were extinguished, Sarah just knew she was about to feel several of the animal's bullets slam into her back as she covered the Frenchman. Instead, she felt and heard a whizzing sound and at the same moment a loud clacking noise. She felt the wetness strike her body from above and she heard the girl her would-be killer was holding scream again. There was a loud thump and as Sarah's eyes adjusted to the dim lighting emanating from down the hallway, she saw the body of Guzman's brother fall in front of her and Farbeaux. He still had the girl's hair gripped in his right hand. Sarah saw the top of the man's head was now gone.

She heard a noise not far from the cell and then the hastily whispered words. "Clear!" Sarah felt like yelling when she saw the dark shape take form as the man advanced toward the cell. She could see the outline of the shape and a reflection of light on glass and then she knew who it was.

"Will," she said as she unceremoniously pushed Henri aside and ran to the cell door.

"Hey, what's up?" Mendenhall said as she started working the key that was still dangling from the lock. "Uh, would you mind telling your young friend there she can stop screaming for the moment? There's still plenty to do tonight, so she'll probably have chances to scream all she wants," Mendenhall said as the cell door creaked open.

"God," she said as she took Will into her arms and hugged him tightly. "It's good to see you. How in the hell did you find me, and how did you get in?"

Mendenhall pushed her back a step and raised the ambient-light goggles. "Well, the colonel was so pissed that you stood him and his mother up, he came personally to kick your ass."

That was when Sarah saw the two figures standing twenty feet away from the cell. Everett raised his goggles up and then started brushing wood chips from his shoulders. The man standing to her direct front also removed his night vision equipment.

"Strange company you're keeping these days," Collins said as his eyes moved from Sarah to the man trying to pick himself up off the floor.

Sarah ran through the cell door and hugged Jack as if she had never hugged anyone before.

"Hey, hey, there's not a lot of time here; gather these girls up."

Sarah pushed back from Collins and looked into his eyes. "Don't tell me you guys are alone?"

"Yes, please don't tell us that, Colonel."

Jack looked from Sarah to the man using the bars as a brace to stand.

"He came here specifically to get me out, Jack," Sarah said, taking his arm before he could enter the cell.

"I bet he did," he answered as he shook Sarah's hand from his, stepped inside the cell, and assisted the Frenchman to his feet.

On his way past McIntire, Everett shoved a white handkerchief into her hand. "In case you didn't notice, your nose is broken." Sarah took it and swiped at her painful break. Everett and Mendenhall stepped in behind Jack and hurriedly gestured for the young girls to be quiet and get the hell out of there. They were young, but they also knew it was time to go. Sixteen girls ran for the cell door all at once, pushing Jack and Farbeaux out of the way as they scrambled into the corridor.

"Jack, you didn't answer me. Are you guys the cavalry?"

"Honey, I'm afraid the only cavalry here tonight has been dead for close to a hundred years."

Everett walked past her and a stunned Farbeaux who had his arm around Jack's shoulder as he too was removed from the cell.

"We are what you would call shorthanded, and probably out of work."

Sarah sighed as she followed the men and young girls.

"Again, Jack?"

The girls were lowered one at a time through the missing floorboards. It was painstakingly slow. Farbeaux came to as he was held upright by Collins and looked around quizzically. He tried to focus on Jack's face and then saw Mendenhall as he lowered Sarah through the small space.

"I thought you had more friends than this Colonel," Henri said as he winced at the attempt at humor.

"Yeah, but with the three I have here, it still makes three more than you have, Henri."

"Touché, Colonel," Henri said and then hung his head again as his arm relaxed around Jack's shoulder.

Everett, who was watching the cell area, poked his head around the corner. "We have company coming down the stairs, and it sounds like whoever it is has more than just three friends with him, Jack."

"The gentleman who is coming . . . is not a particularly nice person, Colonel," Farbeaux said as he again tried to clear his head.

Collins adjusted the Frenchman's weight and then looked back and nodded at Everett.

"Is that your expert opinion?"

"Indeed. Perhaps you better give me one of those weapons you're . . . so fond of . . . carrying."

"Give it a rest Henri. Right now you couldn't see what it was I handed you. In case you didn't know it, you've got one hell of a concussion."

Farbeaux finally managed to get his head up and then looked at Collins. "And that is . . . your expert . . . medical opinion?"

Jack shook his head. "When one bleeds out of his ears, Colonel, the diagnosis is pretty damn plain," Collins answered as he placed Henri behind one of the large barrels lining the wall. He removed his nine millimeter and handed it to the Frenchman. "What the hell, when Mr. Everett opens up, at least add some noise with that thing and make people duck . . . make them duck."

Farbeaux squinted and then half smiled. "Your confidence in my military prowess is . . . overwhelming, Jack."

Farbeaux watched as Jack left to join Everett, charging a round into the suppressed M-14 carbine.

The lights being out gave them a small tactical advantage. But Collins suspected that Guzman wasn't the type of leader who favored saving the lives of his men, so he knew they couldn't make it so expensive that the Anaconda would back off.

As Jack took aim slightly above Everett, who was on one

knee with his ambient-light goggles already down, he looked at his friend.

"We hit 'em hard with no warning. We pile up their bodies until they can't come through."

"Good plan . . . I guess," Everett said as he removed the safety on his carbine. "Okay, they're on the last set of stairs."

The pounding of feet was louder and then they heard before they saw the first man as he gained the bottom floor. Collins placed his hand on Everett, staying him from firing at the first one.

Through the greenish light of their goggles they saw the man stop and stare into the darkness of the now empty cell. He turned just as the Anaconda himself entered the subbasement. Jack recognized him immediately and aimed for his head. Just at that moment the lead man saw the danger and jumped in front of Guzman. The first silenced round, which in the closed space of the subbasement wasn't silent at all, struck the man in the back of his head just as Everett fired.

"Damn it," Jack hissed as he saw Guzman go down with his dead guard draped over him.

They all heard rapid-fire Spanish coming from the darkness ahead and more men flooded through the large open staircase.

That was when Collins and Everett opened up in earnest. They took the first four with no problem and then saw the next two men start to drag the dazed Guzman out from under the dead man covering him. Jack aimed and dropped one, but the other stayed up even as Everett's next three rounds struck him in the torso. His weight falling backward was enough to get the Anaconda near the stairway door where more hands lifted him and pulled him to safety.

"There goes the quick solution," Everett said as he fired another three-round burst at the men streaming through the door. They were now taking cover on the far side of the old cell. Rounds were pinging off the steel and chipping large chunks of old concrete and adobe from the walls as Jack and Carl laid down a withering fire on the attackers.

Just as Collins's first magazine emptied, Guzman's men started to return fire at a far more rapid rate than either career soldier would have given them credit for. Bullets started shattering the corner of the wall that was covering them as Everett stopped to reload.

"Damn fine shooting in the dark," Everett said as he slammed home another thirty-round magazine.

"Remember, Captain, these . . . men have been . . . fighting a real war down here for . . . nearly five . . . years."

Carl chanced a look behind him and saw that Farbeaux had managed to crawl forward and was actually trying to aim the Beretta in the direction of the attack. As he shook his head and turned to fire, Henri's aim proved to be as good as either Jack's or his own as three men fell inside of the cell.

With the flare of the enemy weapons, Jack raised his goggles and then tossed them away, as did Everett. The bright flashes were overwhelming the ambient-light devices and they were firing blind.

Suddenly they heard footsteps directly over their heads and without thinking it through, Collins pulled Everett backward by the body armor covering his back. As they fell back, Henri saw what was happening and fired the remaining rounds in the nine millimeter and then rolled to join his two allies.

Just as they cleared the area, a loud explosion rocked the subbasement, sending wood and concrete downward in a killing arc of shrapnel.

"Damn cheaters," Everett said as he rose and emptied another magazine up and into the smoldering hole that had just been opened up above them.

As Jack added fire to the new opening, they heard another, far louder weapon open up next to them. Will Mendenhall had joined the fight with his MP-5. He sprayed the first fifteen rounds at the men trying to advance through the corridor and then raised the hot and smoking weapon at the same spot Everett and Collins were firing at. As he stopped to change magazines he slapped Everett on the shoulder.

"Time to go! Sarah has the girls heading down the tunnel!"

"Right," Everett said as he stopped firing and then unceremoniously grabbed the wounded Farbeaux by the collar and started dragging him toward the missing floorboards.

There was another explosion and a hole magically appeared just in front of the cell where Guzman's men had taken cover. Collins heard something fall through the opening as the gunfire let up and the Anaconda's men saw what had been thrown into the lower floor. They tried to scramble out, but it was too late. The grenade detonated and men were thrown in every direction.

"Now that's a real nice guy," Mendenhall said as he added bullets to the shrapnel near the darkened cell area.

"I don't think I want to be here when this asshole gets serious. Go, Will, go!"

Mendenhall followed Jack's orders and rolled halfway to the hole in the wooden flooring. He waited as Everett shoved Farbeaux roughly through the opening and then jumped after him. Will heard more men pouring into the basement from the stairs and even saw two or three fall through the second hole they had made. He started to lower himself when he saw a shotgun barrel poke through the blast hole directly where they had been a moment before. He started sliding into the hole before he could aim. Jack was about to be shot from above as Will fired blindly upward as he vanished through the floorboards. One of the rounds hit the man aiming his lethal weapon at the top of his head. Collins never knew how close he had come to having his head blown off as he jumped in after Mendenhall.

Collins missed landing on Mendenhall by a mere foot. He rolled and came up inside the old laboratory. He fired two more times at the spot where he had just jumped, but that didn't stop one of Guzman's men from getting through the missing floorboards. He saw the man struggling with something. Jack aimed and fired, but nothing happened. The man struggled to his knees and then raised his right arm into the air. As Collins froze for the briefest of moments, two aimed rounds struck the man in the neck and chest, dropping him, but not before he managed to do what he came to do. Henri Farbeaux immediately pulled Jack down.

"Grenade!" the Frenchman shouted.

Everett and Mendenhall immediately dove for cover as the small round object sailed over their heads and landed next to the excavated hole they had entered the old laboratory through. The grenade exploded. Several small pieces of shrapnel struck Everett in the shoulder and Will in the right arm. But they would have considered themselves lucky if that had been all the damage done. The bulk of the grenade's power smashed against the dirt opening to the lab, collapsing the ceiling and sending wood reinforcement and dirt cascading down, blocking their escape.

Jack shook himself and then stood, pulling Henri up as he did. "Thanks, Colonel."

Farbeaux didn't answer as he took in the mess around him. Through the smoke and dust he saw Everett and Mendenhall stand and look around—they were both dazed from the concussive effects of the explosion. Then he spied the cave-in.

"I take it that was the way out of here," he asked as he ejected the now empty clip from the Beretta. He looked at Jack and then swiped blood from his right eye.

"You're as observant as ever, Henri," Collins said as he rushed forward, handing the Frenchman three more clips of ammunition as he did.

"You two alright?" he asked as he saw blood streaming from both of his men.

"A little steel and blood is the least of our problems, Jack," Everett said as he bent to retrieve his carbine.

Collins examined the damage and cursed as he kicked at the blockage in front of him.

"Gentlemen, we have more company," Henri said as he dropped the first man who poked his head through the opening above. Then he fired a second time and hit one of Guzman's men in both hands as he reached to move the first attacker out of the way. He emptied another clip up and into the floorboards where he heard men scream in pain. Then all of a sudden it was silent.

Farbeaux had just ejected the expended clip when his eyes fell on something about ten feet away from him. He stepped forward and then kicked at a white object on the dirt floor. Curious, he reached into his pocket brought out a lighter, and then flicked it to life. His eyebrows rose as he spied the misshapen skull staring up at him. He allowed the flame to go out and decided it wasn't worth asking about. He turned and then joined the others at the cave-in while watching the floorboards above him for any sign of movement. He saw shadows through the cracks in the wood but decided not to waste any more ammunition on guesswork. He shook his head as his vision blurred briefly and then turned to face the men who had become his strictest enemies. Jack and Everett were already on their knees digging away at the blockage. Henri could see it would be a painfully slow process.

"Gentlemen, you have made an otherwise boring night into something I will remember for years to come," a man said from above in very good English. "Now, if you will surrender we can—"

The rest of the words were drowned out by a sudden burst of thirty rounds as they struck the floor above. The bullets hit everywhere around the hole.

"You ever notice how assholes like that always want to make a speech when they have the upper hand?" Jack said as he tossed the now empty carbine to Mendenhall to reload as he bent to continue digging. Thirty feet away they heard Guzman laughing near the hole in the floor.

"Do I bore you? What are you, Special Forces perhaps?"

"This guy never gives up," Mendenhall said and then was knocked from his feet as an explosion rocked the large laboratory. Jack, Everett, and Farbeaux were stunned as a large hole opened up against the far wall, knocking jar after jar of the stored chemicals from their shelves. Then before they could react, several men jumped through the new opening before a defensive shot could be fired.

"I think you pissed him off, Jack," Everett said as he came

to his knees and fired his weapon toward the area where the men had taken cover. Several of the wooden tables had caught fire, adding light to the darkened laboratory.

Farbeaux stood on shaky feet and fired twice from the Beretta. He was suddenly struck and went down with a clean bullet hole in his arm.

"That hurt!" he shouted as he scrambled on his belly toward Collins, Everett, and Mendenhall. "I lost your weapon, Colonel."

"Yeah, and you're going to pay for it. I signed that out!" Collins said as his anger at being trapped spilled from his mouth.

Mendenhall pulled two of the poppy-filled barrels over to use as cover while Everett and Collins dug at the fallen earth. He turned in time to see a small opening at the top. They were making headway.

"Jack!"

"Damn it, Lieutenant, get those girls down that tunnel and out of here!" Collins stopped long enough to shout. Sarah had once more disobeyed his order and came back when she heard the explosion that sealed the laboratory from the culvert. When he didn't hear her respond, he once more started tearing at the loose earth.

"She's starting to follow orders like the rest of us," Everett said as he threw a large chunk of wooden beam away. He noticed that Collins was too angry to say anything.

Mendenhall fired five rounds and hit one of the next men through the now large gap where only a few missing boards had been before.

"I see you are trapped, gentlemen. Give up now and the women can go free. Do not and they will be caught and skinned alive before they reach the river."

Jack knew it was Guzman. The Anaconda was actually one of the men who came through the flooring from above them.

"Brave son of a bitch isn't he?" Farbeaux said as he opened fire with Jack's carbine. The rounds struck the shelving above where Guzman and his men were taking cover.

Through the flames of the burning wood Mendenhall saw the jars on the shelves shatter. The he saw more of the samples from a hundred years before break and splatter onto the men below.

Mendenhall changed magazines in the smoking MP-5, which had totally burned out its sound suppressor, and then aimed at the spot he thought the voice of Juan Guzman was coming from. He was about to fire when he saw a man's arm wave from the cover of the burning tables. Then he realized that he wasn't waving as a small object flew from his hand. Will's eyes widened when he realized just what the object was. He angrily stood, and in the flickering light he caught the grenade. In a split-second reaction he tossed it back in the direction in which it was launched.

"Down!" he shouted as Henri fell next to him after seeing the amazing catch in midair.

The grenade exploded amongst the scrambling and now screaming men, sending large pieces of them in all directions. The remainder of the sample jars and more than a few of the wooden barrels of dried flowers erupted as shrapnel tore through them.

Mendenhall stood and emptied the thirty-round magazine in his MP-5 in a spray of bullets in the general area where men were either dead or writhing in pain.

"Hah! Didn't see that one coming did you, you bastards! That one was for Ryan!" Mendenhall screamed just a second before the wounded Farbeaux pulled him roughly to the floor.

"Didn't Collins teach you better than that?" the Frenchman asked with a mask of pain and anger on his face.

"Just thrilled to be here, Colonel, you ought to know that by now," Will said as he changed the empty magazine for a new one.

"If you two are finished, we could use a hand here," Everett said as he continued to widen the gap at the top of the cave-in.

"Go, I'll cover us," Henri said grabbing the MP-5 from Mendenhall.

"Why? I got 'em all!" Will said as he saw Farbeaux fire into the flickering firelight cast by the burning tables and wooden barrels.

"Well, evidently you missed one or two Lieutenant!" Henri said as he loosed more rounds in the general direction of the man who had just risen. Mendenhall, instead of helping Jack and Carl, bent back down near Farbeaux. He saw the man that had thrown the grenade go down when Henri's stream of bullets cut him down.

In the direction where the grenade had detonated, screams of agony were heard—cries of pain so loud and piercing all four men felt like covering their ears. They could all smell burnt flesh, the smell of dried foliage, and something they could never describe—the odor was medicinal, and as the stench grew, so did the screams of Guzman and his men.

"What the—"

His question was interrupted by another four rounds fired by the Frenchman. They both saw the same man go down again.

"That's one hard to kill son of a bitch!" Mendenhall said as he tried to ignore the powerful smell from the burning poppies and the stench of the liquid that had been stored in the jars.

Even as the exclamation left Mendenhall's mouth, Farbeaux's eyes widened. The same man Will had shot, and then hit with the grenade, actually stood up again, this time holding a flaming leg from one of the smashed tables. Henri took careful aim and fired again. This time three rounds left the MP-5. One bullet struck the man in the neck, the next two in the jaw and the cheek. He moved back two steps and then looked up toward where his attacker had fired. Farbeaux was shocked he was still standing. He fired one more round. This one hit the man directly where his heart should have been. Both Henri and Will saw the man's white shirt puff out where the bullet had hit. The man started walking toward them. As Henri's jaw dropped, a sound came from behind the overturned and flaming tables near the wall. It was an actual roar. It sounded like an ape or a bear. Will looked at Farbeaux as the sound reverberated off the wall.

Both Everett and Collins stopped digging long enough to turn their heads to see what was happening. The sound sent chills down everyone's spines.

"Oh, shit!" Mendenhall screamed. "Colonel, we have a problem here!"

As Jack looked on in amazement, Farbeaux emptied the rest of the magazine of 5.56 rounds into the man's body, even striking him on the right side of his head. The attacker was finally knocked down. As Collins started to turn back to widen the hole, he saw the man that had just been hit with fifteen rounds pop up like a Jack in the Box.

"What the hell is this?" Will said as he reached for Everett's weapon, raised it to his shoulder, and took careful aim. This time he loosed a single round as the man drew closer. This bullet hit the bloody guard right between the eyes. Mendenhall was relieved when the man fell back, and this time he didn't move. He looked down at Henri. "You just have to know how to shoot, Colonel."

Farbeaux wasn't listening as he watched two men, one without an arm and the other with his lower jaw missing, stand up from behind the spreading flames.

"Okay, Colonel, I think I want to leave now."

Collins couldn't believe what he was seeing. Men that had been shot, filled with shrapnel from a grenade, and wounded beyond any reason for them to even be moving were growling and walking toward them.

Mendenhall stood and just nodded his head at the two men as they came on. "Okay, okay! They're drug addled or something."

Henri fired until another of the magazines was empty. The man without a jaw was struck in the center of his forehead and went down heavily and didn't move. The second man stood his ground and was about to start forward once more with at least five bullet holes in his abdomen and chest, when another awful and animalistic roar filled the room once more. This time Henri, Will, and Collins actually saw the author of that sound, or rather his shadow, as he rose from behind the makeshift and now destroyed cover.

Henri saw that the man was wearing the very same clothing that Juan Guzman was wearing earlier when Farbeaux was beaten inside of the cell. He stood and then called back to Jack.

"That's Guzman."

Collins saw that the man was at least a foot and a half taller than he was. He had grown so much that the shirt he wore was torn in several places. And what was worse he could now see the man's features in the flickering of the fire. His cheekbones were high and deep lined. His forehead was larger than normal and his arms hung far below his waist. Jack's eyes went from the two men in front of them to the two corpses they had found earlier.

"Jesus, it's got to be that crap from the barrels and the jars. They've changed!"

Henri looked from the monstrosities before them to one of the sealed jars that had nearly decapitated him after the explosion. He involuntarily moved a few feet farther from it as another scream of animal rage filled the old laboratory.

The beast that was once Juan Guzman, the Anaconda, quickly moved, his actions as fluent as a cat's, and took the wounded man standing before them by the throat. He raised his own man off the floor and then they all heard his neck snap. Guzman then brought the man close to his own face and then to the complete horror of the men watching in shock, took a large bite out of the man's face. He chewed once, twice, and then looked toward the men watching. The thing actually smiled, and then before they could react Guzman threw the dead body toward them where it landed against the rubble from the cave-in and slid down at Everett's feet. The roar of triumph pierced their ears.

"Oh, boy, look at this," Will said as he stood stunned and motionless.

They saw several more men rise up behind Guzman. Some were torn to pieces, others had bullet holes across their chests and shoulders. All were changed almost as much as Guzman.

"The hole's big enough!" Mendenhall said as he turned away from the terrifying sight.

Henri saw Will dive next to Jack, pushing the dead man out of his way, and start tearing at the opening at the top of the debris. Everett dove in to help. Farbeaux fired the M-14 until the receiver clacked open and stayed that way. As he was starting to turn and join the flight, Jack jumped over him and dove for something Henri didn't see, nor did he care what it was. As he turned his eyes away from Collins, Farbeaux saw something that made him stop. It was the clear jar of liquid he had almost been killed by earlier. He quickly reached out, took the mayonnaise-sized container, and shoved it into his shirt. He scrambled up and over to help Everett and Mendenhall.

Jack was searching for something in the dark when he heard Everett. "Jack, come on, we're through!"

He continued looking on hands and knees. Then his hand brushed against it. He pulled the twin saddlebag to his chest, not caring that the dynamite inside was sweating. He turned toward the widened hole and started to scramble.

"Don't wait on me, move it!" he shouted as the three beasts came on, slowly, all smiling.

As Mendenhall and then Farbeaux scrambled up and out of the old laboratory, Everett saw what Jack was carrying. His eyes widened and then he turned and went through the opening. He didn't wait for Jack.

Collins made it to the cave-in and then saw the two changed men behind Guzman turn on each other. The brief attack was brutal, but both of them survived. They regained their focus and then followed their boss toward Collins.

"Kiss my ass!" Jack shouted, and then, grabbing one of the fallen M-14s, he tossed the twin saddlebags at the trio of monstrous attackers. He lowered his head, thinking that the nitroglycerine-covered dynamite would detonate upon impacting the floor, but all he heard was a laugh. He looked up and saw Guzman, his misshapen and distorted features looking down at the saddlebags.

"Shit!" Jack hissed as he scrambled to the top of the debris and entered the hole.

Just as Guzman turned away from the saddlebags, he laughed, an evil, cold sound, as he saw his antagonist's legs vanish into the escape hole.

"You should have negotiated," sounded the deep voice.

Suddenly Jack reappeared in the facing of the wall. This time it was he who was smiling.

"You're right, here's my offer!" he shouted as loud as he could.

Guzman's larger-than-normal eyes widened, and just before Jack fired the M-14, the horrid-looking Anaconda raised his hands upward and jumped. Grabbing broken wooden beams, he heaved himself up and out of the laboratory a split second before the red-hot nine-millimeter round struck the saddlebags.

The explosion actually blew Collins backward into the tunnel as it started to collapse. As the excavated hole fell inward upon itself, a split second of fire, rocks, and smoke flew through the hole. The combination of dynamite, and its natural offspring, nitroglycerin, detonated with power triple what the original makers intended.

Everett quickly picked himself up and with his ears ringing out of control, saw Collins lying motionless and face down in the hard, compacted earth of the tunnel. He reached down and handily picked Jack up. Shaking him, not caring if he had a neck or head injury, Everett waited until he opened his dirt-caked eyes.

"Maybe a fuse next time!" Everett screamed.

"Remind me next time, will you?" Jack said, shaking himself to full wakefulness. Then he suddenly remembered. "Jesus, I think Guzman got out!"

It didn't take the genius of Jack's words to get Everett moving. He just turned, helping Collins to his feet, and then they started running for their lives.

The raid on the hacienda called Perdition had ended.

The nearly ten-mile flight from a horror none of the four men could ever have imagined had just started.

4

It didn't take long for the men to catch up with the women who were trying to negotiate the long and dark culvert in complete and utter darkness. The only time they could see anything was when there was a break in the concrete over their heads, which allowed the rising moonlight to penetrate the blackness. Sarah had kept pushing the young girls as much as she dared. All sixteen were close to freezing up in their panic-stricken flight from the bowels of Perdition.

At almost every break in the culvert, the girls would stop, giving them the slightest break and hope at seeing the least bit of light.

"Vámonos, vámonos," Sarah shouted from the rear as the young women stopped just under a large break in the roof of the large concrete tube. "We have to move!" she shouted as she pushed through the block of scared girls.

Sarah saw the wide eyes as the adrenalin rush of their escape had just started to ebb. She saw the fear and terror of what they had been through seeping through them like sweat through their pores. She didn't hesitate as she grabbed the oldest-looking girl and shoved her away from the light streaming through the large hole. The woman just stared at her and then looked down the long dark tunnel.

Just as Sarah pushed the woman again, she heard the girls at the back of the pack scream and surge forward. Sarah cursed at not having a weapon as the girls crowded around her.

"Damn it Sarah, why aren't these people moving?"

Sarah relaxed when she heard the familiar voice of Will Mendenhall as he burst around the small bend just before the break in the culvert. He angrily pushed through the crowd of cowering girls, and when he saw their panic-stricken faces, he tried his best to reassure them.

"Because damn it they're terrified and we have no light!"

Will reached to his side and handed his flashlight to Sarah. "Get them moving! We have company coming this way, and believe me it's far worse than you can ever know. Now let's get them going!" Will angrily pushed two of the girls and then started gesturing for the others to follow Sarah and the light down the tunnel. He had just drawn his nine millimeter, feeling how inadequate the weight was in his hand, when more screams filled the small space.

"Does anyone follow orders anymore?" the angered voice of Collins said, echoing in the tight space. "We have a time issue here!"

Finally the girls stopped screaming when they saw the three men come into view. Sarah pulled the older-looking girl and moved off down the tunnel. The others hesitantly started to follow.

"Will, I have your MP. I'll take the rear, you get ahead of Sarah and take the point. Captain Everett, take our French friend here, who needs to lose weight by the way, and keep these girls on the move. No stops, no rest, Jack ordered."

Mendenhall passed Jack his last two thirty-round magazines and then pushed off to catch up with Sarah and the girls in the lead. Collins struggled out of his body armor and let it fall to the culvert's flow of water. He knew he had at least three broken ribs and assisting Farbeaux hadn't helped. He looked up and in the moonlight could see that Everett was faring no better as he was bleeding from at least three areas of his body from shrapnel wounds. Henri for the most part had exhausted any energy he had left.

"Give Henri the carbine." Jack stepped up to the Frenchman as he changed magazines in the MP-5. "Cover Captain Everett, Henri, you got that? If I go down, you're the only tail gunner we have."

Farbeaux managed to look at Collins and then at Everett who was struggling to hold Henri and himself upright. "Yes, just tell your captain here not to drop any excess weight when the chips are down."

"Don't worry; I won't let it get to that point, Froggy. The chips are already down and I want to drop you right now." With that said Everett headed into the darkness, not feeling much different from the girls who were near panic.

Jack charged the weapon, sending a round into the breach of the MP-5, and then with a last look back and still wondering what sort of horror had befallen them, followed the long line of running men and women.

The group had gone close to a mile when in the rear Jack heard a far-off voice shouting down into the culvert from the spot they were just at not ten minutes before.

"I'm coming gringos, Mama sent me out for supper!"

Jack stopped and looked back into the darkness. The voice was deep and seemed as if it could never have come from the voice box of what Guzman had become. It wasn't brutish like the changed body became. But it was filled with savage intelligence, as if he was trying to scare and panic everyone in the tunnel. Jack knew it was working—he was scared.

He turned and started forward once more, wondering if the creature that was once the Anaconda had entered the culvert. He realized then as he ran, panting hard from his broken ribs pressing on the muscles of his chest and sides, that the smart move for Guzman would be to cover ground up there and try to head them off. He sensed the change had not lessened the man's intelligence.

In just under fifteen minutes, he was proven right.

Sarah turned to make sure the frightened women were still following close by. She decided they would have to take a break if they were to make it to the river. She saw light about a hundred yards to the front where another break in the culvert allowed moonlight to enter the darkness.

"Will, the girls are near collapse. We have to stop for a minute."

"No, keep them moving!" he shouted from the middle

of the pack. You have no idea what's back there. Move, move!"

Sarah took a deep breath and then gently pushed the girls gathered around her forward. It took just under a minute to cover the ground to the next break in the culvert. Just as Sarah moved past the light, she heard a loud scream, followed by another, and then another. As she turned her light on the area where the screams came from, her eyes widened when she saw a large arm and hand reach into the culvert from above. It hit upon one of the girls and grabbed her hair. In her flashlight beam she saw Mendenhall step forward and start bashing at the large, brutal hand as it started pulling the girl upward, out of the culvert.

The rest of the girls panicked and started forward, blocking Sarah's view as Will opened up with his nine millimeter. Sarah grabbed his arm and pulled his aim off for fear of him hitting the struggling girl. Then the girl was just gone.

"What was that?" Sarah screamed as girls started running by her in a blind panic.

"You don't want to know. Now move Sarah, move!"

The panic-stricken girls were now far outpacing Jack, Farbeaux, and Everett. As they passed the open area where the young woman had vanished just three minutes before, Everett turned and saw that Jack was struggling with the wounded Farbeaux. He turned and took the Frenchman's other arm, and together the trio started making better time.

The entire ten-mile flight was one of panic-stricken sprinting, stopping for much-needed air. Then a noise would filter down from above them and the screams of terror would start the stampeding girls off again. Sarah had to fight to keep them as bunched together as she could. She felt naked without a firearm and scared to death that the brave man she knew in Mendenhall was as frightened as the young Mexican girls he was trying his best to protect. As Sarah finally got the last girl past a small break in the upper section of the culvert, a large arm shot through and grabbed her shoulder, knocking her against the curving side of the concrete tube. Mendenhall fired five rounds, with three of them striking the thick-boned arm and wrist. He was amazed when the massive arm didn't pull away from the nine-millimeter rounds but kept working, searching for Sarah. McIntire's eyes widened as the hand and long warped fingers swung back and forth in its quest to grab something.

Will changed magazines, but before he could bring up the Beretta to fire, Everett shot past him and with knife poised to strike, sank his K-Bar deep into the forearm of Guzman. The large knife sank deep until it hit bone, and Carl cursed as he felt the hardened steel of the knife glance off the bone and then break off. His momentum sent him to the running, muddy water on the bottom of the culvert. Mendenhall helped him to his feet as Jack and Farbeaux ran past.

"You okay?" Mendenhall shouted as he dodged the bleeding, massive arm that swiped the empty air.

"Yeah, but I'm out of knives and bullets, so I suggest we get the hell out of here!"

As they covered the last mile to the river, Sarah managed to make her way to the front of the straggling line of girls, making each one scream as she ran past them. She knew exactly how they all felt as she was close to panic herself. Finally Sarah could see moonlight ahead of her. It was distant like the small rabbit hole Alice had fallen through on her journey to Wonderland, only Sarah knew they weren't escaping from that magical place, but from one that had quickly become an underground hell. As the girls started to bunch up behind her, Sarah held out her arm to stop the stampede toward freedom. She had seen a shadow cross the opening, momentarily blocking the light cast by the moon.

"What's the holdup? Let's get them out of here," Will said breathlessly as he caught up to the front of the pack.

"Whatever that thing was back there I think it's ahead of us," she said as she bent at the waist and rested.

Will was about to break for the opening to clear a way for the girls when suddenly the culvert exploded inward from above, showering the retreating party with broken chunks of concrete and mud. Then to everyone's complete and utter horror, the thing that was once Juan Guzman crashed through the hole he had just punched to land directly in front of the screaming women. Will didn't take long to empty the nine millimeter into the torso of the hulking figure ahead of them. In the dark he was lucky to see it at all. The monstrosity bent over as the rounds entered its muscled chest and abdomen. But in the filtered moonlight Mendenhall saw it slowly start to straighten. It was so much larger than it had been just thirty minutes before that it had to bend at the waist to accommodate its size. Will frantically reached into his belt for another clip of nine-millimeter ammunition and then realized when his finger searched the empty pouch that he had just expended everything he had.

"Oh, shit," Mendenhall said as he pulled Sarah back into the bunched-up women behind him. He quickly dropped the useless weapon and then pulled out his own knife.

The women screamed again as Everett crashed through their ranks and then slid to a stop when he saw Mendenhall ahead of him, and to his front, dwarfing the lieutenant, was Juan Guzman. The beastly apparition was standing there, taking deep breaths as it studied the small men and women cowering before it. In the bleached moonlight cascading through the new opening it had just made, Everett could swear he saw the creature smile.

"Damn!" Collins said as he pushed his way through the crowded culvert. He handed Farbeaux off to Sarah and one of the older girls and then slowly stepped to the front in between Everett and Mendenhall.

"It seems I am in possession of something that may become very beneficial to my operations," the beast said as it raised its left arm. It examined the change that had come to it and with tilted head closed its fist.

Collins looked at the man standing before him. Then he saw a strange thing—the creature winced in pain. In the moonlight Jack could see that Guzman's skin color as seen in the firelight back in the laboratory had diminished as the creature had exerted itself. The tough hide that had become its skin was now a sickly looking gray color and seemed to be flaking off in large chunks. It was as if the beast were starting to wilt before his eyes. Collins's eyes followed a long tuft of hair, bunched together with water, mud, and sweat, fall from the side of Guzman's head. Then even more black hair fell in the moonlight.

"It seems maybe you inhaled a little too much of that miracle drug, Anaconda. Feeling a little weaker than you were a moment before?" Jack said, buying as much time as he could.

Everett saw this and then grabbed the first girl he could reach and brought her to his side as he spied one of the first holes in the large culvert they had come across inside the long and dark tunnel. He was just about to lift her up when the beast suddenly turned to face its rear. Something or someone had come up from behind it.

"Rescue team, hit the deck!"

Jack heard the shouted command just as Guzman reacted and charged the new threat that had come upon it from behind. He turned and threw his body into several screaming girls, sending them crashing into the muddy, running water. Everett, Sarah, Mendenhall, and even the Frenchman did likewise. Just as the last girl hit the water, a cacophony of noise erupted in the confines of the culvert. As Jack raised his head he saw Guzman take the first volley of the automatic weapons' fire from the rear. Its body shook and the awful-sounding scream started from deep inside the Anaconda's chest. Then even more fire erupted in the darkness and Collins could see tracers as they hit the beast. More than a hundred rounds slammed home, but Guzman still came forward one faltering step at a time. Jack winced as a ricochet slammed into his hand. He saw tracer fire as it rebounded off wet concrete and he prayed that it didn't find any of the poor women behind him.

Guzman bellowed in anger and then three bullets finally hit the vital part of his malformed head and changed body. Its skull jerked back and Guzman spun around. With its wide eyes staring at Collins, it went to its knees. The right arm came up and then Jack saw a large man in black No-

mex, its shiny material gleaming in the moonlight, step up
to the back of the Anaconda and then fire two more rounds
from a Walther automatic into the back of the large skull.
Guzman, with one last wince of his tortured eyes, went face
down into the running water.

The man who had placed the bullets into Guzman's head
holstered his weapon and stared down at the thing he had
just killed. He raised a set of goggles not unlike the ones
Jack and his small team had had earlier. The man looked
from the giant creature that was once called the Anaconda
and then saw Jack lying a few feet away. The stranger was
soon joined by six others who took up station behind the
first. Collins slowly started to pick himself up in the near
darkness.

"The way is clear. May I suggest you get these people out
of here?" the man in the lead said as he gestured for his men
to assist the girls.

Collins cradled his wounded hand and then stepped up to
the rescuer who had undoubtedly saved their lives.

"Thanks, it was a little dicey there at the end," Collins
said as he looked the man over. His eyes roamed to the left
shoulder where the American flag would have been hidden
under a Velcro patch, but there was none. Jack searched but
could find no U.S.-issued equipment of any kind. As he
studied the man, the girls were pulled and prodded by men
dressed exactly the same. All kept their goggles and their
black nylon masks in place. The leader before him looked
from Collins to the body lying at his boots.

"What in the hell is this thing?" the large man said as he
went to his knees to study the unmoving corpse of Juan
Guzman. "It took at least fifty rounds to bring it down."

"What is your command?" Jack asked as the man raised
Guzman's head up by its hair. Then the sickening sound of
the long black strands tearing free from its scalp was heard
and the head fell unceremoniously back into the murky running water. The man stood and looked down at Collins.

"That was a ballsy thing you did at the hacienda, so I
may ask you the same question: who in the hell are *you*?"

Jack realized he was in a bit of a confrontation and didn't know why. Was he looking at a possible DELTA operative? Were they Rangers perhaps? He felt Captain Everett step to his side and knew the former SEAL was looking their rescuer over just as he had.

"Seems we only lost the one girl, Col—" Everett caught himself before speaking aloud Jack's rank, but not before the large man in black Nomex clothing looked at Carl and a small smile crossed his lips. "We have one down, and it looks like we may not lose anyone except for our French friend, who's lost a lot of blood."

"There's help just across the river. In the meantime we have a large group of men heading this way from the hacienda. I suggest you get the hell out of here. Look, is there anything back there at the hacienda that needs retrieval?"

As Jack waved Everett out and when he saw that Will and Sarah were assisting Henri toward the opening of the culvert, he stepped closer to the man in charge of the highly trained professional group that had come to their aid.

"There's nothing left back there. Again, your unit and rank?" Jack asked again, softening the question somewhat with a smile and an offer of a handshake.

"If you have the training I suspect that you have . . . colonel, is it? Then you should know better than to ask that, especially of someone who just saved your ass. For now let's just say it's just a tad above your pay grade to know."

Jack watched the man turn and head for the opening of the culvert. He saw that Carl was waiting for him. He held out a bottle of water one of the rescue team had given him and Jack took it with his uninjured hand and drank deeply.

"Who in the hell are those guys?" Carl asked as he watched the man splash his way out into the moonlight. "He's not navy, that's for sure."

Jack lowered the bottle of water as he started forward to get out into the night air. "And you know that because?"

"Because he didn't start bragging about what a great operation they had just conducted." Everett smiled, "You know a SEAL would have never passed up the opportunity to gig the army like that."

"You have a point."

Ahead Mendenhall and Sarah helped the weakened Farbeaux out of the opening and into the cool night air along the Rio Grande. Across the river they could see border patrolmen and helicopters as they flew low with their spotlights shining across the way. Mendenhall hit a slick moss-covered rock and lost his footing. He almost went down, pulling the Frenchman with him. As Sarah tried to hold both of them upright, something fell from Henri's shirt. It rolled into the water at their feet and before Farbeaux could react, a large, gloved hand reached out and retrieved the glass jar Farbeaux had removed from the laboratory in the final moments of their escape.

Sarah, Will, and Henri righted themselves and then looked up into the face of the man who led the team that saved them. He looked from the jar of amber liquid to the faces of the three people standing before him.

"What is that, Henri?" Sarah whispered into his ear.

"Something that needs to be handled carefully," Jack said as he removed the jar from the stranger's gloved hand. Holding it, he looked at Farbeaux closely and the Frenchman meekly shrugged his shoulders.

"Bad guy, remember?" he said in a pain-filled voice.

Jack handed the large sealed jar off to Everett and then looked the big man over once more as he heard shouts from across the river.

"Since you can't tell me what your unit is, perhaps you can tell me if we have any air assets nearby?"

The man's eyes were still on the jar that Everett was holding, and instead of answering Jack's question, he asked one of his own. "Does that," he said nodding at the jar of amber liquid, "have anything to do with that thing we saved you from—the Incredible Hulk–looking bastard in there?"

Jack smiled. "I'm afraid that's a bit above *your* pay grade." He stepped closer to the man, happy he could reciprocate this jerk's earlier rebuke. "Now, are there any air assets close by?"

"Number three, radio please?" the black-clad man said holding out his hand while never letting his eyes leave the filthy face of Jack Collins. "TAC three." The man took the handheld radio and then offered it to the colonel who took it without removing his eyes from the strangers. "I believe national command authority has ears on TAC three," the man said as his eyes flitted from Jack toward Everett and the jar he was holding. He slapped Collins on the left shoulder, expertly placing a small tracking device that was radium based and could be tracked from space. Then he stepped a few feet away as Collins raised the radio. Before he spoke he changed the frequency from tactical channel three to another he knew by heart. He turned his back on the others and faced the river.

"Viking Two, this is Berserker. Over."

"Good to hear you voice, Berserker," answered the familiar voice of Niles Compton. "We have company listening in, the CEO in fact . . . do you copy, Berserker?"

"Copy. We are somewhat compromised, so I'll make this as brief as possible. We have to strike at that compound. We have to level it."

The others heard Jack's words and not one of them was surprised to hear the request.

"No can do. We have questions that need to be answered first. The Mexican authorities are almost there to take possession of Perdition."

Jack knew the sound of the president's voice. He grimaced and then raised the radio to his lips, but before he could answer the commander in chief, the large Nomex-clad man interfered.

"Are you saying there is more of this over there?" he asked not too politely.

Jack ignored the large man and stepped away. The man tried to follow, but Everett stepped between him and the colonel. The captain just shook his head, saying that following Jack was a bad idea.

"Listen, we have a mess inside that hacienda," Jack said. "There are chemicals there that are as dangerous as any I've ever seen. If they are not destroyed we could be looking at a bleak situation if they fall into bad-guy hands. I mean serious trouble."

"We are in enough trouble. Stand down, Colonel. That is a direct order."

Jack lowered the radio and then looked at the tired faces around him. That was when he noticed that the large man and his team had vanished. He looked around and saw that Everett pointed to the edge of the river where the last of the darkly clothed men vanished into the water. As he turned back and raised the radio one last time, he angrily hit the transmit button.

"You can send a DELTA unit in to help us, but we can't level the distribution hub of a known terrorist and drug dealer?"

"Just what are you talking about . . . no, never mind, just get your asses back across the border. We'll talk later."

Jack thought the president had gone and then he heard a question that relaxed him a little.

"Colonel, is Lieutenant McIntire alright?"

"Yes, sir, she's been roughed up some, but she's fine."

"Good . . . good," the president said after an eternity of silence.

"Jack, just across the river Pete Golding will meet you with a Blackhawk. May I suggest you get on it so we can go home?"

"Niles, we have to make sure that the hacienda is totally destroyed. If the president can send in a rescue team, why can't we send in air assets to knock Perdition's Gate flat?"

"Colonel, the rescue the president ordered is still in the air and won't land in Laredo for another thirty minutes. There was no rescue OP that came across the border on his orders."

Collins lowered the radio. He then looked at the staring eyes of Farbeaux, Mendenhall, Everett, and Sarah, who were just as shocked to hear Niles's explanation of events as he had been. His head turned and looked at the spot where their rescuers had vanished into the flowing waters of the Rio Grande River. Then Collins cursed himself and suddenly turned and ran back into the large opening of the culvert. Will and Everett followed. Sarah turned with the weight of the Frenchman and watched as the three men vanished into the darkness once more.

"We have to recover Guzman's body or people are going to have a hard time believing this story."

As Jack approached the spot where Guzman had been downed, his eyes saw smoke rising from the running water. Everett and Mendenhall saw the same thing and froze. Lying in the water where Juan Guzman should have been was nothing but a smoking ruin. The clothing was totally eaten away and only a fragment of bone here and there was recognizable. With the jar of fluid still clutched in his uninjured hand, Collins leaned down and looked at the eaten-away remains of the world's most wanted criminal. Jack recognized the chemical smell almost immediately.

"What is it, Jack?" Everett asked as he too scowled at the smoking remains.

"It's something like hydrochloric acid, but different, stronger, a lower ph—but similar."

"Well it did a job on the old Anaconda," Will said. "Good riddance."

As Jack stood up he faced the lieutenant. He held up the jar of fluid. "Now this is the only evidence outside of our own accounts of what this stuff can do."

Will regretted his remark, realizing that the colonel was talking about evidence, and he had just cracked wise about the magical disappearance of Guzman through chemical means. He eventually turned and followed Everett and Collins out of the culvert. He approached Jack, who was looking at the spot where their mysterious rescuers had vanished into the river. Mendenhall stepped forward and faced in the same direction as Collins.

"Okay, those men obviously destroyed what remained of Guzman before they split out of here, so just who in the hell were those guys, Colonel?" Will asked.

As Jack watched the flowing river, he knew he had been had by somebody, but what do you say to a team of men who had just saved your life but destroyed the evidence that you needed?

"I don't know who they were, Will," he answered while looking from the river to the amber-colored fluid in the jar.

Perdition's Fire had left the hacienda, and it would be none other than Colonel Jack Collins who carried death with him back home to the Event Group Complex.

PART TWO

A Journey into Darkness

The path to paradise begins in hell.
—Dante Alighieri

5

The Colorado-based space systems company operated no less than ten satellites in low-earth orbit around the world for a consortium of companies. All privately based and funded, they contracted with this small Boulder operation to download telemetry and feed these companies vital information from their gathering of information—everything from GPS tracking to far more reaching enterprises. Each bit of information is coded and sent to the corresponding company who contracted for the telemetry received by the 130-person operation only three miles distant from the University of Colorado.

On the third floor of the six-story building, a technician was currently tracking a trace program in Nevada. As he bit into a stale Twinkie his eyes roamed over the telemetry streaming in from one of their newer satellites launched just last year. As he chewed he watched as the new KH-21 photo-recon bird made its way across the American Southwest. He noted the red blip on the map and its corresponding latitude and longitude.

The young technician, a young man who never knew

who his work was going to be sent to, was curious as he had never seen a tracer like the one he was tracking. This little gem was priceless in its accuracy—down to plus or minus sixteen inches on the accuracy of the coordinates.

The tech took the last bite of his Twinkie and then leaned forward to examine the small red blip still on the computer-generated map before him.

"Now that is a good old-fashioned 'bug,' " he said as he watched the red tracer hesitate at a spot ten miles north of its original landing position. Then his eyes widened as the coordinates, while changing, started to get strange. At first he didn't understand what he was looking at. Then he tapped a computer command into his keyboard and he smiled as he realized that the tracer he was watching wasn't moving north, south, east, or west, it was moving down—moving into the bowels of the earth.

"Must be a mine of some sort," he mumbled and then punched the send button on his keyboard that would shoot the coded information out to the company or individual who had contracted for the tracking satellite's services.

The technician, who really never got out much, had tracked the tracer blip to a spot fifteen miles outside of the city of Las Vegas. And then he missed the coordinates that would have told him his telemetry streaming from the satellite overhead was looking down on Nellis Air Force Base just outside of Las Vegas.

How could the technician know that the final coordinates before the bug died due to power loss placed his target at 5,700 feet below the desert in Nevada—at the north firing range of Nellis and to a complex that ran almost two miles beneath the desert sands inside a natural cave formation that wasn't on any geological map and was home to—The Event Group.

CIA Headquarters,
Langley, Virginia

Hiram Vickers was sitting in his office going over a file spread out on his desk. He looked up when a light knock sounded on his door. The bookwormish man waved at the girl he recognized as being stationed in the space-based imagery department two floors down.

"Hi," he said as he removed his thin-rimmed glasses. His eyes went from the young girl's face to her small chest. The man in charge of cheap tricks around the globe never lost his smile, but he immediately dismissed the young photography expert as not up to his usual standards. "What have you got?"

The girl stepped into the immaculately cleaned office and held out a large manila envelope. "We just received this from Cassini Space-Based Systems in Boulder. It came coded to you, but the office checkoff doesn't have the director of intelligence in the information loop as it usually does." The girl placed the large envelope against her chest, as if she wasn't about to let the information leave her until she had a little bit more detail on why the agency chain-of-command signoff wasn't included in the package.

"Ah, we're just running a test. We had a major screwup the last time this small company gave us tracking info. They sent it, but it never arrived. Who knows, it probably went straight to the Russians or Chinese," he said with a broad and disarming smile as he stood from his desk and removed his glasses. He stepped out from around the sensibly clean desk and held out his hand for the envelope. "This was to be passed straight to my desk."

The girl didn't look convinced at all. "But we have mandates from the director that nothing goes to the corresponding desks until they get passed to them by their department heads. And since this test originated in Boulder, it should go directly to the desk of North American Operations. Assistant Director Simpson should be the last one on the list before the director of intelligence on this checkoff sheet."

"I believe she was bypassed because of the unimportance of the test and also because, as I understand it, Ms. Simpson is currently visiting relatives in Texas." He smiled and then started to turn away. "But if you would rather wait until she gets back, it's up to you. I can wait for these mundane and boring results."

The courier bit her lower lip and then smiled. "I guess since it's only a test trace it doesn't matter."

Hiram stopped and then turned with his best smile planted on his features. "Now that's the red-tape-cutting imaging department we have come to love around here," he said as he took the offered envelope. "If not for people like you, nothing would ever get done."

The young technician smiled and then turned away. The smile on Vickers's face left as easily as it had come as he reached out and pulled the door closed. He ripped open the sealed envelope instead of untying the string that secured it; after all, the envelope and its contents would be destroyed. This action was something totally against agency policy. He quickly read the transcript of the trace his Black Team had placed on subject one from the Mexico raid. His brow furrowed as he read the report.

"What in the hell is this?" he asked himself aloud as he sat back behind his desk. His fingers followed the line of the track from Laredo, Texas, to Nevada.

"Okay, they obviously landed at Nellis Air Force Base in Nevada. But what in the hell is happening here?" he asked himself as he pulled up a computer-generated and much-classified map of Nellis on his computer. He studied the map and saw where the trace was still operating. His eyes told him he was looking at a firing range that hadn't been in use since World War II. He then punched in a few commands and a real-time image of the base came up. He used his mouse to zoom into the area of interest. All he saw was a large series of dilapidated hangars that looked as if they had seen far better days. The largest hangar was missing most of its rounded roof and he could almost see into the interior.

He looked at the coordinates that had been time stamped

onto the first picture he pulled out of the envelope. Then he cross-referenced those coordinates with what he was looking at. He shook his head and then reached for the phone. He called the number he had memorized in just the last two days.

"Johnson," came the reply on the other end of the phone.

"I have the trace report," Vickers said as he continued to look at the picture of the high desert surrounding Nellis Air Force Base.

"So, where do our mysterious heroes live and work?"

"Before I give you the answer, I have a question, and it comes directly from our British friends."

"Go ahead."

"They want to know what preparations you've made in connection with the Perdition Hacienda. If we complete this assignment for them, there will be no end to their gratitude, which may come in handy for our new operations."

There was a brief silence on the other end of the phone. Then the large man who had just arrived home from Texas cleared his throat. "You can pass it on to those interested parties that the hacienda will cease to exist in just about twenty-seven minutes, compliments of the government of Mexico."

"And this will eliminate any possibility of the drugs getting out into the open?"

There was a small laugh on the other end of the phone. "You can say that, yes." The man became silent as he waited. He knew he didn't have to press the man at Langley for information on the trace because the man he had tagged outside of Nuevo Laredo was now under intense scrutiny by one of the darkest forces in American intelligence.

"The tracer report says that your target landed at Nellis Air Force Base in Nevada, and then according to what amounts to guesswork, the hard target vanishes beneath the high desert."

"Obviously I can't get a straight answer out of anyone in Washington. I don't send my men anywhere on guesswork. That kind of stuff went out of favor a long time ago. If you want us to recover what was taken from that hacienda, you damn well better get me some reliable intel as to who these people are and who they work for. We were lucky to get the body of Guzman reduced to ruins, but they have a sample of the product your British friends want destroyed. Now, I've been doing a little homework myself. The man who led the rescue attempt across the border, I thought I recognized him, but couldn't place him until now."

As Hiram Vickers waited, his incoming e-mail chimed. He opened it and then saw it was from the very same man to whom he was speaking at this very moment. He clicked on the attachment and a picture began downloading.

"Find me this man, and I'll find that jar they took out of Perdition's Gate. Don't find him, and I guess the Brits' dirty little secret will not be so for long."

Hiram regretted having told the Black Team operative everything about who requested their assistance. But the new operating parameters of the Black Teams prohibited them from operating without the full range of intel on their prospective target. He knew this man was determined to keep the Men in Black far more secretive than they had been in the past before they had been dismantled by the federal authorities.

As Vickers watched his computer screen he saw a herky-jerky video of what looked like a C-Span broadcast. As the camera zoomed in on a man in the uniform of a United States Army officer, it cleared up and then the picture froze as the generated name came on below the frozen picture of a big man as he packed up a briefcase with papers. Vickers saw that the video had been purloined from a C-Span broadcast of a senate hearing on the Afghan conflict. Then he looked at the name on the bottom and a flitting memory came to him.

"I think this will help a great deal, if you're sure this is the man you tagged?"

"Anyone in our line of work knows exactly who this man is and what he brings to the table. He's dangerous, not only to me, but to you and anyone who crosses him. If he still has Perdition's Fire it will be hard to get from him. Now send me what you have so I can work from my end."

"Right," Vickers said and then terminated the call. He looked closer at the sun-hardened features of the man frozen in time on his monitor. He then glanced at the printed name below the picture as he placed the yellow envelope and its contents under his arm in readiness to forward what he had to the Black Team in Denver. He reached out and hesitated before he turned off his monitor, but not before Hiram Vickers memorized the hard features of the man.

The C-Span freeze-frame of the soldier known six years before as Major Jack Collins faded to black.

Event Group Complex
Nellis AFB, Nevada

Jack sat at his desk inside the security department cut off from the rest of his people. He stared at the computer screen for the longest time in an attempt to make the words he had written make sense. They were words he thought he never would have placed end to end in his entire life.

They had been in the complex for the past eight hours, and he was waiting for the call that would send him into the director's office. Collins closed his eyes in an effort to make the last few words in the document he had written fade away along with the sight of them.

A knock sounded at the door.

"Come in," he said as he leaned slightly toward the monitor and spoke softly as Captain Carl Everett entered his office. "Europa, file and code document 1877, security one, Collins."

"Document filed, Colonel Collins," answered the Marylyn Monroe voice, one that Collins had finally gotten used to. He had hated it, but finally came to terms that everyone in the complex liked the sexiness of the computer-generated voice synthesizer.

"Jack, we have an update on Ryan," Everett said as he watched Collins lean away from the computer terminal.

"Is he screaming bloody murder yet?"

"You know he is. He said to tell you that if he's to stay put in the hospital he wants a transfer to one that has better-looking nurses." Everett watched the colonel's face for any reaction.

"Tell him he's damned lucky to have been moved from Texas to Las Vegas, and if he's not careful, you'll send him right back there."

Carl noticed that Jack said *he* would have to send him back, not Jack *himself*. Everett smiled and took a seat without Collins offering it to him.

"Other than that, what are they saying about our flyboy?"

"He's doing better than expected. He's sore as hell and has two dueling scars he can thrill women with, so all in all the kid got off lucky." Everett smiled hoping to get Collins to react to something. "I didn't know hearing about the security department's loss in our football game had upset you that much?"

Jack didn't hear the question and looked at his second in command. "Excuse me?" he said.

"Okay, what's going on? You've been in here since we came home. Sarah's been in twice and even Charlie Ellenshaw dropped by to collect his winnings from the game and wanted to see you, but you told him to go away. I guess you sort of hurt the fuzzy-haired guy. You've been locked up in here doing God knows what—so, what gives?"

Jack took a deep breath and then looked at Everett. "Did you get to Doc Gilliam and have that shrapnel taken out of your shoulder?"

"I'll get in line behind you as soon as you get that hand checked out. In case you didn't notice, you have a bullet hole in it."

Collins looked at his bandaged hand and then looked back at Everett. "I have to stop by the director's office first. You want to tag along?"

"As long as it's on the way to the infirmary, sure," Everett answered as he watched Jack leave his chair for the first time in hours.

Collins led the way from the security offices, nodding at a very tired Will Mendenhall as the lieutenant sat at his desk adjusting the security roster for the absence of Lance Corporal Udall and Jason Ryan.

As they gained the hallway just to the left of the elevators, Jack turned to Everett.

"How many men do you have on our French friend down in the infirmary?"

"Two in the room, two in the hallway."

"As soon as he's able to be moved, put him in isolation down on level eighteen, with only a cot and a blanket."

Everett nodded as they waited for the elevator. "The president wants Farbeaux turned over immediately to the FBI. He says now that we have him, he's going to stay a guest of the United States for a very long time."

Jack looked at Everett and then raised his left eyebrow. "I want you to conduct the debriefing of Colonel Farbeaux. The president doesn't get him until that's concluded," he said as the elevator doors finally opened.

"I thought you would have wanted to have that little conversation with Henri?" Carl said as he watched Jack step into the elevator. Finally, when no answer came from his boss, Everett stepped in beside the colonel. "Europa, level seven, please."

"Level seven."

The elevator started up on its air-cushioned ride as Jack leaned back against the rear of the glass car.

"Europa, location of Director Compton, please," Jack inquired as he closed his eyes once more.

"Director Compton is currently on level seventy-two, specimen vault 789000."

"Location of Lieutenant McIntire, geology department?" he asked next.

"Lieutenant McIntire is currently conducting research on geological abnormalities found in current volcanic cones in the Central Pacific."

"Have Lieutenant McIntire stop her research and join us on level seventy-two at the appropriate vault please. Now stop the elevator and take us to level seventy-two."

"Yes, Colonel," said Europa as the elevator came to a very fast and hissing stop. Then as Collins looked at Everett the elevator reversed and started down into the bowels of the Event Group Complex.

"You going to tell me what's going on?" Carl asked.

"Any word yet on the properties of that magic elixir we took out of Perdition?" he asked instead of answering his friend.

"They haven't touched the sample yet. The director wants some of our people currently on assignment to be in on the opening phase of the research. He's also recalled the former head of our infectious disease department who now works for the Centers for Disease Control in Atlanta. The doctor and his daughter are on the security clearance list. So I guess if the director is recalling old personnel back into the fold, this stuff must worry him to no end."

"The director thinks it may be a virus?"

"He doesn't know yet, but he says if a reaction can happen that fast on Guzman, he can't take any chances." Everett turned and faced Collins. "But I guess you would have known that if you had read the same report I did."

"Patience, Captain."

As the elevator doors slid open and Europa announced their desired location, Jack shook his head when he thought Carl was going to ask another question. Both blue-clad men stepped into the hallway on level seventy-two and went directly to the security arch that led to the vaults. One of their security men was at his station at a small, clear desk and stood when they approached.

"Is the director still in the vault area?" Jack asked as he placed his hand on the glass security scanner and had his prints and the moisture content in his hand analyzed for his DNA. Europa cleared the colonel for entrance and then did the same for Everett.

"Yes, sir. He and the assistant director are classifying

several new artifacts that have been transferred down to the new vault level."

Jack went down the curving, plastic-lined hallway that hid the granite strata underneath. Level seventy-two was one of the newest vault areas in the complex and was just now starting to fill up with the treasures of the world's past.

Collins ran his large hand along the wall as he headed toward the only vault door open on this level. Everett watched him and noticed that it was like Jack was taking it all in for the first time.

"We've done, I mean, the Group has done good things here, right?" he asked before stepping up to the open thirteen-foot steel door.

"If you mean has the Group fulfilled its charter? I think so. How many parallels in history have we uncovered that may have averted a war? Given the president something extra that he would never have known if it wasn't for the Group? Yeah Jack, we've done some very good things. Everyone at the Event Group, past or present, has all done what was asked."

Jack just nodded his head and gave Carl a ghost of a smile. "That helps."

Everett watched Jack knock lightly on the sill of the giant vault door and then step over the threshold. He was about to follow when he heard a voice that usually gave him pleasure.

"Hey, Captain, we having a clandestine meeting down here?"

Everett smiled as he took in the battered face of Sarah McIntire. Both of her eyes were black and blue and the right was still nearly closed. She had a large bandage on her head where she had received sixteen stitches from Dr. Gilliam just two hours before. He lost his smile as he realized at that moment why they were there. It didn't enter his mind until he saw the shape that Sarah was in. It all clicked as he allowed the diminutive McIntire to enter the vault first.

Jack was impressed with this particular acquisition they had uncovered in a small valley just inside the South African province of Natal. The vault was lined with artifacts and weapons from a period of revolt in what was once a part of the British Empire—Zululand.

Collins watched as Niles turned toward him with pride. He and Assistant Director Virginia Pollock were standing near a glass enclosure with hydrogen hoses running into it. There was another hose that fed the small enclosure with humidified air to keep it at a constant 67 degrees.

"What have we here?" Sarah asked in that never-ending wonder she always had for the vault areas of the complex. Collins turned and looked at his beaten but happy Sarah McIntire and wasn't surprised at the wonder of a schoolgirl as she took in the new find.

"Actually, you can thank the colonel's department for this one. They went on a hunch and raided a very wealthy South African gentleman and relieved him of this and other valuable historic finds. It turned out that this gentleman still longed for the days of apartheid. He stole everything here and was responsible for one of the most blatant grave robberies of the twentieth century," Niles Compton said as his eyes flitted from Sarah to those of Colonel Collins. Niles patted the glass enclosure. "You're looking at the remains of a great king, at least in most of the world's eyes. Here is a man that took on the British Empire in their more heady days. His body was stolen from a simple gravesite back in 1981. No one even realized the theft had taken place."

Jack smiled at Sarah and both he and the lieutenant turned to study the body inside of the enclosure. Everett stayed back and just watched. Not the enclosure, Niles, Virginia, nor Sarah, but Collins.

Sarah rubbed up against Jack as she looked at the shriveled but somehow still proud corpse of a man from their past.

"Say hello to the onetime king of the Zulu nation," Niles said proudly. "I give you Cetshwayo—the man who defeated the British army at Isandlwana, Transvaal Province. It amounted to the Empire's version of Custer's Last Stand. It would be like us standing here looking at the body of Crazy Horse."

Jack's eyes moved from the body lying in its enclosure to the weapons lining the vault's walls. There were spears, muskets, and lion's skins, along with zebra skin shields. Large crates of more short-handled spears and artifacts sat on shelves.

"This man had all of this stuff in his possession?" Sarah asked as she smiled and looked at a far-away Jack.

"All of it. We were mostly interested in collecting the stolen remains. The president wants to make it a gift to the Zulu people, after—"

"We study and release," both Sarah and Virginia Pollock said at the same time. They knew Niles wouldn't give anything up until the old king had been documented from head to toe for their records.

Niles lost his smile when he looked from the enclosure to the face of Jack Collins. He cleared his throat and then his eyes traveled to those of Carl Everett. He patted Jack on the shoulder. "So what brings you down to my territory, Jack?" he asked, knowing full well what was about to happen.

Jack turned and walked over to the far wall and Europa's temporary computer terminal.

"Europa, are you online?" Jack asked, looking at the blank screen that would one day soon hold a talking tour of the vault they were now standing inside.

"Yes, Colonel Collins."

"Please give me a hard-copy printout of document 1877, security Collins, please."

Without comment, Europa did as ordered and started printing out the document Collins had been working on since his return to the complex. He waited out the moment in silence and then pulled the single page from the printer. He handed the single paragraph to Niles, who refused to look at it. Instead he nodded at Virginia and she moved out into the rock-lined hallway. Niles followed.

"Before we see what Jack's brought us, I want to show you a few more things of recent acquisition," Niles said as he waited for the three people to catch up with him and Virginia.

All of the vaults on this level were brand new. Niles walked to a large vault thirty feet away and then slid his ID card down the security lock.

"I had these flown here from our original complex inside Arlington National Cemetery." Niles swung open the door and waited for his people to enter.

Sitting on tables and on the vault's floor was what remained from the evidence taken in the 1916 raid on Perdition's Gate.

"We hope to get some answers here. We'll start analyzing what we have as soon as our people get in from the CDC in Atlanta."

Jack once more tried to hand Niles the sheet of paper Europa had printed out for him. Compton once more stepped out of the vault and waited for the others to follow.

"I think all of us will get a kick out of this one," Virginia Pollock offered as Niles opened one last vault at the far end of the level. This vault, being the last on the level, was by far the largest. It rivaled the vault used to house the Ark in size and dimensions.

Collins shook his head but followed the director and assistant director inside.

"Wow!" Sarah said as she took in the display inside of the giant new vault. Even Collins and Everett were impressed with what they were looking at.

"Jack, do you remember when Virginia and I went on vacation at the same time last year?" Niles asked.

"Yes. Are you telling me you and her are responsible for finding these?" Jack asked, amazed at what he was looking at.

"Well, no, not exactly, but we wanted to be in on it, and we both knew you wouldn't let us out of the complex without a security detachment tagging along, so we lied and went on vacation to South Florida. We had to be in on this expedition. After we found them, well, we arranged to have them misplaced, and to tell you the truth, the National Geographic Society who funded the expedition is tossing a fit all the way to Washington over us 'borrowing' these artifacts.

After we've had our fun with them, we will arrange for their find to be . . . well . . . found once more."

On the polished tiled floor of the vault and arranged in a semicircle around the stainless-steel vault were some of the most recognizable aircraft the world had ever known. There were five Grumman TBM torpedo bombers from the forties as clean and shiny as the day they rolled off the assembly line.

"Are these aircraft what I think they are?" Everett said, knowing the old tale from not only his navy days, but from every program on the Bermuda Triangle he had ever seen.

Niles stepped up to the computer terminal next to the large vault door and hit a small switch that activated Europa's description of the contents of the vault. The sound came over the speaker buried into the rock ceiling far above their heads.

"United States Navy Training Flight 19 out of U.S. Naval Air Station, Fort Lauderdale, Florida, lost on 5, December, 1945. The Operational Archives Branch, Naval History & Heritage Command, had ordered the Board of Investigation convened at NAS Miami to inquire into the loss of the five TBM Avengers in Flight 19 on a clear day. The flight and its training crews were never heard from again, and it was concluded by the Board of Investigation that the flight was lost due to pilot error. On June 3 of last year, the National Geographic Society commissioned a search of the area after underwater depressions had been found inside the original search area. The five TBM Avengers were located exactly where the search parties in 1945 had estimated the flight went down. The Avengers were found in 375 feet of water and were located inside of an immense underwater cavern. The aircraft were in pristine condition as they didn't show any sign of salt water deterioration after sixty-five years in Florida's hostile waters."

Niles reached out and shut off the presentation. He didn't need it, as the event regarding the lost flight was a private indulgence that the director of the Event Group had taken a special interest in, even as far back as high school.

"Ammunition, fuel, everything was intact. There was no deterioration of the aluminum used in the Avenger's manufacture. The cockpits were dry and their canopies were closed. The aircraft show no sign of being ditched after running out of fuel. Well, we know now that they didn't run out as each torpedo bomber had at least 300 gallons still in its tank. There were no signs of the pilots or their crews."

"How could these planes still be intact?" Everett asked as he ran his hand along the wing of one of the giant single-engine aircraft.

"That's why we have to study them," Niles said as even the preoccupied Collins reached out and touched one of the dangling belts of fifty-caliber ammunition hanging from an exposed port in the left-side wing. The rounds on their belt looked to be new. There were no signs of water corrosion or crash damage anywhere on the dive Avengers. The tires on the landing gear were still pliable and filled with air.

"It's like they were snatched out of the sky and placed inside that seamount and the cave at its base. Then it seems they were protected by something in the water that we don't understand . . . yet," Virginia said as she too looked up at the first large Avenger sitting before her. "But we will get to the bottom of this, before the FBI gets into the full swing of investigating the disappearance of such a valuable military find."

"Amazing," Sarah said gazing up at the magnificent aircraft every man, woman, and child would probably recognize thanks to the rampant Bermuda Triangle theories being pushed by the media. "The next time you two sneak out to go on vacation, please take me with you. This had to be as exciting as it gets."

Jack stopped touching the aircraft and turned and smiled at Sarah. She returned his smile. He was never surprised by Sarah's take on the historical world. She was like a small schoolgirl giddy over everything the vault levels had to offer. He loved her for that. Her enthusiasm for her work was something that he himself was having a hard time coming to terms with. Collins once more pulled the printed sheet of paper from his pocket and again offered it to the director. Niles looked from Jack to his assistant director, Virginia.

"I guess our toys didn't do the trick we had hoped they would on the outlook of Colonel Collins here, Virginia," Niles said taking the offered paper from Jack's hand. He started reading aloud so everyone, including Everett and Sarah, could hear.

"I, Colonel Jack Collins, U.S. Army, currently attached to Department 5656 of the National Archives, an entity of the federal government; hereby tender my resignation as colonel in the regular United States Army, effective immediately."

Niles Compton looked up from the resignation letter and then removed his glasses. "I think we can find a better way than this, Jack. I do know how to handle the president; he's bound to cool off. He doesn't want to lose you or Sarah. You'll be reprimanded officially for disobeying a direct order, but I'll take the brunt of that and absorb anything the president orders our punishment to be. You knew we were headed for serious consequences over the raid when we decided to go."

Jack smiled and then placed his arm around Sarah who was absolutely speechless when she had heard Jack's decision.

"The letter stands. The president may feel better later," he looked down into Sarah's bruised and swollen eyes, "but I will not. Out of personal reasons I have placed members of my command and the people I am charged to protect in extreme jeopardy. I disobeyed a direct order from not only you, Mister Director, but from the president of the United States. I find these facts to be unacceptable." He reached down and kissed Sarah on the forehead, at the same time wiping a tear that had slid from her half-closed left eye. "Don't worry, short stuff, I'll be around for you, just not here. I'm not a very good officer anymore, but neither am I stupid."

Sarah tried to smile as Jack let her go. They all watched in silence as Collins stepped to the vault door. He turned and looked at the five aircraft once more. That was one thing he would have to get used to, and that was not being in on the world's great archaeological finds. But he knew as long as they had people in the Group as dedicated as the four men and women inside this new vault, the Event Group would still do its job. Then his eyes went to Captain Everett. He stood silent as the moment was just too much to take in. Instead of saying goodbye, Everett saluted without looking the colonel in the eyes.

"The navy doesn't salute indoors, swabby. Only the army, of which I am no longer a part," Jack said and then walked out amid the stunned silence inside of the vault.

Sarah turned to face Niles Compton. "Of course, you won't accept his resignation, right?"

Niles handed the single sheet to Virginia and then looked at the lieutenant and replaced his glasses. He looked over at the much taller and stockier Everett who just stood inside the doorway. Sarah, to her shock, saw Everett shake his head negatively. Then he looked at Sarah.

"Can't you see it, Sarah, Jack's had it. He can't do his job here and protect those he's supposed to protect with you in the field."

"Then I quit," she said, starting to walk toward the vault door, but Everett placed his arm across the wide opening.

"Jack won't allow that and you know it. So don't hit your head up against that particular wall; you'll end up looking worse than you already do."

Niles stepped to the doorway and watched the form of Jack Collins head for the archway and the elevators beyond. He saw a man that wasn't broken, just one that was afraid he couldn't do his job any longer in the manner he was used to doing it. He turned and faced Everett and Virginia.

"Virginia, I need those CDC people on station in the next ten hours to start the study on this chemical that was recovered from Perdition's Gate. Captain Everett, I need extra security on the labs where the work will be done. Don't take any chances. Our former Event Group members who now work for the CDC in Atlanta know their stuff. They have top security clearance and they'll have the run of the sciences divisions while on site."

"Yes, sir," Everett said, noticing how matter-of-factly the director had turned over the security department to him without so much as batting an eye. For the director, the Event Group had to go on, with or without Jack Collins safeguarding those seeking the truth of history.

With that said, the director of the Event Group stepped from the vault area and left behind a stunned and seething second lieutenant—Sarah McIntire.

After years of training not much different from that received by Jack Collins during his years in the United States Special Forces community, Colonel Henri Farbeaux, regular French army, Ret., had developed the same sixth sense that Collins himself had. He knew when he was being observed, and even in sleep his brain reacted to the danger. The Frenchman forced his eyes open. At first he saw the dim light coming from the fixture just above the headboard. As he tried to focus his eyes, his brain detected from which direction his observer was sitting. He saw the face and then the finer details came into view. The young female doctor who had attended to him upon his arrival at the Event Group Complex, Gilliam, he thought her name was, was just finishing up wrapping his observer's hand in white gauze.

"So, you've come to see the drugged and caged animal, Colonel?" Henri said as the etched features of Jack Collins sharpened to a fine point.

Collins nodded at Gilliam in thanks and then flexed his left hand. The good doctor said the through-and-through bullet wound was pretty much cleaned, but she admonished him for being so late coming in for treatment. There was still a major chance of infection. Jack listened to Denise Gilliam without really hearing her words as he continued to look at Farbeaux. His eyes went to the handcuff holding Henri's right hand to the chrome bedpost.

Collins looked up and nodded to the first of the two

guards inside of the infirmary's single-bed room. Jack tapped
his wrist and the large army sergeant took a few steps toward the bed and unlocked the restraint holding Farbeaux's
hand to the rail. Henri turned his head and watched the
guard move back into the shadows. He lifted his right hand
and then rubbed his wrist with the left. His eyes focused
on the small room in general and avoided Jack's gaze alto-
gether.

"No, Henri, I didn't come in here for that."

"So when may I expect a meeting with my attorney, and
when is my arraignment?"

Jack smiled as he sat in the chair next to Farbeaux's bed.
The Frenchman could see Collins was going on zero sleep.
His face, although clean, hadn't seen a razor since their return from Nuevo Laredo. His jumpsuit was clean and pressed
and his wounds had now been tended, but there was still
something wrong with Collins outside of him needing a
shave.

"I think our department will want to keep the court system out of this one, Colonel. We have no evidence to offer a
U.S. court of law that would place you in any crime scene
that we know of. Oh, there's no doubt that the FBI will have
some questions for you, but as for the Group, we have nothing we can charge you with."

Henri continued to rub his wrist where the handcuff had
chafed his skin. He looked at Collins and then slowly reached
for the control that raised the bed to a sitting position.

"I seem to be quite sore," he said as the whine of the
bed's motor ceased.

"Two bullets, ten small pieces of shrapnel, three broken
ribs, and a severe concussion. All in all you could qualify to
be a part of my security team the way you get busted up like
you do."

"If that is the prequalifier to becoming a true blue
blooded American hero like you and your men, I think I'll
pass, Colonel."

Jack didn't respond and remained silent as his eyes moved
away from the Frenchman. After all of the years of chasing

the Frenchman, Jack found he had little or no animosity toward the former commando. Collins had long suspected that Henri on several occasions had just been the bogeyman everyone believed him to be—a convenient one. Appearances, Jack knew, could be as deceiving as the Group sometimes found history to be.

"Okay, so you didn't come here to read the charges against me. You didn't bring in flowers or a get-well card, so just what is it that brings you to my sickbed, Colonel?"

Jack leaned back in his chair and then looked toward the darker recesses of the room. With a nod of Jack's head Farbeaux watched the two large security men leave the room silently, closing the door behind them.

"Oh, I see, shot while trying to escape?" Farbeaux joked.

"With you, Colonel, I wish it were that easy. If anyone shoots you, it won't be me."

Farbeaux saw the complex look on the face of his adversary—a man he hated for causing the death of his wife, Danielle, deep in the Amazon Basin four years before. But he was also a man he had begrudgingly come to respect.

"Your wife, Danielle, tell me about her."

The question took Farbeaux by surprise, mainly because he had just thought of her himself. It was as if the American had read his mind, and he didn't like that one little bit. Henri gathered his senses and then looked Collins over.

"I loved her, Colonel, that's all that needs to be said. She was the only woman, besides one other, that knew me for what . . . ," he looked away from Jack's eyes, "knew me for something other than someone's psyche evaluation in a foreign intelligence report."

"You said Danielle and one other?" Jack asked.

Finally Henri turned and faced Collins. "What do you want of me, Colonel Collins?"

"I guess I'm here to say I'm sorry. Sorry for your perception about my having anything to do with your wife's death."

Henri stared at Jack for the longest time. He reached out and took a plastic cup from the rolling table at the bed's side and drank water from a straw. He placed the glass back down and looked away toward the door of the room. Jack looked down at the bandage wrapping his left hand.

"The thought of losing Sarah . . . if that had happened, I don't think I would have reacted any differently than you have been toward me."

"There is one major difference here, Colonel," Farbeaux said, finally turning angry eyes on Jack. "Sarah is breathing, while my wife, Danielle, is not."

"Yet you risked your life, your fortune, and at the very least your freedom to try and save the woman I love. Why is that Henri?" This time Jack's eyes never left those of Farbeaux.

"Some things in my life are not to be found in that thick little folder that Senator Lee started on me and my exploits many years ago. I too have my secrets, Colonel."

Jack nodded his head once and then stood. He removed a small notebook from his breast pocket and then with a pen jotted down some words. When he was done he tore the sheet from the pad and then paused.

"When you're transferred to Washington and turned over to FBI custody for your trip to the Justice Department, I have no doubt you will find a way to escape. When you do," Jack handed the Frenchman the note, "call this number; you can reach me anytime."

Henri looked the paper over and then looked up at Collins.

"So we can finish whatever it is we have to finish." Jack leaned in closer to his onetime antagonist. "Stay away from Sarah, Henri. Despite what you may be inclined to believe, she is not Danielle."

Farbeaux was silent as Jack turned and headed for the door, but just before he opened it and without turning around Jack said, "Henri?"

"Colonel Collins?"

Farbeaux didn't think Jack was going to continue as he pulled the door open. Then he let it close a few inches.

"Thank you for doing what you did in Mexico, no matter what the reasons behind it were."

With that the colonel left the clinic's sterile room and disappeared.

Denise Gilliam came through the same door a moment later along with the two security men. She took Henri's wrist and checked his blood pressure.

"Well, your B.P. is not as bad as I would have thought it would be after your little meeting," Denise said as she released Henri's wrist. "You need to get some rest. If you need anything, just ask one of these two rather large gentlemen."

"He quit, didn't he?" Farbeaux asked as his eyes finally went to those of the doctor.

"I don't listen to, nor do I confirm, rumors, even if I know them to be true, Colonel Farbeaux."

Denise walked away as Henri's eyes moved to the door.

"Goodbye, Colonel Collins. I suspect I'll be making that phone call sooner than you may think."

Henri Farbeaux turned off the light above the steel headboard and then placed his hands behind his head and went into deep thought.

*One Mile East of Hacienda
Perdition's Gate, Nuevo Laredo, Mexico*

A small man with a paunch and a sweat-stained baby-blue blazer adjusted his field glasses as he watched the Mexican National Police force come and go from the hacienda. Every once in a while he would see an old woman, his files said that she was the late Juan Guzman's mother, start haranguing the officers as they compiled their evidence packages inside of the main house. He knew the police hadn't actually removed any evidence from the hacienda to this point.

The man worked for the Centro de Investigación y Seguridad Nacional, Mexico's version of the CIA. The National Security and Investigation Center, or CISEN, was one of the more corrupt agencies in the Mexican federal establishment. For years they had been trying to clean up the factions at work deep inside of the agency, but they had thus far been unable to curb the avarice thrown to certain members of the corrupt agency. The man with the field glasses was one of these men.

He lowered the glasses when he heard a car drive up from behind his hiding place. He knew who it was so he just waited for the report. A man dressed as a Mexican state policeman walked easily toward the man, tearing away a false moustache and removing his blue hat.

"It is done."

The small, rotund man nodded his head and then raised the powerful field glasses once more. In the lenses he saw the old woman once more, and this time it looked as if she had two of Guzman's younger children in tow. She was still shouting out indignities as she waved her arms wildly about some offense or other.

"Señor, you realize there are still women and children inside of the targeted area. And many, many of our Mexican police brethren?"

The man sniffed as he watched the hacienda but kept his glasses steady on the main building.

"It is a shame, but the situation cannot be helped. We have orders to destroy the hacienda and all of its contents. Now, are you sure the package was delivered to the right area of the building?"

"We followed your precise directions. The entire structure should be nothing but a large hole in the ground. It should destroy everything in the lower levels, along with everything and everyone within a thousand feet of the hacienda."

"Very well. Do you have the transmitter?"

The uniformed man reached into his jacket pocket, brought out a small box, and then extended the small antenna and held it out for his operations manager. The smaller man finally lowered his field glasses and then looked at the transmitter and shook his head.

"You can have the honors."

The man in the state police uniform looked uncomfortable. He turned his back on the hacienda one mile away and then quickly raised the small plastic cover and depressed the black button underneath.

The man with the field glasses was taken by surprise when the thousand pounds of special explosives provided by their CIA contact in Langley literally blew the ground the hacienda was sitting on in a vaporous, rolling ball of hell. The entire hacienda and the land it sat on vanished in a split second of destruction that Mexico had never seen. It was so powerful that the small man was shoved as hard as he would have been if a rugby player had slammed into him.

The explosive, octanitrocubane, is the most powerful nonnuclear explosive ever made. Octanitrocubane consists of a cube of eight carbons with nitro groups (oxygens and nitrogens) attached to each carbon. It is an explosive that doesn't require an external oxygen source to decompose, meaning that it could blow up in every environment, including water and even in the vacuum of space.

As the small mushroom-shaped cloud rose above the small valley, the man rose and shook his head. As he raised the field glasses to his eyes once more he was shocked to see that between the rolling clouds of dust and sand and smoke, there was absolutely nothing left of the hacienda or the areas beneath it or around it. He couldn't even discern the bodies of police or family members.

He lowered the glasses and removed his cell phone from his suit jacket. He hit the preselected number and then waited.

"Vickers, it's your dime," came the answer.

"Excuse me, señor?" the small man said, not understanding Vickers's play on words.

"Oh, just a joke. What have you to report?"

"The explosives your man delivered were quite adequate for the job. I am afraid that there were many collateral pieces on the chessboard however."

"The bastard Guzman led his family to this end. Make no sympathies for him or his family. They're not innocents in all of this."

"Sí, we knew what kind of man we were dealing with." The small man closed the cell phone and almost raised the field glasses to his eyes once more but stopped short. He didn't need to see the smoking ruin of this particular piece of Mexico. No, he didn't need that. He stood instead and tossed the field glasses to the uniformed man.

"Sí, Señor Vickers, we do indeed know what kind of man we are dealing with. He's a man not far removed from your own desires and aspirations," the man said to himself.

Event Group Complex
Nellis AFB, Nevada

Collins sat for the longest time on his bed looking at the two packed suitcases sitting by the door. He looked at his wristwatch and then his eyes moved back to the cases. He was waiting for the arrival of Sarah McIntire. The knock on the door soon came and Jack stood to answer it, kicking one of the suitcases out of the way as he did. He opened the door and Sarah was leaning on the frame, looking down.

"Hi, short stuff."

Sarah looked up, and with her eyes black and blue and her nose bandaged she imagined she didn't look her best. She stepped into Jack's large room and then faced the far wall.

"You didn't feel the need to discuss this with me before springing it on the world?"

"So you could do then what you're going to do now?" he asked as he placed both of his large hands on Sarah's shoulders. She reached back without looking and took his bandaged hand in her much smaller one.

"Jack, if it's us and the military etiquette involved, I can resign and still keep my post as the geology department's head instructor."

Jack squeezed her shoulder and then turned her around and kissed her deeply. Then he pulled back and ran a finger close to her left eye, which was showing signs of opening all of the way for good. The bruise was deep and purple with tinges of yellow under the skin. Collins shook his head and then smiled.

"That wouldn't stop me from showing favoritism toward you. That wouldn't stop me from losing any more people in the field." Jack removed his hands and then took a few steps back before turning to face Sarah. I'm afraid it's much more than just us, baby. Do you know that on the plane trip back to Nevada, I couldn't recall what Lance Corporal Udall looked like? A marine I have spent the past five years training?"

Sarah watched as Jack's face clouded over with self-doubt and he closed his eyes. He took a deep breath and then looked at Sarah again. "All of the faces of all those boys, from Iraq, Afghanistan, and here at the Group, they all seem to merge and form themselves into . . . ," again he tried to smile, "well, you. All of my fears, all the terror I feel when I order men to their possible deaths, all come back to you. The loss of you would be my punishment. Do you understand that?"

Sarah remained silent as she reached up and placed her arms around his shoulders and pulled him to her. He felt her soft sobs as she said goodbye in her own quiet way.

"You know, short stuff, my mother thinks you're a figment of my overworked imagination."

Sarah laughed through her tears as she finally looked up at Collins. "She does?" she said as she wiped a tear away from her very sore face.

"I think we better allay her fears. She's coming to Las Vegas so I thought maybe we can have dinner tomorrow night?"

"It's a date . . . Mr. Collins," she said as she started crying one more time.

Jack didn't realize that he would not be addressed by his military rank any longer. As he hugged Sarah he smiled for the first time in a long while, while meaning it.

Jack Collins was very comfortable with the *mister* aspect of the change. He was tired. Tired of the death that had always surrounded him even since the days of his father. Now, he would wake up tomorrow and would never have to feel that hopelessness again.

Yes, he thought, *Mr. Collins was something he could get used to being addressed by.*

Niles Compton sat at his desk and read the report that had just been forwarded to him from Pete Golding down in the Computer Center. He shook his head and then looked up at the faces of Carl Everett and Virginia Pollock.

"The explosive used in the destruction of Perdition's Gate was an exotic mixture. Octanitrocubane is made here in the States and a few countries in Europe, mostly NATO members. We can assume someone wanted the hacienda reduced to dust. That, coupled with the fact that this savior of yours and the colonel in Mexico destroyed the body of Guzman, coincides with someone not wanting some detail of Perdition's secrets out in the open."

"Do Pete and Europa have any leads as to who these gentlemen were that have so graciously covered up someone's mess?" Everett asked as the new head of security. He looked at his watch, knowing that Jack was due to sign out of the Group in fifteen minutes.

"None, but I'm willing to bet that someone over at Langley may have some answers for us. This smells like their work. I've talked to the president and he's looking into it."

"How is he taking Jack's resignation?" Virginia asked what she and Everett both were curious about, at least hoping the president wouldn't accept the request for retirement.

"He's not speaking to me on any matters not related to this fiasco in Mexico, with the exception of the colonel. I think he will order Jack back to the Group, but that will be the colonel's call. One he has to make on his own." Niles tossed Pete's report on his desktop and then looked up at his two people. "Virginia, how are we handling this sample we removed from Mexico?"

"As of right now, we are treating it as we would a viral

compound. Until our cleared Event Group members of the CDC arrive to classify it, that's all we're working with."

"Good. I don't want anyone near it until we can get some recommendations. I also want that crap out of the complex as soon as that assessment is made. Do we have anything yet on the 1916 raid into Mexico?"

"Pete is putting together a package of everything Europa can dig up on this Professor Ambrose. I just cannot believe that a man with his credentials could come up with a compound such as this in the 1890s. It's impossible, especially for what he was a professor of. At least we have the good professor Ambrose's journals that our famous general Patton recovered from the hacienda."

Everett looked from Niles to Virginia, who just shrugged her shoulders as she didn't know what Compton was talking about either. "Just what was he a professor of?" Everett finally asked.

"Believe it or not, this Ambrose character was only a botanist. No chemistry experience, no genetics, just a botanist—a brilliant one to be sure, but still just a botanist."

A U.S. Army sergeant stepped into Jack's room, took the suitcases, and left for the loading-dock area of the complex. He was followed by Sarah and Collins. As they passed people in the hallway many of them stopped to shake Jack's hand, and he graciously spent a minute with each as they slowly made their way up to level five. As the elevator doors opened, both Jack and Sarah were shocked at what was waiting on the massive concrete loading dock.

"Damn it," Jack said beneath his breath as over a hundred of the off-duty Event Group staff were there to send him off. The rumor of his resignation had spread like wildfire from the moment he had left the vault area that morning.

As the hundred men and women broke out in applause, Jack waved them off. Sarah placed her arm through Jack's as they stepped onto the dock. The first to greet him was a man with wild white hair and small round glasses. Charles

Hindershot Ellenshaw III stood before Collins with his white lab coat buttoned askew and his eyes wet.

"Colonel, on behalf of everyone at this complex, I want to say thank you. I . . . I . . ."

Jack took Charlie's hand and shook it. "No Doc, thank you," he said as he looked up at the faces trying to get a glimpse of him as he left. "Thank all of you." He looked down at the professor and head of the Cryptozoology Department and smiled. "Thank you for giving me back my humanity in the last six years. Everyone here reminded me of what my job was truly all about." He again looked at those around him. "You made me care about whom and why I do what I do. And now I leave that to others. Goodbye."

Ellenshaw released Jack's hand and without another word turned and burst past both he and Sarah, removing his glasses and swiping at his eyes as he did. Collins took a deep breath and then looked at Sarah. He gestured toward the lone transport car at the edge of the loading dock. With a few more handshakes he finally got a chance and whispered into Sarah's ear that he loved her. Then as he was about to step into the plastic-reinforced magnetically controlled car, Sarah pulled on his sleeve and nodded to the right of the loading dock where the Security Department kept a small kiosk for inspecting incoming shipments. Will Mendenhall watched from the glass enclosure.

"I'll be damned," Jack once again said. Collins stood as straight as he could and then raised his hand.

Will Mendenhall stepped from the security kiosk, and then just when Collins thought he wasn't going to respond to his goodbye, Will saluted him.

Jack nodded his head, and then looking directly at the best man he had ever trained, a man who had risen from staff sergeant to second lieutenant through sheer talent and ability, he returned the salute. Will snapped his head down, half smiled, and then turned away from the departing soldier who had replaced a father Will had never known. Jack watched the black man move away and knew he was leaving the best people he had ever known.

"Well," he said as he finally looked down at Sarah.

"Yes, Mr. Collins?"

"Until tomorrow night then?"

"I'll be there, and I'm going to tell your mother you did this," she swam her hand around her blackened eyes, "to me."

Collins smiled and kissed the top of her head. He then stepped into the small transport that would carry him the seven-point-seven miles to gate number two at the Gold City Pawn Shop in Las Vegas.

"After meeting you, she just may agree that you needed that beating Lieutenant McIntire."

"Goodbye, Jack," Sarah said as she turned and walked away.

Collins watched everyone start to file back into the complex. And for a fleeting moment he saw the diminutive shape of the woman he loved disappear among the many military, science, academia, and other professions that made up the personnel of the Event Group.

"Europa, gate number two, please."

"Yes, Colonel Collins, gate number two."

"Hey!" came a shout that made Collins tell Europa to hold the magnetic-driven car. He looked over and saw the blue jumpsuit and then Everett stepped clear of some large crates on the loading dock.

Jack slid the plastic door up and into the frame of the bullet-shaped car. He stood and waited for Carl to reach him.

"Thought you would get out without having to face me?" he asked as he held out his hand to Collins.

"Something like that," Jack answered as the two men shook hands.

"It's been a hell of a ride, Jack."

"That it has, Carl. A ride I wouldn't have missed for the world."

Everett took a step back and literally examined the battered frame of his friend. He knew Collins was at his limit. Most men hit that mark after it's too late, and they end up getting a lot of people killed. Jack had lost people, a lot of them, but had yet to get anyone killed out of negligence to duty. No, Everett thought, Jack was leaving on his own terms and he for one would not ever mention the why's of his leaving. Instead, Everett just raised his right hand and, like Mendenhall a minute before, saluted.

Collins returned the gesture and then shook his head.

"Any advice, besides run as fast as I can out of here?" Carl asked with a smile as Collins sat back down with his hand poised over the glass-enclosed door.

"Yeah, Senator Lee once told me, 'Jack, you're in command, so goddamn it, command.'" With that and a return smile, Jack Collins closed the door and the car zoomed away down the centerline rail toward the city of Las Vegas and whatever future he could carve out for himself.

6

CIA Headquarters
Langley, Virginia

The same photo and trace technician who had questioned Hiram Vickers earlier about the chain of custody for the tracer tract forwarded to her department from the Cassini Corporation in Boulder stood at the far end of the hallway from Vickers's office. She half turned with the large envelope in her arm, pressed it tightly to her chest, and then looked down on the signoff sheet. Only her department had signed the receipt of service from Cassini. There was a long red arrow from the top of the custody list straight down to Hiram Vickers's name near the bottom. She looked at the name bypassed by the arrow—the person in charge of intelligence for the North American Desk, Assistant Director Lynn Simpson. Once again the woman bit her lower lip; after all, maybe Vickers had a point about not filling up the desks of people who didn't have the time to look at test patterns from one of their CIA contractors.

"Penny for your thoughts," came the familiar voice that had come up on her unawares.

The young girl looked at Hiram Vickers and the cold smile he always gave women he thought far beneath his station. While he looked at her chest, the technician easily pulled the chain-of-possession list from the front of the envelope. She then smiled and held out the large envelope.

"Ah, the second part of the test came through, excellent," he said as he reached for the envelope. "Uh, do I have to sign for it anywhere?" he said as she released the intelligence report from Cassini.

"Since you said it was a test that came to you only, we didn't bother, since here you are, and it is only a test, right?"

Hiram kept his smile on his lips far longer than was necessary. "Right, as I said, yours is the red-tape-cutting department. Thanks again for this," he said holding the envelope up and then turning away.

The technician looked down into her hand at the chain of possession list and the first name at the top. She didn't quite know how to handle Vickers and his test that didn't seem to show up on their daily "to do" list. She thought about it and decided on what course of action to take. She turned and walked to the elevator and took it to the sixth floor. She saw the empty area where the North American Intelligence Department usually was, but saw that they must have gone home for the night. She looked at her wristwatch and saw that it was almost seven o'clock. She looked around and spied the old pigeonhole mail slots for the North American Desk. She went over and looked at box number one: Lynn Simpson, Assistant Director, North American Intelligence. She looked at the signoff sheet, folded it, and then placed it in Lynn's mailbox. That ought to get her to wonder why her desk was bypassed on an intelligence target deep inside the United States . . . test or no test.

As the girl turned and left the large area, she only hoped she was doing the right thing. Unknowingly, she had placed

the intelligence trace report coming in on compromised test
subject Collins, Jack, U.S. Army, into the mailbox of Jack's
very own sister, the head of the North American Intelligence Desk, Lynn Simpson.

The young technician was wrong about the North American
Desk having gone home for the evening. Since Lynn Simpson's return from Texas, she had been steadily working on
the Juan Guzman case and had every single one of her people in a large meeting room one floor up.

She knew beyond a shadow of a doubt that her brother
Jack had been involved in the illegal rescue of Sarah McIntire and fifteen kidnapped girls. Lynn had managed to learn
through her law enforcement contacts down in Texas that
Jack and the mysterious entity he worked for had not been
identified as being related to the U.S. government at all.
There was only the fact that the rescue element had crossed
the Rio Grande into United States territory.

As she read the statements of the fifteen surviving girls
as told to the FBI and the Texas Rangers, she thought someone had been drugged or at the very least beaten until all
reliability had vanished. Words such as *monstruo*, *satanás*,
and *criatura* had come from the lips of the women being
questioned about their rescue regarding the man who had
abducted them. Lynn knew the three words most of the girls
used to describe the Anaconda on their harrowing flight out
of Mexico—*monster*, *Satan*, and *creature*.

The bulk of her staff recommended they should start looking into either the American military, or a corporate security group. "No," she explained, "we'll not follow that angle."

Although Lynn knew her desk had to pursue answers to
the raid into Mexico, she didn't want to because she knew
Jack, Carl, and Mendenhall were up to their eyeteeth in the
cover-up. As she passed the mailboxes she noticed something in her box. She closed the folder on the Anaconda and
pulled free the folded paper.

As Lynn walked to her desk she still hadn't given instructions to her people as to where to start their search. She was

hoping to buy time until she could get a hold of Jack, Carl, or Sarah. As she placed the thick file on her desk, she unfolded the piece of paper. It was a signoff chain-of-custody sheet that had been originated in the imaging and trace section. She scanned the sheet and then slowly sat down. She saw the person who had signed for the information received from that section. She also noticed that the subject header was "Surveillance and Tracking Test" from Cassini Space-Based Systems. Her brows rose as she reached for her phone. As she punched in the appropriate number for imaging her eyes roamed to the name that did eventually sign for the test results—Hiram Vickers.

"Imaging and Tracking," answered the voice on the other end of the line.

"This is Simpson at the Intelligence Desk for North America; your section forwarded an intelligence package from Cassini Space-Based Systems in Boulder to Hiram Vickers."

Suddenly and before she could continue with the person on the line in imaging and tracking, her awareness rose as she suddenly remembered who this man was. He had started at the company a year or so after Lynn herself. He had begun his intelligence career down in Games and Theory. Now there was a rumor of a new section, a small one to be sure, but new nonetheless—Field Incursions, a special operations teams used by the CIA to infiltrate any country, any place. She suddenly remembered she was talking on the phone.

"Listen, do you people understand your protocols down there? I know your department doesn't get out much, but any intelligence that comes through North America, is about North America, or is even rumored to be information derived on this continent, gets forwarded to me." Lynn stopped talking and listened. "Okay, I need the contents of both of these so-called test evaluations brought to me in five minutes. And Mr. Vickers is to know nothing of this." Lynn hung up the phone and then wondered why Hiram Vickers would be interested in a test subject in Nevada.

As Lynn Simpson waited on the information from Imaging, those same tracking details were being passed to that organization that didn't exist—the Men in Black.

Denver, Colorado

"This is Smith," said the deep voice of the large man who was now dressed in Levis and a pullover golf shirt. He glanced over at the door that opened to the hallway outside and the few guests he had over for dinner. He stepped to the den's wide door and closed it as he pressed the cell phone to his ear.

"I have a little surprise for you," Hiram Vickers said on the other end of the cell phone call.

"Surprises in my line of work are never a good thing, Mr. Vickers. You should know that."

"Yes, yes. Now, before I give you the information you've been waiting on, I just wanted to say that was a real nice piece of work south of the border this afternoon. Real nice."

The man known as Smith didn't respond. He didn't need the adulation of some desk jockey in Washington to critique his work. He waited in silence.

"Well, anyway, the man with the hard bug on him has left whatever hole in the ground he was in. The signal is weakening, but we are able to maintain the trace for the time being. Not for long though. The man is definitely the officer you know as Jack Collins. I cannot get into his file other than his regular 201 file, which basically only tells us he's not dead. As for his current assignment, no luck there either. I do know that he is now a full-bird colonel not, as you said, a major. At one time everyone inside the military world thought this man would one day wind up running the whole army corporate arm, until his command had been shot to hell thanks to some generals and rats in Washington a few years back. That was when he was on Capitol Hill testifying before the Ways and Means Committee."

The large man known to Vickers as Smith made no comment but did reach over for a pen atop his desk and started writing.

"Where can our good colonel be located?"

"I'm waiting on the next package from Imaging, but you can start at 1267 Flamingo Road, Las Vegas. After he appeared downtown, he was traced to this address, and that data is only fifteen minutes old."

"Now, I'm going to ask this but one time. When I trace this colonel to wherever he is based, what kind of executive power do I have to recover this substance?"

"The highest. These orders come down from on high. But we'll never have to prove that since you can get what we want and not get caught doing it, and with as few unpleasant things happening as possible, am I right?"

"You know, without knowing who this Collins works for, this thing could get messy. This could involve the elimination of American citizens."

"The substance that was removed from the Mexican hole in the wall must be recovered or destroyed at all costs."

"Now you see, Mr. Vickers, that is why I hate dealing with you intel types. First you wanted the substance found and destroyed; now you want it recovered. Which is it?"

"Our financiers would like it destroyed. However, we here at the home office believe you can recover at least a sample; that wouldn't be a bad thing either. But if you doubt recovery is possible, destroy it for our friends."

Smith just pushed the end-call button on his cell phone and then looked at the address he had written on the pad. He heard the den door open and a small scream of delight. He turned to see his six-year-old daughter run into his study followed by his wife of ten years. They were both smiling.

"Honey, did you forget about our guests?" his dark-haired wife asked as Smith sweeped his daughter into his arms.

"I'm afraid you're on your own tonight sweetheart; Daddy has some work to do."

The daughter frowned and the wife only shook her head.

"It can't wait?" she asked as she removed their daughter from his large arms.

The man known to certain aspects of the intelligence community as Mr. Smith looked from his wife and daughter to the address on the notepad. He tore it off and then reached for a black suitcase and placed the address inside.

"No, the country is in danger and Daddy has to save the world from the bad guys!" he said dramatically, making both his daughter and wife laugh as they kissed him and then left his study to deliver their guests the bad news.

Smith watched them leave and then the smile vanished from his face. He made the necessary phone calls and then looked out of his window at the fine Denver night.

He joked about saving the world from the bad guys, but little did his wife and child know that he was the biggest and baddest of them all.

Las Vegas, Nevada

Jack rang the doorbell several times, but no one answered. He knew someone was home because he could hear the deep bass thump coming through the door. Someone was blasting the old Credence Clearwater Revival song, "Green River." As Jack was just about ready to knock loudly on the door, the music was lowered inside of the modest house. He turned slightly and looked at two of those plastic flamingos that always drove him crazy. Their black eyes looked accusatory to him, so he sneered and turned away. As he did there was the sound of a chain being removed and then he saw the door open. Standing there smiling was Alice Hamilton.

Since Senator Garrison Lee had died three months before, Alice had kept pretty much to herself. Jack and the others figured she needed the time to grieve and allow the senator's memory to settle into its proper place. But as Collins looked down upon the eighty-five-year-old woman, he could see that if she were grieving, it was one dirty process. She had paint covering most of her face and even more of her arms and hands.

"Jack," she said loudly and then reached up and put her arms around him and squeezed him so tight he lost his breath.

"And how are you doing?" he asked when he was able to pry her arms off of his neck.

"Just rockin' out here and painting the old place. You know, adding a little color now that . . . that the ogre has gone to the great beyond."

Jack could see that as much as Alice tried to hide it, the loss of Lee was still etched into her mind.

"Ogre, yeah, whatever you say," Jack said as he stepped into the foyer of the small house.

"Now, I understand you've had some excitement?" Alice said as she walked a few steps to the bar, a new addition to the house Jack noted. She started pouring whiskey for both of them. "Ice?" she asked, holding up the amber fluid, which reminded Jack of the substance they removed from Perdition's Gate.

"No ice, and yes, much excitement."

Alice stepped from behind the bar and handed Jack his drink, which he looked at curiously because of its color.

"So, tell me, Jack, what's it like to be a civilian?" she asked as she took half of her drink down in a swallow.

"How in the hell did you know about that already?"

Alice smiled and batted her eyelids, just the way she used to do with Garrison Lee, which drove him insane. "Now, just because I haven't returned to work yet, doesn't mean I don't have my sources."

"Sarah," Jack said as he downed his entire drink in a swallow.

"Well, actually I received calls from Sarah, Carl, Niles, Virginia, and Charlie Ellenshaw."

"Did they think you could do something about my resignation?"

Alice took Jack's empty glass and returned to the bar and refilled them both. Before she could return, the phone rang and she answered it.

"Hello?" she said.

"Yes, I've heard. I know it hurts, but you have to let him

sort through this. I know you do, but like the rest of us have to do, you just need to give him his space. Yes dear, thank you, and yes, you can come over anytime. Yes, goodbye, Will." Alice hung up the phone and then brought Jack his drink.

"You can add Will Mendenhall to the list."

Jack shook his head and then had to smile.

"Hey, since you're no longer an officer and a gentleman, Mr. Collins, would you care to get drunk with an old woman and tell me a story?"

Jack downed his second drink and then pursed his lips as the whiskey burned its way to his stomach.

"It would be a pleasure, Mrs. Hamilton. But get this straight, young lady—I am not helping you paint. I draw the line right there."

Event Group Complex
Nellis AFB, Nevada

Will Mendenhall had actually worn his Class "A" uniform just two times since his promotion two years before to that of a second lieutenant. As he walked through the reception area for incoming aircraft he noticed for the first time how empty the uniform looked without his old E-7 rank on his shoulders. He missed being a staff sergeant on most days, but now that he had officially been promoted to second in command of the security detachment at the Group, he realized he really wanted to be just a soldier again. As he rounded the corner he saw the four men and two women he was there to meet and escort to the Event Group Complex. The first person he saw caught his attention and he came to a stop thirty feet from the mingling group.

The young black woman saw Will and she smiled. She held the handle of a small rolling suitcase in her right hand and with her left she waved at Will. For his part, Mendenhall turned around to see who she was waving at. When he saw no one behind him but the two crewmen of the Blackhawk that took him to the reception center, he turned back

to the young woman who held her smile as she looked the young officer over. Will realized then that the girl had actually been greeting *him*. He tried to smile and felt it faltering even as he attempted it. He decided he better just do what he came to do and leave the smiles for another time.

"Hi, are you the escort we're supposed to meet?" the young lady said as she held out her small hand to Mendenhall. He cleared his throat as he tried to speak but quickly decided that he would also abandon that thought. He couldn't take his eyes off of her gorgeous brown ones. "Hello, anyone home?" she said jokingly as she was joined by a rather stern-looking man dressed in the uniform of a lieutenant colonel, U.S. Army. Finally Will saw the rank staring at him and instead of shaking the girl's hand, he saluted the colonel.

"Never saw a second lieutenant that would refuse the handshake of a beautiful woman in order to salute an old man," the colonel said shaking his head.

"I don't think he's capable of speech, Dad," the beautiful woman said as she lowered her hand just as Will raised his to shake. She laughed and tilted her head and looked at Mendenhall. "Maybe we'll start over later; right now we're supposed to be met and escorted through to the Group. It seems our security badges have lapsed, at least that was what Director Compton told us."

Will started shaking his head up and down and then after a few insane-looking minutes he finally found his voice. "Sir, I am here to bring you into the secured area of Nellis. Can you give your identification cards over to this man," he said gesturing to the crew chief standing behind them. "He'll run your security clearance and then we can be on our way." Mendenhall's eyes locked on the woman again and this time managed a small smile that was returned instantly. He then managed to pull out the folder he had been carrying. He looked at the list of names and then checked them off as the crew chief gathered their identification cards. He noticed immediately that the woman's name was Gloria Bannister. Then he saw the letters following her name. He

stopped counting after sixteen, which all boiled down to the woman having just about fifteen years more education than Will had. And that made her—

"Dr. Bannister," she said once more holding her hand out when she saw Mendenhall looking at her name on the Event Group recall list. This time Will didn't hesitate; he shook her hand. Her eyes traveled to the bandage covering his hand and then rose to meet his. That was when she saw a small bandage covering his jawline from just below the ear. "It's too bad I'm not that kind of doctor; it looks like you could use one," she said as she released his hand. "You're new since my last trip back to the Group."

"Oh, uh, this," he said looking at his hand. "Just part of the job around here. And I don't think I'm that new; I've been here for six years."

"Well, I guess we missed each other."

"They all check out Lieutenant," the crew chief said as he started handing the IDs back to their owners. The crew chief had to tug and pull Dr. Bannister's ID from Will's grasp.

"I'm Lieutenant Colonel William Bannister, young man, and I am supposed to be in charge of this band of fools from the CDC, including my daughter here, Dr. Bannister."

Mendenhall's eyes slowly moved away from the now grinning girl to the large man in the same Class "A" uniform he wore.

"Although it's written into army regulations that anyone, and I mean anyone, above the rank of first lieutenant can make a fool out of second lieutenants, I will forgo that right at the moment. Right now I understand we are needed for some particularly dirty work at the complex, so may I suggest we get to it?"

"Yes, sir, right this way." Will turned away after placing the file under his arm and with eyes wide shooed the two chiefs away ahead of him.

The young doctor slapped her father on the arm and then placed her arm through his. "You're just plain mean sometimes," she said and they both laughed as they followed the scared second lieutenant out to the flight line. "Sometimes I

think working too closely with Senator Lee all those years has made you mean at heart."

The Blackhawk flew for only seven minutes. It circled the ancient hangar where at one time B-25 Mitchells and P-51 Mustangs sat like waiting dragons to take to the war-torn skies of the world. It had been over sixty years since the propeller-driven beasts ruled the air and just as long since the giant hangar had housed anything other than insects and Gila monsters.

The Blackhawk swept the area twice so the security detail surrounding the hangar could clearly identify them. Then it circled to the front of the old hangar and the large rotored craft settled to about ten feet off the desert scrub. Wind and sand blew up and obscured the Blackhawk as it eased itself through the giant and dilapidated hangar door, so it would look to the casual observer to be hanging from only five of the twenty giant hinges on either side. The helicopter hovered for the briefest of moments before the experienced pilot sat it down onto what looked like a cracked and broken concrete center floor.

Suddenly every one of the reactivated Event personnel from the CDC gave out a loud breath when they felt their stomachs heave up slightly as the Blackhawk was lowered down by the massive lift.

As the twenty-seven-ton lift operated on ultraquiet hydraulics, it was hard to tell once your stomach settled if you were still moving or not. Finally the elevator came to a stop and Niles Compton was there to greet his returning team.

Will jumped free of the Blackhawk and then handed the file folder to Niles.

"On behalf of our department, I would like to welcome you back home to Nevada," Niles said.

"Whatever this is about, Mr. Director, I sure hope you can afford my fees," Colonel Bannister joked with his old friend as he held out his hand.

Niles took the colonel's hand and shook it. "Good to see you again Billy," he said looking over at the colonel's daughter. "Gloria, sorry to drag you back to the Group on such short notice, but budgeting for a full-time disease control staff is a little beyond us."

"It's good to be back, Niles," Gloria said as she waited for their mission to be described to them.

"We have an element in house that needs to be treated with respect, and I trust you to see that it's analyzed and then, if need be, destroyed after study."

"Sounds fascinating," Colonel Bannister said as he followed the soldiers carrying his suitcase toward the elevators. The others followed Bannister.

Gloria smiled as she walked by Will. Compton half smiled as he watched Mendenhall's eyes follow the attractive doctor as she walked away.

"What's wrong, Lieutenant? You look sick. Aren't your new expanded duties meeting with your approval?"

"Huh?" Will stammered, not hearing a word Niles had said. "Sir?"

Niles turned his head and watched the group of doctors as they entered the elevator. Compton smiled and then raised his eyebrows as he turned and looked at Will.

"Carry on, Lieutenant," the director said.

"Huh?"

Niles smiled as he turned away and strode to the elevator, leaving a confused second lieutenant in his wake.

McCarran International Airport
Las Vegas, Nevada

The large man going by the name of Smith stepped off the chartered flight from Denver. He was met by a team of three men and they were backed up by four more in a car he knew was there but couldn't see as per their training.

As the large well-dressed man stepped up to the black Chevy Tahoe, he looked at his watch and then turned to the man holding the door. He saw that he was wearing a black windbreaker.

"How much longer does the transmitter have before it

dies?" he asked as he eyed the man who led the Black field team inside the Las Vegas city limits.

"We lost the signal five minutes ago, Mr. Smith."

"You have GPS locations for all of the stops the target made?"

"Yes, sir, we do. Actually, he made only one stop after appearing at 2896 Koval Lane, and that was a private residence out on Flamingo Road."

The man named Smith shook his head and then buttoned his blue blazer. As he stepped by the smaller man who held the door open, he looked down at him and without his other men hearing said, "What's with the black windbreaker?"

The man was taken aback as Smith seated himself in the backseat of the Tahoe. He opened his mouth to speak, but nothing came out. After all, he had heard the rumors about Smith and his famous temper. He had also heard that the man really had one passion in life, and that was to end other people's aspirations for a long one.

"We never wear black when the need to intimidate isn't called for," he said as he looked over at the man who was now having second thoughts about running the Las Vegas office for him. "And investigating doesn't call for the intimidation factor. Don't wear that shit again unless I specifically order you to." Smith reached out and closed the door in the man's face. The former U.S. Army Ranger swallowed and then ran around to the opposite rear door and climbed inside.

Smith once more looked at his watch. "Take me to where our target first appeared. That's quite a jump from Nellis to Koval Lane in downtown Las Vegas with the route the subject took. According to the report, he cut through rough desert and the basements of several casinos to get to this location on Koval Lane. I'm interested in knowing how he achieved that little stunt."

"Yes, sir," the driver said as he placed the large Tahoe into gear.

"What's the name of this place again," he asked the chastised man next to him.

The man pulled out his notebook and then decided at that

precise moment to remove the offensive black windbreaker. He opened the notebook and studied his notes, infuriating Smith even more than he had been.

"The Gold City Pawn Shop," the man finally answered without looking up.

"Then why aren't we at the Gold City Pawn Shop already?"

The Tahoe screeched out of the charter area of McCarran airport heading to downtown. As they pulled out onto the main drive heading toward the city, another black Tahoe pulled out after them.

Las Vegas, Nevada

As Collins ran the paint roller across the den's wall, he tuned with a sneer and looked over at a very messy but very satisfied Alice Hamilton.

"No wonder the senator didn't like you much. You purposefully plied me with drink, and then the next thing I know I'm painting, and I'm doing most of the work."

"Yes, and soon I'm going to go into that backyard of mine and then grill you a steak, Mr. Collins." Alice looked up after she poured more light-green paint into the pan she was using just to see if she got a rise out of Jack by calling him mister. But Collins just kept painting. Badly, but he kept painting nonetheless.

"You're not going to get to me, you know?" he said as he almost fell over when he tried to get more paint on his roller. "This is only the first day of my retirement, so my mind is still strong young lady."

Alice looked up at Jack and smiled. She lay the paint brush down inside of the pan of paint and then walked over to where Jack was trying his hardest to apply paint to the roller, but every time he tried he would almost fall face first in the opposite direction. Alice took the roller and then placed it in the pan at Jack's feet. "Come on, soldier boy, I think you're ready for that steak now."

"See, I knew if I did a bad-enough job you would call an end to this . . . this farce."

"That's right, Jack, I'm surrendering," she said as she guided him through the now empty house and toward the back sliding door. "Let's get some air, and then I'll bring you out some coffee."

"Air? Yes, air would be nice," he said as she placed him not too gently into one of the chaise lounges.

"Okay, just stay put and entertain yourself for a few minutes."

"And how do I do that, my dear Mrs. Hamilton?"

"Hum 'Row, Row, Row Your Boat' or something."

An expression of confusion came over Jack's face. "I . . . I . . . don't know Row, row, row . . . row, row . . . your boat."

Alice wanted to answer, but she had to turn away or she would have lost it right there. She went back into the kitchen, trying her best not to laugh out loud at Jack's butchering of the children's song title. When she made it into her kitchen, which she hadn't really used since the death of Garrison Lee, her cell phone rang. If it was someone public, they would have called on her landline. But since it was her cell phone she knew it was someone at the Event Group calling from the complex.

"Hello," she said, knowing who it was before the words came through the atmosphere.

"Uh, hello, Alice?" came the voice full of worry and concern.

"Hello, my dear. And before you worry yourself too much, he's here. A little plastered right now, but I can also attribute that to painting, and not just my twenty-year-old whiskey. He's out in the back trying to sing."

"Thank God," Sarah said on the other end. "He's not answering his phone and I—"

"Stop it now. You listen to what I have to say. My words may be a little bit slurred, but you should understand them well enough. Jack needs time. I don't know what happened in the field, but I know something inside of him snapped. I've seen it before, Sarah. Garrison resigned no less than fifteen different times. He and Jack are a lot alike you know?"

"That's why I knew where I had to call. Look, Alice, I have to give our field report to a group of recalls from the CDC in a few minutes, but do you think afterward I can stop by? I won't bug him about his decision. I just need to see him."

"I would be angry if you didn't come by, young lady. He needs you now, not an old woman who knows songs he doesn't know."

"What?" Sarah asked.

Alice turned away from the open sliding glass window where she heard Jack trying to recall the words to "Row, Row, Row Your Boat," but he kept going off track with a mixture of that song and the theme from *Gilligan's Island*.

"Nothing, I'll see you when you get here." Alice hung up the phone and then as her eyes moved away from her back-yard, she caught a glimpse of the only portrait she had on her walls. It was of her and Garrison Lee fifty years before when they took a field trip to Egypt. She saw the angry look on his face for having to be still for so long just for a portrait, but it was the only thing she ever asked of him, so he did it, complaining all the way. She smiled at the picture of herself and the one-eyed ex-senator and former general in the OSS, the Office of Strategic Services, and then she looked at Jack out on the back porch.

"Just like him."

The Gold City Pawn Shop
Las Vegas, Nevada

The man inside the Tahoe was parked across the busy street. The Black Team had been out front watching for the better part of thirty minutes. Smith never uttered a word but had held up his hand several times when one of the three men inside the Tahoe attempted to ask a question. His eyes never left the pawn shop.

As far as he could discern it was a busy place of business. He saw very little out of the ordinary. Smith looked to his left and the field supervisor he had chewed out earlier. He looked at the man's hand and then smiled to himself. "Give me your ring and watch," he said as he held out his large hand.

The man next to him was about to ask a very stupid question, especially stupid considering how his day had gone thus far with the director of the Black Teams. Instead of doing the stupid thing, he removed his watch and his wedding ring and gave them to Smith. He would have asked why he didn't use his own watch, or his own wedding ring, but stopped short when he saw how much more expensive the man's wedding ring was compared to his, and with the Rolex he wore, well, he decided not to break the bond of trust he was now trying to develop.

"Thank you. I'll be back in a few minutes."

Smith left the large Chevrolet and then waited for a city bus to pass before he sprinted across the street and entered the Gold City Pawn Shop without a second's hesitation.

The agent from the Las Vegas district watched Smith go and then turned away and looked out of the side window. He knew the man as the most ruthless person he had ever met in his life. He had been recruited by Smith right out of the army, claiming he and others were about to rebuild an elite paramilitary unit that would work closely with the CIA and NSA. Needless to say, he had jumped at the chance. But now he realized that if the job didn't kill him, the man named Smith surely would.

Smith looked down at the ornate door handle that was probably cast sometime in the 1940s. He depressed the thumb plate and knew immediately that he had touched something other than brass. Under his thumb he felt slick, cold glass. He opened the door without pausing and stepped into the pawn shop. He held the door open a moment as two teenage girls left holding a bag full of CDs. He smiled and nodded as they giggled their way past. He closed the door and then looked around the shop. There were musical instruments hanging on the walls, large screen LED television sets, and stereo systems. *If this was a front*, he thought, *it was convincing.*

Smith started up the aisle toward the back of the store where he noticed an older man leaning against the glass cases reading a magazine. As he looked at the many pawned items on display, he watched the man without him ever knowing it. He saw the clean-shaven face and the well-trimmed hair. That was when Smith smelled military. As he stepped to the counter he also saw that he was being observed by no less than fifteen cameras, far too many for a small pawn shop. The older man noticed his approach and then closed his magazine.

"Howdy, what can I do ya' for?" the man asked as he looked Smith up and down.

"Well, I just want to get these appraised," he answered with a return smile as he held out the wedding ring and the watch.

The older man behind the counter looked at the two items and then smiled. "Without looking through my jeweler's loupe, I can tell you the ring isn't what you probably think it is, and the watch, well," he started to say as he pulled a large cardboard box out from under the counter, "as you can see, I have a bunch of that crap already." He looked at Smith, and then he relented a little. "Having a hard stay in Vegas my friend?"

Smith smiled and tried to look embarrassed. "You can say that."

"Okay, partner. I'll give you fifty for the ring. On the condition you take that fifty, put gas in your car, and go home. Do we have a deal?"

Smith placed the ring on the countertop and then nodded his head as if he were embarrassed to no end.

"Ah, don't sweat it my friend, we all have our moments. You just had yours and now you've learned from it." The man, a staff sergeant in the U.S. Army and part of the security team for the Event Group Complex, took the ring and then slid a paper form toward Smith for him to fill out.

"Name, address, phone number, and sign at the bottom of the page. And I'll tell you what, I'll treat this as a loan, so you can get it back before the wife finds out."

"Thanks, buddy—thanks a lot." Smith watched as the clerk turned and went into the back room. When the thick curtain parted he could see two other men standing in the back with the refuse of junk collected by the gambling low-lifes that frequented this place. He saw one of the men look up at him just before the curtain slid back into place. The man was medium sized, and he was black. Their eyes locked for the briefest of moments, but in that short time Smith had confirmed what he already suspected. The place was a front for something. What, he didn't know yet. But the black man with the bandage on the side of his jaw was the very same man from Mexico they had pulled out of that culvert outside of Perdition's Gate. Smith would recognize him anywhere.

As the old man returned from the back room, he handed Smith his fifty dollars in cash. He read the receipt of exchange and then smiled. "ID please."

Smith produced the fake license that corresponded with the fake name and address he had given on the loan form. The old man wrote down the license number and then slid the ID back.

"Now, you go home," he looked down at the receipt, "Mr. Smith, and we'll see you when you come back to get your ring."

"You bet," Smith said as he pocketed the cash and then placed the watch that he couldn't pawn into his pocket.

Smith strolled confidently through the pawn shop and then hesitated at the door to see what was happening behind him thanks to the reflection in the thick glass. The old man watched him for a moment and then went back to the magazine he was reading. Smith opened the door and left. As he crossed the street he felt inside of his coat pocket. The watch that he couldn't pawn appeared and he smiled as he dropped it into the gutter beside the Tahoe. He entered the backseat and handed the man his fifty dollars.

"They took both the watch and the ring."

The man just looked down at the cash in his hand. That was all he received for the wedding ring and the watch his wife gave him last Christmas.

"This place has something under it, I can smell it. A passageway, something . . . ," Smith said as his words trailed off in thought. "We may have to call in another favor and get some geological data of the area leading to and from that pawn shop." He smiled to no one but himself as a plan started to form. "Now, let's go to the private address out on Flamingo Road."

Inside the Gold City Pawn Shop, Will Mendenhall stepped out from behind the curtain and watched as the large man crossed the street and vanished. He shook his head as he tried to think.

"What is it, Lieutenant?" the sergeant asked as he again closed his magazine.

"Did that guy look familiar to you?" Will asked as he watched the gathering darkness outside to see if the man would reappear.

"Familiar? One thing you should remember from your time at this counter, sir, is that everyone looks familiar."

Mendenhall smiled at the memory of the boring days on gate duty. He slapped the sergeant on the back. "Yeah I do remember." He turned as one of the marines in the back room looked out from behind the curtain. He made sure no customers were in the shop and then faced Will.

"The director called and said they're ready for your deposition to our newly arrived CDC people."

Mendenhall perked up as he realized he would get to see the young Dr. Bannister again. Then his smile faded as he remembered she would be with her father, Colonel Bannister.

Mendenhall turned and left as he was starting to realize he didn't stand a chance with someone like Gloria Bannister.

The reactivated Event Group personnel from the CDC were sitting around the large conference table on the seventh level. Niles Compton was at his accustomed place at the head of the table and next to him was Virginia. The doctors from the Group and now the CDC were all facing the large-screen monitor as they took in the information compiled by Pete, who was busy using his pointer on the large 3-D screen while explaining about Perdition's Gate and its ownership through the years.

"We have thus far met a block wall as far as getting the history of Professor Lawrence Ambrose. His academic credentials, his research grants, his employment history seem to have been misplaced by everyone in government. Where he received the millions upon millions of dollars to conduct research has not been discovered—yet," Pete added. "We hope to have that question answered very soon as we are just now starting to pore through the old data compiled by the Group back in 1916. The material is volumes in length and extremely detailed so it may take a while. We have decided that at least one of you should assist in the archival research. You may see something we don't."

"So, until two days ago you had never heard of this Lawrence Ambrose before?" Colonel Bannister asked.

"No," Niles answered for Pete Golding. "We discovered the results of his work and the sample we brought back after our security detachment's raid into Perdition Hacienda south of Nuevo Laredo one day ago."

"And the subject of this raid had no knowledge of the hacienda's ownership at the turn of the century?" Dr. Emily Samuels, one of Virginia's old nuclear science students, asked.

"Thus far our search has turned up no relationship between Professor Ambrose and Juan Guzman," Pete answered as he pointed at the picture of the Anaconda in the right-hand corner of the screen. "As far as we can see, it was just a fluke, a coincidence that they ended up owning the same hacienda, one hundred years apart."

"In the earlier portion of your brief you said that the area of concern at the hacienda was two levels below the main floor of the house, and that level had been sealed earlier in the century in an attack by the American military searching for the bandit known as Pancho Villa, am I correct?" Colonel Bannister asked as he checked off the question from his list of about a hundred.

Niles nodded his head.

"Then it seems the answer may lie in the auspices of the Department of the Army. Wouldn't that be the next logical step in your search?"

"Dead end. There were no such orders, at least officially, issued for the 8th United States Cavalry to cross into Mexico on that day and date. It is well known that on that particular night, Pancho Villa was raiding a Mexican federal pay shipment from Juarez. He was a far distance from Perdition on the night of the raid." Pete looked at his notes and pushed his horn-rimmed glasses back onto the bridge of his nose.

"Then how do you know the raid on the hacienda actually took place?" Gloria Bannister asked.

"A journal—little known and kept in a family trunk for many, many years," Virginia Pollock added.

"And whose journal are we speaking of?" Gloria asked.

"A first lieutenant who actually commanded the raid that night—George S. Patton," Virginia answered, stealing Pete's thunder. "We not only know he led the raid that night, but also that the Event Group was there right along with him. That's how we came into possession of the artifacts from 1916."

"*The* George Patton—General George Patton?" the colonel asked, raising his brows.

"The family of the general always thought the raids into Mexico did nothing to enhance the general's reputation after the war years, so that was one piece of information they kept pretty close to the vest, only stating that the general was in on the pursuit of Pancho Villa. They never once uttered the words *Perdition's Gate* or *Professor Lawrence Ambrose*," Pete said as he lowered his pointer and then looked at his notes. He then nodded at Virginia who stood up and walked to the large screen where the navy signalman replaced the scene from the spot where Perdition used to sit to a large picture of Lawrence Ambrose himself as he was just after he finished his studies.

"Professor Lawrence Jackson Ambrose was born in the third year of the American Civil War in 1863. His father was a greenhouse keeper and gardener in Indianapolis, Indiana, and was killed the same year his son was born at the battle of Gettysburg. After that Ambrose was raised by a doting mother, Isabel, and eventually went off to college. He graduated from the University of Indiana with the highest honors of his academic class."

"What were the main courses of study?" another doctor, Pierce, asked from the end of the group.

"Botany," Virginia answered. "The man, according to graduation reports from his professors, was a genius, as was his father in the breeding, cross-breeding, and pollination of plant life. He was the foremost authority on splicing and was one of the first to conduct such experiments on wild flowers and plants from exotic areas of the world. It was these experiments that led to the disappearance of Ambrose in 1885. At the time, the professor was only twenty-two years of age and the most brilliant man in his field. We suspect he was hired into private practice, for what reason we do not know. He literally vanished from the face of the earth and didn't show up again until the raid by the United States cavalry into Mexico in 1916."

"Now, I have three people that were at Perdition Hacienda the night of the Guzman raid. They will fill you in on the effects of this sample that was recovered from the sublevel of that building. They are witness to the change that occurred on more than one man and its subsequent effect on their minds and bodies," Niles said as he nodded for the blue-clad marine to allow the three people into the conference room.

Captain Carl Everett, Sarah McIntire, and Will Mendenhall stepped into the conference room, each clad in their military-designated coveralls of blue and gold trim. All had their military designation on their sleeve and collars. Carl waited for Mendenhall and Sarah, who still had most of her face hidden behind a large pair of glasses. She looked at Director Compton and he lightly tapped his own glasses. She took the meaning and removed her glasses. She saw the look on the lead doctor's face as he took in Sarah's large black eyes and broken nose.

"I don't know what function your people perform for our government, Dr. Compton, but I hope you get hazardous-duty pay," Colonel Bannister said as he looked back at Sarah who actually smiled back at him.

"They do get hazardous-duty pay, and believe me, Colonel, they earn it here," Compton said as he removed his glasses and then nodded at Virginia to offer up the questions for Everett and the other two witnesses to the amazing transformation of Juan Guzman the night of the raid.

Virginia smiled and then looked at Captain Everett who looked as if he really didn't want to be in the conference room at all.

"Doctors, this is Captain Everett, the head of our security staff. He . . . ," she hesitated a moment, choosing the only words that came to mind. "He led the assault on Perdition Hacienda two nights ago. Captain, can you explain to our guests from the CDC what happened in the brief firefight between your forces and those of Juan Guzman?" Virginia smiled and nodded her head at Carl.

"First, to be accurate, we discovered approximately fifteen barrels of dried flowers. We assume these flowers were grown somewhere other than Mexico. After a brief and not very knowledgeable examination of the contents of these stored flowers, it was suggested that they were poppies of some variety. The barrels were marked *2370*. Lined up next to these barrels were several hundred jars of a substance consisting of an amber fluid. These jars were sealed with not only rubber stoppers, but also had been waxed over to secure the contents."

"Excuse me, Captain; my name is Dr. Gloria Bannister. Were these jars marked with any form of identification?"

Mendenhall allowed his eyes to move across the table for the first time and was shocked when Dr. Bannister made eye contact with him after asking Carl the question. Everett saw the exchange and wondered what Will was up to.

"Yes, they were all marked with what I assumed was a batch number as they were all different, with one exception. They all had a number in bold print—batch number 2370."

"Please continue, Captain," Colonel Bannister said as he looked from Will and then slightly turned to see his daughter lower her eyes.

"Well, Juan Guzman and his men assaulted our team before we could get clear of the laboratory spaces below the hacienda. They had us cornered and we were taking fire from a covered position. Lieutenant Mendenhall here held them at bay until heavier ordnance was introduced into the fight from the Guzman faction. A grenade exploded in their covered position, breaking open several of the barrels containing the dried vegetation, and unfortunately this brought down the shelving where the liquid material was stored. Our young lieutenant here was the first to notice something was wrong. Will, what happened after the smoke cleared?"

Mendenhall wasn't expecting to speak to the group of doctors. He shifted in his chair and then with a great deal of concentration tried to recall and account for what happened that night without everyone thinking him an idiot.

"Several of Guzman's men were killed in the initial detonation of the grenade." His eyes moved from the tabletop and locked with Gloria's. He felt a little better when she lightly smiled. "Several others were just injured. As one of these men rose to continue his assault, he was hit by several rounds, from not only me but another part of our team. The man took hits from at least ten different bullets. He went down."

"Perhaps we can write that off to injuries, causing shock to the system, and also a rush of adrenalin?" asked Dr. Lewis, a balding man from the CDC who was looking at Mendenhall with the slightest bit of skepticism written in his face and laced into his words.

"Perhaps," Will said, not liking the condescending tone in the doctor's words. "But I quickly eliminated any speculation as to the man's condition when he once more rose up and continued his attack."

Several eyes of the visiting CDC doctors rose and they started paying far better attention to the young army officer's account.

"Perhaps your defense did not hit any vital organs. Maybe his being alive was just a fluke?" Gloria said, hoping to point out something Mendenhall had maybe missed in his eyewitness account.

"Well, yes ma'am, while my initial thoughts may have leaned that way, my second thoughts included the sight of half the man's head missing. After at least fifteen more rounds to the body and finally the front of the man's head, he went down. This attack was repeated by others who had been inundated with the material stored in the jars."

"Sounds like the effects produced by the PCP studies of 1975," Gloria said softly to her father.

"Can you tell us of any odors you may have caught during this time?" Colonel Bannister asked.

Mendenhall looked over at Carl who only shrugged his shoulders. "Uh, no, sir. The vapors from the liquid seemed to be confined to the floor area near the impact zone where the men had taken cover."

"Confined to the floor you say?" another of the doctors asked.

"Yes, sir. It was like a shroud of fog."

Gloria leaned forward so her statement could be heard by the rest of the CDC team from Atlanta. "Obviously heavier than air and a possible chemical breakdown that produces a gas when exposed to the air?"

"Possibly," Colonel Bannister said. "Lieutenant, can we have your description of the major changes that occurred in this Juan Guzman as you witnessed that night?"

Mendenhall slightly shook his head and then looked into the colonel's eyes. "I don't think you could describe it as a change. It was more of a transformation. As far as I could see, Guzman took the brunt of the spill. He had been right under the fall of specimen jars from their shelves. But as I said, it was more of a transformation right before our eyes. His body resembled that of Guzman, but that's where it all ended. His height even changed. I could venture a guess, but I would have to say by at least a good foot. His musculature had tripled, enough so that his clothing couldn't contain his body any longer. The teeth were different, larger somehow. But all of that wasn't the strangest part."

"Go ahead, Lieutenant," Bannister said when he saw Will hesitate.

"The material he ingested, breathed in, seemed not to have affected his higher brain functions at all. He was able to articulate his words, and . . . and . . ." Mendenhall looked into the eyes of Gloria Bannister. The return look told him to go ahead, that he was doing fine. "I could actually see intelligence behind those larger-than-normal eyes."

The visiting team of viral, germ warfare, and toxicology specialists looked at one another. They were clearly stumped for the time being.

"And each one of these affected men was hard to kill in the extreme?" Gloria asked.

"Ma'am, I have been in more than just a few firefights. Been though what a lot of people would call harrowing situations, but after seeing what happened in Mexico, I can honestly say I have never been that scared. I guess it was the fear of the unknown. What we saw there wasn't natural. And one last thing doctors . . ."

"Go on, Will," Virginia encouraged from the head of the table.

"Guzman actually killed several of his men for simply being in his way when he started to come after us. He went through them with his bare hands and tore them to pieces. He was enraged but still able to function. He not only escaped, but stalked us all the way back across the border. He hit us at differing ambush points in the underground culvert. Yes, he was a monster, but a calculating one that was relentless."

At that moment one of Compton's four assistants came through the conference room doors and then nodded at Niles. He then went to where Sarah was sitting and handed her a folded piece of paper. She thanked the assistant and then read the note as the CDC personnel talked amongst themselves. She refolded the note and then looked at Niles.

"Dr. Compton, our other guest is causing a little problem down in the clinic, uh, may I—"

"Do you need Captain Everett to accompany you?" Niles asked as his worries about keeping Henri Farbeaux a prisoner inside of his complex came to the surface with his stern look.

"No sir, I think I can handle our friend."

Carl leaned over and whispered. "If you think it necessary, shoot the bastard in the head and call it a day."

Sarah looked down at Carl as she stood. "We need to talk later about that very subject, Captain," Sarah said, causing Carl to raise his eyebrows when the venom in her words hit him like a slap in the face. She placed her sunglasses back on and then nodded at the doctors across the table before she left the conference room.

Mendenhall chanced a look at Gloria across from him, but she was deep into conversation with her colleagues and didn't pay him any mind.

"Thank you Lieutenant Mendenhall and Captain Everett, I think we have a picture of the change this possible pathogen may have caused. Now I think it's time we get to work." Bannister looked over at Niles Compton. "I assume you have a clean room we can work in?"

"Dr. Pollock will take you to your new labs; quite a bit has changed since you were here last. There you'll be set up with anything you may need. One thing I want to make clear ladies and gentlemen is that I want that crap out of my complex as soon as you deem it safe to either destroy or move."

"That's why we're here Niles, old friend."

Gloria Bannister gathered her notes and stood along with her father and other members of the CDC. She happened to look up one last time and smiled at Will. It almost looked as if she wanted to say something, but she shook her head and then followed her father and the others out of the conference room.

Both Niles and Carl looked from Gloria's back over to the lieutenant. Will tilted his head and then caught himself. He tried to smile as he looked from Everett to Compton, but failed miserably.

"Smart girl," he said.

"Not bad looking either," Everett said as he looked over at Compton.

"Cute," was all Mendenhall could say as he quickly stood and hurried from the conference table with worried eyes following him all the way.

"Are you sure our young second lieutenant didn't get a dose of that stuff along with Guzman?" Niles asked.

"Whatever Will's got in his system, although I do suspect it's chemical in nature, has nothing to do with Perdition, Lawrence Ambrose, or Juan Guzman. Our friend has been overwhelmed by someone he doesn't understand and he realizes that because of that, he's attracted to her."

Niles smiled as he stacked his file folders. "Sounds like you've been there before, Captain."

Everett smiled and stood from the conference table. "I have, and I don't recommend it."

With that said, the investigation into Perdition's Fire began in earnest.

Sarah stood in the open doorway of the clinic's ten-bed area and watched Farbeaux as he slept. She took a moment and leaned against the doorframe to study the man. With his blonde hair tousled and the way he turned his head from time to time, it was as if Henri were but a small boy lost in a world he couldn't control. Of course Sarah knew she was only speculating, but she knew the Frenchman wasn't what he appeared to be. And now that the famous thorn in the side of the Event Group had been caught, she supposed it was true—he was nothing but a lost man who had done a kindness and now was a prisoner. That kindness had been done for her, and it only confused things in her head to the point that she had to know more about him. As she touched the overly large sunglasses and took a tentative step inside, she reminded herself that Henri had killed people—their people—all for the sake of more money and priceless objects. She set her mind to a course and entered the semidark room.

As she approached the bed, one of the security men in the far corner cleared his throat. Sarah looked over and nodded at the man. As she continued, another security man stepped into the doorway she had just left, blocking out the light from the clinic's offices. She was self-conscious about Jack's men even seeing her in Farbeaux's room.

She stepped up to the bed, quietly pulled over a chair, and sat down. She ran a hand through her short brown hair and then eased the glasses back up the bridge of her nose, suddenly self-aware of how she must look. She came here because Henri requested her to, but now she knew she had made a mistake in not allowing Carl to accompany her. She started to rise from the chair.

"My dear Sarah, it must have taken a lot of courage for you to come here unescorted by your rather large navy friend. I'm sure he wasn't happy about it." Henri reached up and moved a strand of hair back behind Sarah's left ear. She started to flinch away from his touch, but found she couldn't. She swallowed as his hand came away.

"I don't think I have to worry Colonel; Captain Everett seems to be well represented here."

Farbeaux looked up at the marine standing in the door and the army sergeant sitting in the chair. Both were watching him very closely.

"Yes, I suppose he is," Henri commented with a smile. "I did notice little Sarah that you didn't disagree when I said 'the captain's men'."

"Why should I? They *are* his men."

"This afternoon I received the distinct impression that Colonel Collins relieved himself of his duties. Is this true?" Henri sat up with some amount of pain showing on his face so he could see Sarah more closely. He would detect a lie if one was told to him. He knew the small woman in front of him had little affinity for that particular sin.

Sarah only looked at Farbeaux through the dark sunglasses. She placed her hands in her lap and took Henri in.

"He did. And yes, it was his choice. Unlike a lot of professional soldiers, and others, Jack had filled up with loathing over war and other things. He needed to step away for a while."

"A while?"

Sarah didn't answer the query, but she did start to rise from the chair, and this time Henri reached out and took her hand, making her stop. As he did, the marine at the door took a few steps toward Farbeaux's bed and the sergeant in the corner stood—his hand was on the holster flap where his nine millimeter was secured.

Sarah looked over and shook her head slightly at the marine. Then she turned and did the same for the sergeant in the corner. They both relaxed. But neither one moved back to their original positions.

Sarah twisted her hand free of the Frenchman's grip. "What did you want to see me for, Colonel?"

"Please, sit," he said as his eyes looked up and into his own reflection in her sunglasses. That was a view Henri never liked—one of himself.

Sarah took in a deep breath and then slowly sat down once more. She adjusted her glasses and then looked at Henri. "I have a lot of work to do, Colonel, and I still have plans to track Jack . . . er, uh, Colonel Collins, down before the night is over."

Farbeaux smiled. "I doubt very much if his resignation will affect the way he feels about you, dear Sarah."

"I know that, as it won't affect the way I feel about him. He's the love of my life, Henri; I want you to know that." Sarah watched the former French commando for a reaction. His smile remained, but as for understanding what she had just stated, there was no way she could know.

Henri looked over at the two security men who just stood watching the exchange. He held his hand up so they could see, and then he slowly reached out and removed Sarah's sunglasses. He held them as he examined her face. The large bandage covering the bridge of her nose and the blackened and bruised eyes shocked the Frenchman and for a moment he lost his smile. He reached up and touched McIntire's cheek and tried once more to bring back the ghost of a smile he had just a moment before.

Sarah tried not to flinch at his touch, but she did and she resented her weakness. She touched his finger and then took hold of his hand and lowered it.

"Colonel . . . Henri," she said, remembering that Jack, the man Farbeaux wanted to kill, never called Farbeaux by his last name, but mostly by his given name. "Thank you for coming after me. I . . . I don't know what to say, and I don't know why you did it. But thank you," she finally said the words and then she released his hand and stood.

"You don't know why?" he asked as he looked her in her bruised and swollen eyes.

"Colonel, I don't know why. And I am going to leave it at just thank you for doing what you did." She turned away toward the door.

"Have you forgotten, dear Sarah, I asked *you* here? Not to profess my inner soul to you, but to pass on something that I remember from Mexico."

Sarah turned and then purposefully walked back. She made a large pretense of snatching her sunglasses from Henri's right hand. She placed them gingerly on her nose and then looked down at him.

"That man who came to our rescue, the rather large one who seemed to be in charge of his group. I suspect that Colonel Collins and his sidekick, Captain Everett, found out that no one sent this man and his team in to rescue us . . . am I correct?"

Sarah stood still as she took in the question, one that she had no idea was coming. She felt she had shorted Henri for what she had been thinking. But then she corrected herself when she saw the way he looked at her. It was the same way Jack looked in their quiet moments together. She could see in his blue eyes, the same color as Jack's she noted, that there was far more to Henri's request for her to be here than just answering his one question, so her original fear of his feelings for her quickly returned.

"No, the director said the president had a team of DELTA operatives in the air, but at the time our large friend and his commandoes showed up, they were still an hour out of Laredo."

Henri turned his head in thought. He then turned his burning gaze on Sarah once more.

"I'll tell you what, little Sarah, if you can manage to bring me a bottle of wine and a menu from that American slop house you call a cafeteria, I'll tell you a secret that would be of very much interest to your Director Compton."

For the first time since McIntire entered the room, she had to smile. Henri was starting to heal and that made her happy. His French sense of humor was returning.

"Colonel, I will bring you that menu, or I can have our chefs cook you up anything special you may want, but unless I get orders to allow you access to the Ark Lounge and the spirits sold there, you can forget about the wine."

"The Ark?"

"We're not barbarians here, Colonel—we actually have a lounge for off-duty personnel."

"Then that is where we will sit and have many drinks."

"I doubt that very much."

"Then I will divulge my suspicions for the offered menu and your obviously fine military chefs."

Sarah shook her head and sat back down in the chair. "I'm waiting."

"So you are. That man at the river; I have seen him before, a very long time ago. When I was contracting out to various corporations, I met him once. He is not a very nice man. If it were not for my face being covered entirely in blood, I am sure he would have identified me in seconds, at which point he would have not only ended my life, but everyone that he rescued from Guzman."

"Who is he?" she asked, becoming concerned simply because a man she knew as fearless was obviously frightened of this person.

"When I met him he went by the name of Smith, obviously not his real name. Tell your Captain Everett to start a search for him by designating him as possibly former CIA. He is ruthless and he was at Perdition's Gate for a particular reason, and it was not to the benefit of your Group."

"Thank you, Colonel. I'll pass this on to Captain Everett and the director. But regardless of what they say, I will get you that menu."

"Lovely, Sarah, there is but one more thing I must say." Henri tried to sit farther up in his bed and when he saw out of the corner of his eye that the nearest security man took a step toward his bed, Farbeaux ignored him. The marine saw that his move wasn't threatening and relaxed.

"Can you come a little closer? I promise not to bite."

Sarah took a deep breath, not wanting to get any closer to Henri than she already was. There was no telling what was running through this man's head. He was adept at getting out of tight spaces, and she also knew he would use any means to get out of this one. She leaned forward and before she knew what was happening Farbeaux kissed her. She was so shocked that she froze. If anyone could see her eyes under the dark-shaded glasses they would have seen them wide as saucers. Finally she broke away and stood so suddenly that she knocked over the chair, bringing both security men to her side.

"Are you okay, Lieutenant?" the marine asked as he steadied her.

Sarah couldn't say anything; she just stared at Henri. As she did, the other security man walked up to the bed and then slapped the handcuff on the Frenchman once more.

"Captain Everett said your comfort was a privilege . . . one that you just lost, Colonel."

Henri smiled as the click of the cuff sounded louder in the room than it should have. He kept his eyes on Sarah as if the two security men didn't exist.

Sarah went through the open door and passed Dr. Gilliam as she was coming in to check on her patient. The doctor smiled, but Sarah rushed right past her without saying a word.

* * *

Sarah had her arms crossed over her chest as she strode through the hallway heading toward her classroom where she was now officially ten minutes late to instruct on the hidden rock formations inside of natural caves that give off mineralized light. She stood outside of the classroom, adjusted the glasses on her face, and was about to open the door when she looked up and saw Charles Hindershot Ellenshaw III walking past reading a report and eating an apple. The crazed white hair of the cryptozoologist was in its accustomed state of disrepair. His glasses were propped up on his forehead holding his hair in place, necessitating his need to read the report closely held to his face.

"Doc," Sarah said as she sniffed and swiped a tear away before it ran out from under the large glasses.

Ellenshaw, or Crazy Charlie as he was known to the other science departments, looked up startled. He stopped abruptly as Sarah reached out and removed his glasses from his forehead and then slid the wire frames onto his nose.

"Oh, that's better," he said as he smiled and then looked more closely at Sarah. "Thank you . . . my dear you are looking terrible."

"Thanks, Doc. Listen, do you have an hour and a half of free time?"

Ellenshaw looked at the report in his hand and the half-eaten apple and smiled crookedly. "It seems the head of cryptozoology always has an abundance of time on his hands."

"Would you take my class for this evening?"

"Your geology class?" he asked as several of the papers he was studying fell free of his folder. Sarah reached down and retrieved them for him.

"What instruction do you want me to give?"

Sarah stood and removed the crumpled folder from Charlie's hand and then replaced the papers. "Nothing as mundane as I had planned, Doc. Just regale them with your exploits in the Amazon, or in Canada."

"Well, I suppose—"

Ellenshaw didn't have time to finish as Sarah abruptly turned and headed for the elevators. He watched as she vanished around the curving hallway. Charlie shook his head, quickly piecing together what he thought was happening. Knowing that Jack Collins had left the complex, he thought for sure that was the main reason Sarah needed a break. So, with the apple clutched in his teeth and the file folder in one hand, Ellenshaw opened the door to Sarah's classroom and entered. As the door closed there was a group exhale of excitement as they realized that they would not be quizzed this evening on the factors determining the mineralized phosphorescent nature of geological formations. Instead they had Crazy Charlie and his crypto exploits. What better time to hear about monsters and aliens?

The Gold City Pawn Shop
Las Vegas, Nevada

Sarah felt the single car come to a whispering stop. She even heard the computerized voice of Europa announcing they had arrived at gate number two, sublevel three. The automatic cover of the car slid back and still Sarah sat unmoving. One of the security men, alerted at the pawn shop that a car had arrived but thus far no one had signed into the gate, greeted her.

"Lieutenant?"

Sarah finally looked up and seemed to be lost for a moment. Then she realized where she was. "Sorry," she said, "it's been a long day."

"Are you signing out of the complex?" the air force sergeant asked as he gave Sarah a hand stepping out of the car.

"Yes, I'm signing off base for the next twelve hours," she answered as she headed for the elevator that would take her up to the gate.

"Uh, ma'am?"

Sarah grimaced, stopped, and looked back, irritated that

her leaving was being delayed by one of Jack's former men. If she received one more look of sympathy from that department she was going to hit someone. "Yes?" she hissed.

"Lieutenant, you're breaking about fifteen different regulations. You know you can't sign out in that jumpsuit, right?"

Sarah looked down at her Group-issued military blue suit. She even had her ID tag still hanging from the pocket. She lowered her head when she realized she had to go all the way back and change into civilian attire. She started to return to the magnetized car on the single track that ran down the ten-mile-long tunnel far beneath the city of Las Vegas.

"Ma'am, we have clothing upstairs in the shop. It's in the locker room and you're welcome to it. Shorts and blouses is all we have."

Sarah looked up at the sergeant and nodded her head. "Thank you," she said.

"Going into town?" he asked as he escorted her to the elevator.

"No, I'm going to see someone."

The team had been stationed in the nondescript van outside of the Gold City Pawn Shop for the past hour as they observed the comings and goings of customers. One saw a small woman step to the door escorted by one of the large men from the counter of the shop. He opened the door for her as she stepped out into the hot night air of downtown Las Vegas. The man inside the Tahoe raised his small camera with the miniature telephoto lens. He snapped off several pictures of the small dark-haired woman. He noticed she was wearing sunglasses even though the sun had slipped behind the western mountains hours earlier. He watched until she hailed a cab and left.

The man removed the digital chip and then inserted it into the laptop computer. He brought up the pictures of the woman in short pants and a black blouse. He recognized her from somewhere but couldn't place her. He looked into the back of the van and waited for one of his technicians to give him some answers. The man examined the pictures of the woman and then shook his head.

"Nope," he said shaking his head. "She never entered the shop through the front. I don't know where she came from, but it wasn't through this side of the building. And we can see that in the back there is nothing but an alley, and she doesn't look the type to go strolling through an alley at night in downtown Las Vegas."

"Right," said the man in the front as he turned in his seat and examined the woman again. He shook his head as his memory failed him. "Send this on to Mr. Smith, and get a tail on that cab."

The technician in the backseat started talking on a set of headphones, and as he did he e-mailed the blown-up pictures to Smith, who was observing the house where Colonel Jack Collins was.

As the cab holding Sarah turned away from the curb, heading toward Flamingo Road, a tan Plymouth pulled out of the pay parking lot across the street and quickly followed. The tail on the woman was on the move.

One minute later, parked only a block away from the house under surveillance, Mr. Smith looked at the photos that had been forwarded to him from his pawn shop team.

"Well, it seems we have confirmed that all of our eggs came from the same basket." Smith smiled as he started to formulate a plan to finish what his team was paid to do.

"We may have just found our way into wherever this woman and Colonel Collins have been hidden away."

"When do we move?" one of the men in the backseat of the car asked, eager to get moving toward a more action-filled night.

"I think when this little darling returns to her secret hide-away, she just may have company."

The two men in the backseat exchanged looks just as the yellow cab pulled up in front of the tract home they were watching.

"Yes, indeed, it is a small world," Smith said as he compared the photo on the laptop to that of the actual woman stepping out of the cab.

Smith closed the lid to the laptop and then watched as the small woman headed for the front door of the house.

"Inform our friend in Langley that we have a way in to this mysterious lair. And we should have the formula destroyed soon." Smith was careful not to include the word *recovered*. He remembered the smoking corpse of Juan Guzman and what this material may have done to him. He knew he wouldn't touch the stuff nor would any of his team.

As the call was made, Smith watched as the woman entered the house, and then he looked at the driver.

"Sound the alert for the assault team. We move at a moment's notice," Smith said as he turned back to the man on the phone in the backseat. "And ask for orders concerning American personnel at this location and the pawn shop."

After a few moments, the man on the phone hung up and looked at the man who ran everything concerning the Black field teams.

"He says that the priority is the destruction of the formula. All trace of it is to be eliminated, and as far as collateral damage is concerned, he said you were supposed to be good enough to do this without killing. He suggests you do that. But elimination is authorized for self-defense . . . his words, Mr. Smith." The man added the last part quickly when he saw the brief flash of anger in the dark eyes of his boss.

The man known as Smith shook his head in disgust.

"Sometimes the people we contract out to have the morals and patriotism of a pig."

He reached into the glove compartment of the car, removed a handgun, and then pulled the magazine out and checked the loads. After reading the file on their main adversary, this Colonel Collins, he wanted to be ready for any surprises he may get from whatever the pawn shop was hiding.

"Okay, I want a flyover of the pawn shop. Get me thermal

images of the personnel inside. Mark them expendables and number them for confirmation purposes after the raid."

As the men followed his orders, Smith thought of the formula they were there for and the dangers that may exist in destroying it.

"Who in the hell would invent such a thing as Perdition's Fire?"

7

Vauxhall, London, England
Office of MI6

Sir John Kinlow listened as their man inside CIA headquarters in Langley, Hiram Vickers, explained the situation. The call was a conference session between a secure phone in Langley and three others in London—MI5, MI6, and the Defense Ministry.

"Are you saying that the formula actually still exists?" asked the defense minister.

"That's what's being reported," Vickers answered from his Virginia location.

There was silence on the three connections in London. Vickers was actually thinking that the three men had severed the connection with him.

"This could be a bigger bloody mess than we first thought," said the defense minister.

Sir John cleared his throat. "Mr. Vickers, you are indeed a kind and loyal friend to Her Majesty's—"

"Gentlemen, let's cut to the chase here," Vickers said as he was starting to lose his patience with the British old guard. "We can destroy the Ambrose element, but there could be collateral damage to American personnel involved in carrying out this rather touchy mission."

"Of course you can bill us for the agency's services Mr. Vickers, and you may include the overtime," the defense minister said.

There was silence on the other end of the line stretching across the sea to America.

"That was in very poor taste, Joseph," Sir John said, trying to calm the anger he felt through the phone connection.

"We're talking about the elimination, no damn it, the cold-blooded killing of Americans on their own soil, upon the shores of an ally state? That's what we're discussing here Minister. This could mean a noose for all of us. Mostly, I dare say, for myself."

"Mr. Vickers, how good is your field team?" the minister of defense asked.

"They're the best. But one thing you gentlemen must realize. If you kill American citizens, or military personnel, in this quest, I will not answer for your crimes. If I am caught, gentlemen, you'll swing on the rope right next to me. I want that understood."

"Sir John, what say you?" the defense minister asked.

"I think this is all madness. But what choice did our ancestors leave us? I vote Mr. Vickers the power to destroy the Ambrose serum—at any cost."

"I'm afraid we have no choice, Sir John. Mr. Vickers, please pass along instructions to your field element to destroy any and all British property in and around its current location."

"Yes, sir, I will pass on the instructions. Now I will pass on the thoughts of my boss. This is an expensive proposition that you have thrown our way, gentlemen. My superior believes it may be too costly, friends across the sea notwithstanding."

"Mr. Vickers, you are stammering like a reluctant stickup man stumbling over his holdup note. Can we get to the extortion part of this passion play, please?" the defense minister asked.

"Very well, I'll do that, Minister. Our price is 100 million pounds. That's the cost of doing business so close to home.

There you have it, gentlemen. I can assure you that the funds are appropriate for the action to be taken. There will also be a compensation package for any American killed in the operation. This will of course be supplied by Her Majesty's government for services rendered, even if we are the one killing these poor souls. This will cost you five hundred thousand pounds for each one of these unfortunates who, after all, are citizens we here at Langley are under oath to protect."

"How very moving, Mr. Vickers, extortion brought on by patriotism."

"Yes, that is a nice touch. You can never imagine the better feelings restored to those who order the deaths of others when they know the victim's family will have their needs met. After all, we are not barbarians here in the West, are we gentlemen?"

"Extortion is a light term where you are concerned, Mr. Vickers. I'm sure there is something other than British pounds that we can come to terms with. I am sure—"

Sir John heard the connection end. He slammed down his finger on his own disconnect button and then angrily stood.

"This is bloody well out of control," Sir John said as he turned to face his open window and the rainy early morning of Vauxhall. *They are actually going to kill American personnel over a formula that turns men into raging, cunning animals*, he thought as he placed a hand through his gray hair.

As he looked out of the window into the gray and diffused morning light, he knew that Jack the Ripper would raise his ugly head one more time, and now it was he and the other ministers who would have to cover up once more the mistakes of the past.

CIA Headquarters
Langley, Virginia

Lynn Simpson yawned as she signed off on a report confirming the death of Juan Guzman. Earlier she had spoken to her mother, informing her of Jack's decision to leave the service. She had been taken aback as much as Lynn herself had been when informed by Carl Everett from whatever location he was holed up in out in the desert. She had tried several times to call Jack on his cell phone, but had no luck in reaching him.

She heard the knock on her door. She looked up and saw her assistant standing there.

"I have the report on that trace test that was run earlier by Hiram Vickers?"

"Did we dig up the test subject's name?"

"No, but we do have the results of the target's route and the final destination where Mr. Vickers's tracer test was terminated."

Lynn folded her hands in front of her and smiled. "Well, I'm all ears. Where did the test terminate?"

The woman looked at the report and then placed it in front of Simpson.

"The test terminated at 1267 Flamingo Road, Las Vegas, Nevada. The home of an elderly woman who owns the house free and clear," the assistant said as she looked down at her notes so Lynn wouldn't have to bother with the official report. "Her name is Alice Hamilton."

Lynn lost the smile as the name rang a bell for some reason. She looked down at the folder in front of her and then waved the assistant into her office. "Close the door," she ordered.

Lynn quickly perused the one-page trace report. "I don't see a list of calls coming in or out of this residence, by either landline or cell."

"Oh, it's right here," the woman said as she opened a second folder and slid it across the desk.

Lynn's eyes scanned the report of listed numbers and then moved down to the unlisted phone numbers. Her eyes

saw one that looked familiar, almost as familiar as the name
listed as the home's owner. She read the numbers aloud.
"702-545-9012?" Her face lost all of its color as she pulled
out her own cell phone and hit her contacts list. As she ran
down her list of names and their phone numbers she immediately saw two that made her catch her breath. The first was
702-546-1190, Sarah McIntire. The next name and phone
number made her far more frightened than the first: 702-
545-9012—Jack.

Lynn Simpson, the sister of Jack Collins, stood from her
desk so suddenly she made her assistant jump. Lynn headed
for the door.

"What is it?"

"I have someone I have to talk to, and he better have a
good reason for tracking a government employee on my turf
without informing me."

Lynn, with folder in hand, left the office and headed
straight to the bank of elevators on her way to see a man that
was attempting to run an operation behind her back and in
her territory.

That man was Hiram Vickers.

Event Group Complex,
Nellis AFB, Nevada

The Event Group personnel from CDC watched from behind the sealed glass window as the robotic arm eased the
old and clouded jar onto the stainless-steel table. As the articulated claw released the glass, the technician operating
the Honda Corporation's latest robotic human-assist device
took a deep breath. Colonel Bannister placed his hand on the
back of the air force sergeant, impressed by how he handled
the unknown substance with the advanced robotic arm. He
was also impressed by the facilities Niles had managed to
finagle out of the federal budget—indeed, times had changed
since the colonel, his daughter, and the others had been an
official part of the Group's roster. Their equipment was on

par with anything they had in Atlanta, and in some cases surpassed it. The main reason for this he noted to the rest of his team, was the computer-assisted actions of everything within the complex. He understood that the system was called Europa, and he had never seen anything like it. It was far superior in computing power to the old system they used to have when he led the Infectious Disease Department at the Group.

As their team took a deep breath, the air force sergeant eased his hand off of the control yoke and flexed his fingers.

"Now, this is the tricky part," the sergeant said as he looked over toward Virginia Pollock who stood slightly away from the CDC team as she watched the procedure. "I will hold the container in place with robot assist arm number two, but the Europa-operated arm, number one, will slice into the beeswax seal holding the rubber cork in place. Only the correct pressure of blade against wax can sever it without damaging the cork—something only Europa can gauge correctly. It's far beyond the scope of human touch to consider trying."

"Yes, keep the genie in the bottle and us in control," Gloria said as she watched the procedure.

As they watched, the arm controlled by the sergeant took a firm hold on the center of the glass jar as Europa manipulated the second arm into position. Attached to the three-fingered claw was what looked like a shortened scalpel. As the stainless-steel device eased into the wax, Europa started measuring the exact thickness of the old and dried beeswax by the use of a laser that measured the density of the wax before the blade struck it. As the scalpel sank into the hardened organic matter, the team watched as its thickness was measured by the distance it traveled through the wax. As the arm started to rotate and start its run around the rim of the jar, the team saw the numbers start to vary as it spun around the seal.

"Actually, I am surprised at the almost exact nature of the placement of the beeswax. It's almost the same thickness all the way around the cork," Colonel Bannister said as the cut

around the wax was completed and Europa eased the wax
seal free of the jar. Everyone took a breath as the wax came
free without shaking the material inside.

The sergeant then started operating a third robotic arm.
He brought it down and used it as an assist to the first. It
grabbed hold of the jar at center mass to stabilize the container as Europa, this time minus the scalpel, moved across
the top of the now brownish-looking, cracked, and old rubber stopper. As the team examined the rubber cork on the
large monitor, they saw in intricate detail that the rubber
was brown with age and cracked throughout, creating another possible escape route for the highly unstable serum.

"Even with the wax seal, that rubber would not have
lasted another ten years. If this formula is as powerful as the
witness testimony described, there could have been a disaster in Mexico as these seals failed one by one and the serum
found its way into the groundwater or, worse, the Rio
Grande," Professor Franks, the eldest of the CDC people,
said as he examined the close-up view of the container.

The air force tech brought his microphone closer to his
mouth. "Europa, you may insert the tube at this time."

Without answering the command, Europa started to slide
the articulated arm closer to the top of the cork. Attached to
the claw this time was a ten-inch-long tube, only 2.8 centi-
meters in diameter. This was something the CDC people
had worked with many times. The small stainless-steel tube
was worth just short of a million dollars and was a piece of
engineering genius. It was actually a large syringe and had
opening and closing valves at each end of the tube. Once
inserted, the computer would have definite control of any
flow of fluid from the container, but what was more important, it could also be used to pump high-octane fuel into the
container for destruction purposes if the seal failed at any
time. Again the Event Group under the Nevada desert had
equipment that the CDC only heard about a few years ago.

Colonel Bannister looked over at Virginia Pollock. "Doctor, just how in the hell does Niles come up with equipment
others of us can only dream about?"

Virginia smiled and shook her head only slightly. She nodded toward the glass wall as Europa inserted the tube and then removed the arm. "Dr. Compton is hard to argue with when he states that this department needs something, and most people are smart enough to know that if Niles wants it, the country needs it. He's never, ever frivolous with the taxpayer dollar."

"Okay ladies and gentlemen. You are now in control of the sample. We can now safely insert your probes without exposing the substance to the air."

Colonel Bannister just shook his head as Virginia kept her smile on her face.

"Okay, let's get to work," Bannister said as the air force tech stood and moved away.

The secret of Perdition's Fire was about to be revealed.

Pete Golding sat in the chair inside of the clean room as the robotic arms behind the glass enclosure started placing program after program into the giant Cray computer system. Thus far Pete and Europa had examined almost every report ever filed by the United States Army concerning the punitive raids into Mexico from 1899 to 1917. They had not come across the name Lawrence Ambrose in any of those reports. They had only the documents they had uncovered concerning the ownership of Perdition Hacienda in 1917, and that in and of itself gave them nothing but the fact that Ambrose had really existed. The technicians involved in digging through the old Event Group material recovered after the Patton raid still had not come across any journals or chemical traces of the compound. He looked closer at a picture sent up from the vault area of several small brown bottles that still contained liquid of some unknown variety. Because of the clear color it was suspected that this substance could not be Perdition's Fire. It was sent up to the infectious disease area nonetheless for safekeeping.

Pete shook his head just as Niles Compton walked into the room. He received an immediate dirty look from Pete. Then he remembered to place the cover over his head in case any hair fell from his balding scalp, Compton gave Pete a return dirty look.

"How come you didn't freak out when Jack refused to wear the clean-room garb?"

Pete returned his eyes to Europa as she worked behind the glass. "Because Mr. Director, I was terrified of the colonel because he could kill me with that same dirty look," he turned and faced Niles as he sat in the chair next to Pete's, "whereas I am not afraid of you doing the same."

"Point taken." Niles turned and watched Europa as she placed the last of the new programs into her hard drive, which was the size of the entire rear wall of the clean room. "Nothing so far?"

"We came across a Lawrence Ambrose mentioned in a Ministry of Defense document generated in London in 1883 that mentioned a Professor Ambrose. But upon review we decided it couldn't have been the same man. The document was never a classified one and stated that this Ambrose was a citizen of India, thus the British Empire. It made no mention of him being an American citizen. And of course he couldn't have held both citizenship in the United Kingdom and the United States at the same time; it's against American law. It says he was paid an initial sum of ten thousand pounds sterling for the purchase of a shipping facility in the south of London. We checked, and it was an actual company called the LJA Import Company, and their main shipping revenue was generated by importing tea."

Niles nodded his head, knowing the name *Ambrose* was not a unique name in the slightest.

"So we moved back to this side of the Atlantic. Now Europa has started poring through diaries kept by United States military personnel during the time in question, particularly any documentation written by either George S. Patton or John J. Pershing. And I can tell by the fast movements of Europa's arms placing and removing programs that she hasn't hit on the name *Ambrose* yet. This is particularly frustrating. It's like searching for a needle that should be big enough to find in a field of haystacks. I mean, the man must have been a brilliant scientist in order to have conducted a genetics research project seventy years before the science was even invented."

"I see your point," Niles said as he watched Europa placing her programs. Niles looked down as he went deep into thought. "The man worked with flowers; at least that's what we suspect the substance is made from. So what do we know of Ambrose and his history?"

"Well, it's pretty straightforward. He graduated in 1881 from Colorado State University, or as it was known then, Agricultural College of Colorado, and later Colorado A&M. CSU records state he graduated head of his class in biology. The Department of Biology said he had earned an undergraduate degree in botany. That was not a very lucrative franchise at the time unless you went into food production or placing flowers in rose competitions, which we know now that Ambrose did not." Pete exhaled in exasperation.

"What is it?" Niles asked.

"From his graduation on, Europa cannot track his movements. He went to work for a small pharmaceutical concern in Dallas, Texas, where he lasted all of one year, and then poof, the man vanishes. His employment records from that time, and these were sketchy at best, state the man was impossible to work with; that he was always flying off half-cocked until he was terminated for insubordination. After that there is nothing until he shows up in Mexico, and Ambrose has only the briefest of mentions in the memoirs of George Patton."

"Nothing more specific from his days of legitimate employment?" Niles asked as he saw Pete starting to stress out over his not being able to find anything on Ambrose.

"Europa, list the reasons for the Ambrose termination of employment."

"Compiling data," Europa answered. It only took fifteen seconds. "Infractions listed by Killeen and Knowles Pharmaceutical Company are as follows:

1. Theft of company property— ten thousand dollars of investment capital for laboratory equipment
2. Insubordination
3. Embezzlement of departmental funds
4. The illegal import of apothecary supplies
5. The illegal import of Macleaya microcarpa poppy native to China
6. The illegal import of Papaver somniferum poppy native to India
7. The destruction of company records regarding the splicing procedural on above-mentioned plants for genetic-modification purposes and the destruction of company property and records of the invention here known as phencyclidine

"Poppies, and what in the hell is that last one?" Niles asked.

"Europa, give us the definition of phencyclidine," Pete asked.

"Phenylcyclohexyl—piperidine—officially developed in Germany in 1926 and first patented in 1952 by the Parke-Davis pharmaceutical company and marketed under the brand name Sernyl."

"Did she understand the question?" Niles asked.

"Europa, if this product was invented in Germany in 1926, how is this possibly related to Lawrence Ambrose in 1882 Texas?"

"Insufficient data stated for requested information."

"Europa, could this, this, whatever the hell this thing is, be invented at two different times on two different continents?" Compton asked, now getting as frustrated as Pete had been a few minutes earlier.

"Probability factor is 5–1 in favor of near simultaneous matrix construct of said formula."

"Okay, that's not bad odds," Pete said. "Europa, what is the purpose of phencyclidine?"

"It's original grant was for use in the anesthesiology aspects of its properties. Sernyl, after it was synthesized,

was taken off the market in 1931 for its adverse hallucino-
genic and neurotoxin effects. Sernyl was brought back into
favor after World War II and at that time patented by Parke-
Davis."

"Pete, what in the hell is that stuff?" Niles asked.

"Europa, is the drug still in use today?"

"Sernyl has been banned from pharmaceutical usage but
maintains a high level of illegal use."

"Europa, does this drug have a street name?" Pete asked,
playing a hunch.

"Yes, it is also known in street level illegal activities as
PCP or, more commonly, angel dust."

Pete looked over at Niles as he realized what Ambrose
had synthesized forty years before it was supposed to have
been invented.

"Europa, the two poppy variations you mentioned, what
are they commonly used for in today's society?" Compton
asked.

"Foodstuffs, but the most common usage is in the manufacture of diacetylmorphine or, in 1874, as the anesthetic
coded as morphine or, in today's street terminology, heroin."

"Okay, he was splicing poppies and creating heroin. Jesus, what was this guy working on?" Pete asked.

"I think Jack and the boys found out the results Ambrose
was seeking in Mexico a day and a half ago."

Niles stood to leave. "Keep digging and find out who
Ambrose was working for. He could not have financed such
advance research on his own. Find them and we'll know just
what in the hell he was up to. And pass what Europa has
formulated up to our CDC team in biology."

Before Pete could answer, Niles had left the Europa clean
room.

"I'll tell you what he was working on, Niles my friend.
He was working on a better way to control and kill people."

Pete was surprised when Europa commented on his statement.

"Probability of question is 98.6 to 1.4 percent in favor of
statement."

"Thanks. Now stop eavesdropping and get me some useful data."

Las Vegas, Nevada

Sarah paid the cab driver and with borrowed clothes on her back, she walked up to the front door of the house and past the two stupid-looking plastic flamingos Jack and she always teased Alice about, even though Alice always explained that they had come with the house. She saw the door ajar and there was music pouring through the open space. She adjusted her sunglasses and then tapped on the door's frame. There was no answer. As she knocked a second time, she realized that she recognized the song being played, an old 1960s song, at least she thought it was from the sixties. She just didn't have Jack's memory for rock and roll. The song was called "Nights in White Satin," by one of Jack's favorite groups of that era, the Moody Blues. She did remember that much, and she also remembered that Jack usually played the Moody Blues when he was, well, in a blues state of mind. The song was one that his father used to play when Jack was just a baby. He had told her many times about his father's music collection and how his mother had saved it all for him for when he was old enough to understand the depth of his father's passion for music. Sarah shook her head, wondering in just what state she would find Jack in. She pushed the door open and stepped into the small foyer.

"Hello?" she called out.

Suddenly Alice appeared in the hallway and smiled as she wiped her hands on a paint-stained cloth.

"I was wondering when you were going to be able to break away from that slave driver Niles," Alice said as she came forward and hugged Sarah.

Alice Hamilton pushed Sarah away and examined her face. She reached up and removed the large sunglasses and then winced at the bruised and swollen eyes. The bandage across her nose was plastered like a white strip of war paint.

"Oh, dear, what did those animals do to you?" she asked as she again hugged Sarah.

"It's nothing. I fell off my bike once and did worse to myself."

"I take it you fell off your bike going over a hundred miles an hour then, huh?"

Sarah laughed and then patted Alice on the back as she was released. "So, is Jack three sheets to the wind?"

"He started to go out that way," Alice said as she tossed the rag she had been using over her right shoulder, "but I found him something to keep him busy."

Alice turned and waved for Sarah to follow. When they entered the hallway, Sarah had to smile when she saw Jack down on one knee painting the mopboard at the bottom of the wall. He cursed when his brush ran away from him and the trim and swathed a section of wall. He quickly used a rag and wiped the paint away. He started to look around.

"That's right, I saw that, Picasso," Alice said with her arms crossed over her chest.

Jack turned and saw Sarah standing beside Alice. He tossed the brush into the paint pan and then stood. Without preamble, he walked the short distance and then picked up Sarah into his arms and gave her a kiss.

"Did you come to rescue me from the Wicked Witch of Southeast Las Vegas?"

Sarah smiled after wincing at the kiss Jack gave her. She looked into his eyes the best she could with her own damaged ones. She could see Collins flinch at the sight, becoming angry all over again at what had happened to her. She started to say something to try to calm him when Alice cleared her throat, gesturing for them to come into the kitchen.

As the three sat, Alice brought over a pot of coffee and turned to get three cups. "I was telling Sarah that you started out wanting to get your brain soaked in whiskey, but you decided against making a fool out of yourself."

Jack looked at the paint on his hands and then at Sarah. "She won't allow me one minute to feel sorry for myself."

Sarah reached out and took his hand. He squeezed it and then smiled as Alice placed two cups in front of them.

"I contacted my mom, and these two old women here concocted a plan for her to come to Las Vegas. She should be here anytime," Jack said, looking to see if there would be a reaction.

"Jack, I cannot meet her looking like this!" Sarah said, snatching her hand out of his.

"Oh, it isn't that bad, dear," Alice said as she poured the coffee, intentionally not looking at Sarah for fear of laughing.

"How are things coming along at the complex?" Jack asked as he took Sarah's hand once more.

"Jack, Colonel Farbeaux said he recognized the man who came to our rescue in Mexico two nights ago. He said he met him once when Henri was working contractually for various corporations. He says to tell you he isn't a very nice man."

Collins allowed his mind to drift back to the image of the large man and his team of black-clad rescuers. How Niles had denied that it had been the president that sent them across the border. He knew something was wrong.

"Did you pass this on to Carl?" he asked as he sipped his coffee.

Sarah looked from Jack to Alice, who finally sat down to drink her own coffee. She couldn't hold his eyes or those of Alice as she flashed back to her encounter with Henri Farbeaux. For a reason she could not begin to fathom she felt ashamed and guilty with the memory of the confrontation between her and Henri. And what scared her most was the briefest second of what could only be described as excitement. And that made her feel horribly guilty.

"I . . . I left in kind of a hurry before I remembered to talk with Carl. I'll call him now."

Jack thought about what Sarah was saying. He knew she would never have left the complex without informing Everett about a possible breech in security. How this man knew about his rescue attempt into Mexico was something Jack was worried about, now more than ever since he heard the warning from the Frenchman. And what would upset Sarah enough to make her leave so fast that she spaced out on doing her duty first?

"How is Henri?" he asked instead, watching the swollen eyes of the woman he had loved for the past five years. What really worried him at this point was the small fact that Sarah could no longer meet his eyes.

"He's recovering at his normal superhuman rate, I guess," Sarah finally answered as she reached for her own coffee.

Alice sat quietly, but she could see Sarah was in conflict about something. The girl was scared of far more than what had happened to her in Mexico, and Alice was wondering if the Frenchman had something to do with it.

Sarah placed her cup down and inexplicably started to cry. "You're not resigning are you?" she asked, unable to be the trooper she wanted everyone to think she was.

Jack looked at the top of Sarah's head as she lowered it to wipe away the tears. He then looked up at Alice who returned his look with a raised right brow, angry that Jack was putting her through this.

"I just need some—"

Alice saw Jack go rigid in his chair. Sarah heard his voice stop and how quiet the kitchen became. She looked up, wiping the last tear away. She started to ask something, but Jack held up his hand.

"Are you armed?" he asked Sarah. She shook her head, frightened at Jack's sudden change of demeanor.

"Kitchen drawer beneath the knife rack," Alice said quickly as her fear also rose. After so many years with the greatest spook the United States government had ever produced, Senator Garrison Lee, Alice picked up some of his habits of knowing when something wasn't right. And she knew Jack was just like her late Garrison.

Collins quickly stood and started to make his way to the kitchen counter when the rear sliding glass door burst inward and the front door came crashing in. Before Jack could reach the counter, he was quickly surrounded by ten men dressed in the exact same black Nomex clothing that he had seen two nights before. They leveled small but deadly look-ing automatic weapons at all three people inside the kitchen. Collins stood there angry that he hadn't caught the sound of the men getting into the house before they had time to strike.

"Colonel Collins," a voice asked as it entered the house from the smashed-in front door. "Please have a seat at the table as we have some matters to discuss."

As Collins watched, the large man from the raid into Mexico walked into the house. He wasn't dressed like the rest, with his face covered in Nomex material. He was the same as he was that night. Jack knew he didn't fear being identified, and that meant only one of two things: they couldn't identify him, or the three of them wouldn't be around to do so even if they could.

The large man with the clean-shaven face and combed hair came into the kitchen as Jack was roughly pushed into his seat. Collins looked the man over and then settled for just eye contact.

"Colonel, I understand your feelings. I have read your 201 file, what was available of course. I know your capabili-ties, so I will only state that the first bullets will not be for you, but the two lovely ladies sitting with you. So please, Colonel, no heroics tonight."

"You have my attention and my cooperation—for now."

The large man nodded his head and then looked around the kitchen. He spied the rack with the coffee cups on it and used a handkerchief from his sport jacket to place one on the counter. He stepped up to the table and with kerchief in hand removed the coffee pot from the table and returned to the counter to pour himself a cup. He sipped the coffee and nodded his head toward Alice. "That's the good stuff."

"What do you want?" Jack asked.

"Colonel, we could just raid the Gold City Pawn Shop, or maybe even breach the other security gates of your . . . your . . . what do I call it, lair, complex, whatever the case may be. But I am offering you a chance to save some lives here tonight. I wish returned to me what was taken from the hacienda in Mexico two nights ago. And I am willing to negotiate its return and not allow to happen what my men are very good at making happen, as you saw the other night. If needed, I will kill everyone inside your . . . whatever the hell that place is . . . for what I came for. Perdition's Fire must be in my hands before sunrise tomorrow. And before you ask Colonel, no, there is no dark motive here. I am here to destroy that which should have never been invented."

Jack didn't respond. He just kept his eyes locked on the man leaning against the counter, sipping coffee.

"We do have other contingencies, Colonel." The man placed the cup he was drinking from on the counter and then stepped up to Sarah who was facing away from him. "You have weathered your treatment at the hands of that pig Guzman rather well, miss," he said as he placed his hands on Sarah's shoulders. He looked at Collins as he slid his hand down the front of Sarah's chest. She winced at his touch, and Jack's eyes went from the man's face to his hand as it inched ever downward toward Sarah's breast.

"Alright, whoever you are, that's quite enough."

The man stopped and looked over at the very angry Alice Hamilton.

"Do what you came here to do and leave off with the cheap bad-guy antics. We've seen it all before and it hasn't worked yet."

The large man took a step back with a smile. "Just who in the hell are you people?" he asked.

No one at the table answered. Sarah bit her cut lower lip but held strong, even though for the first time in her life she didn't feel it. As for Collins, he was now glaring at the man in front of him. He hadn't muttered a single word.

"No matter," he nodded at someone behind Jack. The next thing Alice and Sarah heard was the sound of a crack and Jack falling out of his chair. He hit the floor and tried to rise back up. Another man stepped up and slammed the collapsing stock of his weapon in to the back of his head once more, and Collins hit the floor, out cold. Sarah jumped from

her chair and went to Jack's side. She looked up and through
the haze of her bruised and mangled eyesight started to
glare at the man just as Jack had a moment before.

"Quite unexpected, wasn't it?" the man said as he reached
down and took McIntire by the arm and lifted her free of the
floor. He shook her and then brought her close. "I am full of
the unexpected, miss. Now, if you want to see these two
alive again, you'll do what needs to be done, or you'll lose
far more tonight than just your two friends here."

"If you think—"

Sarah stopped as suddenly as she had started when another
man stepped up to the back of Alice and placed a gun to her
head.

"I do think, miss; I think I have gained your full support
in my endeavors here tonight."

Alice snorted and then laughed. "Have you ever noticed
these assholes have practiced speeches and smart-ass little
soliloquies for moments in which they wish to impress
people?"

The man smiled and wanted to laugh at the old woman's
bravado. "Jesus, lady, it would be a pleasure to shoot you
right in the head."

"Be my guest dickhead."

The man allowed his mouth to go ajar for the briefest moment and then caught himself. He pushed Sarah into the
arms of two men and then looked over at Alice.

"Please try something stupid. You will have the deaths of
many people on your conscience if you do. I admire your
spunk, but in my business ma'am, it gets your buddies killed.
This isn't a fictional setting where the colonel here is going
to come off the deck and save the day."

Alice smiled as the words were said. She could see that it
made the man uneasy. He turned to follow Sarah and her
escort out. He stopped and looked back at Alice Hamilton
one last time and then whispered to the man following him.

"We'll leave you one of the transport vehicles. I didn't
want to do this if I could help it, but leaving this man behind
is something I would later regret; I know this for a fact. I'm

afraid we have to kill them both. Wait fifteen minutes after we leave so we have time to get to the pawn shop and then meet us there after your duty is completed."

The man, with Sarah in tow, left with the others following close behind.

The remaining mercenary raised his hood and looked at the unconscious Collins and then over at Alice. He raised the noise-suppressed handgun and smiled at her.

She returned the smile with one of her own.

Outside of the house the men entered three Chevy Tahoes and then left heading south on Flamingo Road.

CIA Headquarters
Langley, Virginia

Lynn Simpson walked past the assistant sitting at his desk and strode straight into Hiram Vickers's office. She immediately saw the man wasn't in. She slapped the file holding the report on Jack twice into her left hand and then turned to face the assistant as he came up behind her.

"He's not in," the smallish man said looking at Lynn.

"Did he go home?" She took a menacing step toward the man and he retreated.

"Uh, he checked out, that's all I know."

"Then I guess my next stop is the director of operations," she said squeezing past the assistant. "I'm sure I can get the information I need from his immediate boss."

The man swallowed and watched as Lynn quickly made her way to the hallway and the elevator beyond. Then he pulled his cell phone out of his coat pocket and selected the correct number. "Sir, the North American Desk was just here, and it looked like she had the Cassini tracking report with her. She said she was on her way to the ADO's office. Yes, sir, let me see," the man said and then crossed over to his desk and the rolodex there. He quickly spun the reel and hit on the name Vickers wanted. "Yes, sir, I have her cell phone number right here."

* * *

Lynn was almost to the third floor when her cell phone chimed. She reached for the phone and saw that it was a private number. She shook her head and came close to not answering. She thought about Jack and Sarah and decided it may be one of them.

"Hello," she said as the doors slid open on the third floor. She stepped out and waited.

"Ms. Simpson? Hiram Vickers, I understand you were looking for me?"

"Yes, we have some things to discuss, or rather you, me, the director of operations, and possibly the director himself. Does the ADO know that you are tracking a possible confidential military asset?"

"Military asset? Why no, we just picked a person at random, or rather Cassini did."

"Mr. Vickers, if you think I'm going to buy that, you don't know me very well or the duties of my desk."

"Okay, I better come clean. Go to the director of operations and tell him what you found and he will explain everything. He's new to the job, but he has been briefed on this tracking operation. Then we'll sit down and discuss the test subject. How's that sound to you?"

Lynn said nothing as she closed the cell phone and continued across the expensively decorated foyer. She saw the door to her own boss's office, the director of intelligence, but his assistant wasn't there and the area looked closed down for the night. She started to walk to the right side of the large office area and saw that the director of operation's assistant was still on duty.

"Ms. Simpson, the director of operations is expecting you. Please go right in."

Lynn looked at the woman and knew she had never seen her before. She and her boss were both new to the job. She was an older-looking lady whose smile never reached anywhere else on her face other than her lips. As Lynn walked past, she quickly lost her smile and then raised her right, well-groomed brow.

Lynn stepped into the office and a man of about fifty-five or so stood from behind a large desk. His hair was gray and he wore half-rimmed bifocal glasses, which he removed as he stepped forward. Lynn and everyone else at Langley had heard about Samuel Peachtree's appointment from the Overseas Desk in London. And the placement of the man had infuriated not only CIA Director Harlan Easterbrook, but the president of the United States as well. The man's appointment had been pushed through by the Senate Oversight Committee on Intelligence, led by Senator Giles Camden, one of the president's staunchest enemies.

"Well, we finally get to meet," Peachtree said as he came around the desk with his hand held out. Lynn saw the expensive suit, the harmless-looking bowtie, and the way the man stepped gingerly, as if he were walking on a cloud. Nonetheless she held out her hand. "I apologize for this thing getting past you, but being new to the job and all that—"

Lynn shook the man's hand and felt uncomfortable when he placed his other hand over her own as his left hand shook hers. She didn't like the feel of it.

"There are protocols that cannot be overlooked, sir. My desk has to be informed, no matter how trivial your section thinks it is, about anything coming or going from North American soil." She released his hand and looked at the man's crooked smile, disliking that even more than his handshake. "And this could be far more serious than you realize. The trace test was on an American military officer of some stature inside of government circles. I have to inform Director Easterbrook about this."

"Well, of course you do, and I would have it no other way. As I said, I'm learning as I go; there was never any offense intended," he said as he again smiled, returned to his chair, and started writing something on his letterhead. "But before you do, I want you to be able to go to the director with all the information I have available, and the only man that can fill you in properly is my assistant director, none other than Hiram Vickers. He's at this address, and he's expecting you," he said as he folded the letterhead and then slid it across his dook toward Lynn. "He's going to come clean, where I cannot because Mr. Vickers knows the details far better than I. He's currently debriefing one of our people at that location. The homeowner is Mr. Dylan Weeks and he allows us to use his Georgetown brownstone from time to time for expedience sake."

Lynn hesitated in picking the note up. She looked the man over once more and as he continued to smile at her, she saw the vein running just beneath his temple throbbing. She returned the smile only halfheartedly and reached for the address.

"I'll listen to the why of it, but afterword I have to bring this matter straight to both the director of intelligence and, if she deems it necessary, the director himself."

"I insist. I want everything to be aboveboard on this. If not, I'll hold Hiram Vickers for you and let you kick him in the knee."

Lynn nodded her head and turned to leave.

"Have a nice evening, Ms. Simpson," Peachtree said. This time there was no smile.

It took Lynn twenty minutes to travel the distance to Georgetown where the address was located. She checked out at Langley at 1:00 a.m. and left the address and name of the man, Mr. Dylan Weeks, where she could be reached by cell.

As she pulled into the drive of the beautiful brownstone, Lynn saw most of the bottom-floor lights on. She saw one of Langley's vehicles parked in the drive and she parked behind it. As a precaution, she looked into her bag and checked to make sure her nine-millimeter Beretta was handy. She opened the car door with the Cassini file in hand, walked up the winding steps to the front door, and rang the bell. She rang again when no one answered. Then as she started to turn away, Hiram Vickers was suddenly standing in the now-open doorway. He smiled and stepped aside.

"Boy, you made good time," he said as he gestured for her to come in. "I'm glad we can get this taken care of so you can at least explain to the director our innocent intent."

Lynn came inside the very-well-appointed brownstone. The house was immaculate.

"Come this way, our man said we can use his study for our talk."

Lynn followed Vickers to a large double door. He opened one side of it and then stepped through. The room was dark and her instincts kicked in, but her internal warnings made it to the surface of her brain a bit late. As the lights came on she felt a hand grab her wrist as she reached into her bag. She dropped the file she was carrying as the nine millimeter was twisted from her grasp. She swung around to strike Vickers, but his fist beat her to the punch. She was struck on the jaw and went down.

"I guess this will be a lesson you won't forget soon." Vickers stood over Lynn and looked at her as she shook her head, trying to clear it.

He reached down, grabbed her by the blouse top, and pulled her to her feet, ripping the blouse material as he did so. Then he pushed her onto a large couch and she flew back until she struck something that kept her from falling onto the floor. She shook her head again and turned to see what was behind her. Her breath caught as she recognized the young girl from Imaging. She was lying half on and half off the couch. As she studied the young girl, she couldn't see any rise or fall of her chest.

"You son of a bitch," she said as she pushed herself away from the recently murdered girl. "You killed her because she did her job?" she asked angrily as she finally gained her feet, only to see that Vickers had replaced her gun with one of his own. This one had a noise suppressor attached, and it was aimed at her head.

"Curiosity killed the kitten as they say." Vickers looked from Lynn to the young Imaging and Tracking technician from the basement at Langley. "Mr. Peachtree said that she was expendable. Sad I know, but securing the country sometimes has its drawbacks."

"No matter what you do to me, they'll find out," Lynn said. "There are those that won't rest until they know the truth."

"I'm sure. Even though your kind can never understand it, there are elements involved here that stretch far beyond anything you know. You see, that's our real job silly woman, one that your bosses at Langley would never understand. It's the lengths we have to go to protect the American people. Everyone is expendable, Ms. Simpson, everyone."

Lynn closed her eyes and waited. Her last thoughts were of Jack and her mother. She wanted Jack to save her, but knew he wouldn't be there this time.

"Jack—" she started to say, hoping his name would calm her.

The shot caught her in the exact center of her chest. Lynn Simpson-Collins fell back onto the couch with her big brother Jack's name still on her lips.

8

Las Vegas, Nevada

Alice Hamilton never took her eyes off the intruder as he stood watch over them. She saw him glance at the watch on his wrist every few minutes. Jack started to move on the floor near the man's booted feet. Alice planned to try for the gun in the kitchen drawer when the man made the move she expected was coming. The mercenary had no idea how spry a woman she was at age eighty-seven. She could outrun most women half her age. Besides, if it was her time, it was her time, and she would gladly sacrifice herself to give Jack a fighting chance.

The man kept looking from his watch to the chair where Alice sat. "I don't know why you're smiling, lady. If you think you're making me nervous, you're out of your gray-colored head." The man reached over and pulled the Velcro straps from the front of his body armor, loosening it so his body could get some much needed air. Then he thought a moment about the threat the unconscious man at his feet posed, along with the old woman, shook his head, and removed the body armor completely.

Alice continued her smiling ways. She tried to keep her eyes focused on the man when she heard the noise. It was the most subtle of squeaks she could ever remember hearing. She cleared her throat, hoping that her and Jack's intended killer didn't hear the same thing.

The man looked at his watch and shrugged. He looked down at Collins as the colonel was trying to raise himself up from the floor.

"Well, it's been wild," the man said as he aimed his silenced weapon at the back of Jack's head. "Sorry I have to do this, but orders are . . . well . . . you know?"

As the flash of movement caught her eye, Alice only hoped the gun wouldn't discharge. There was a quick-sounding thud and then the man froze for the briefest of moments as his eyes lowered to the two steel prongs sticking through his chest just to the center of where his body armor would have protected him. His eyes widened just as Jack came fully to and staggered to his feet. He reached for the back of his head just as he saw the man look up and into his own eyes. Collins saw the two three-foot-long steel prongs protruding from the man's chest. Jack quickly reached out and shakily pushed the assailant's gun hand down and then removed it completely from his grip.

Alice, with her mouth firmly set, stood and rushed to the stricken and speared man and then slammed her fist into his face, sending him over onto his left side.

Jack's eyes went from the sudden movement of Alice's attack to the spot where the man had been standing. His eyes widened when he saw none other than his own mother standing there with a shocked look on her face. She was dressed in slacks and had a new blouse on. Her blue eyes moved from Jack to the man she had just killed. Collins was amazed to see one of the pink plastic flamingos from the front yard pushed all the way through the man's back. Its black plastic eyes were once more looking at Jack, but this time he didn't mind the look.

"I . . . I . . . I have to sit down," Cally Collins said as she reached for a chair.

Alice shook her hand in the air, knowing she had broken at least one knuckle and maybe two on the man's face when she had struck him. She also knew she wouldn't trade the pain for anything in the world. She then helped assist Jack's mother into a chair, stepping easily over the dead man.

Jack looked around with blood still running from the top of his head and over his left sideburn. He was still feeling woozy and knew he had better join his mother and Alice at the table.

"I . . . I . . . had a hard . . . time . . . finding your house," Cally said as she tried to look up at Alice.

"Well, thank God you did, Mrs. Collins, or Jack and I wouldn't have been here to greet you."

"Ma, what made you think of the flamingo?" Jack asked as he wiped blood from the side of his face.

"Don't you remember when you were a boy and you were scared to death of those things? You had nightmares about them . . . I'm not really making any sense am I?"

Jack reached out after placing the gun on the table and took both his mother's and Alice's hands in his own.

"Thank God for pink plastic flamingos," he said.

"I just wanted to be here to meet your girl. Where is she?" Cally asked worriedly.

Jack looked up and released both of the women's hands. He stood on shaky feet and then collapsed onto the table's top.

"Oh!" Alice said as she ran to get the phone. She lifted the receiver and dialed while Cally tended to Jack.

The United States government offices you are trying to reach are temporarily experiencing technical problems with their phone lines. Please try your call again at a later time.

"Damn it!" Alice cursed as she looked from the phone in her hand to Cally and then to Jack. She made a quick decision and dialed a special number she knew by heart after so many years at the Event Group.

Cally looked up in confusion as she ran a hand over Jack's face. She heard the words coming from Alice's mouth, but couldn't believe it.

"This is code 5656-01, Hamilton, Alice D. I need to speak to the president of the United States immediately."

Event Group Complex
Nellis AFB, Nevada

Gloria Bannister watched as the spectrograph started printing out the known substances that were used in the synthesized production of Lawrence Ambrose's chemical formula. As she read the printout she checked off the substances that had already been verified by the supercomputer Europa. She shook her head as she tore the printout away from the machine and then handed the report to her father. Those from the CDC crowded around the list of names, matching them perfectly with what Europa had already told them. Colonel Bannister also shook his head.

"I've got to get me one of those computers," he said as he looked up at the others dressed as he was. They all wore the same environmental chemical suit with hoods that attached but hung down the back, giving them a little breathing space. The chemical-genetic agent was placed behind two separate panes of sealed glass, and that was behind a steel wall that completely closed the clean room off from the laboratory on the seventeenth level of the complex. "I wonder if they sell this Europa thingamajig at Best Buy."

The seven biologists from Atlanta laughed as they surrounded the colonel.

"Can you imagine the advanced science this Ambrose used? I mean, splicing poppies together as if he were doing nothing more than breeding roses? This was impossible science for that time period," said Dr. Emil Harris, a brilliant man who headed the Viral section in Georgia. "The chemical properties alone would have made this man a giant in the field of chemical engineering."

"Yes, but what in the hell was his goal? What was this genius after?" Gloria asked as she relieved her father of the chemical analysis report and started going over it again. Something at the bottom of the page that the spectrograph picked up caught her attention: agent 00012—unknown. "What do you suppose this could be, and this, an organic substance that is unidentifiable?"

Colonel Bannister looked over her shoulder. "Maybe some sort of binding agent perhaps. Something to keep the chemicals mixed—who knows? This other, the matrix of the substance, looks familiar. Almost like a DNA strand. But that would be impossible."

"It's something," Gloria said, surprised her father wasn't more concerned about it. As she looked over the printout, she walked to the far corner and sat down while the others started talking about the properties inherent in heroin and PCP. They all knew that the two poppy species alone produced high-grade hallucinogens, but when spliced together what chemical properties did they produce?

As Gloria looked at the report, she happened to look up at the observation window and saw several people watching their procedures from the area next to the clean room. She saw a familiar face talking with the assistant director of this strange complex, Dr. Pollock. Will Mendenhall happened to look up at the same moment she did. Their eyes met, and Gloria found she couldn't help it; she smiled and then gave the lieutenant a quick wave of her hand. She was actually happy when Mendenhall returned the smile and waved back. Embarrassed when Dr. Pollock turned to see her schoolgirl gaze on the young black man, she quickly averted her eyes and looked down at the report. She just as quickly looked back up to see Will still staring at her. He nodded at something the doctor said and with one last smile turned and left the observation room.

"Gloria, shall we run the agent through the Agilent atomic spectroscopy? We'll destroy some of the formula, but we'll get a much clearer picture of just what we're dealing with here." The others nodded their heads in agreement.

Gloria stood from her chair and, with one last look back at the observation window in the hopes that Will had returned, went to the window looking into the clean room where Perdition's Fire was still sitting atop the stainless-steel table, held in place by the robotic arms.

"I don't think we should jump the gun here," she said looking at the simplified spectrograph report. "We just don't know how this will react to flame. And this other biological source, what in the hell is that? You're right, it looks like a DNA strand, and we don't know if the extreme heat will destroy it completely without getting it analyzed."

They all knew that when the formula was burned by the atomic spectroscopy, it would release a momentary burst of evaporated material for the machine to pick apart and analyze. The problem as Gloria was seeing it was that since they were dealing with an unknown agent as listed on the report, they didn't know what reaction the flame would have on the chemicals. It was a minimal chance of contamination she knew, but in their business a minimal chance could be deadly.

"Oh, I think we can safely say that it is statically speaking very unlikely this Ambrose created something that also reacts to heat. I mean the agent went through the spectrograph just fine, and that's almost the same principle. As far as the second unknown is concerned, we always have more formula."

Gloria Bannister bit her lower lip and then shook her head. "That was utilizing much less heat than the atomic spectroscopy. It's just an unknown factor in all this. I think we need to study, and maybe even postulate, just what in the hell this man Ambrose was trying to accomplish with this. We have time to find out, and coupled with his goal we may be able to see where it was he was going."

The colonel looked from his daughter to the others. They were on his side as they wanted to know exactly what made up the complete formula.

"It's my call, and I say let's go for it."

"Here, here," said one of the doctors. "I for one am certainly looking forward to seeing what this man has created and how."

"Okay, let's do it," Bannister said, looking away from his daughter's warning look.

Gloria didn't like the shortcut, but she fell short on taking a stand. The combined brain power of the group standing inside the clean room outweighed her by about ten thousand pounds in degree and letters after their names, so she decided to ride out the storm.

She just hoped that storm was not a hurricane.

Pete Golding was actually dozing at the clean room desk as Europa continued to cross-reference anything having to do with Professor Lawrence Ambrose. He had his hand resting on his cheek with his horn-rimmed glasses propped onto his forehead. He started to slip forward and the change made him awaken with a start. He scratched his head and then rubbed his eyes. He looked down at the half-eaten sandwich that had been delivered to him by the stewards in the cafeteria. He gave the ham and cheese sandwich a dirty look and then stood from his chair just as the clean room door opened.

"Dr. Golding?" the young man asked as he stood just outside the clean room door looking in like a curious child glancing through the windows of a toy store.

"Yes?" Pete said after stretching his arms over his head.

"Sir, I'm Scott Walton from Archives. I was told to give this to you."

Pete looked down and saw the battered leather journal and his brows rose just below the paper hat he wore for clean room purposes.

"This was buried in files also."

Pete stepped forward to look at the journal and his flesh turned cold when he saw the initials on the front of the leather-bound volume. "LJA," Pete said in a low tone as he reached out and took a rather thick and very old folder from the archivist's hand. He read the bold print placed there by an old-fashioned typewriter almost a hundred years before.

"Lt. Colonel John Henry Thomas—Department of National Archives."

Pete knew they had uncovered a great amount of material and he would have to start immediately because this was an eyeball job where Europa would be of no assistance to him. It was good old-fashioned paper-pushing detective work.

Pete nodded his thanks, closed the clean room door, and then turned and placed the found materials from one of the very first Event Group missions on the desk. He then pulled the microphone down and leaned over.

"Europa, I'm going to take a break. Continue to—"

"Dr. Golding, excuse me, but I have a vague reference to a Dr. Ambrose listed in a Scotland Yard report filed November 8, 1888."

Pete realized the time frame fit the earlier discovery about the Ambrose that owned the shipping company. They had rejected the possibility due to his profession. The company was mainly a tea importer.

"This may be the same Ambrose as the person rejected earlier."

"Would you like to see the Scotland Yard photographic report, Doctor?"

Pete shook his head to try to clear it of the fog of sleep. "Europa, where did you secure this report?"

"The Europa system is designed for computer mainframe penetration, Doctor, as you well know. The report is listed as an MI-5-1 coded secret."

That got Pete's attention. Europa had actually gained access to the secure system inside of Scotland Yard and retrieved a top secret file originated through the intelligence services of Her Majesty's government. What was most shocking was the fact that Europa did it all on her own without Pete's guidance. The Cray computer after six years in operation was learning to analyze data and move in many directions of tracking without being told.

"Uh, Europa, the Scotland Yard system mainframe didn't detect the backdoor break-in, did it?"

At first Pete didn't think Europa would answer.

"The protocols as set forth by Director Niles Compton, and yourself, Dr. Golding, are clearly programmed into my system. I would be required to report such an occurrence immediately. The system being utilized by the British government is far inferior to that of the Cray Corporation's standards."

Pete thought Europa, with her Marilyn Monroe voice synthesizer, sounded insulted.

"Just checking, no offense. Please bring up the Yard and MI-5-1 file please."

"Yes, Dr. Golding."

As Pete watched the main viewing screen, a document that had been catalogued and filed away by photographic means many years before came up. The head of the Computer Sciences Division stood to study the document. To Golding it looked like a security report filed by a man named Frederick George Abberline. Below his name were scrawled the letters *CPI*.

"Europa, any guess as to the letters written below that of the reporting name?"

"The letters refer to rank: chief police inspector."

"Makes sense," Pete said as he read the brief report directed to someone with the initials H.R.M.A.V. Pete read the words on the Photostat.

H.R.M.A.V—

Madam, on this night, 8, July, in the year of our Lord 1889, it is my sad duty to inform you of the demise of Colonel Stanley of Her Majesty's Black Watch. His demise came at the hands of the man known in certain circles as Professor Lawrence Ambrose. It is now my suspicion that Ambrose has left this country in favor of his homeland. I am also obliged to inform you that all material related to this professor's work has been removed to a location unbeknownst to Scotland Yard. Since the discovery of the body of one Mary Kelly in the early morning hours of last year, this problem in Whitechapel should

*have been resolved. This is the final report that will
be filed from this office on an official letterhead concerning the case mentioned.*

Your loyal and obedient servant,
Frederick George Abberline,
CPI, London

Pete read the letter once more and then a third time as he
reached for the phone on the desk facing the now-still Europa handling system inside the protective glass cover of the
clean room. He slowly removed the paper hat that covered
the thin coating of black hair that remained on his head. As
the phone buzzed several levels up, Pete reread the woman's
name once more—Mary Kelly.

"Charlie, are you still teaching Lieutenant McIntire's geology class?" Pete listened as his eyes scanned all the names
listed in the Scotland Yard report. "Good, could you come
to the Europa clean room? I think I have something here that
you may be able to help me with." Pete hung up the phone
and then studied the images on the screen more closely.

"No, this has to be a coincidence."

Twenty minutes later Niles Compton, coming straight from
a late dinner in the cafeteria, entered the clean room. He saw
a crazed-haired Charlie Ellenshaw standing and looking at
the large-screen monitor. Pete was pacing in back of Ellenshaw and looked up when he saw Niles.

"I think we found him," Pete said shaking his head. "And
you're not going to believe this one."

Niles placed the hair cap on his head and Pete shook his
head. "Never mind that; Europa is all finished except for a
few questions. You can erase the screen Europa."

"Yes, Dr. Golding."

As the main monitor went blank, Charles Ellenshaw
turned and smiled at Niles as he took his seat.

"Dr. Ellenshaw lent me some of his obscure history knowledge and helped confirm what we found. Europa, please
bring up the letter found in the archives of Scotland Yard."

"Yes, Dr. Golding."

As they watched, the photocopied letter was placed on the screen. Niles read the words and as he did Pete started to smile.

"Is this the same man that operated out of the warehouse we disassociated with the professor we were searching for?"

"Yes it is." Pete spoke into the microphone. "Europa, the name Mary Kelly; please confirm for the director Professor Ellenshaw's statement."

"Mary Kelly, the last known victim of the mass murderer known to London at the time as Jack the Ripper."

Niles had to sit down. "Who is this man who filed the report?"

"Frederick George Abberline, chief inspector for the London Metropolitan Police. The man in charge of the Jack the Ripper case," Charlie said, knowing the story from memory.

"And the person he sent this letter to?" Niles asked.

"Europa, verify and report on the initials of the recipient of this letter dated November 8, 1888."

"The initials are used for private communication when names are not permissible in official communiqués. The letters *H.R.M.A.V.* appear in many secret documents from the law enforcement and intelligence communities in various reports."

"The name?" Pete insisted.

"Her Royal Majesty Alexandrina Victoria," Europa answered.

"Ha!" Pete said loudly, making Niles jump and Charlie laugh.

Niles sat stunned.

"Queen Victoria herself!" Pete said even louder. "She knew our Professor Lawrence Jackson, or Jack if you wish, Ambrose."

"The warehouse?" Niles finally managed to ask.

"That was harder, but once we knew he was our man, not too hard to confirm. Oh, he was an importer of tea alright, and where in the hell does the best tea come from in the known British Empire at the time?"

"India," Niles answered sitting up in his chair.

"And what have we learned about dear professor Ambrose?"

"He was a botanist," Niles said, and then his face froze as the reality hit him. "Poppies?"

"Correct, poppies from India and China. Both species smuggled into London hidden in barrels of tea shipments," Pete said as he leaned against the desk.

"And what's the strangest part of all this?" Charlie Ellenshaw asked.

"The queen knew about Ambrose and what he was doing. That means her people knew what Ambrose was doing and didn't stop him."

"Now look at this," Pete said, "Europa, display paymaster record 191037462 dated July 1884 on the monitor, please." He faced Niles. "This is another surprise Europa dug up at Charlie's suggestion. It was an outlay for payment from the Ministry of Defense bearing this Ambrose's name."

On the screen Europa placed an old ledger document that had also been photocopied.

Payment delivered and signed for service rendered to Her Royal Majesty—Lawrence J. Ambrose, one million pounds sterling for investigation into military science on aggression.

"My God," Niles said. "They created a formula that transforms men into superhuman soldiers, or possibly a weaponized agent that would send enemy troops into a self-destructive and murderous state against their own."

"Or a dose fed to a soldier at just the right time would become what the old Viking tales called 'Berserkers,'" Ellenshaw said as he slowly turned and looked at Niles and Pete. Both men just stared at Charlie, wondering how he came up with this information on ancient legends around the world. When they shook off Charlie's observation it was the director who broke the silence in the room.

"Unbelievable," Niles said for both men. Compton then rubbed the bridge of his nose, raising his glasses as he did. "There's still a lot of speculation involved here, gentlemen."

"Yes, but as I am reading it right now, and until we get something that takes us in another direction," Charlie said wiping his glasses on his white lab coat, "I would have to say that Ambrose tested his formula out on the foggy streets of Whitechapel, possibly utilizing smaller doses than what was witnessed in Mexico. In essence he used himself as a guinea pig, and the whole damn nightmare was paid for by the queen's own military."

Niles stood and looked at the two scientists.

"And together they created Jack the Ripper."

At that moment a red light started flashing over the doorway leading to the hallway and an alternating tone sounded throughout the giant complex.

"A Code One contamination alert on level seventeen has been detected. All departmental personnel are required to gather in secure locations for possible complex-wide evacuation."

Niles's face turned white, as did those of Charlie and Pete, at Europa's announcement. Niles Compton was the first to realize what it meant.

"Oh, God, level seventeen is the biological clean room."

The Gold City Pawn Shop,
Las Vegas, Nevada

The black Chevy Tahoe was parked across from the pawn shop while the Black Strike Team waited to get into position. The plan was to hit the security gate hard and fast with overwhelming force to bring about the capitulation of the forces inside the building. The goal: to remove any threat from the security personnel stationed at the gate.

"I hope the men and women you utilize for security aren't the brave or stupid kind," Smith said to Sarah in the backseat as he pulled his cell phone from his jacket. "This could get real messy."

Sarah remained silent, not liking the feeling of being close to the large man. Her mind was on Jack and Alice, and that was all she could focus on. She turned away from Smith and looked out of the darkly tinted window toward the well-illuminated Gold City Pawn Shop. She could see at least two of the Event Group security staff inside. One was speaking with a young man who looked to be haggling over a guitar that was displayed on the north wall of the building. As Smith made his call he saw what McIntire was looking at. Then his eyes moved to Sarah's hands, which were folded in her lap. Without saying a word Smith reached over, removed her sunglasses, and tossed them on the floor.

"That idea that's running through your mind about breaking free of the car and running to warn your people, that, my dear lady, will result in a lot of needless deaths. We are going to destroy that formula no matter what it takes to do it."

Sarah looked away from the shop and stared into the man's eyes. Without replying to his threat, she turned back to look out of the window.

"Yes, we're in place. Are there any last-minute instructions or developments?"

Sarah listened to the one-sided conversation but felt Smith move his free hand over to her shoulder and once there, the large hand squeezed, letting her know he was in control.

"You seem to be covering your tracks well. I just hope this Simpson person doesn't lead to my Black Teams. Are you sure she is eliminated and won't cause a problem inside Langley?"

With the name *Simpson* and the word *Langley* spoken in the same sentence, Sarah froze. She knew Jack's sister was named Simpson, and she was in charge of the North American Desk in Virginia. She swallowed, hoping she was wrong in her guess as to what Smith was talking about.

"Well, it seems you do have a set of balls on you. I just want you to know that if this is discovered it could blow your whole operation right out of the water, and that would lead government sources not only to your door, but mine as well, and if that happens, nothing will stop me from killing you, supposed good guy or not."

Smith closed the cell phone and then pulled Sarah from the backseat of the car as his Black Team moved into place. From the far side of the large Tahoe he watched as a four-man team went into the alleys on both sides of the square building. Once there they quickly set up a transmitter that would send a burst of electronic jamming noise straight into the video surveillance cameras on each corner of the building. His eyes then moved to the large step van as it pulled up in front of the pawn shop. His fifteen-man assault element was now in place and waiting for him to enter the building. He reached into his pants pocket and brought out a small roll of tape. Sarah watched as he tore a strip off and placed it in his hand.

"This is your big moment. You can do as I say or die with the men inside of that building if they resist. It's up to you. Either way I'll still be the happy soul I am right at this moment."

"What's happening with Jack and Alice?" Sarah asked, her blackened eyes looking upward into the dark at the black shape before her.

Smith looked at his watch, raised his small radio, and then placed a small headphone in his right ear. He hooked the small microphone close to the corner of his mouth and smiled at the diminutive McIntire.

"Do as I say and in less than an hour you'll be back with them again. Do not act accordingly and my man has orders to kill both of them. Now, if you please?" he gestured toward the street.

Sarah was taken by the arm, and as he started across the busy road Smith contacted his men.

"Team One, fifteen seconds after we enter the shop you will initiate the blinding of their optic security systems. Team Two, at that time you will enter the area through the front and back doors."

Sarah knew the drill well and understood that Smith was receiving responding clicks through his earpiece telling him their individual teams were ready. She knew she had to do something to warn Jack's men inside the shop.

The two stepped up to the door. "Smile miss, you're about to see the best assault team in the world go to work— something very few people have ever seen and lived to talk about." Smith gestured for Sarah to open the front door. "And be sure to place your thumb properly on the pressure plate located in the center of the door handle please. We do need them to read your thumb print accurately."

Sarah cursed deep inside as she realized the man had figured out the first line of defense for the pawn shop. The scan would be read and the security men in the back of the shop would not be alerted to any trouble, especially from one of their own. She pressed down on the thumbplate, knowing that Europa was sending a precise rendering of the swirls and valleys of her thumbprint through her security system. She pulled the door open and as she entered saw the first of the Event Group security men turn away from the customer he was assisting. He gave her a half smile, nodded, and then turned back to his customer, not aware of the danger posed by the man accompanying her inside.

As soon as they were inside, they heard a slight buzzing sound as the electronic burst of energy from outside struck the security cameras on the building's sides and back. Smith quickly pushed Sarah to the floor and pulled the silenced nine millimeter from where he had it hidden behind his back. As he placed his foot onto Sarah's back, the security man reacted far faster than Smith would have thought possible. He had his own weapon out almost as quickly. Smith fired only once, catching the marine security man in the head, knocking him into the stunned and shocked customer. Then he moved the large silencer a few inches and placed another bullet into the young boy who had been inquiring about the guitar.

"You bastard," Sarah said as loud as she could, eliciting a sharp kick delivered by Smith to her kidneys.

Smith took a quick step to the left and saw the clerk behind the glass counter look up at the sound of the muffled weapon's discharge and Sarah's shout of anger. The two bullets flew down the crowded aisle of CDs and other possessions given up. The rounds struck the man in the chest and neck, dropping the air force sergeant in an instant.

At that moment his assault element entered through the front door and quickly started up the four aisles toward the rear of the shop. That was when a sharp tone sounded. Smith knew the alarm had been tripped.

"Damn it," he said, knowing that the security element had been far faster than he realized they could be. He gestured for his men to move forward.

As the black-clad men jumped the counter, one was taken down by a security marine coming from the back. A spray of red-colored mist filled the air as the shotgun blast removed his hooded head in a microsecond. Before the marine could turn the shotgun on the next man, three Black Team members cut him down. They moved quickly through the curtain. Sarah heard several discharges of automatic weapons that could only have come from security personnel in the back. As she flinched on the tile floor, she saw another of the Black Team thrown back through the curtain separating the front of the shop from the back. She head Smith curse at the fast response of Jack's men. Then she heard the muffled reports of several weapons as they finished the task at hand. Sarah shook her head as she was harshly pulled from the floor.

"Your assistance is needed in the back," Smith said as he pushed her forward, angrier than ever over the loss of three of his men.

As he and Sarah pushed through the curtain, Smith looked around and saw a small storage area and then the two security personnel that had opened up on the assault team. One of the men moaned on the floor as he lay in a pool of his own blood. Sarah closed her swollen eyes when she recognized the man. *No*, she corrected herself, not a man, just a boy. He was Albert Petrakis, a U.S. Army sergeant that had only been on the security team for a year. As he moved his head, Smith stepped over the boy. Sarah turned the sergeant over and cradled his head as Smith took in the back office. He made a cursory inspection for more traps.

McIntire was beside herself. She had never seen such ruthless behavior from anyone, much less Americans as these men obviously were. She was pulled up from the floor by one of the black-clad men, but she angrily shook him off, still holding the sergeant's head. The shoulder wound was serious and she knew if she didn't stop the bleeding the massacre of the security element at gate two would be complete. She looked up and saw Smith looking down at her with a bemused look.

"You had better shoot me too, because I go no farther."

Smith kept the strange look on his face and nodded, making Sarah think he was about to grant her request. Instead he nodded toward the wounded soldier. "Bring him along. I think he'll be the key to what's behind door number one." He looked back at Sarah as he reached down and pulled her to her feet and actually tossed her farther into the office area. Two of his men yanked the sergeant up with a ruthlessness she had never witnessed before. Smith passed by Sarah as she leaned against one of the desks.

The large man placed his silenced weapon into a shoulder holster and walked past the spilled blood of the sergeant but came to a stop when he saw that another one of his team was down in the back-office portion of the pawn shop. He angrily grabbed Sarah by the arm and shook her. "Before I leave here I'm going to find out just exactly who you people are. To have a security element that is capable of killing my men with such abandon, well, let's just say that I'm impressed."

As McIntire looked down, she saw the darts protruding from the men lying on the floor. The anesthetic projectiles had been exploded outward from a false-fronted computer and the facing of the large desk it sat upon. She could still see the smoke rising from the wood and plastic as the security man, who was now lying dead on the floor next to the desk, had triggered the booby trap that had sent three hundred darts into the Black Team's faces and necks. As they stepped over them, she could see the men were out cold and would be for hours.

"I am duly impressed. Booby traps and such a fast response could only mean your man Collins trained his men well." Smith angrily hit Sarah on the side of her head as he saw the red flashing light illuminating the room. Sarah went to one knee from the harshness of the blow to her head. She shook her head but refused to wipe the blood away from her slashed cheek.

The entire assault team was shocked when the synthesized voice of Europa sounded through a small speaker overhead. The suddenness of the announcement made the armed team jump and aim their weapons in every direction.

A Code One contamination alert on level seventeen has been detected. All departmental personnel are required to gather in secure locations for possible complex-wide evacuation.

Sarah was stunned and angry that the warning wasn't about the security breach at gate number two but about another emergency somewhere deep inside the complex.

"It seems your people have a larger problem than just a break-in at the pawn shop." Smith again reached down and pulled Sarah to her feet. "I think this could be rather fortuitous. You men bring the sergeant along." He glared at Sarah. "If you don't get inside, the sergeant here will take many more bullets to areas that merely cause pain. Then I'll personally place one into his head. Understand?" Sarah was pushed toward the wall. "I didn't want all of this damage, especially to American personnel, so that should tell you the seriousness of the matter at hand. Now my dear, shall we go see what all of the commotion is about?"

Sarah lowered her head but placed her palm on the disguised plate in the wall so the security system of Europa could read her palm print. As it did, a small false-fronted wall slid up and into its frame. Beyond the false wall Smith was amazed and pleased to see a set of shiny stainless-steel elevator doors.

"Now *this* is impressive."

Event Group Complex,
Nellis AFB, Nevada

Everett and ten members of the Group's security team were the first to arrive on level seventeen. They were greeted by the flashing red emergency lights lining the upper portion of the curving hallway. The Europa computer station was flashing green and the audible warnings she produced alerted everyone on that level to evacuate. Carl waved men left and right to viral contamination suits that were kept every fifteen feet along the wall. Carl moved quickly to the Europa station and placed his thumbprint against the glass. Europa quickly identified it.

"Europa, shut down the alarm warnings on seventeen; we can't think down here."

"Yes, Captain Everett."

As he looked around, the alarms ceased, but the red flashing lights continued as a visual warning. Several Event Group staff hurried down the hallway and Carl held out an arm to slow them down.

"Take it easy, nobody's dropping dead yet. Europa is routing all of the elevators to the center hallway and the far end away from lab 700-2."

The man and the woman, two people Everett recognized from the Biology Department, nodded their heads, gaining confidence when they saw the ex-SEAL giving orders. "How many Group people on this level?" Everett asked.

"I'm not sure. I think I saw Dr. Pollock earlier inside the lab where the viral alarm sounded," the thin male technician said trying to catch his breath.

"I know Lieutenant Mendenhall was here also; that's every one of our people," the woman added.

"Good, now take the elevator to the gymnasium; everyone will go there for the evacuation."

Carl watched the man and woman turn and start walking at a fast gait toward the elevator he just used. He shook his head and turned as one of his men handed him the plastic package with the viral suit inside. As he tore it open he heard a voice from about fifteen feet away. He looked up and saw Colonel Bannister and Virginia Pollock walking toward him.

"You don't need that, Captain," the colonel said as he stopped in front of the stern-looking Everett. "The spill is contained inside of the clean room. We have lost about three CCs of the material."

"How in the hell did this happen, Doc?" Carl asked Virginia, not trusting the opinion of a man that has had his status as a Group member deactivated.

"The atomic spectroscopy unit didn't burn the sample at the specified temperature. Instead of burning the sample to vaporize it, it only evaporated into the air. The protocol was right; they just didn't make the correct entry." Virginia looked over at the colonel with a shake of her head. "It seems our guests were in too much of a hurry."

"That's not fair, Doctor. We don't know your equipment as well as you."

Everett saw that Virginia was about to respond when he shook his head.

"I don't think the need is there to evacuate your facility. We have been through this before. As long as the room remains sealed, we can clean up any leftover particles using robotic means."

Everett looked from the colonel to Virginia just as Will Mendenhall ran up to the trio. He was soon followed by the other Dr. Bannister. Carl made a quick decision and then stepped up to the Europa terminal once more. He placed his thumb on the touch screen again.

"Europa, continue the alarm on all levels. Order the evacuation of the complex authorized by Everett, Carl C. Security 11789, code 1-1-A."

Virginia looked from Everett to the colonel. "We don't take chances with our people, Colonel. You should remember at least that. The captain knows what he's doing."

Everett lifted the phone next to the terminal and made the announcement himself. The protocol would have the four hundred and twelve personnel on base that night gather in the gymnasium and sports field for a head count, and then they would take the massive cargo elevator up to level one where they would exit through gate one inside the old dilapidated hangar to be met by fifteen air force buses supplied by Nellis.

"I know this is just a precaution, but it's totally unnecessary," Bannister said even as Gloria took his elbow and shook her head.

"No, we don't know the unknown element that was in that formula. If it's a fogging agent, we don't know what the lessened burn will do to it. We need these people out of here until we get that sample sealed and under control. We can utilize the supercomputer and verify it's under control," Gloria said.

The colonel was not pleased with his daughter's overestimation of the strength of Perdition's Fire.

"You're qualifying this formula as a possible viral agent, whereas we are not convinced."

"Dad, we have this gentleman," she turned and faced Mendenhall, "and the lieutenant's testimony that says it's more than likely a viral inhalant. That means any sample not cleaned up could be missed and spread."

"That's good enough for me," Everett said as he nodded to Mendenhall. "Will, take the doctors back to the lab and make sure protocol is followed. Have Europa and Virginia take them through it step by step with not so much as a period or comma overlooked."

"Yes, sir," Will said as he gestured for the two Bannisters to follow him back to the lab.

Everett faced Virginia next. "Doc, get this thing under control as fast as you can. As long as I have people on the surface, this Group's security status is compromised."

"Carl, get Niles to the surface. He's the priority. I'll be here, that's enough."

Everett knew his duty as laid down by Jack's new safety standards initiated not long after he took over the Security Department. The number-one rule, and Compton hated it, was to get the director out of the complex.

"Good luck, Doc. If you think things are going to go south inside that lab, get to the sports complex," he said smiling. "You remember where that is, Bronko Nagurski?"

"You bet," she said returning the smile.

Everett watched her leave to follow the CDC people being herded by Mendenhall back to laboratory number 700-2—the chemical and viral containment clean room.

Everett only hoped the expensive laboratory held up to its impressive name.

CIA Headquarters
Langley, Virginia

Director of Operations Samuel Peachtree angrily closed his door and turned on Hiram Vickers. He paced to his desk but didn't sit down. He made sure to reach under his desk and switch off the office recording device.

"Do you think that was low key?" he asked angrily, placing his hands squarely on his desk and leaning far enough forward that Vickers thought he would fall over.

Hiram took the anger in stride. "I did what was necessary."

"Those two people were not only citizens of the United States, they were fellow agents. How could you allow this to get to that level of dysfunction? All you had to do was follow protocol and inform her desk of the fucking test!" Peachtree angrily straightened and turned toward his office window, looking out into the woods surrounding the complex at Langley. "It's such a natural function of your office that she probably would have ignored it."

"Not her type. She's one of those people who happen to take her job seriously, thus we couldn't allow her to see we were tracking a possible American military asset."

Peachtree turned so suddenly that Vickers was impressed with the old man's agility.

"That is exactly my point, you idiot. She was good at her job, which was why trying to sneak this test by her desk was a moronic move! We could have explained it far better if a goddamn spotlight hadn't been placed on it."

"Regardless, the problem has been solved."

"May I remind you that our job with this new department is to gather corporate intelligence through the use of the Black Teams, not the killing of innocents? If you can't do that without killing people you work with, we obviously chose the wrong man for the job," he hissed as he glared at Vickers.

"If that's the case we better stop our Black Team in Nevada because they just eliminated one hell of a lot of American citizens for the same exact reason I did—self-preservation, Mr. Director of Operations. Sometimes the money collected comes with hidden costs," Vickers countered.

The director of operations managed to ignore the comment about money, as that was the dirtiest part of their covert operations—the gathering of wealth. It wasn't just for themselves for their hard work and patriotism, but because utilizing the Black Teams was an expensive proposition. The older man calmed visibly as he tried to put his house back in order.

"Now, this Lynn Simpson just happened to be a favorite of Director Easterbrook."

"You sent her to me in Georgetown. How was I to interpret that?"

"You idiot, I knew what you had planned; the point is you let it get that far!"

"Do you want to cancel with the British?"

Peachtree exhaled and slowly sat down in his large chair. "Of course not. Things have progressed too far for us to end up with nothing. Who in the hell would have thought that the CDC had a lab in place in Nevada? Order Mr. Smith to get this business over with and get out of there, preferably without anyone else dying."

Hiram Vickers stood while buttoning his jacket. "Have you a list of this Simpson woman's next of kin? We don't want someone coming out of the woodwork asking too many questions. As it stands she was ambushed in Georgetown by unknown elements and the technician just disappeared—happens all the time."

Peachtree looked down at a file on his desk and opened it.

"Well, the girl has parents living in Wyoming; they shouldn't be a problem. Ms. Simpson has a mother in Texas, no other next of kin."

"See, if you don't panic everything works itself out." Vickers smiled and then turned and left the office.

The director of operations watched Vickers leave and then looked at Lynn Simpson's picture in her file once more. He shook his head as he remembered the beautiful face of the young woman.

"At least she'll only leave behind a grieving mother and no one else." Peachtree closed the file and slid it away from him.

"Pity."

The Gold City Pawn Shop
Las Vegas, Nevada

The man talking with the four Las Vegas police officers didn't feel the eyes on him from across the street. Jack Collins ripped the bandage away from his forehead, not feeling the pain of the tape Alice and his mother Cally had applied earlier. He watched as another man came from the deepest reaches of the pawn shop to join in the conversation with Las Vegas' finest. Jack watched as another policeman examined the large hole in the wall on the left side of the shop with a flashlight and then walked back around the building to join his fellow officers. The two strangers were gesturing and laughing with the officers as if they had merely had a break-in at the Gold City Pawn Shop.

The employees signed a report and Jack watched as the police returned to their cars, shut down their overhead lights, and then drove away, being watched until they were out of sight down the road. The two men turned and reentered the shop, placing the *closed* sign in the door. With one last look around they locked it and pulled down the shade. It was completely understandable after a break-in to shut the doors for repairs. There was only one problem: Jack knew these men weren't a part of his security team.

Jack ducked back behind a large van, reached behind him, and pulled the nine millimeter from his waistband. The weapon had been given to him by Alice, and Jack had taken it with the knowledge that Alice was one of the better-armed elderly ladies in Las Vegas. Before he left the house he made sure both she and his mother Cally were properly armed. Jack pulled back the slide and made sure the weapon had a round in the chamber. Then he straightened and crossed the street after a short burst of traffic passed by.

In the twenty minutes Collins had watched the shop, he had only seen the two men inside the shop. He realized that the kids he had spent the past five years training for their security positions were all more than likely dead. He just hoped they had taken as many of those bastards down as they could. As he made it across the street, he slid past the overhead street light, made his way to the right side of the building, and slid along the brick wall toward the first of the two blast holes in the building. He stayed on the far side of the three-and-a-half-foot break and stayed against the wall, waiting.

He knew that the imposters would have to cover the hole eventually, and as he didn't just want to knock on the front door, Jack waited. It didn't take long. As the light inside the shop filtered through the man-made hole, he saw a shadow, and then as he leaned forward slightly, a piece of cardboard was placed over the hole. Jack reached out and with his left hand made a scratching noise on the makeshift patch the man was using to seal the hole. Suddenly the light inside flared as the man pulled the cardboard away. Jack almost had to smile when the mercenary stuck his head through the hole.

"Hi," Jack whispered as the man's eyes widened to the point of popping free of his skull. The momentum of the barrel of the heavy nine millimeter caught the mercenary

squarely on top of his head. He collapsed and Jack easily
pulled him free of the hole. With one look toward the street,
Collins raised his right foot and brought it down on the unconscious man's neck, crushing the windpipe and severing
his spine just below the jawline. Collins reached down and
pulled the man along the alley and then placed the lifeless
and broken body beside the Dumpster, silently covering him
with discarded cardboard and newspaper. He then returned
to the hole.

As Jack stood still next to the entry point, he listened intently. When he heard no movement he quickly risked a look
through the damaged brick. He saw no movement. Then the
front bank of lights went out, meaning that the remaining
man was in the back at the breaker box. He bent low and
squeezed through the hole, scraping his back against the
damaged brick as he did, but he wasn't feeling any pain at
that moment. As he entered, he straightened and heard the
lone man in the back call out to his partner whose job it was
to seal the holes leading to the outside.

"As soon as you're done, head down that elevator and join
the strike team," the voice echoed from the back.

Jack quickly looked around in the semidarkness and his
eyes fell on the silenced weapon that the recently deceased
man had been carrying. He reached down and retrieved the
heavy automatic. It was a Glock nine with a large noise suppressor attached. Collins placed his own weapon back into
his waistband and then made sure the dead perp's weapon
was loaded and charged. It was. He heard the curtain leading to the back room part and as he sped, the second man
came through with a mop and bucket. Jack stepped into the
darkened aisle. He caught the man's attention as he stood
straight, knowing he had placed his silhouette directly in the
killer's line of sight.

"You get the holes sealed?" the man asked as he leaned
the mop against the glass counter. The man stood still when
the figure standing in the aisle didn't respond. Jack realized that the man he was facing most definitely had years of

military training as he didn't hesitate in reaching for his weapon.

Jack's training was far better and practiced for many more years. He raised the silenced weapon and shot four times in rapid succession. The first two rounds struck the man in both shoulders, making his gun hand go numb and forcing the weapon from his paralyzed grasp. The second set of rounds struck him in the upper thighs, sending him crashing into the glass case filled with jewelry. As Collins approached, he heard the moaning of the perpetrator as he tried to extricate himself from the shattered glass of the case. Collins on his way past reached down and grabbed his collar, pulling him free and ruthlessly dragging him along until he was through the curtain and into the brighter area of the storage room. He let the man fall to the floor as he scanned the area like an automaton to make sure he was the only one left in the pawn shop. His eyes fell on the blood the man had missed when he was cleaning.

The blue eyes of Collins managed to lock on several things at once. The door to the rear office was open and he could see the damaged desk and computer where the anesthetized dart system had been activated. Then he saw the two army cots where the results of the booby trap were lying, unmoving. With a stern countenance he walked up to the cots and fired two not-so-silent rounds into the men's foreheads, making their bodies jump with the impact of the bullets. Collins was on automatic, and anyone that knew him would have realized that Jack could be a cold and proficient killer.

When he saw that the shop was indeed empty, he returned to the bleeding man who was trying to hold the wounds to his thighs with his two broken arms. Collins reached down and with one arm swung the man up and onto one of the dead he had just killed now lying still on the cot. Jack then looked down at the man, unscrewed the now, damaged silencer, and pulled it free of the Glock. His eyes locked on the man writhing in pain. As the wounded man

opened his eyes, they widened when he saw up close who he
was dealing with. He shook his head to try to clear the pain
that wracked his mind as Collins continued to look the man
over.

"Son, anything you tell me that doesn't have the ring of
truth to it will bring on pain such as you've never known.
Normally I'm not a cruel person. I treat enemies by the rule
book, even terrorists." Jack ejected the clip in the Glock,
pulled back the slide, and popped the lone bullet from the
weapon. He then tossed the gun on the floor and pulled Alice's weapon from his waistband. "But you are neither a
warrior nor even a terrorist with an agenda. You are a mercenary who gets money for wet work—a traitor." Jack leaned
over to make sure the man was hearing him. "I am a colonel
in the United States Army, and son, you fucked with the
wrong man at the wrong time."

"Colonel, I . . . I . . . was . . . am a former member of the
SAS. I work for men that want no harm to come to this
country. I—"

Jack simply reached out and hit the man with the barrel
of the nine millimeter, smashing and breaking his nose and
sending blood out in a spray where it hit Collins in his face
and shirt.

"The queen must be proud of one of her boys that would
kill innocent men and attempt to kill unarmed women. I
don't think she would approve of your job choices, son."

"Please, don't—"

The gun barrel again. This time it was on the left thigh
directly over the large hole where the nine millimeter round
had entered. "I talk, you listen."

The man could only nod his head as the pain from the
blow coursed through his system.

"Good. I have your attention then?"

The mercenary nodded again, tears streaming from his
eyes from the blow to his shattered nose.

"The man's name leading the assault, who is he?"

"Ssssmith," he struggled to answer.

Whack, a blow was delivered to the other thigh, bringing

a silent scream of pain as the man rolled to one side. "Smith, that's all I know."

"The lie meter says you're telling the truth," Jack said as he pulled the man back into position for further questions. "How many on the strike team?"

"Twelve," the man said, managing to open his eyes as the weapon was raised again. "Twelve, I swear! Your security team eliminated four of us!"

Jack closed his eyes for the briefest moment when he heard that his men had managed to take four of the attackers down. Then he opened his eyes and became that cold and calculating killer again.

"The woman that was taken, is she dead?"

"No, she was taken below," the killer said as he cried in pain.

"Your mission?"

"To . . . destroy . . . the formula . . . from Mexico."

Jack pursed his lips as the words were spoken. "Who hired your team?"

"I . . . I . . . don't get that information. My team is stationed in Arizona. We—"

Collins was done with the questions. He had enough experience in these matters to know that grunts like the man on the cot had no knowledge of the men pulling their strings. His business lay with the man named Smith. He placed the automatic to the man's forehead before his sentence was finished and pulled the trigger.

"Thank you," Jack said and turned for the back room.

Event Group Complex
Nellis AFB, Nevada

Everett knew he was going to have to force Niles Compton from the complex as he stood before him in his office. The large monitor was on and he was watching the procedures happening at that moment down on level seventeen.

"Virginia is now in charge of the complex, Doctor. You

need to get above ground and into the loving arms of the air
force, and if I have to call the president to get that done, I
will."

Compton looked up at Everett and saw him set his jaw. At
that moment he knew that arguing with the former SEAL
would be like arguing with his boss, Jack Collins. He angrily tossed the pen he had been fiddling with onto the desktop and pushed his chair back.

"I should never have allowed that crap into this complex," Compton said.

"I'm as much to blame as anyone. It was my duty and
Jack's to see what a potential hazard we had on our hands. It
was us who saw what this stuff can do. So quit kicking yourself in the ass and I'll get an escort for you to take you
through security at gate two."

"I'm leaving under protest," Niles said as he stomped toward the door. He waited when he saw Everett pick up the
phone on his desk to alert the gate he was sending Niles
through the tunnel.

"Your protest will be duly noted in the security log," he
said as he waited for his men to pick up the phone inside the
pawn shop.

Compton shook his head and saw the concern cross
Carl's features. He saw him hang up and then try pushing
the buttons again. Everett waited and then slammed the
phone down.

"I'm going to have someone's ass," he said angrily as he
turned to the Europa terminal on Compton's desk.

"What's wrong now?" Niles asked stepping back into his
office.

"No answer at gate two," Everett said as he slammed the
communication link down with his finger. "Europa, what in
the hell is happening at—"

"Alert, alert! We have an intruder alert on level three,
loading dock east. I repeat, we have a security breach on
level three, loading dock east," Europa said, interrupting
Carl's question. "All security personnel are required at this
time to report to loading dock east, transport rail."

Everett couldn't believe what he was hearing and Director Compton felt his face go flush.

"Maybe with all that's happening, Europa has blown a circuit," Niles said as he quickly moved to his desk next to Carl. That question was soon answered when the doors to his office opened and Charlie Ellenshaw and Pete Golding burst through.

"Captain, we think we heard gunfire somewhere on the upper levels," Pete said breathlessly.

Everett looked up and then went into action. "Get the director the hell out of here," he said as he ran through the double doors.

As the intruder warning sounded again, Charlie was the first to take Niles by the arm and pull him from the office.

"You know the drill," Charlie said as Pete took Compton's other arm.

"Damn it let go of me!" Niles protested.

"Sorry, the captain is a little bigger than you. Let's go," Pete said as the warning notice sent by Europa continued.

All around them the warnings blared.

As they hit the elevator in the large area where Pete's assistants normally sat and worked, they stopped as the sounds came down from above them and entered the office through the closed doors of the elevator, making Pete and Ellenshaw come to a stop while still holding Compton's arms.

The sounds wafting through the double doors were of gunfire and screams.

The assault was well coordinated by a group of men who had served in Special Forces units trained by the United States government. They were all patriots and believed deep in their souls the righteousness of the missions they were sent on.

After the larger of the tram system cars had transported the teams to the loading facility, it had only taken a brief moment for the two-man security team manning the dock to succumb to the assault team inside the first transport. Sarah cringed as the two men went down without firing a shot. The confusion generated by the biohazard alarms and evacuation announcement by Europa had contributed to the quick subjugation of marine and air force security men.

The two men had at least been spared. Sarah was so angry and felt so helpless that tears were rolling down her cheeks. The most horrible aspect of the initial phase of the assault was the death of the young soldier they had brought along to force Sarah's cooperation. Smith had performed the murder himself, placing two quick shots into the dying security man's head even as he sat wounded on the rear plastic seat of the magnetic transport. She didn't understand why he spared some and not others.

As Sarah was pulled from the car and pushed onto the concrete loading dock, she took a hard swing at Smith who moved easily away from her blow and then backhanded her once more across her face. Then he again grabbed her by the arm and pulled her into the complex following the team-by-team movement of his men.

"Is there a code to get into the elevator system beyond this point?" Smith asked as he slid into a heavy set of body armor.

"Kiss my ass!" Sarah shouted as she spit blood weakly toward the man who was handed an M-14 carbine and bandolier of thirty-round magazines.

Smith smirked, admiring the small geologist's desire for vengeance. He then scanned the large facility that housed the incoming freight destined for either the vault levels or various other facilities inside the complex. As the large man passed a crate of apples, he used the folding stock of the M-14 to break the wood covering the crate. He reached in and brought out a bright red apple and bit into it. He then gestured for one six-man team to cover the first set of elevator doors and then, as he chewed a bite of apple, pointed to another set of stainless-steel doors on the far side of the warehouse. He then tossed the apple away and, pulling Sarah along with him, walked over to the first set of doors.

"The target level is seventeen," he said into the microphone near his mouth. "It looks like we'll end up at opposite ends of the level, so Team Two set up from that end and wait for my word to cover us if needed. In and out in fifteen minutes gentlemen or it will screw up our timetable." As Sarah watched, Smith reached into his vest and brought out a small device. "How much security is on level seventeen?" he asked Sarah.

"There's a team of twelve heavily armed men on seventeen," she said with a smirk, hoping to throw a kink into Smith's plans.

Sarah tried to pull away as the elevator doors opened and the first team of six black-clothed men and Smith stepped in.

"Level please?" asked the Marilyn Monroe voice of Europa.

Smith smiled at Sarah and then clicked the on button of the small recorder, making McIntire close her eyes in frustration. He rewound the small digital recorder to the point he wanted. He then held it up to the small Europa terminal just beside the door and pushed the play button.

"Seventeen," Sarah's voice said through the electronic trap he had set for her.

"Thank you, Lieutenant McIntire, level seventeen. You must be aware there is a current state of emergency on that level. Please follow supervisory procedure for entry onto the affected level."

Smith smiled as Sarah grimaced in frustration at the way she was outsmarted.

"Level seventeen, formulas, serums, colognes, and after-shaves, all aboard," Smith joked as he pulled a fuming Sarah McIntire in with him.

As the first elevator started lowering on a tube of compressed air downward into the bowels of the Event Group Complex, the second Black Team waited for the second set of doors to open. They weren't stupid in their method, as they didn't want a surprise to greet them when the doors opened. They were broken up into three sets of two, covering the doors as the level indicator above signaled that the car was arriving. The one flaw in their coverage was the fact that they didn't know about the stairwell to the far right of the warehouse area.

Without warning and according to the "Use of deadly force is authorized for trespassing onto this federal reservation" signs they walked past with just a cursory glance, a security team of ten men led by Sergeant Jessie Sanchez, a U.S. Marine with ten years experience, opened fire on the men before they knew what was happening.

Sanchez had been in the process of securing the facility and, as protocol dictated they not use the elevators, had entered the stairwell when the security team on the dock didn't answer his calls. Without checking with Captain Everett, Sanchez fell back on the training he had received from Carl and Jack. Within three-and a-half seconds the six-man Black Team had been cut down with clean shots either to the back of their heads or to their exposed necks. The sergeant was the first man to stand from behind some of the incoming freight. His ears were still ringing from the unsuppressed gunfire as he examined the dead men on the floor.

"Clear!" he said loudly as his team also stood from their positions of concealment. "Security Unit 3-5 to officer on watch. We have intruders in the complex. Over."

Sanchez used his boot to kick one of the dead men over to examine him. He reached down and yanked the black hood from the man's face and stood as his radio was answered.

"This is the watch officer. We have gunfire on level seventeen. Bring your unit to level sixteen and meet Captain Everett. Nellis security has been informed and the base is now shut down."

"Roger," he said and then gestured to his men. "Use the elevator, we're out of time," he said as he ran forward and entered the car that was supposed to send the second murderous Black Team to join their comrades.

Once more, a battle was raging deep beneath the sands of the Nevada desert.

Henri Farbeaux was awakened by something he had heard while dozing. As he sat up in his bed he was reminded where he was by the clinking of the handcuff on his right wrist. He shook his head to clear it of sleep when he heard what had awakened him—the sound of the complex computer system announcing the emergency on level seventeen. The larger of the two security men used his radio to check into the security center. He listened for a moment and then quickly walked over to where Farbeaux was lying. Without comment he produced a second set of handcuffs, fastening the Frenchman's left wrist to the bed rail. All the while Henri watched the man with bemusement.

"Uh, gentlemen, I believe that fancy computer of yours said there was a biohazard alert. Do you think maybe—"

"Now's not the time, Colonel," said the large air force sergeant. He looked at the marine standing and watching. "You have orders to join Sergeant Sanchez and his team. They're securing the complex. Meet him on level seven with your body armor," the marine told him.

Without asking questions, the air force sergeant left the room.

"Is this necessary?" Henri asked, clanging both sets of handcuffs against the stainless-steel bedrails.

"Maybe, maybe not, but your reputation does precede you, Colonel."

"Oh, that again, huh?" he said with the ever-present smirk on his face.

"Always, sir, always."

As the elevator fell free into the airtight tube down to level seventeen, Smith tried to contact Team Two on his radio. He tried a second and third time with the same result—static.

"It seems your security element inside the complex reacts just as fast as your gate security," he hissed, finally allowing his frustration to show through his hard exterior. He charged a round into his M-14 carbine and looked down at Sarah who wiped some more of the flowing blood from her mouth. She took the chance and returned Smith's arrogant smirk. "I wouldn't be so smug miss; you're going to be the first one out of these doors." Smith was now convinced his Black

Team was in over its head. He had opened a hornets' nest of highly trained men, and if he could retreat he would. But now he had a possible hostile element in his rear. His thoughts on the situation were quick and decisive. He would continue on mission and destroy what it was he came there to destroy.

The elevator finally came to a hissing but smooth stop on level seventeen. Europa announced the location of the car as the doors slid open. Sarah was roughly pushed through the door first, followed by two men who covered the hallway right and left. Sarah turned and looked at Smith.

"Lies always come out," Smith said as he stepped free of the car with the other four men. "I guess your supermen can't be everywhere at once." He once more grabbed Sarah and pushed her against the wall. Before he could question her as to where the appropriate lab was, three people, two women and one man, came around the bend of the white plastic corridor in a hurry to meet the evacuation deadline. Smith pushed Sarah into the waiting arms of one of his men and then raised the M-14 and shot the Event Group man in the chest, making the lab-coated women scream and look up in shock.

"What lab has the emergency?" he asked, still pointing the weapon in their direction.

The two biologists saw Sarah being held by one of the hooded men. Then in an act of quick thinking the one nearest the wall reached for the alarm based at the Europa station. She only made it a foot before she was cut down by Smith. "I'll ask once more," he said angrily with the echo of his shots still ringing their ears. He was starting to think these people, whoever the hell they were, were all crazy, or they all had been taught to be a hero.

The woman with tears in her eyes shook her head. Then, knowing what was coming, squeezed her eyes shut just as three rounds caught her in the chest and head, spraying blood on the white plastic wall just as another two men in white coats came around the corner and froze.

"No more!" Sarah shouted.

Smith ignored her, turned to the two men, and shot the one on the right, closest to the alarm terminal. In the flashing of the red emergency lights, Sarah saw Smith aim at the other man who stood frozen to the spot.

"You better be sure, miss," he said to Sarah.

"It's the next lab over," she said as Smith grinned and then shot the other unsuspecting man.

"In for a dime, in for a dollar. They can only hang me once."

"Ahhh!" Sarah screamed and pulled free of the man holding her. She almost made it to Smith with her arms near his throat when he swung the carbine up and smashed her in the jaw, dropping her at his feet. He looked at his men and then pointed down the hallway in the direction the men and women had come from. With one look down at the unconscious Sarah, he followed the rest of the Black Team.

As they approached the laboratory area, they saw the warning lights and the flashing biohazard sign warning them not to go any farther. Smith waved the men down, moving his right hand to the right and left of the clean room doors. He managed a quick look inside and saw a black man standing next to a tall, thin, black-haired woman. There were seven others at some very large windows and they were watching something in another part of the clean room.

As Smith was about to step back, the black man wearing a blue jumpsuit that Smith recognized as the military apparel the dock security team had been wearing turned, each man catching the other's eyes. He recognized the man immediately as one of the men he rescued in Mexico. Smith quickly brought up his weapon and pointed it through the double-paned window. He gestured for everyone inside to raise their hands as the rest of his team entered through the unsecured door. The black man jumped at the first man through the door. He hit as a linebacker would and they both went down. It was Smith who quickly kicked the black man in the head, sending him off and over Smith's fallen team member.

"Next time I'll let him kill you," the Black Team member said to Will as he lifted himself from the floor. Smith watched the man point the weapon down at the black man's head and then Smith moved the barrel away angrily. "You afraid he's going to rise and come at you again?"

The man stepped away angrily and then pushed the tall woman away as she knelt to attend Will Mendenhall.

"Which one of you is named Bannister?" Smith asked as he took in the group of eight people.

A small and light-skinned black woman stepped forward but was pulled back by a large man in a white coat. He pulled the woman until she was behind him.

"I am Colonel Bannister. Who in the hell are you?" he asked angrily, looking from Smith to Mendenhall who hadn't moved yet. "Can't you see we have a situation here?"

Smith stepped forward and looked through the glass. He saw immediately what they had come to Nevada to retrieve. The old and weathered jar was sitting between three robotic arms. It looked as if it were still sealed.

"Don't even think about it," Gloria said as she stepped out from behind her father. "That thing can be airborne. We are dealing with an unknown element that we haven't identified yet."

Smith looked from person to person. "No," he said as he gestured for two of his men to enter the sealed room. They tried the door, but it wouldn't open. "The formula is called Perdition's Fire; it can only be inhaled or digested to be effective. The unknown element you are referring to is a little something our esteemed professor Ambrose invented about a hundred years before its time. The unknown is called Lazarus Mist. It's a compound that when added to liquid and exposed to air will fog or mist. My superiors weren't sure on the result, but it was listed and described in the good professor's journals. But we did see the results in Mexico with that stupid bastard Juan Guzman. The Lazarus Mist performed pretty well I would say in creating an airborne cloud of Perdition's Fire. Anyway ladies and gentlemen, we may have just saved you from uncorking that bottle and releasing a genie you could not control. Now, have your safety systems unseal the clean room please." He looked at his watch. "We are on a tight schedule."

"No," Colonel Bannister said.

"What is with you people?" He then aimed his weapon at the woman the large man was trying to protect.

"Europa, security override, Pollock, alpha 11-7."

Without Europa answering Virginia's request, the Black Team heard the click of the locks on the clean room door pop open.

"Damn, finally someone with a little sense," Smith said as his men entered the clean room. Smith turned to the others and waved them inside the room as well. He stationed two men by the door and gave them the eye, meaning no one gets in. "Ladies and gentlemen, I assure you there is no danger as long as you cooperate."

As they entered along with the four Men in Black and with Smith taking up the rear, the seven CDC men and women were confused as to what was happening. Only Colonel Bannister understood the gravity of the situation. Virginia was just buying time for Carl's security to react to what was happening. She remained silent as they were herded into the clean room.

As Smith watched, his men tried lifting the jar from the claws of the Honda robotic arms. The first man turned and shook his head at the larger Smith. Smith shook his head, reached into his vest, and produced a small black object. He clicked a switch and a six-inch blade emerged from its handle. He walked over to the arms and then, seizing the hydraulic hoses in his free hand, swiped the knife through them, severing all three hoses to the first arm. Fluid shot out of the pressurized system as Smith merely pushed the large arm up and out of the way. He repeated the process with the arm holding the base of the jar.

As he started to reach for Perdition's Fire, gunfire erupted out in the hallway. As he turned he saw the black man rise and once more tackle the man closest to the door, sending Mendenhall and Smith's man into the exposed corridor. He gestured for his men to take cover, but it was too late. Colonel Bannister acted first. He raised his long arms up and pushed all of his people through the still-open doorway. Virginia saw this and dove herself. Bannister then quickly closed the door and locked it just as sixteen bullets struck him in his back, sending his head into the glass inside the door.

Gloria hit the floor, turned on her back, and looked up just in time to see her father's face hit the glass in the upper half of the door. He looked in shock as he was shot in the back. Several rounds hit the safety glass, sending shards into the observation room and making the lone mercenary turn away from the action in the hallway. Virginia, with her football prowess still intact, sent her body in a headlong plunge at the man's ankles. He stumbled and fell backward, and she was struck in the face with hot blood as one of the attacking security team members placed a bullet into his hooded head. Virginia rolled and was soon picked up by Will Mendenhall who pushed her into the arms of another man. Virginia looked up and saw Captain Everett.

Mendenhall frantically gestured for the others to crawl forward out of harm's way. As they did, he reached down and pulled Gloria Bannister to her feet. She immediately wrapped her arms around Mendenhall as he threw both her and himself back against the wall as more bullets started flying out of the clean room.

"My father!" she screamed as Will held her in place.

Mendenhall just shook his head as he pulled the CDC doctor onto the floor.

"How many?" Everett shouted over the gunfire inside the clean room.

"There are four, plus their commander," Virginia answered.

Everett nodded and turned to the twenty men he had lining the hallway. He gestured for them to take up station on either side of the open doorway. Then he turned to Will and tossed him his headset and radio. "Get on the horn and have Sergeant Sanchez bring up an assault package. We need flash bangs and gas."

"Yes sir," Will said as he placed the earphone into his ear and made the call. "Then get to the Europa terminal and order the rest of the staff out of the complex. Tell them not to wait for the buses; get into the desert and stay there." Everett turned to Virginia and the CDC team. "Did you hear any names?" he asked them, covering his head as more gunfire erupted from inside.

"Smith," said a voice from their right.

Everett turned and saw Sarah as she limped forward. She was literally covered in blood. He ran to her and eased her onto the carpeted hallway.

"Jesus," he said as he used his large hand to wipe some of the blood from her head.

"I think he killed Jack and Alice," she said as the words threatened to catch in her throat.

Everett acted as though he didn't hear her as even more bullets came flying out of the clean room. Large holes stitched random patterns in the plastic wall behind them. Then he lifted Sarah's bruised and battered face upward.

"He's been dead before—he didn't like it much."

"Smith is the same man that rescued you in Mexico," Sarah said as she started to regain her senses. She saw Everett go blank for a moment. Then anger set into his features as he placed her against the wall.

"Goddamn it," Everett said as he crawled back toward the doorway. He looked up at Will and he nodded his head, letting Everett know that his orders had been successfully passed on. Carl then got as close to the doorway as he dared and placed his nine millimeter next to the frame. "Will, get these people to the gymnasium and then up through the cargo platform to level one."

"Captain, I think—"

"That's an order Lieutenant," he hissed through gritted teeth.

"Yes sir," Mendenhall answered with a sour look on his

face. "But I'm coming back," he said, daring the captain to say something to the contrary.

"Don't worry; I'll save pieces of these guys for you," Everett said as twenty more rounds smashed through the remaining glass in the double-paned windows above. "Will, get to a phone and get Farbeaux out of here. Tell his guard to put one in his leg if he has to to make sure he doesn't run."

"I'll perform that little task myself," Will said as he started herding the civilians away at a crawl.

Everett turned and looked at Virginia. "You too, Doc, take Sarah and meet up with the director. He should be out of here by now."

Virginia nodded her head and helped Sarah up as they both bent low and ran for the elevators.

Carl nodded at his men as he saw them ready to strike. He held up a hand.

"In the clean room, cease fire!" he called out.

"No, I think we'll keep up the Lord's work," came the reply. "We have quite a bit of ammunition to play with."

"Mr. Smith, the complex is now sealed. There's nowhere to run," Carl called out.

"I like that old song, never believed in the theory of running before," Smith said in his irritatingly smug voice.

"Then it will be my pleasure to kill you, Smith."

Inside the clean room Smith was behind the cover of the largest of the three robotic arms. He looked around at his men as they covered the only opening. He closed his eyes in thought as he seemed to recognize the voice coming from the hallway. He figured there was no reason to taunt the man about the murder of his companion in Las Vegas, so he tried to formulate a way out of there without getting himself killed. He realized that surrendering was just a slower way to make that happen.

As he opened his eyes and scanned the clean room, he looked up and saw the jar filled with the amber liquid.

One of his Black Team looked up just in time to see Smith

reach up, take hold of the jar, and then bring it down to floor level. Smith knew this could be his only negotiating tool.

"Exactly to whom am I speaking?" he shouted out into the hallway.

"Captain Everett, United States Navy," Carl answered.

"Well, Captain Everett, you seem to have an eclectic outfit here as far as I can see. There is an old rumor in the outfit I work for that said there was something like this little day care center situated in the desert somewhere. I guess some rumors are true."

"Surrender now, Smith, and I'll give you the grand tour."

"I think I may have another solution to our predicament, Captain. How about you give me and my men safe passage out of here, and in exchange I won't contaminate this entire facility with Perdition's Fire. Sound reasonable?"

Carl leaned back against the wall and mentally cursed himself for thinking this would be an easy situation. He waited for a few seconds and then leaned to his right without exposing himself to the open doorway.

"You of all people know what that would do to everyone, including yourself. So just lay down your arms and give it up."

Just as Smith was about to react to Everett's command, one of Smith's own men gaped wide-eyed at the jar Smith was holding and tried to slide a few feet farther away. Before he could move Smith shoved the jar into the hands of the startled soldier.

Smith made sure the man was stable enough to hold the jar, and just as he was about to demand once more the surrender of his antagonists, Smith's own eyes widened at a sight that froze the unvoiced demand deep in his throat. As he looked from the startled soldier's eyes to the jar the man held, he saw that the rubber stopper, cracked with age and with a new three-cc-sized hole in its top, was *leaking*. Drop by drop it hit the floor.

In a panic the young soldier reacted without thinking, dropping the jar not a foot in front of him just as Smith

started to back away. It shattered. Almost instantaneously
the fogging agent mixed with the formula and both agents
started to do their work. As soon as a massive amount of air
struck the compound it started to fog. Smith and the soldier
were the first to feel the sting of the mixture as it hit their
nostrils. Smith placed a hand over his mouth and tried to
stand and run, deciding that surrender would be far better
than the fate of Juan Guzman, but his boots hit the hydraulic
fluid that had been released from the hoses and he fell back,
knocking the air from his lungs. As he tried to reach for the
table over his head, his fingers found instead the blue set of
hoses that ran from the floor to the robotic arms. He pulled,
trying to gain purchase when the hoses separated from the
valve in the tile. A sudden burst of air, one that supplied
pneumatic power to the arms, sprayed onto the pooling formula, sending a large cloud of vapor toward his stunned and
shocked men, engulfing them and burying their black-clad
bodies in a veil of whitish-brown mist.

The screams of pain and anguish from what was left of
Smith and his remaining Black Team started almost immediately.

A flaw in the design of the Biology Department's fail-
safe system became immediately apparent. The system was
a separate entity from Europa, and as soon as the "sniffer"
inside the clean room detected the release of the formula,
the safety system went into effect.

Perdition's Fire had been released just as every door inside the complex except for the emergency exit in the gymnasium and sports arena shut down and locked automatically.

Sarah and Virginia were near the elevator doors when
Europa became aware of the second protocol warning of the
biohazard system inside the clean room. On her own Europa
and entirely under her emergency directive that was designed separately into her system by Pete Golding and the
onetime supervisor of the Computer Sciences Department
ten years before, Dr. Niles Compton, that order could not be
overridden without a code sent out by the president of the
United States—she had immediately sealed the Event Group

Complex to the outside world, literally cutting them off from any form of rescue.

Hell had come to Department 5656, and Jack the Ripper, a biologically created beast, was reborn. Only this time he was not only one but five supermen.

PART THREE

The Seventh Circle of Hell

Satan, having betrayed God, is himself trapped at
Hell's core,
at the sunken tip of the inverted cone he created when
he fell to Earth, cast out of Heaven . . .
—Dante Alighieri

9

The president stood silently at the window that looked out onto Pennsylvania Avenue. The street was clear of any protesters for the day and that was when he liked looking out at the quiet Washington night. He felt the Oval Office was most secure at that time. His visitors thought he was intentionally ignoring them, and the two men sitting on the two couches facing each other waited for the president to speak.

Harlan Easterbrook, the director of the CIA, sat with his glasses at the end of his nose and read the report from the man in front and opposite of him, Director of Operations Samuel Peachtree.

Finally the president turned and faced his guests. "And we have no idea the location of your agent?" the president asked as he sat on the edge of his desk and rubbed the bridge of his nose.

"No, sir. According to our records Agent Simpson checked out and went to Georgetown. We checked out the address, and as it turns out it's a model home that is up for sale," Easterbrook said as he looked up from the flimsy report that had been offered up by Peachtree. He handed the paper over to him and then looked at the president. "I know you had met the agent in question before, so when she came up missing we thought you would like to be briefed."

"I do know Agent Simpson, and my concern for her safety is of paramount importance, but no more so than any other American intelligence employee. Why isn't Ms. Simpson's boss here with you gentlemen?"

"The Assistant Director of Intelligence is currently visiting his counterpart in London, Mr. President. He has been informed about the absence of the North American Desk supervisor."

The president looked hard into the dull eyes of the recent appointee by the Senate Oversight Committee to the position of director of operations, Samuel Peachtree.

"She has a name, Mr. Peachtree, not just a desk or an assignment or a title."

"Of course, Mr. President, Miss Simpson," Peachtree said feeling the heat of the president's glare.

"Okay gentlemen, keep me informed."

With that the brief meeting was over. The two men waited for a word before they left, but the president kept his head down in thought. The two CIA men left the Oval Office.

The president took a deep breath, hit the intercom switch, and then mentally calmed himself. "Please send in General Caulfield."

A moment later four-star marine general Maxwell Caulfield walked into the Oval Office and greeted his boss. The chairman of the joint chiefs of staff stood rigid at the center of the office.

"Jesus, Max, knock it off and have a seat will you?" the president said as he tossed the pen he was holding onto his desk and stood and walked over to the couch opposite of where Caulfield sat. He rubbed his face and looked up at his own appointee from almost two years before.

"Max, I need your help with something, and I need you to keep it close to the vest and not ask any questions. Do you understand?"

The general matched the president's move and leaned forward. "Of course, anything; you know that."

"That group you think is just a think tank buried under Nellis Air Force Base?"

"The one run by that little bald fella that shows up here from time to time?"

"You know damn well who I'm speaking of so don't play games; it's too late at night."

"Yes, sir, I know of the rumors that have circulated inside the military for years. I first heard of it at the Academy. Everyone thinks we have secret bases and covert operations all over the country, why—"

"We have a problem in the desert, Max. We need an assault team put together that can not only pull off a hard job, but is able to keep their mouths shut once the operation is complete. A small unit if possible."

Caulfield looked offended. "My people always keep their mouths shut, Mr. President."

"No offense, Max, but what I'm talking about is beyond anything you know. For the first time in American history I am bringing a military officer into the loop on this agency. It exists, and that is all you will ever know, Max. Is that understood? There will be no questions, no official answers. Now I have to say this; if I didn't, the ghosts of every president since Woodrow Wilson, hell, possibly even Abe Lincoln, would turn over in their graves, and the ones still alive would crucify me and then throw my rotting corpse in jail. Which, Max, is the same thing I am now threatening you with on an official basis. I will have you skinned alive if this leaks from anyone under your command." The president held up a hand. "Think, Max, before you speak. This group is special and they have just declared a state of emergency. The complex they utilize has been attacked. Most of the personnel have been successfully evacuated, but there are over seventy men and women still down in that hole in the ground." The president looked hard into the general's eyes. "And it's one damn big hole."

"What size assault element is it we're speaking of?"

"Colonel Collins estimates no more than twenty, maybe less. But he also says these people are good."

"Jack? Jack Collins?" the general asked with his eyes growing concerned.

"Let's just say he's involved with this group and needs assistance in regaining control of the facility. That's another name you will forget about after tonight, General," the president said with a sternness he had never used with Caulfield.

"I need details," the general said raising his left brow after all of the threats were delivered.

The president went to his desk and returned with his laptop. Instead of sitting across from Caulfield, he sat next to him on the couch.

"Okay, Max, officially you're the only one outside of this office that will ever be told directly about this group. Some have guessed at its existence, especially after the Atlantis thing, and then the space shots, but no one could ever prove it. Throughout the modern history of this country they could never prove a thing." The president opened the laptop and brought up a file after he entered his personal code. "This is a layout of the complex. Study it and commit it to memory because you can't have any drawings for planning."

As Caulfield looked at the detailed layout of the eighty-seven levels of the Event Group Complex, his eyes widened. "What in the hell is this?" he wondered. The massive complex was laid out before him and he couldn't believe the scope of the construction.

"Max, I said don't ask. I'm breaking about a thousand laws laid down by my predecessors about secrecy where this group is concerned. I need you to come up with an assault plan to help Colonel Collins and his men. I need you to get my friend Dr. Compton the hell out of there. The operation is to be kept tight and small. You run it for me. Just an officer and as tight a unit as you can find. Who do you have in mind?"

Caulfield had a hard time drawing his eyes away from the underground structure he was looking at. It was shaped like an upside down bowl with a large stem coming from its center, followed by another inverted bowl, then another, and still another.

"This son of a bitch is a nightmare, Mr. President."

"I know, I've been inside and said the same thing," he answered, again rubbing his face in frustration.

"And we have to keep it tight and quiet?" The general didn't expect a response. He looked away and then glanced back at the tired and even grayer-haired man than the one who appointed him to his current position. "Thank you for trusting me with this. I knew that quirky little bald man was something, but running a joint like this? I guess we have to help save him, don't we?"

The president placed his hand on the general's shoulder. "Thanks, Max, I would hate to have you . . . well, dealt with."

Caulfield looked up after the president's small joke, but when he saw that he wasn't smiling the general turned away with his eyes a little wider and the threats to him that much more vivid.

"I think maybe you better save the thanks for the DELTA team I have to send in there, and please don't make me threaten them like you did me. I don't know if these boys would take it as well as I did."

"Oh, they would take it if I sent a regiment of FBI agents to their front door. Now, where are these gentlemen?"

"Right now they're at Fort Lewis, Washington, conducting their mountain training on Mount Rainier. I can have a team at Nellis in about three hours with luck. Mr. President, you said most of the personnel were evacuated successfully. Wasn't Dr. Compton one of those people?"

"No, he's missing, along with many others. They are cut off far underground." The president turned and faced the general. "Max, besides Collins and his security force, the people that work inside that complex are only thinkers—doctors, professors, and God only knows what else. They are the best people this country has to offer as far as brains. They need your help and the silence of you and the men you choose."

Maxwell Caulfield stood and removed his uniform jacket. He placed it on the back of the couch and sat back down to study the layout of the Event Group Complex underneath Nellis.

"I need a direct line to Fort Lewis in Washington State," he said as his eyes started roaming over the large gates that were the entrances to the giant complex in the desert.

"Get them out of there, Max," the president said.

The general raised the phone to his ear. "This is General Caulfield. Connect me with the JSOC immediately."

The president overheard the chairman of the joint chiefs of staff request the Joint Special Operations Command.

The JSOC and the DELTA team they planned operations for were about to assault the underground complex that housed the most secret organization in the history of the United States—the Event Group.

The Event Group Complex
Nellis AFB, Nevada

The three men had almost made it down to level twelve by the stairwell when Niles said he had to return to the office level up on seven. Charlie shook his head no and Pete just sat down and tried to catch his breath.

"If we go back the captain will shoot us instead of any intruders," Charlie said as he helped Pete to his feet in the semidark stairwell. "We had one job to do and we can't even do that."

"Look, I'm not leaving while I have people still inside the complex. Now you two can either come with me or continue on to the evacuation point, but I would prefer you come along. Pete, Europa could be helpful in what's happening. How many men are left here with the expertise to get her up to spec enough to help out Captain Everett?"

Pete shook his head negatively. He finally took a couple of deep breaths and looked back up the stairs. The distant sounds of gunfire had ceased for the moment.

"I haven't heard any shots in a minute or so. Maybe it's all over," Pete managed to say.

"Maybe, but why isn't Europa telling us anything? You of all people should know her programming. We're literally in the dark here," Niles said as he turned and started back up.

Charlie Ellenshaw looked at Pete and then nodded his head upward. "Well, the office on seven is ten levels above the danger on seventeen. Niles has a point; I really don't relish the thought of running out on the rest of them."

Pete took the first few steps back up the stairs. "Neither did I, but someone could have mentioned that just a bit earlier—like when we were on level seven."

The three men went back up the stairs where they thought it would be safe.

They were wrong.

Level Seventeen

The silence coming from the clean room was overwhelming. Everett didn't want to get men killed by rushing the outer office, knowing the killers of his men were one room beyond that. Where were Will and Sanchez? They needed the assault packages before they could chance a move into the room. Carl scowled and motioned for his men to stay down. He had to keep this Smith talking to know he wasn't making a move out of the clean room.

"Smith?"

There was nothing other than the moans of someone wounded inside the room. Then they heard a grunt, followed by another. Everett closed his eyes because he knew he had to risk exposing himself to gunfire from inside. Making a quick decision, he rose to his knees and raised his head to the shattered window above. With a quick glance he saw that the observation area was clear. He lowered his head and grimaced. Then he chanced another look. As he rose he quickly saw that the clean room was filled with a fog that was just starting to roll free. He thought he saw several shadows moving about. There were more screams of pain and then, not believing his ears, he heard the laughter of not only one but several men from inside the clouded and fogged clean room. Everett quickly ducked back down, not believing what he had just seen. It was the same fog that had engulfed Guzman and his men at the hacienda.

"We can't wait for the assault packages," he called out to the twenty men lining the wall. "When I give the word, we give those bastards everything we have."

The ten men on the right and the ten on the left gave him the thumbs up. Everett quickly noted the twenty weapons his men had. Most were from the smallest of the three armories located in the Security Department, not the heavier-caliber weapons in the main armory down on level forty. The ones his men were armed with were light M-14 carbines, the small version of the M-16. He counted four shotguns in the mix, and they weren't the solid-shot rounds he would have preferred, but double-ought buckshot. He knew that would have to do.

"One—two—three—now!" Everett shouted.

The men as one rose ten on the left and ten on the right with Carl taking up the middle ground with his nine millimeter. The opening salvo was so fierce that each man couldn't believe anything could live through it. The weapons' rounds ricocheted off the robotic arm and smashed through any remaining glass inside the clean room. As Everett emptied his Beretta into the fogged-up room, he heard the discharge of the four shotguns. As the rounds and pellets were blasted into the clean room, Carl could see the streaking rounds create eddies and rolling fog as they sliced through the mist.

"Cease fire," Everett called out, but as he did he saw one of his sergeants, a marine, start to inch toward the door. "No, hold back!"

The sergeant started to take a step backward when a large hand pierced the fog that now covered the entire observation room. One minute the man was there, the next he was gone. Then they heard the scream and most chilling of all, more laughter. One laugh was joined by many more. The screaming stopped abruptly, but the laughing continued. As Everett took in his men he could see the unsettling effect the situation was having. They were looking to him for the strength he usually possessed.

"Open fire!" he called again.

This time the barrage was intense, and for the first time they heard other screams of pain as they were finally striking something other than glass, steel, or plastic. The men were firing and dropping empty magazines at a furious rate until Everett called a cease-fire yet again.

"Smith!" Everett yelled as he waved three men away from the fog that was starting to roll out of the observation room and beginning to touch the carpeted floor in the hallway.

"Yes?" came the deep, unnatural voice.

That was enough for Carl. He had heard the same change come over Guzman in Mexico.

"You ten men, get to the stairwell and down to the main armory on twenty," he said to the men on his right. "You ten, come with me. We can't fight this with what we have."

For the first time ever Captain Everett saw hesitation in his men.

"Move!" he ordered as he quickly turned right and started for the far stairwell as the first team made a dash for the closest elevator and the stairwell doors next to it.

As they moved, something crashed through the plastic-and-concrete-reinforced wall. It was huge, and as the last man passed, he was taken in the arms of a man with torn, black-colored clothing. The security man was pulled inside and his screaming was heard in the ears of the men that were making a run for the stairwells.

Everett managed a look back to see three more of the transformed Men in Black as they burst through the fog with a childish-like glee of laughter and animalistic roars. As Everett forced his nine remaining men in through the stairwell opening, he saw a much larger man step out of the fog and into the hallway. His eyes locked with the altered orbital

structure of the man he had met in Mexico. As Everett
watched, the man's four men spread out and went in opposite directions, two coming at him and his team, the other
two heading in the opposite direction.

Carl could see that their firing hadn't been in vain as
blood was coursing down the bodies of the men who had
grown so much that they had broken free of their body armor and most of their clothing. Everett quickly aimed his
nine millimeter at the head of the beast he thought was
Smith and fired five quick shots in succession at the man's
head. The creature Smith had become smiled even as he saw
Everett aim his weapon and ducked quickly back into the
fog bank now moving like a rolling wave into the hallway.
He remembered the description of the formula and how it
may boost the IQ of the user, or guinea pig, if it was ingested.
With that thought, he didn't wait to see if he had hit anything. He turned and entered the stairwell and started the
retreat back into the depths of the Event Group Complex.

Behind them two of Smith's men, their teeth elongated
and with both drooling spittle, started convulsing as even
more of Perdition's Fire was inhaled. Then as one they
started bashing their ham-sized fists into the walls, creating
giant holes with each blow. Farther down the hallway as
Smith once more rose from the fog laced with Perdition's
Fire, he saw what the two men were doing and nodded his
massive head and laughed as he and the other two started to
repeat what the first men were doing. They needed to get
into the walls and the spaces behind them so they could
control the complex from directions its defenders would
never believe possible. The first two broke through to the
empty and nonfunctioning elevator shaft at the far end of the
hallway, even as Smith started laughing uncontrollably as
his men were tearing into the walls like they were papier-
mâché.

The Security Department had lost the first round with
Lawrence Ambrose's chemically improved soldiers, with
four security personnel dead and level seventeen lost.

* * *

On level eight, Niles stopped to get some air into his lungs. It was right about then that he regretted excusing all officers and supervisors from the intramural activities such as the football game they watched just three days ago. As he sat down on one of the steel risers to catch his breath, he was soon joined by the other two scientists that could have used a prescription for exercise as both Pete and Charlie virtually collapsed on the steps just below him.

"Did you hear that gunfire a minute ago?" Charlie asked as he leaned against the sealed elevator tube that ran along the stairwell. "That was a serious firefight."

"I wouldn't know a serious one from two gang members banging it out on a street corner," Pete said as he reached up on his chest and felt his racing heart.

"Pete, why is Europa off-line? The warning lights have stopped and she hasn't made any announcements about the evacuation since we started back up the stairs."

Pete managed to look up at the director. They were all soaked with sweat because one of Europa's last commands was to shut down the air conditioning systems because of the threat of spreading the contaminate to other levels.

"When the intruder alarm was sounded, Europa had programming instructions to shut down everything so she cannot be compromised by the intruders. A serious programming error by yours truly I'm afraid. I just couldn't fathom any scenario where I could not override any of her protocols." Pete looked away. "I'm sorry."

Niles reached down and patted Pete on the back as he rose from the stair he had been resting on.

"Well, that's another reason for returning to the office level. You can get her going once you reach the computer center, right?"

"You bet I can, as long as nothing interferes once we get there."

The white-haired Charlie Ellenshaw was still leaning against the steel and plastic tube of one of the eighteen different elevator shafts when he thought he felt something inside of the sealed tube the elevators rode on with compressed air. He removed his glasses and tried not to breathe for a moment as he listened. He shushed Niles and Pete as he placed his ear closer to the tube.

"Pete, Europa shut down everything you said?"

Pete saw what Ellenshaw was doing and nodded his head. "The elevators were the first thing cut off after the intruder alarm sounded, Charlie."

Ellenshaw leaned back onto the stairwell. "Uh, maybe we better get to the next level because something seems to be coming this way—it's noisy and very much in a hurry."

Pete placed his ear to the tube and listened as Charlie shot up a few steps, took Niles by the arm, and started pushing him up the remaining stairs. As Golding listened he could hear grunting coming through the round tube that activated the elevator system just like an everyday drive-through bank deposit tube. His eyes widened when he heard the impact of something as it traveled upward. Pete wondered if something was in the tube but didn't wait for an answer as his frightened imagination produced any number of possibilities after Captain Everett's description of the nightmare in Mexico. He started running after Niles and Charlie.

"Oh, this is bad," Pete said as he tried to catch up with the suddenly fast-moving director and cryptozoologist.

Virginia, Mendenhall, Gloria, and Sarah were having the same problems getting down to level thirty-four where they could evacuate. Sarah was just now getting her senses back and refused to slow the others down. She leaned against the stairwell wall and wiped the last of her bleeding wound to the top of her head away. Virginia again ripped part of her lab coat to dab at the large cut in Sarah's scalp.

"Girl, you're not doing too well the last few days, are you?" Virginia said, trying not to hurt the small geologist anymore than needed.

Sarah looked up with her swollen and blackened eyes and touched the large gash on her cheek. "I have had far better weeks."

"Sarah, is what you said about the colonel true?" Will

asked as he placed an arm around the still-sobbing Gloria Bannister.

"I don't know, Will. When I was taken Jack was still alive, but these men are ruthless."

"Do you think you can get to level thirty-four from here?" Mendenhall asked as he pulled Gloria's arms from around him where she had been holding on to him with a death grip.

Sarah and Virginia looked at him at the same time. Sarah removed the blood-stained rag from Virginia's hand and glared at Will.

"We've already been separated from everyone else, and in case you didn't hear what I heard, Carl has his hands full up on seventeen. So consider that if you want to get yourself into the fight, because we're going to go with you if you attempt to leave. We follow orders remember?"

From somewhere high above them they heard a crash and a moment later several large chunks of plastic and concrete flew past them on the stairwell. Each person standing on the stairs ventured to look up into the darkness over their heads. That was when they heard loud, very heavy footsteps on the steel steps several levels up.

"What in the hell is that?" Virginia asked out loud.

"I don't know, but it doesn't sound like kids playing on the stairs," Sarah said as she tried to penetrate the darkness with her damaged eyes.

Suddenly the stairwell was filled with an animalistic roar that reverberated off the concrete walls. The sound vibrated the steel stairs beneath their feet and shook the handrails.

"Oh, shit," Will hissed as he started pushing the women before him down the stairs. "I've heard that before and I didn't like it much then either!"

The four people started their flight down the stairs and just hoped beyond reason that unlike the regular elevators, the cargo elevator was up and working.

That was when the lights went out.

As Everett and nine men ran upward after being cut off by two of Smith's enraged giants, he heard something breaking

into the elevator tube on seventeen that was even more terrifying than the roars, laughter, and screams of the transformed men. He called a halt to their flight so he could listen
more clearly. His men came to a stop and immediately went
into a defensive position with weapons aimed up and down
the semidark stairwell. Everett leaned over and placed a
hand on the steel tube, feeling the shocks from the blows
and then something else—the steady thump of something
that sounded as if it were running, or worse, climbing or
descending the tube itself. He leaned back and looked at a
marine gunnery sergeant who had just spent two full tours
overseas, one in Iraq and the other in Afghanistan.

"I think the damn things are using the tubes to move
around."

The sergeant unzipped his body armor, lazily scratched
his chest, and then looked from Everett to the tube and back
again.

"Well, Cap'n, not knowing just what in the hell we have
going on here is throwin' a kink in my train of thought," the
old sergeant said as he reached out and felt the tube himself.
His eyes widened and he pulled the nylon glove on his right
hand free and then touched the tube. "Damn," he hissed.

"What we have here is what amounts to a genetic, or viral, experiment gone bonkers, Gunny. One that's damn hard
to kill," Everett said.

"Okay," the sergeant said with a wry look at his squad of
men around him.

"From what I learned, they can't last that long. The substance starts eating away at their brains if there was too much
of the formula taken into their system. It was invented to be
given out in light doses to soldiers to bolster their aggressive-
ness. It has properties that can open up the unused portions of
a person's brain." Everett again felt the tube and realized
that the movement inside was moving away from them, traveling farther down into the complex. "But that in and of itself starts a fast process of something akin to brain cancer."

"Some kind of super trooper, huh?" the gunnery sergeant
said with a grin and shake of his head.

"Something like that," answered Everett.

"Sounds like something the army needs," quipped the gunnery sergeant.

"Hey!" came a shouted protest from farther up the stairwell.

"It feels like the movement is heading down."

"Yeah," the gunnery sergeant said spitting a large stream of tobacco juice onto one of the steps, "but what about the fifteen other tubes inside the complex, Cap'n?"

Everett closed his eyes as the point the sergeant just made hit home.

"What kills these bastards, Cap'n?"

Everett looked around at his small band of men. "One hell of a lot of bullets," he said in frustration, noticing that his words didn't have a very good effect on his men. "Head shots men. They can't very damn well function if they have no brain."

The men started shaking their heads in response to the captain.

The gunnery sergeant pulled the magazine from his M-14 and inserted a full thirty rounds. "Well, I hate to be the bearer of bad news here, but we're running low on ammo."

"Yeah, and I don't think we're going to run into Sergeant Sanchez with his assault packages before we run into more of these monsters. We're heading in the wrong direction to get more bullets. It's either make it down to level ten and resupply at the security office, or make a run to the main armory on thirty-two."

Before the gunnery sergeant could say anything, they were caught completely off-guard when a loud hollow-sounding bang came from the tube. A large dent appeared in the steel right where Everett had placed his hand. The men on the landing stepped back as another large dent appeared. The steel of the elevator tube was only an eighth of an inch thick and was standing up too well to the assault from the inside.

"Jesus," the gunny said as he stood and backed away

from the fifteen-foot-diameter elevator shaft. "Whatever that is has been waiting right there, probably hearing every word we were saying."

"I think it's time we start fighting back and get our asses to the armory," Everett said as he checked the remaining rounds in his Beretta. "I want something a little heavier than this cap pistol."

"Then may I suggest we beat feet the hell out of here?" the marine said as he waved the men farther up on the stairs to start back down.

"If they're smart like the docs say, they may be able to cut us off. And if they're real smart they will make it to the breaker boxes on each level. Smith will know we can't fight in the dark without the right equipment."

Suddenly the already-dim lighting in the stairwell went completely out, followed by the flash and start-up of the battery-powered floods on each level. They were now almost totally in the dark.

"Well, I guess they're real smart, Cap'n."

Everett turned away and motioned downward as his squad started a headlong flight back down the stairs and into the darkness below.

The man once known as Smith had stayed the longest inside the cloud of Perdition's Fire. He had inhaled deeply knowing that he and his men were done for. In his mind-set he had quickly realized that he wouldn't go down without a fight. Without regard to himself or his men, and needless to say the thought of the many lives inside the underground complex. He had been fully briefed by Hiram Vickers on the properties of Perdition's Fire and knew exactly what it was he was in store for. He quickly figured he would rather go out this way than placing a bullet into his own head as the Black rules of engagement called for.

As he had inhaled the toxic mixture of Perdition's Fire he felt the burning as the mist penetrated his eyes, nose, and throat. At first he couldn't catch his breath while all around him his four men writhed on the floor, covered in fog. He felt the dreamlike sensation of actually floating off the floor but also had the wherewithal to realize he was still there, covered with the wetness of the mist. He had shaken his head when the effects started to take hold. He felt the bones in his body start to ache. The pain set in as the bones started their growth spurt, contracting the muscles around them like a vice grip. The marrow inside was reacting far faster than the tissue surrounding it. At the time he didn't realize it, but the section of brain that had lain dormant his entire life started firing on all cylinders, sending endorphins through his system to help expand those body parts that it felt were the weakest.

Smith remembered rolling over onto his back in sheer agony as the formula coursed through his system. He felt his clothing expand until his arms burst through the material. He felt the crunching as bone met bone and cartilage was torn free from tissue. He felt his eyes bulge and his teeth separate. His body began to convulse even as his system started to heal itself. Even through the excruciating process Smith realized that Ambrose had not only hit on an aggressive formula of absolute mind control; he had hit on a miracle drug that made the expanded brain system produce chemicals that could heal, escalating the natural process of blood clotting and bone marrow production. All this because for the first time in human history the key to unlocking the unused portion of a human brain had been introduced by pure chance by expanding the brain cells in the operating portion of the mind. With the correct and lighter dosage, Smith would have realized without the severe pain he was going through that Ambrose had actually accomplished what he had started out to do. He would have created a soldier that not only was brighter, but could heal faster and take more punishment than a normal man would have been able to achieve on his own.

After the transformation was complete, there was the problem of clothing. His muscles and bodily tissue had expanded so much that his circulation was being cut off and robbed of blood by the tightness of his clothes and boots. He remembered ripping free the vent, most of his shirt, and the waistband of his pants. His massive hands had torn through the laces of his boots until he could feel the cold floor beneath him. As he had risen from the mist covering the clean room floor, he felt free for the first time in his life. His mind was seeing and understanding things he never realized possible. His vision was perfect. He could see shadows and knew that through the mist he could actually see his men around him. He felt so good he had to laugh at the newfound power he was feeling. He found he was near hysteria as his nose widened and flattened, expanding his nasal cavity to allow smells and odors to penetrate that he could never have smelled before.

The biggest difference in Smith was his desire to hurt, destroy, and render flesh into pulp. The thought of taking life from anything and everything overwhelmed his mind as he shook his head with an ecstatic swelling of near perfection. He remembered laughing uncontrollably.

Since he had intentionally breathed in far more of the formula than his men, he had immediately taken control of the altered men before him. He was the dominate of the group according to the millennia-old adage that the strong will out. He had had to make an example out of a soldier who had thought he could control the group by smashing the man's head through a wall. The man was still alive but was now far more receptive to control. This was all due to Smith's much larger stature.

He was also aware that his brain could only take so much before the sensitive synapses overwhelmed the very tissue that contained the electrical firings. Its material could not expand fast enough, nor was the cranium strong enough to hold the enlargement. The brain was dying and Smith knew he had only a short time to extend the magnificent feeling he was experiencing. The drug had made him not regret anything in the slightest as he saw beyond the mere death of the body and knew he was truly living for the first time. He was now seeing what life for humankind would be like millions of years in the future with the expansion of the mind. The evolutionary growth was an intoxicating mix that sent euphoric riches into the thought process. He realized that this is what being God was meant to feel like.

And a vengeful God he was.

The clinic on level nine was silent for the moment, but Farbeaux had the sense to know that something had gone quickly to hell as men and women were seen running through the halls and his senses could fathom that there was more than just a biohazard happening inside the complex. He cursed his luck as he felt the cold steel of the handcuffs that secured him to the bed. He looked over at the security man who had been trying to raise someone on his radio. Henri watched the man step into the clinic, look around, and then step back inside the room shaking his head and trying the radio once more.

"Sergeant, how long have you been in the military?" Farbeaux asked.

"Five years, eight months," the young airman said as he again walked to the doorway.

"That's long enough for you to have developed a sense that all soldiers get over the years."

"And what's that Colonel?" the sergeant asked as he angrily turned away from the activity in the hallway.

"A sense that should tell you, as you Americans would put it of course, that the proverbial shit has hit the proverbial fan."

The kid didn't say anything as he turned back around, ripped the headphones off his head, and walked over to the phone beside Henri's bed. He lifted the receiver, but then Henri saw his face flush with even more anger when he heard the continuing announcement by Europa to evacuate. The guard started to slam the phone back down into its cradle when he felt the Frenchman's eyes on him. He looked up and saw Henri raise his right eyebrow. He was about to say something when Denise Gilliam strode quickly into the room, walked over to the bed, and started removing the tape that held the IV in place on Farbeaux's left arm.

"Hey, Doc, what are you doing? I have orders that say he goes nowhere," the guard said.

"I override any authority inside this clinic, young man. Now free up Mr. Farbeaux's restraints; it's time we get the hell out of here," the young dark-haired MD said as she started to pull the bed away from the wall. "Now, Sergeant!" she said far harsher than she would have liked.

"Ma'am, this is a very dangerous man," the sergeant said even as he produced the handcuff key.

"I suggest you follow the good doctor's orders, son. Smell that?" Henri said as he jangled his right cuff against the steel bedrail.

"What?" both Gilliam and the sergeant said at once.

"Cordite. There is one hell of a battle taking place somewhere, more than likely below us on another level, possibly even on level seventeen where the emergency was declared."

Both the doctor and sergeant looked at each other, realizing that the Frenchman was telling the truth. The airman started to unlock the right handcuff as Denise finished pulling the IV line free of Henri's arm.

"Help me push him to the elevator," she said as she started tugging on the large bed.

"Doctor, if you would release this other restraint, I assure you I can walk, possibly even run, which I think may factor into this situation any moment."

"No, we can get you to safety," the sergeant said as they reached the doorway.

"Then may I possibly persuade you to get my clothes out of the closet?"

"No!" both the sergeant and doctor yelled at once.

Event Group Complex
Nellis AFB, Nevada, Gate One

As the load of over a hundred and fifty staff rose into the ancient hangar on level one, the perimeter security element of the Event Group was waiting for them. They were in the process of herding the last of the science staff off the giant cargo lift to join the first lift of men and women out in the scrub of flat desert to await orders and transport to a safe location when the exterior lights flickered and then went out. The twelve men of the outside security team whose job it was to secure gate one were frustrated in not being able to join their mates down inside the complex, especially when they started hearing the stories about heavy gunfire coming from level seventeen.

Every man, woman, soldier, doctor, professor, or technician knew the Event Group was compromised, and its largest element was sitting out in the open where the world could discover a secret that had been buried in the sands of Nellis Air Force Base for the past sixty-one years. Even more, they wanted to return and assist those men and women who were now trapped inside that darkness that may have become a mass grave for their friends and colleagues.

And what was worse, they knew there was now something in that darkness that had a functioning and scheming brain and worst of all—teeth.

As Niles Compton, Pete Golding, and Charlie Ellenshaw banged through the doorway of the stairwell and into the main reception area they heard the crashing through the steel conduit that allowed the elevators to ride on a cushion of air. Niles could see enough through the battery-powered lighting to know that his staff had successfully evacuated, a load off his mind. Still, he had to know there was something and as he moved away from the two scientists they were shocked to see him move toward the elevator doors. Their eyes widened when they saw their boss start to pull the doors apart.

"Niles, what in the hell are you doing?" Pete called out as Charlie reached him first and tried pulling his hands away. Just as Charlie reached the doors Niles slammed backward into him and he was forced to catch Compton before he fell to the floor. Something had impacted the double doors leading to the shaft. As they watched, there came a loud bang and then a large bulge appeared in the stainless steel.

"How are they moving up that shaft?" Pete asked as he pulled the two men away from the elevator.

"With the description Captain Everett gave us, they must be using the guide rail that centers the elevator inside the shaft, and with no compressed air they have no resistance to impede their climb."

Both Pete and Niles turned and looked at Ellenshaw, who returned the look with a "what?" expression. All three jumped when the left side of the steel door bent outward and for the first time they saw the hand of the thing inside of the tube. It grasped the corner of the steel door and pulled down. The screech of metal was deafening as the creature wrenched and warped the elevator doors, first one side and then the other.

"Uh-oh," Charlie said even as Niles started pulling them toward the double doors that led to the main hallway. The only other way was through the conference room, which was a dead end.

As they inched their way toward the doors, in the battery-powered and very weak light they saw a massive head poke through the widened gap of the twin doors. The creature actually saw them and smiled, showing elongated and crooked teeth with wide gaps between each. The eyes were overly large and it was Niles that noticed large patches of hair that had fallen out of its scalp. The remnants of a black military uniform hung around its neck and chest. The men were so shocked at the sight that Niles stumbled, taking all three men down to the floor. The creature that had once been a human being actually laughed, sending fear and chills down the men's spines.

As they watched, trying to rise, crawl, crabwalk, any-thing to distance them from the Perdition's Fire–created monstrosity before them, the beast reached through with both massive arms and started pulling the left-side door away from the frame with a sickening crunch of steel. As it did so blood was coursing out of the creature's ears through the exertion it was placing on its body and brain. Little could Niles and the other two men know that the beast was dying but was too hopped-up and euphoric to realize it. The altered man finally managed to tear free the door, letting it fall eighty-seven levels down the elevator tube. Then with little effort it finally extricated itself from the shaft.

"Oh, shit!" Pete said as he leaned farther into Charlie and Niles.

The beast stood in the darkness and they could see the whiteness of its teeth. The massive arms hung like those of a giant ape as it leaned to the right and then to the left, taking the three men in. The smile was ever present as its long fingers closed and then opened, only to close again. They saw tatters of skin hanging from its hands that it had damaged on its climb up the shaft. The blood was flowing far more freely from its large ears even as it kept staring at them. Then its eyes enlarged and it took the first step toward Niles, Pete, and Charlie.

Suddenly a heavy stream of gunfire opened up from somewhere behind the cowering men. As they watched, a line of tracer fire stitched its way across the beast's expanded chest. Then another line of bright phosphorescent bullets struck the creature and made it take three steps back toward the open shaft. They saw the M-14 carbine hit the carpet next to them and looked up in time to see Colonel Jack Collins dressed in civilian clothes as he advanced toward the beast with his nine millimeter drawn. Jack started firing into the head and neck of the creature, not giving it a chance to recover as the colonel advanced on it. Finally the creature was backed into the shaft where it grabbed the elevator doorframe and held on tight. Jack fired the Beretta until the clip was expended and then without missing a beat ejected it and resumed firing. He caught the beast three times in the head and it still hung on to the frame. Then he took careful aim, still walking toward the creature, and fired all of his remaining rounds, striking the altered man in the wrists and hands. Finally the rounds to the head and hands did the work Jack was hoping for, and the beast was forced to let go. It fell back into the darkness as Jack ran the short distance to peer into the dark shaft. He arrived just in time to see the beast falling. It struck the side of the tube and finally vanished. Collins turned and ejected the empty clip from the automatic. He looked at the three men with resolve.

"You three alright?" he asked as he finally reached down and started pulling them up from the floor one at a time.

"Thank God you came in. I don't think that gentleman cared for us all that much," Charlie joked as Niles placed his hand on Jack's shoulder and lowered his head, thankful for his sudden appearance.

"Jack, is Alice alright?" Niles asked when he thought his heart could stand the exertion.

"She's at home and the last I knew was trying to get you some help down here. Now where are Captain Everett and the rest of security?"

"Colonel, the entire security team is spread out inside the facility. As far as we know there are at least four more of those monstrosities around. We heard one hell of a lot of gunfire coming from the lower levels," Niles said as he looked away from Jack. "I should never have allowed that formula into this complex."

"Well, sometimes it takes a lot to get a policy changed. You know that, Mr. Director." Without waiting for comment from Niles, Jack turned and faced Pete. "Can you get the complex systems up again, especially Europa?"

"That's what we came back to do, Colonel."

"Then may I suggest you get to it, Pete. Niles, you go with him; you know the system almost as well as he does. Charlie, you're with me. You get to play John Wayne. We have to get below. Are you game?" Jack reached down and retrieved the M-14 carbine, inserted another magazine, and handed it to Ellenshaw.

Ellenshaw looked the lightweight weapon over and grinned, his white hair flying in all directions. "I'm always game, Colonel."

Echo Five Three Seven—Sierra
Somewhere Over Southern Utah

The Lockheed Martin C-130J Super Hercules had left Mc-Chord Air Force Base under tight security. There had been no witnesses to the rollout of the special-operations aircraft and even the normal air force personnel that manned the tower had been replaced by a unit of "special" technicians that always traveled with the unit that had loaded onto the massive transport plane. Under cover of darkness, the Hercules lifted free of Washington State and was in the air less than five minutes after her rollout from the giant hangar. Inside were men that had received more special-operations training than any unit in the United States military. They were so special that they knew their missions would be few and far between.

Special Forces Operational Detachment-Delta, also known as the Combat Applications Group (CAG), or simply DELTA, were the United States' most elite tactical combat group.

Contrary to rumor, DELTA wasn't an army Special Forces detachment. Delta Force was a unit unto itself, composed of members from all branches of the U.S. military. Its home base was considered to be Fort Bragg, North Carolina, but its training took place all around the world. The special men inside of the Hercules were not really soldiers at all but were called operators and were said to shun the traditional philosophies of military life. They most often wore civilian clothing and were rumored to work for everyone from the FBI to the CIA. The three groups on this mission were made up of twelve men to a section. All thirty six men, plus their commanding officer, Major Jerry "Grateful Dead" Garcia, were dressed for one of their most trained-for assignments—a high-altitude, low-opening jump, or HALO. The need to get to their target quickly without being seen by anyone at Nellis Air Force Base was of particular interest to the powers that be, but when the president of the United States said to get to Nevada, they were going hell bent for leather.

Each man had been briefed on the rescue. They were going into a scenario that few had ever trained for, the taking back of an underground complex that may be held by an opposing force that may or may not be genetically altered. Each man in the three teams took the mission parameters with a grain of salt. They understood that someone up the chain of command was either out of his mind or very near to it.

Major Garcia checked his watch one last time as the Hercules climbed to their jump altitude. They would jump at 32,000 feet and low open at 2,000 feet from the desert scrub, hopefully below the radar of the Nellis tower.

He looked over at Sergeant Major Reynolds and winked.

"Major, I have one hell of a stupid question for ya," Reynolds said in his Texas drawl.

"And what pray tell can that be, Sergeant Major Reynolds?" Garcia said as he studied the other thirty men inside the cavernous hold of the C-130J. He saw that most of them had their eyes closed, bored as always with the "getting there" portion of a mission.

"Who in the hell is in charge of naming these missions? I mean, come on, my fifth-grade niece could come up with something better than this."

"Well, according to my sources, Sergeant Major, this one comes from the very top."

"Besides the name of the mission, I also noted a name that wasn't entirely blacked out on the mission parameters. I guess it got through some egghead sensor."

Major Garcia turned away and saw that no one else was listening over the drone of the four powerful engines.

"I saw that myself. I'm glad most of these boys are too young to have noticed and recognized the name, or maybe they just didn't care. But it did add a little element of surprise to the game." He looked over at the smaller man from Texas. "I mean, if the man that trained most of the officer corps in this outfit is in deep shit, it definitely means we're not headed for a picnic."

The sergeant major nodded his head and adjusted the oxygen tank on his back. He closed his eyes and tried to sleep but leaned over and said, "Yes, sir, if the Jack Collins I know is in trouble, there must be one large shitstorm where we're goin'."

The huge aircraft increased power as it slipped out of its planned flight path and climbed with its four engines screaming.

Operation Nerdlinger was nearing the sand and scrub of Nellis Air Force Base.

Spring Valley Hospital,
Las Vegas, Nevada

Jason Ryan was feeling the course of light-dose morphine as it rushed through his system. He watched as the duty nurse administered the injection through the IV line attached to his right hand. For the first twenty-four hours the doctors had been worried about infection setting in, but since his three bullet wounds had been treated right away by the attending physicians in Laredo, that fear had been laid to rest very quickly. With the drugs running through the naval aviator's body, he had decided he hadn't felt this good since his Annapolis days. And the nursing staff was on the receiving end of that feel-good situation.

The young nurse looked down at the dark, short-haired Ryan and shook her head as she finished administering the morphine into the IV tube.

"Look, if you persist, I'll write your fantasies down on your chart and then you'll have to deal with the nurse we call Ratchet."

"That doesn't sound too good," Ryan said as the warm feeling started streaming through his head. "Did you know I was shot taking down the largest drug dealer on the American continent?" he said as his hand wandered down to the nurse's leg and "accidentally" brushed the white nylon stocking.

"You are so humble," she said as she took a step back.

"Yeah, that's me, humble and shy."

She shook her head and wrote down her injection on his chart. "With any luck to the staff, you can leave here in a couple of days."

"Ah, come on, I don't want to go back to work. You don't know my boss like I do."

"I'm sure he knows you though," she said as she left the room with a smile. Jason tried to sit up in time to see her hindquarters but was too late. Instead of lying back down he reached over and grabbed the cell phone from his table. He had one of the younger nurses buy it for him in the gift shop and actually talked her into purchasing minutes for him on the promise that they would all be used talking to her. He opened the cover and dialed the security cover number for the Group. As the TV in the corner of the room showed some of the devastation wrought by a massive explosion south of the border in Nuevo Laredo, Jason smiled. His smile faltered somewhat when there was no completion to his call other than a recording administered through the office of the National Archives. *The United States government offices you are trying to reach are temporarily experiencing technical problems with their phone lines. Please try your call again at a later time.*

"What?" he said as he tried again.

After receiving the same message again, he punched in Will Mendenhall's cell number he knew by heart. Again there was no answer as his call went straight to voice mail.

"Ah, to hell with it," he said as he set the phone down and changed the channel on the television. After perusing the channels three times he snapped off the set. He again picked up the cell phone and tried Will and the complex once more. He closed the cover in frustration.

"Damn, this isn't right," he mumbled. He again opened the cell phone cover and dialed a number he had only used one time—Jack Collins. "Goddamn it!" he cursed as the colonel's phone also went straight to voice mail. The hair on the back of the aviator's neck rose as he dialed one number that was always answered, Charlie Ellenshaw's. As he listened, the phone rang ten times before he heard Charlie's voice on the recording. *You've reached Charles Hindershot Ellenshaw the third. If I'm not answering, that means I either don't want to talk to you, or my music is so loud I can't hear the phone. Either way, call back later.*

Jason's face turned whiter than his lack of blood could account for. He swallowed as he realized that something was wrong. He tossed back the blanket and sheet and then sat farther up in bed. He started to place his legs over the side, became lightheaded, and then paused while his equilibrium settled back down into its rightful place. Jason tried to reach over and pull himself to the right with his left hand, but the connected IV pulled his hand back with a slight stab of pain. He cursed and yanked the needle out of his vein, tossing it to the floor. Then he slowly placed his right foot on the cold tile of the floor and hissed. His head felt fuzzy, but he persisted in getting his left leg off the bed. As he braced himself as best he could, he used his ass to push up and off the bed. He felt a sharp stab of pain from the bullet wound closest to his heart. It had passed through cleanly between his heart and lungs, and the doctors said he had been far more than just lucky that there hadn't been any more significant damage—that it had been a small miracle.

Right now Ryan wasn't so sure about the lucky part as he realized he had never felt this horrible in his life, even after ejecting from an F-14 Tomcat over the Pacific Ocean five years before at over a thousand miles per hour.

After holding on to the bedrail for as long as it took for his head to clear, he realized that his ass was hanging out of the back of his hospital gown. As he half turned he saw his reflection in the mirror attached to the bathroom door. He saw the white of his butt and tilted his head. "Not bad," he mumbled as he attempted his first step. He actually felt that things were going well as he raised his right leg and stepped. The one thing he didn't realize until too late was the fact that he raised the right leg just a little too high and brought it down where he thought the white tile was located. He was wrong—about a foot off as a matter of fact. If he hadn't been able to grab the rail in time he would have flipped completely over.

"Okay, let's try that again," he muttered.

Still holding the bedrail, Jason cautiously tried again. This time his right foot came down where the estimation of distance and space had been calculated. Then as he removed his hand from the bed he tried it again, this time with the left foot. Success. Moving at a snail's pace he reached out and again calculated correctly as he grasped the doorknob to the closet. He took a deep breath and waited for his heart rate to slow and his mind to scan his wounds for any leaking that may have happened. There was none.

"Okay, step one complete." Jason twisted the knob and pulled the door open, once threatening to continue on with the momentum of the heavy closet door but stopping and arresting his movement with a fancy balancing act. Once straight again he looked into the closet. He immediately realized he was in trouble as he didn't know how to cover his body with the ten wire hangers that hung there. "Houston, we have a problem." Jason remembered that his clothes were probably somewhere in Laredo, Texas. He closed his eyes to think, even though he knew for a naval aviator that usually meant trouble. So before he could do some damage to his brain he slowly walked to the door and opened it a crack.

As he scanned the darkened and half-lit hallway he spied the nurses' station where he saw the tops of two heads as they sat working on the reports. A candy striper came around the corner and spoke to the nurses there for a moment and then turned away and continued her rounds. Jason managed to take a step out of the room and into the hallway. His eyes widened when he saw a rack of clothes still in their plastic wrap from the dry cleaners. With his feet freezing and his coordination returning, he made it to the rack and quietly started going through the hanging clothes, hoping beyond hope for a doctor's smock, surgical clothing, or anything he could find to cover his nakedness. He cursed when he realized as he moved the plastic-covered garments aside that he was looking at nothing but nurse's uniforms and candy striper's dresses. He rolled his eyes and wanted to scream in frustration, that is, until he felt the cold draft rushing up his spine from his open hospital gown. Shaking his head, he removed the white nurse's uniform from the rack. He realized that this must be the only hospital in the country that made nurses wear skirts instead of pants or surgical greens.

"Las Vegas," he said under his breath as he moved back into his room to change and grab his wallet.

It took U.S. Navy Lieutenant J.G. (Junior Grade) Jason Ryan nearly an hour to wind his way past the nurses and another forty minutes to travel the stairs from the third floor to the first. The trip hadn't been all that unlucky as he did manage to at least snag some paper shoe covers. Now he had his feet somewhat covered and the color did match the white of his skirt and the blouse with the small red cross on the breast. He also had a surgical cap on his head and knew he must look the sight as he stepped from the shadows of the hospital emergency room.

Another fifteen minutes passed as he waited for his cab to take him to the Gold City Pawn Shop where he would undoubtedly find the Security Department running some kind of a drill that Colonel Collins was fond of designing. As he gave the cab driver the address he saw the man looking into his rearview mirror every five minutes. His eyes roamed over the nurse's face. Ryan realized that although he thought he was a passable nurse, he forgot that he hadn't shaved in three days.

"These long shifts are killing me," Ryan quipped and continued to stare at the cabbie's eyes until he looked away.

The man with the dark hair and arrogant aviator's walk, who guessed he looked at least decent in his nurse's outfit, was in for a shock when he pulled up to a closed and locked pawn shop.

Event Group Complex,
Nellis Air Force Base, Nevada

As Dr. Denise Gilliam waited in front of the elevator to take them to level thirty-four, she felt the Frenchman's eyes on her. She looked from the elevator to the airman who watched Henri and finally at Farbeaux.

"What?" she said louder than she intended.

"Hear that?" Farbeaux asked.

"I don't hear anything. The gunfire has stopped."

"That's not the only thing that has stopped, dear doctor."

Denise looked around as the overhead fluorescent lighting flickered. Then she realized what the Frenchman was referring to.

"What's he talking about?" the airman asked.

"The bioalarms have stopped," Gilliam said as she looked up and down the small clinic, not liking the empty feeling of it for the first time since she joined the Group.

"Not only that," Henri said as he too glanced around, jingling his cuffed hands as he did, "that sexy computer you people rely on so much seems to be on her lunch break."

"Jesus, that isn't right," the airman said as he moved to the phone at the small nurse's station to try to reach someone again. As he clicked the disconnect button several times, he knew they were in trouble. No radio, no phones, and worst of all, no Europa to tell them what to do.

"Where's that damn elevator?" Denise said as she placed her hand on the scanning screen to see if Europa would react.

That was when the lights went out.

"I hope this is budget cuts," Farbeaux said as his senses started their small dance inside of his body.

"Shit," Denise said as she wheeled the bed Henri was restrained to back around and away from the elevator. At that moment the dead circuit tripped the battery-operated lighting in the distant corners of the clinic. "This isn't right. The clinic and other facilities are on an emergency line. We have a separate backup generator. Why isn't it kicking on?"

"Because Europa isn't there to tell it to," the airman said as she returned.

"Uh, may I suggest the stairs?" Henri said as he once more jingled the cuffs on both hands.

The pounding made all three go rigid. The noise came from several directions at once, the closed elevator doors, the doorway leading to the stairwell, and even more strange, from the walls itself.

Farbeaux watched the doors to the elevator. In the semi-dark of the clinic his hackles rose to an all-time high on his danger meter. He again jingled the handcuffs.

"Airman, I would feel much better if I was able to move about. Release me from this bed—it may be a bit too heavy to run with it on my back."

"Colonel, you know I can't. Captain Everett was specific in his orders about you."

"I think the colonel's right. I'll take responsibility," Denise said as her eyes turned from the elevator doors to the far wall where the stairwell was located. "I'm officially saying that his circulation is being cut off and am ordering the cuffs removed."

The sergeant looked hesitant but then pulled his sidearm and tossed the key to the doctor.

"A wise decision, Airman," Henri said as he watched Denise undo his restraints.

"Colonel, make no mistake; I will shoot you if you try anything."

As the cuffs were removed Henri flexed his wrists and sat up enough to place his bare feet on the floor.

"I'm afraid by the sound of that racket in the walls and elevator shaft, you may have to shoot something."

All eyes were on the elevator doors as the pounding got louder and louder. The tension was building as whatever was making the horrible sound was growing closer. Suddenly the door to the stairwell burst open. The sergeant turned with his nine millimeter poised to blast their visitor. It was Henri who reached out and forced the gun barrel down just as Virginia Pollock, Sarah, Gloria Bannister, and

Will Mendenhall came through the door. They watched as Will closed the door and then slowly started backing away from it as if he expected something to burst through it at anytime.

"God," the airman said, grateful that the Frenchman forced his aim off as he had come close to killing Dr. Pollock. "Doctor, Lieutenant McIntire, I almost shot you!"

Farbeaux watched as Sarah caught her breath. His eyes told him that she had received far more damage to her head and face. Still breathing hard, Sarah saw Henri and their eyes locked. She immediately went to the side of the bed where the Frenchman was trying to get to his feet. She took his hand but said nothing. As for Farbeaux, he just felt the warmth of her touch but made no move to comfort her.

"What in God's name is that noise?" Denise asked as Mendenhall joined the group, still looking at the stairwell door.

"Something real bad," Virginia said as she hurried to the opposite side of the clinic and placed her ears to that door, hoping she wasn't hearing anything from there like they had heard at the door they just exited.

"Sergeant, we need more weapons. Is that all we have on this level?" Mendenhall asked as his eyes never left the stairwell they had just left.

"Yes, sir, and the radios are out. We're not picking up anything."

"Our security teams are scattered all over the damn complex. As long as we are keeping to the stairwells, any signals will have one hell of a hard time getting through all of this steel. The radios are meant for use in the complex, not its inner workings," Will said as an even louder bang sounded from the elevator shaft. Mendenhall reached out and took Gloria's hand, pulling the frightened woman close to him when she jumped at the sound.

"What in the hell is in the tubes?" Dr. Gilliam asked as another large bang sounded from either two levels down or maybe even closer.

"The men who attacked the complex, they've changed.

The formula is reacting just the way it did in Mexico, only this is different; it's like they have actually grown far more than Guzman and his men. The higher dose of Perdition's Fire, it was in the clean room like a fog—the exposure was far more than at the hacienda," Will said as he stood in front of the weakened Sarah and frightened CDC doctor.

"Dr. Pollock, I know this is not your field of specialty, but perhaps you can give us something that could explain the impossible way in which these men have grown. It cannot just be the hallucinatory effects of poppy splicing," Farbeaux said as he reached out and took a pair of green surgical pants from a rack on the far wall. Trying to keep his balance, he slid his legs into them with much difficulty until Sarah stepped out from behind Mendenhall and held him up. Henri placed his arm around her and squeezed as he finally accomplished the task.

Virginia walked quickly back into the main clinic and to the elevator doors, sliding her lab coat off as she did. She stopped in front of the doors and then without looking tossed the coat over to Farbeaux.

"Thank you, Doctor," Henri said as he tossed the hospital gown away and slid into the coat.

Virginia listened intently as the grunts and scraping continued beneath them. The sound was getting louder, as if whatever it was was checking each floor for people before it moved on.

"I don't know, but I do have a guess. That unknown element that the CDC doctors ran across, Europa was close to identifying it before she went down. She tagged the unknown as human tissue, but that was as far as she got. It was too arcane for the CDC's analyzer to identify," she said as she started backing away from the elevator doors until she bumped into the now empty bed. "The only thing it can be that explains the unnatural growth of these men has to be an HGH synthesis that Ambrose created during his experiments."

"HGH? That's impossible," Gloria said, finally thankful she had something to think about. "He couldn't have synthesized anything close to human growth hormones, not at the turn of the century." Gloria allowed her mind to wander into the realm of impossibility for a moment. Then she vigorously shook her head, frightened at the prospects of the growth hormone in conjunction with the human brain power that had been opened up in the men who had basically overdosed on Perdition's Fire. "The second unknown?" she said as she went into deep thought.

"What's that?" Virginia asked seeing the stunned look on the face of the CDC doctor.

"Could it be possible that this man was working on something related to stem cell research? There is no telling what he could have achieved. But that would have been impossible at the time. Ambrose was a barbarian compared to today's scientists. He didn't have the equipment necessary for the work."

"Regardless of the impossibility of it, Miss Bannister, we're facing something that is a direct enemy of the natural laws of nature here. There can be no other explanation. The human body is capable of so much, but add to that the fact that the human brain has only used 10 percent of its power throughout human history and now it has been expanded to use 100 percent. What you have in the end is what is out there: the brain mixing with a human growth hormone and possible embryo research, fetus material, if you prefer. The consequences are phenomenal," Virginia said just as the first crash of steel sounded on the other side of the elevator doors, creating the smallest of bulges.

"I'm leaning toward the good doctor Pollock's theory and the young lady's guesswork," Farbeaux said as he stood next to Mendenhall. "Lieutenant, I know I'm not a citizen of your country, at least legally speaking, but I vote we get the hell out of here, and I would prefer to be armed as we run like hell for the surface of this menagerie."

Will looked at Henri and nodded his head. "You don't have to convince the U.S. Army, Colonel—everyone to the stairwell. Sergeant, give me the weapon and go with them. I'll draw that thing's attention."

Gloria reacted first as the second, much larger dent appeared in the double elevator doors, creating a small separation between them. She reached out and grabbed Will and just shook her head. "No, please don't," she said with pleading eyes.

"You go with Dr. Pollock and the others. Sarah and the colonel are too weak, they need a hand."

"We all go, Will," Virginia announced loudly. "For once in my life, with Niles out of the complex, someone is going to damn well follow my orders."

"Perhaps we can discuss this when we're headed upward in the unaffected stairwell?" Henri said as he pulled Sarah to the left, heading for the opposite set of stairs just as eight very large and grotesque fingers pushed through the opening.

"Jesus," the airman said as he pushed everyone in the direction Farbeaux had taken with Sarah trailing. "Lieutenant, go!" he shouted at Mendenhall and the others.

Suddenly the doors separated and in the dark they saw the glowing eyes. The impossibility of it struck everyone as the eyes were radiating like those of a night-hunting animal. The brain of the affected was altering the way humans were seeing—Perdition's Fire was adapting to its situation.

As everyone turned and ran, the airman who was responsible, at least in his mind, for this level opened fire, catching the retreating Mendenhall off-guard. The lieutenant shoved Gloria forward toward the far exit door and turned as the airman emptied his nine millimeter into the creature that was even now balancing itself in the right half of the empty elevator doorframe. It was too large to squeeze through such a small opening so it angrily started battering the left section of steel door, warping and bending it even as the powerful nine-millimeter rounds struck and penetrated its upper body. As each round hit, it would yell and roar in pain as it continued to battle with the steel of the remaining door.

Just as Mendenhall reached out to grab the young security man, the beast had a similar thought as it leaned as far into the clinic as it could, bending the remaining door even further until it caught the airman while he was reloading.

The beast's grip was wrapped so powerfully around his neck that he dropped the Beretta with the clip still only partially inserted. Will reacted fast as the man was pulled toward the towering beast. As his struggles continued, Will retrieved the weapon and finished inserting the clip. He quickly took aim at the monstrosity still struggling in the elevator opening. When he saw he couldn't get a shot in without hitting the terrified security man, Will placed the gun in his waistband and attacked.

The beast was caught off-guard by the blows raining into its face delivered by Mendenhall. It reacted by squeezing his grip even harder on the airman. The beast roared with insult as Will continued to fight for the young security man's life. Then, even through the screams of outrage from the creature, Will heard the airman's neck snap. It was a sound the lieutenant would never forget. The struggles of the giant and the security man ceased at once. The beast let the boy slip through its grip as the large, unnatural eyes fell on Will. The giant brows rose and the creature smiled. With its bare chest almost through the door it reached out with lightning-quick speed and grabbed Mendenhall around the neck. The lieutenant knew that he hadn't moved fast enough just as his life force was being squeezed from his body.

Suddenly the grip was released and a roar of pain sounded that actually shook the pictures from the clinic's walls. As Will fell to the floor he looked up in time to see Henri Farbeaux step away from the flailing, infuriated giant. Then Mendenhall finally saw why the beast had let go as it pulled the ballpoint pen from its right eye. Farbeaux and Sarah were there to pull him up and out of the creature's flailing arms.

"Thanks!" he screamed.

As they ran for the stairwell door being held open by Virginia and Dr. Gilliam, Farbeaux looked back as the creature now began to concentrate on the only remaining obstacle trapping it, the second door.

"This is the second time I've been here, and I must say

you people go out of your way to make my stay vigorous and exciting," Henri said.

A choking Mendenhall reached the door and allowed Henri and Sarah to go through first just as the beast bent over the remaining door.

"That's what we're here for, Colonel, to make sure your days are filled with wonder and awe."

Virginia cursed and pulled Will into the complete darkness of the stairwell.

For the first time in Compton's fifteen years and Pete Golding's ten at the Event Group, they saw the computer center go dark. With Europa being down for the first time ever, the sight was surreal for both men. As Pete pushed the large bulletproof glass security door open, he realized with the only lighting coming from the battery-powered floods in the corners and center of the large room, that the cavernous area with its empty theater-style seating and main-floor desks looked ghostly. The fifty-foot main computer screen with the flashing red light at its base was a reminder just how vulnerable the complex was without Europa running things.

"How long to reboot the system, Pete?" Niles asked as he walked down the main aisle of seating while looking through the glass walls out into the main hallway. He felt like they were being watched. He knew that was probably a wrong sensory input due to the stress of the situation.

"She should come right up," Pete said as he practically ran down the steps to his large desk on the main floor. He immediately checked his personal system and then paused as his security code challenge came up on the monitor. He entered Golding-Hercules—Marilyn 11900-A-1.

"You better not let Jack see the Marilyn part of the code—he'll kill you."

"Ah, what the colonel doesn't know won't hurt him."

Even through the terrifying situation they were now locked into, Niles Compton had to smile and shake his head. After all of this time he just learned that it had been Pete

Golding all along who had programmed Europa's voice synthesizer to mimic the sex symbol Marilyn Monroe's voice. Collins had been looking for the culprit from the first day he started at the Group.

"Come on old girl, come on," Pete urged. "I'm feeling mighty exposed here."

Suddenly the main screen flashed a bright white. Then it did it again. Finally it went to a solid blue and the code Pete had entered started flashing at the top minus the numbers in case Pete wasn't alone. This was a very good indication that Europa was regaining her programming. Golding lowered the microphone on his desktop and leaned in. He swallowed and closed his eyes.

"Europa, are you online?"

Silence filled the giant room. Then: "Good evening, Dr. Golding. With my systems down, can you tell me if the emergency on level seventeen has been resolved?"

"We need you to help with that assessment."

"I will need five minutes, thirty-seven seconds to regain sensory input from that section."

"Hurry, please hurry," Pete said as he pushed the microphone away from him and looked at Niles who was looking up through the bulletproof wall upstairs. As Pete started to inform Niles of the delay in case he hadn't heard, the lights flickered overhead and Golding breathed a sigh of relief. He waited, but the lights didn't come back on. He grabbed for the microphone once more. "Europa, is that you getting the power grid back up? Is that the first protocol?" Pete asked as he tried his hardest to remember the sequence of her reboot program.

"Dr. Golding, the power has been severed at the source. With my surveillance systems still down, that is my best estimation."

Niles heard that. He turned and faced Pete who lost all the feeling in his legs and had to sit. Then he caught himself and sat back up.

"Europa, do you have a status report on nuclear reactors one and two?"

"I must source query by utilizing the programs that are currently available, Doctor. Standby."

"Pete, what are the odds that one of those soldiers could access the reactor area on eighty-four?" Niles asked, no longer concerned about the boogeymen in the darkness outside the walls.

Pete shook his head. "Niles, with her systems down, the area could have been unsecured to allow our reactor technicians to get to the evacuation point. God only knows, but if Europa shut down her systems for a security breach, resecuring that area may have come too late."

"Doctor, by accessing the main water systems and the sublevel systems such as distilled water storage, I have calculated that the hard-water levels in all four reactor pumping stations are down 46 percent," Europa said.

"Is this an occurrence due to the emergency shutdown procedure?" Pete asked, doubting his own question.

"Negative, Dr. Golding. The pumps have been shut down at the source and both reactors have scrammed."

"They can't be capable of that!" Niles said as he ran over to Pete's desk. "Europa, we need you to bypass normal startup procedures and go directly to your surveillance systems. Reboot now!"

Before she could react, the red flashing of her warning systems started back up with the irritating buzz of the alarm.

"Doctor, we have a biohazard warning on level seventeen and a security breach on levels one, four, eight, eighteen, and eighty-four. Untagged persons are inside the complex."

By *untagged* Europa meant that all Event Group members had a microscopic bug placed in their thigh area just under their skin that told Europa where every member of the Group was currently located. Event guests like Gloria Bannister and Henri Farbeaux had been tagged on a temporary basis. The untagged people she was currently picking up on her security scan were obviously the intruder element inside the complex.

"God, they made it into the reactor section and shut down the cooling pumps and water," Niles said as he reached for the phone on an empty desk "Europa, I need communications ASAP!"

"Estimate two minutes until program reboot on communications, Dr. Compton. I am now receiving security video from level eighty-four. Low-quality night vision has been achieved."

As the two men watched, a hazy and greenish picture came on the main screen. At first they saw nothing out of the ordinary except for the flashing red and yellow lights indicating that the reactors, both one and two, had scrammed automatically or had shut down as per fail-safe protocol when they started being starved of coolant.

"Location of Colonel Collins?" Pete said into the microphone.

"Colonel Collins is currently on level eight, south stairwell."

Pete realized that they had to get people down to the very bottom level of the complex to restart the distilled water pumps and get the reactors to start their cooldown. Without getting them up again, the reactors would blow, taking all of Nellis and Las Vegas along with the complex, and also leave a radioactive hole in the ground half the size of Lake Mead.

"Niles, you have to leave here, get to some radios, and pray that the colonel pops out someplace where he can receive."

Compton didn't hesitate as he knew where there were at least a dozen radios—his own office. He ran up the stairs knowing that if they didn't get this stopped, growing giants would be the least of the problems for his Group.

"Dr. Golding, security cameras on thirty-four have picked up nine members of Department 5656 that have not achieved egress from the complex."

"What? We still have more people down there?"

"Correct, Doctor, they are trapped."

"Can you get any kind of emergency power to the main cargo lift and get them out of there?"

"It may be possible to reroute my battery power to the cargo lift."

"How will that affect your backup power system?"

"Total drainage in seven minutes, ten seconds, Doctor," Europa replied.

"And how long to get the lift to level one?"

"Five minutes, thirty-seven seconds."

Pete felt the knot in his stomach grow larger. If he ordered Europa to assist the trapped men and women in the gymnasium and sports complex, she wouldn't have but one minute and thirty-three seconds of power to either get the men and women help or go up with the reactors.

"Europa, reroute your power to the cargo lift and get those people out!"

Jack placed his hand on the chest of Charlie Ellenshaw when he not only felt something below them on level eight but smelled it. It was an odor he had smelled on every battlefield he had ever served on. It was the smell of blood—a lot of it.

"Stay here, Doc," he said just above a whisper, knowing that Crazy Charlie didn't understand military hand signals.

"What is it?" Charlie asked gripping the M-14 as tightly as he could. He looked up at the weak lighting of the floodlight and then cursed that he couldn't see the landing on the next level down.

Jack took the steps one at a time without any weapon at all. He was only ten steps away from the sharp curve in the stairwell when he saw an arm stretched across the landing. Jack cursed as he took another step and then suddenly felt a presence behind him. He turned as fast as he could and almost gave Charlie a coronary as well as himself.

"Damn it, Doc!" Jack hissed, "I told you to hang back and cover me."

"Colonel, from that angle, the trajectory of any form of cover fire would not have accomplished what I was asked to do, if—" In the darkness Ellenshaw saw Collins and knew that he better not continue his geometry lesson at that time. "Sorry," he said as a way of completing his sentence.

Jack took another step, and another, and then was at the

next level. His jaw set when he saw the six men sprawled on the large grate leading to level eight. They were torn to pieces. Jack had to grab the handrail as Charlie moaned behind him. The worst thing they saw was the head of Sergeant Sanchez placed directly on top of his own chest. Collins knew it was meant to frighten. That was the only statement the killer of his reaction team could have meant, to send fear down the spines of anyone who saw the decapitation. Instead of shaking in his boots as the beast who did this foul act intended, Jack simply reached down and grabbed three of the assault packages that were scattered on the landing. As he passed his men, stepping over them with care, he stopped and waved Charlie over.

"Take two more of these, Doc—we're going to need them."

"There is no sign of Captain Everett and his men, Colonel. The last we heard, he was off to find," he hesitated as if saying the sergeant's name would bring on more bad luck, "Sergeant Sanchez."

"Remember that the captain is not only good, he's the best at evasion, even from these assholes."

"Yeah, the captain can be on my team any day," Charlie said with as much bravado as he could muster.

Collins came to the thick steel door and paused. He tilted his head and listened for anything coming from the far side. Then he placed a hand over the door and felt the cold steel. He looked back at Ellenshaw and shook his head.

"Pete and Niles should have had the power up by now. Where in the hell is Europa? That expensive bitch better not have bailed out on us."

Collins reached into one of the bags and brought out a small box. He felt better just seeing what was inside. Six hand grenades were packed in foam and looked like diamonds in the rough to him. He started filling his pockets.

Above Jack, Charlie's eyes widened. "Can I have—"

"No," Collins answered before the stupid question could be voiced. Jack turned and tossed Ellenshaw three new magazines one at a time. Charlie fumbled but managed to catch them all. He then reached inside the canvas bag and brought out a sawed-off twelve-gauge shotgun. He quickly loaded it with the blue plastic-cased solid-shot shells, adjusting the strap and then placing the shotgun over his shoulder. Next came the Ingram submachine gun. He quickly taped two of the long clips together, both facing in opposite directions, and then slammed the magazine home. "There, that feels better," Jack said.

"I must admit it, you look better, Colonel," Charlie said, happy that Collins was happy.

Collins brought the Ingram up and slowly reached out in the light of the floods above him and cracked the door open. He looked inside the dimly lit corridor and into the clinic. He saw that a bed had been pushed up close to the heavily damaged elevator doors, which lay bent and crumpled on the tiled floor. The colonel then opened the stairwell door wide enough to get his head through.

Charlie Ellenshaw winced as Jack's head disappeared through the opening, wanting to say that that's how teenagers get killed in all the slasher movies—by sticking their heads into dark rooms. He managed not to warn Jack of the danger.

Collins quickly saw that the clinic was empty. He let the door close and then turned to face Charlie.

"It looks like they managed to evacuate Colonel Farbeaux."

"Oh, joy," Ellenshaw said.

"Okay, we know the only ones above us are Pete and Niles in the computer center, so it looks like we're headed down, Doc."

Charlie had his throat catch in midswallow but managed to nod his head.

"Don't worry, Doc, it's all downhill."

10

The attack had come upon Everett and his nine men so suddenly that two of the men were dead before a shot was fired in their rushed defense. Just before the creature came through the plastic-lined wall, they had been up two levels and then back down three as the maze of trying to reach anyone still alive was quickly becoming fraught with pitfalls. The creatures had torn free steps in the steel staircases, wrenched away handrails, and rolled large chunks of concrete down upon anyone who might be traversing the stairwells. Everett felt the intelligence of these creatures, even before they came upon several bodies of technicians he recognized as being a part of Virginia Pollock's Nuclear Sciences division. Somehow they had missed the evacuation order, had been cut off, and then tried to make their way in the dark down the stairwell, where they were ambushed and then busted to pieces. As they examined the bodies they could clearly see that every bone had been smashed.

They had hoped to be at level forty-two and the main armory far before this, but with the obstacles around them they were slowed to the point of crawling. Just a moment before the attack came, Carl had thought he heard voices from the stairwell they were traveling in at least two levels below them. As one of the sergeants started to call out, Everett hushed him.

At that moment he heard a woman's scream from down below and simultaneously the concrete wall beside the middle part of his remaining nine men crashed inward. Standing in front of them was one of the creatures, which had grown so much that its remaining tattered clothing had been completely shed. The beast was standing on one of Everett's men as the others, including the captain, opened fire at point-blank range. The beast ducked and covered its head with its massive forearm, and in the darkened stairwell they could not get a clear shot at its head. It quickly swung outward and caught Lance Corporal Jimmy Dolan across the chest, sending him crashing into the hardened steel rail, snapping his back, and tumbling him over the edge. Then the monstrosity before them reached out with a backswing and grasped a young corporal by the neck. With its free arm guarding its most vulnerable area, the head, it pulled the young marine into the wall and then vanished into the honeycomb of the cave system that lined the entire complex.

Everett shook his head and watched as army staff sergeant Frakes emptied his M-16 into the large hole. The return flash made Everett turn away. The captain was now down to seven men. Hanging his head, Everett took a moment to collect himself. Then he remembered the scream he had heard just before the ambush hit. He steeled himself and waved his men on. The blackness of the staircase loomed and Everett realized for the first time that Smith's men had smashed the remaining battery-powered light to bits.

"It didn't take them long to discover the cave system," Sergeant Frakes said as he came up on Everett's rear.

"Yeah, well, we have a few surprises left also if we can just get to the damn armory," Carl said as he looked back at Frakes. "And if I ever see you empty a weapon like that again, with the chance that my man is still alive, I'll toss your ass right off this stairwell."

Frakes gave a nod, happy the captain still had the fire to chew on his ass.

They would all need that fire in the next hour.

Echo Five Three Seven—Sierra
Operation Nerdlinger, Ten Miles North of
Nellis AFB, Nevada

At thirty-five thousand feet the giant Lockheed Martin C-130J Super Hercules opened her rear ramp as the thirty-seven

mon operating under the auspices of Presidential Order
122213, designated Operation Nerdlinger, lined up as the
high-altitude, freezing air blasted into the open ramp. As
Major Garcia stepped forward, the U.S. Air Force Special
Operations team waited for the red light to flash to green.
"Grateful Dead" Garcia didn't have to turn to check on his
DELTA element as he knew they were ready. Each man was
self-sustained from radios to weapons. And their weapons
were of the special kind. They each carried three of them
and ammunition. Garcia felt the cold air coming from his
oxygen system and knew it was just enough for the four-and-
a-half-minute freefall to the desert below. He made sure his
ambient-light goggles were secure on his helmet until he
would need them as he neared the ground.

"Gentlemen, the U.S. Air Force Special Operations
Command wishes you all good luck!" the loadmaster called
out through the secure radio channel just before the red light
flashed green in the red tint of the sight-saving lighting inside the Hercules. "Go, go, go, go!" the loadmaster called
out as four rows of men jumped from the ramp at the same
time. As he watched, a single man brought up the rear and
delayed his HALO jump by ten seconds. Then the plane was
empty and the Hercules turned away to the West where it
would head to March Air Force Base in Southern California
to be hidden from prying eyes and immediately prepped as
the special operations crew rested. In just ten hours the Hercules would be ready to be called upon once again to deliver
any secure package anywhere in the world.

Event Group Complex,
Nellis AFB, Nevada

The group of nine men and women huddled in the far corner
of the football field, not far from the goal line where Virginia
had scored her winning touchdown not three days before.
That event now seemed like it had taken place a thousand
years before.

The eldest of the group, and by far the most tenured person on the Event Group staff was Professor Henry Thomas, a man who graduated from Cal Berkley in 1977. He kept all those around him silent as they heard time and time again loud, roaring screams, gunfire, and then as now, complete and utterly terrifying silence. They had been hiding since the power failed and the giant lift failed to return from level one.

"Take it easy. Captain Everett and old Pete Golding will do something soon; you can bet on it," said the totally gray-haired professor of Middle Eastern philosophy.

In the near darkness of the sports complex he examined the young, frightened faces of technicians and chemists, photo analysts, and chefs. They all looked to him as the elder statesman for the nerve it took to sit in the dark and tell themselves time and time again that there was no such thing as the boogeyman, that there was never a monster under your bed, and that the thing in the closet was nothing but your own fertile imagination.

As Professor Thomas moved from person to person, reassuring as he went, a sudden crash sounded right above the high-ceilinged gymnasium. He flinched as several large chunks of plastic and plaster fell from high above and struck the fifty-yard line of the football field.

"Must be rats up there," he joked, but when no one laughed he felt terrible for making light of the sound of the concrete as it hit the artificial turf.

The sound of laughing froze everyone, and those that were sitting stood. The old professor froze as the sound chilled him to the bone.

"It seems your friends have abandoned you," came the deep, raspy, and booming voice from somewhere in the darkness. This elicited more than one of the frightened people to scream, and that alone made the others want to run in the opposite direction of the voice.

"Who are you?" Professor Thomas called out.

More laughter. "Why I am Darkness. I am Fear. I am Satan and you are in the ninth level of hell," came the voice with almost hysterical laughter. "My hell!" the booming voice echoed.

A woman screamed and turned away, only to be kept still by two men next to her.

"Do not panic; it's trying to frighten us," Thomas said.

"Trying?" the voice asked with a chuckle. "I have achieved at least that," came the horrible sound.

They heard the sound of something moving above them. Thomas looked up at the spiderweb of girders above the athletic field. His old eyes could not penetrate the darkness, but he thought he saw movement. Then he saw something move hand over hand above them that made him move away toward the group of frightened men and women.

Suddenly a screech sounded to their far right. Several men and women screamed as they thought whatever was taunting them was right behind them. They all realized at once that it was the sound of the cargo elevator descending the great carved-out shaft of natural rock. They heard the eight-inch cables as they creaked and whined in its powerful descent.

"Everyone move toward the elevator gate. Get ready to enter it and then close the gate behind you. Now move! Go as quietly as you can."

"You're coming too, right?" asked a young woman who had spent the past four years analyzing the download of information from the Group's KH-11 Blackbird satellite, code named Boris and Natasha. She sounded as if she were near tears as she realized what the old professor had planned.

"I'm afraid not dear. Now get moving and I'll see if I can keep this thing, whatever it is, occupied."

Just as they started to move away, the laughter came once more. The professor nodded at his small group of survivors and moved off into the dark. The others started moving toward the back of the sports arena. They heard the elevator drawing closer as they moved, stumbling and cursing in the dark, but still doing as the professor ordered. Then suddenly they heard the cargo elevator hit their level and stop with a loud whine. First one, then another, and then the others started a blind and panic-driven run toward the gates that housed the lift.

Professor Thomas started a run of his own. He ran toward the center of the field and then tripped immediately over the rubble that had fallen. He rolled onto his back just as something large fell from the girders above him. It fell the one hundred feet and landed with a thud only five yards from his prone body. He heard the growl of whatever it was immediately. He raised his head and saw the darkened shape standing before him. The figure looked like the largest primate he had ever seen. It was at least seven feet tall and built like a tank. He could see the outline of its body and knew it to be naked.

"What in the hell are you?" he asked as he tried his best to sit up, but his body would not cooperate.

"I and others like me are dead men, just as you are," came the deep and menacing voice.

"Who are you?" Thomas said in a low voice, shocked when he realized that the creature standing before him heard the question. Its hearing must have been like that of a timberwolf in the winter months.

"Who . . . am . . . I?" came the lowered voice, which had lost the menacing, just-beneath-the-surface growl. "My . . . my name is . . ."

Thomas saw the line of drool fall from the beast's mouth. It shimmered in the weak lighting from the emergency floods. The professor chanced a look behind him and tried to see where his people were. He heard the opening of the large cargo gate and the hollow thump of footsteps as people started to fill the giant floor of the elevator. He knew he had to stall for more time.

"Yes, tell me your name," he asked, trying to use as much sympathy-laced injection as he could.

The shadowy beast before him tilted its head as if it were deep in thought. It was still drooling and it shifted its massive weight from foot to foot.

"Car . . . Car . . . Carmichael, Sam . . . uel, rrrrr, serial num . . . ber . . . 556 . . . 67 . . . 48 . . . 79."

"That's a nice name, son,"

The beast straightened up and with a shake of its large head lifted its face to the dark area above them and screamed in rage. It started forward and Professor Thomas said a silent, quick prayer as the creature came into full view. The old man crossed himself as he realized he had been speaking to a beast who said his name, and then offered his serial number, just as a soldier would have. He hoped it wasn't one of Captain Everett's security men just as he closed his eyes at the exact moment the giant soldier stomped him literally to death. Then its green and glowing eyes looked up and penetrated the darkness as it caught sight of the lift and the people inside who were just lowering the gate. It started running for the elevator and its occupants.

The men and women inside were screaming for whoever was operating the lift to step on it. They realized that they weren't going to move in time. The beast was almost upon the steel gate as it reached out. Suddenly the giant cargo elevator started to rise and it was the sudden movement that made the beast miss the mark. It was left grabbing at empty air as the lift rose on its sixteen massive cables. As the lost souls rose from the depths of the ninth circle of hell, they looked through the steel grating and watched in abject horror as the large gate sealing the shaft crashed inward.

"Oh, God!" one of the men shouted as the beast rose in the darkness, leaped from the shaft, and grabbed hold of a trailing cable. It started to climb.

The giant lift started to climb faster as the large motors on level one coiled the cables and took on the massive weight of the elevator. Still, the creature came hand over hand on the slippery cable.

"Jesus, what do we do?" asked one of the women.

The beast hit the bottom of the lift before any answer could be given. Everyone screamed as the thick and elongated fingers came through the grating that made up the flooring. The beast held on as it ripped and pulled at the steel mesh. It was now in a frenzy of madness as the men and women tried to get as far into the opposite corner as possible. Soon, the beast was able to get its entire arm through the steel floor. It swiped at those closest and nearly managed to snag a woman's bare foot.

It would be through the floor of the lift in less than a minute.

Gate Number One
The Old Hangar

As the thirteen security men watched, they could see the top of the lift as it rose. They had been caught off-guard when the giant elevator started down into the complex. The sergeant in charge of gate security cursed his luck that he hadn't been closer so at least six of the team could have lowered themselves into the complex. As it was, they were stunned when the lift started rising once more. They could hear frightened screams of men and women coming closer out of the blackness below.

"Stand ready to cover these people," the sergeant said as he backed away from the gate where the elevator would arrive. "It sounds like they may have company coming with them."

Finally they could see the anxious, scared faces staring up at them from the terrified men and women on the lift. "Stand back," the sergeant shouted as the concrete flooring parted fully. The gap they had been looking into separated into a massive thirty-foot-long chasm as the lift neared the top.

The sergeant quickly opened the steel gate that protected the open pit and readied his M-14 carbine as did his twelve men. The lift finally appeared and as it cleared the opening the steel gates that made up its side slowly lowered on their hydraulics until they were flat against the old concrete of the hangar. He didn't have to order the men and women off the lift, as they came at his men in a stampede. Shaken, the sergeant was yelling for them to slow down and tell him what was happening. Then he heard one of his men shout as another sound came into the mix, the tearing and wrenching of steel as the beast finally tore away the last of the flooring.

"My God," the sergeant said as his men's gunfire drowned out his exclamation of shock at what he was seeing. The beast covered its head and face and charged the security detail. It was only focused on getting through them and their gunfire to kill everyone that had been on the lift. It was as if its brain had locked on to one desire only: get those that had escaped it.

The security men saw that their 5.56-millimeter rounds were just punching holes in thick, pulsing skin while not doing any real damage.

"Fall back, out of the hangar!" the sergeant yelled as he started to back away, pushing and pulling his men as he did.

The beast roared and advanced. It moved with purpose as Jack and Carl's well-trained security men maintained their fire until they were clear of the giant hangar doorframe. They backed away while keeping up a withering fire at the beast. They watched as large pieces of flesh were torn free of its chest, legs, and arms, but still it advanced.

The camouflaged security detail ventured into the dark night where the desert surrounded them but offered no hope of cover. They realized too late that they were walking the creature directly into the path of every man and woman they had pulled from the complex, over three hundred of them, most of which were yelling and screaming in fear as the beast was free of the hangar and bearing down up them.

"This is it, no farther, hold the line!" the sergeant shouted as the beast was only fifteen feet from them. Men were firing and quickly emptying their weapons.

Suddenly they heard the command coming from behind the creature. The order was loud and clear, even over the crackle of gunfire.

"Soldiers to our front, hit the deck!"

Collins had trained his men to not hesitate. He had drilled into them that any form of hesitation got people killed. The thirteen men of gate one security hit the ground just as a withering, powerful eruption of heavy-caliber gunfire opened up at almost point-blank range. The heavy-caliber rounds, most fired from fifty-caliber weapons, struck the creature, forcing it to turn and face the new threat behind it. That was its fatal mistake. It thought that it was going to face more of the light-caliber rounds of the security men, but instead it faced heavy fire that tore the front of the beast to pieces. It roared in pain and shook its massive head. It continued forward. Suddenly the altered soldier was dropped as a round fired from a fifty caliber Barrett single-shot rifle struck it between the eyes. The creature's head literally exploded into mist. Still it took one, two, and then three steps forward before it fell into the desert sand outside of the old hangar.

Suddenly the frightened group of civilians and the security element from gate one saw over thirty shadows rise up from the still-hot sands of the desert. One of the men still held the smoking M107A1 fifty-caliber Barrett rifle.

"Jesus Christ!" the sergeant from the Event Group said loudly. "Where in the hell did you guys come from?"

A small man that held the large-bore fifty stepped forward and removed his ambient-light goggles and then his bush hat. He wiped sweat from his face as he stared down at the monstrosity he and his men had just dropped.

"We just dropped in from Never Never Land Trooper," Major Jerry "Grateful Dead" Garcia said as he motioned his men forward. "Tommy, it looks like we'll be rapelling. Get the gear ready."

The sergeant stepped forward and held out his hand to the smaller man. Garcia noticed the civilians in the desert start to come forward. He ignored the sergeant's handshake gesture.

"Sergeant?"

"Reggie Anderson, U.S. Air Force," he answered.

"Well, Anderson, Reggie, Sergeant, U.S. Air Force, would you please keep your people back? If you were trained by Jack Collins, you can guess as to why we cannot mix with the civilian element of . . . of . . . hell, whoever you people are."

The sergeant realized as he looked from the smaller man to his other rescuers that he was dealing with the highly deadly group of men known as DELTA. He understood immediately, turned, and waved everyone but his security team back into the darkness of the desert.

"Thank you, Anderson, Reggie. Now, can you tell me where Jack is?"

"I have no idea. The last I heard . . . well . . . the last I heard was that he was off base. Captain Everett has been stuck below since this mess began."

The major looked down again at the beast at his booted feet. He reached over and removed a flashlight from his collar and snapped it on. His eyes roamed over the transformed man and he looked up at the sergeant once again as he snapped off the flashlight.

"One of yours?" he asked.

"Not exactly. This is one of the intruders. From what I understand, he didn't come into the complex that way."

"Must be the water down there, huh?"

The sergeant remained silent even as the major slapped him on the shoulder.

"Sorry, it was a long freefall, and I don't handle it as well as when I was a sprout."

One of Garcia's men came over and handed him a small bag of gear.

"What's you plan?" the sergeant asked.

"Well, the president said he wants those people down there brought out in one piece, so I guess we're going in."

"Can my men and I come along?"

Garcia looked up as he handed the heavy-caliber Barrett over to the man who had given him his rapelling gear.

"Thanks, but we work better alone. Grateful for the offer though." Garcia turned away and then stopped and faced the Event Group security man once more. "By the way Sergeant, from two hundred feet up, we saw that you put up one hell of a defense. Pass that on to your men. I can see Jack Collins's training there. You did real well. You and your men can fight with us anytime—just not tonight."

The sergeant watched the small officer and his thirty-six-man team move off toward the hangar and the black hole that awaited them.

"Good luck."

Level Seven

Niles had never been as frightened in his life as he walked the long and curving corridor. The white plastic helped in reflecting the weak lighting from the emergency floods but did nothing to dispel the shadows that threatened to give him a stroke every time he saw his own as reflected in the plastic wall and ceiling. In the million times he had walked this very corridor heading to either his office or the conference room he had never given one thought to the darkness that would prevail in the underground complex if power had ever been lost. If they survived this night of horrors he swore to himself that he would line every hallway, office space, and stairwell with so much backup emergency lighting that the heat would fry an egg if needed. With billions of dollars in high-tech equipment and millions more for a military arm, right at that moment Niles would trade half of it for more emergency lighting.

It was amazing how his ears and mind were playing tricks on him. In the almost empty complex, echoes and sounds from many levels away could be heard wafting up through stairwells and elevator shafts. Screams of his people and gunfire from what remained of the security staff kept Niles praying and moving. As he approached the double doors leading to his office, he slowed when he heard a faint echo. To him it sounded like a deep breath had been taken in and then exhaled. He froze as he came to the last curving bend. He knew the curve of the last corner didn't offer the protection a straight-lined wall would have, but he tried not to expose much of his body. Somewhere in the distance, perhaps three or four levels down, the thump of gunfire wafted through the soles of his shoes and popped in his ears.

As he looked around the bend he finally saw the offices where he, Pete, Charlie, and Jack had been but an hour before. The doors were still propped open and he could see the desks of his assistants inside. His private elevator was to the left of the door and from his vantage point he couldn't see the damaged shaft. He shook his head, moved as fast as he could to the door, and then stopped.

This time it was something else. Not breathing like he thought he had heard before, but something else he couldn't put his finger on. Cursing himself for his deep-seated fear of the dark, Compton stepped into the outer offices used by his four assistants. He quickly looked around. It seemed everything was still as it was. The damaged elevator doors and the empty tubular shaft inside looked as if they held no hidden monster waiting to jump out at Niles. He cursed himself again as he remembered the nine-millimeter Beretta Jack had slipped into his hands. He again wanted to stomp his feet in anger as his frightened state was fast becoming something that was as deadly as the unnatural soldiers prowling his complex. He angrily reached back and pulled the heavy handgun from his waistband. He felt the pressure plate designed into the new Beretta disengage the safety on the weapon as he gripped it tightly. He felt better for at least the moment as he scurried across the reception room thinking that at least now he could shoot something, even if it was himself. Niles paused at his large oak doors, just waiting and listening. His eyes caught the large portrait of Abraham Lincoln at the centermost point of the main wall. Niles rolled his eyes.

"Don't look at me like that—all you had to deal with was the Civil War," he whispered to himself, realizing that the humor of his small joke had made him feel better.

Collins and Everett had always told him that humor came out in the most pressure-filled situations for the simple fact that in a terrifying moment, a soldier's brain will fall back on something that was familiar. In the American military, humor was the most common thread they had. Niles remembered what they always taught—keep it light even in times of stress; it will free your mind to think. He shook his head and for no reason he could think of, nodded up at old Abe. Then without further thought he opened the left side of the office doors.

As soon as he was in he was grateful that all fifty monitors situated around his curving walls were still on. They were all bright with the snow of no signal, but it still gave him more light than he was used to in the dark of the complex. The main thirty-foot monitor was on and the blue picture showed that Europa was still fighting to bring her systems back online. He noticed a clock in the far corner winding down from two minutes and thirty seconds. Above the clock it read "Time to power loss."

"What in the hell does that mean?" he asked himself. He shook his head and walked quickly toward his desk and the credenza on the back wall. He knelt and as he did he suddenly looked behind him when he thought he heard something move in the outer offices. He froze for what seemed like ten full minutes but was actually only three seconds. He again shook his head to clear it of the fear and started to open the credenza drawers, hoping his radios were still there and that they had held their charge. His eyes widened behind his wire-rimmed glasses as his hands hit the first of five radios and their headsets. He pulled two of them out and turned the first one to the on position. He wanted to scream "Yes!" when the green light came on indicating a full battery charge. He stood and placed the Beretta inside of his belt and the headset onto his balding head. He looked down at the frequency and prayed that it was still set to complex security.

"Compton to Colonel Collins, come in," he whispered, remembering the things that were stalking not only him but possibly anyone with a radio. "Compton to Colonel Collins, come in please," he hissed.

Suddenly Niles heard a sound that stopped him cold, and it had definitely come from somewhere in the outer office.

"I hear you," said the deep, raspy, and absolutely terrifying voice that had the quality of a bass speaker. "Come out, come out, wherever you are."

Niles closed his eyes and went down hard on the carpeted floor.

"Damn it," he murmured to himself, "these things are really getting to me." Niles slowly raised his head to look over the top of his desk and into the reception area of his office. His blood froze when he saw the large shadow as it moved from desk to desk in the office outside.

"This position is untenable," he said quietly, trying to allow his own voice to give him the bravado he needed to take action.

As he thought, he lambasted himself for all of his inactivity over the years. If he had been in shape he would risk it by running as fast as he could out of his office and through the reception area in a break for freedom before the beast inside could react. But he knew he was fooling himself to the extreme. He could be Jessie Owens and still be caught by this thing from his deepest nightmare. He had seen how fast the creatures reacted.

"I can smell you little man," said the voice as it tipped over the desk of one of his assistants.

Niles closed his eyes as he tried to think of something humorous as before, but nothing came. He realized that it must take practice for humor to come to your mental rescue in a stressful situation—something he would have to speak with Jack or Carl about.

When the thing had seen that there was no one hiding behind or under the first desk it went into a rage. It roared like an out-of-control animal and started smashing the other desks to pulp as it circled the office. Then it suddenly stopped and looked toward the double doors leading into Niles's office. Its eyes next went to the adjacent double doors. The conference room was closed. Niles prayed that the beast went there first.

"Stop, think, plan, initiate," said the deep voice as Niles heard calmness overwhelm the anger of the creature. The beast laughed again, an insane-sounding giggle-like noise that reeked of schizophrenia.

The laugh and trailing giggle were unnerving as they

rumbled into his hiding place. As the beast came to his office doors Niles could swear he heard the giant sniff the air. What kind of a nightmare were they truly dealing with? Could this thing be the future of men, or their eventual doom? If this was evolution at its height, he could see no way that mankind could ever survive. Intelligence and violence advancing through evolution together? If this is what the human brain is capable of, Niles now feared for the very soul of the human race. A world of supermen and soldiers that were hard to kill, acted and hunted as animals, and could think as fast on their feet as Einstein? No, he wanted no part of that future, and he knew that this thing wasn't going to outthink him. Not today.

The beast sniffed again, but for the first time one of its animal-like senses failed it. It went left instead of continuing into Niles's office.

As Compton listened he screamed when he heard the beast suddenly fall into a rage again as it battered down the double oak doors and burst inside where it began to tear into the giant conference table and chairs that lined it, looking for its easy prey. Niles took that opportunity to start creeping around his desk and crawl from the office to the reception area and then to the hallway outside. Once there he knew through his frightened state that there wasn't an animal wild or domestic that would ever catch him. At that moment he knew he was capable of flying.

As he finally reached the center of the reception area on his hands and knees, he chanced a look up and realized he would make it because the beast was even more frenzied as it tore through the inside of the conference room. Compton closed his eyes and had hope for the first time in what seemed like hours. Then disaster struck.

"This is Collins. Come in Compton. Over."

The call could not have come at a worse moment. Niles had never adjusted the radio volume and it seemed anyone could have heard it through the entire complex.

"Oh, shit," he said, not waiting for the beast to come at him. He leapt to his feet, his heart practically flying out of his chest. His feet spun on the slick floor of the main office. It was like a nightmare where he was stuck in sand or, even worse, syrup. His shoes finally caught traction just as the beast roared and burst out of the conference room. The enraged beast was just in time to see the backside of Compton streak into the hallway.

The chase was on between a heavyset, balding, beyond-middle-age director and a genetically altered superman.

Mendenhall led the way down the stairwell. He was down to three shots in his Beretta as they finally made it to level forty-two. He paused so the others could catch their breath before they ventured into the corridor outside the stairwell door. He looked back and nodded at Gloria, giving her a reassuring smile. Virginia was speaking softly with Sarah and Farbeaux, reassuring the Frenchman that they had made it to the level where the armory was. The Frenchman nodded his head and with the help of Denise Gilliam squeezed past Sarah and Virginia.

"What's the plan?" Henri asked Mendenhall, interrupting his vision of Gloria Bannister.

"That's what we need to discuss," Will said as he moved over to the side of the landing to allow Farbeaux to stand next to him. "The armory will be locked, but unlike everything else in the complex, it's not sealed magnetically, so power or not, we can open it with this," he said as he pulled out a large key.

"Finally, a security design I can understand," Henri said as he looked back at Sarah, now looking better than she had in the past hour. Her eyes managed to look up at him and she gave the Frenchman a ghost of a smile.

"You think maybe Sarah's a little vulnerable right now, Colonel?" Mendenhall asked as his own eyes blazed at Henri when he saw the looks exchanged between Farbeaux and McIntire.

Farbeaux smiled and looked at Sarah and back again to Mendenhall. He could see Will was angry about Colonel Collins not being here, and possibly being dead. Still Henri could not resist. He looked back at Gloria who was anxiously awaiting Will to tell her to come the rest of the way up the stairs. Farbeaux's smile broadened as he glanced back at the young black man.

"It's highly possible she is vulnerable, Lieutenant Mendenhall, perhaps as much as Dr. Bannister is at the moment."

Will got angry for the briefest of seconds, and his eyes went to Gloria as she looked up at him and smiled once more. The air was let loose from his lungs like a punctured tire. His shoulders slumped as he realized the Frenchman was right in his assessment. He was no better than the colonel and he knew it. He just nodded his head.

Farbeaux returned the nod and lightly slapped Will on the left shoulder.

"It is hell being human sometimes, isn't it, Lieutenant?" Henri again smiled. "But then again if we weren't, we would end up something like those creatures out there. And I thought I was inhuman at times."

"You are inhuman," Will said and again nodded to the Frenchman. "Well, what do you say we go and get something to fight back with, Colonel?" Will said as he turned to the stairwell door.

"After you," Henri said looking back at Sarah and winking in the weak lighting.

"Let's just hope we don't run into trouble," Mendenhall said with a confident move to open the door.

He swung the heavy steel door open and his eyes widened as one of the giants was standing right in front of him. Mendenhall quickly closed the door and threw his body against it just as it was struck with the weight of the beast in the corridor. Farbeaux saw the lieutenant's predicament and quickly threw his weight behind the effort to keep the abomination at bay.

"Okay, we're in trouble!" Mendenhall yelled over the roaring outside.

Jack and Charlie stared into the black abyss where the stairwell had once been. At least three levels of steel landings

and steps had been torn free from their mountings by the
intelligent creatures they were struggling to survive against.
Collins shook his head in utter frustration as he knew they
would have to brave the hallway outside and the long curving corridor to get to one of the other three stairwells that
were situated in a semicircle along this particular level.

"Doc, now you wait here while I see if there's company
waiting for us on the other side of this door. Do you understand?"

Frightened to death after he had peered into the darkness
far below and seeing the stairs ripped out, Charlie could
only manage to nod his head up and down several times.

"Damn it, Doc. I asked if you understood," Jack barked
angrily and then immediately regretted it.

"Yes . . . Colonel," Ellenshaw finally managed.

"Alright, do as I say and maybe I'll let you have a hand
grenade," Jack said with a wicked twist of his lips, knowing
he would never give Crazy Charlie one of the small explosive devices, one that he could pull the pin on and hold until
it went off in his hand. But the mere offer worked on the old
hippie turned soldier wannabe.

Collins turned to the door, took a deep breath, and then
opened it slowly. The hallway as far as he could see left and
right seemed to be clear. The emergency lighting was still
functioning, meaning that the creatures more than likely
had not visited this level. He looked back at the wide-eyed,
crazed-haired Charlie who waited without breathing for
Jack to say something.

"Okay, come on, Doc."

Charlie followed Jack into the curving corridor. He raised
the M-14 carbine, careful to aim it away from the colonel's
back as he had numerous times since their journey had begun and been stingingly admonished for it. There were several flashes from the emergency floods likely due to weakened
wiring that made the two men pause as they moved down
the seemingly clear hallway. They passed the brand-new
nuclear science labs and made sure to duck beneath the broad
windows in case there were surprises waiting in Virginia's

laboratories. Collins raised his hand up in the air and Charlie stopped, but not before running into the colonel's backside. Jack looked back and shook his head.

"Wipe your glasses off, Doc; they're all fogged up."

Ellenshaw did as he was told, surprised when he placed the thick glasses back on at how he had seen anything before he was told to clean them.

Just as Jack started to move forward again the radio at his side sent a message through to his earpiece. Collins was instantly ashamed that he had actually jumped at the suddenness of the noise, which in turn made Ellenshaw yelp. Collins hissed for the hundredth time in the last thirty minutes. He quickly placed a finger to his lips, making sure Charlie remained quiet, but still ashamed for acting just as frightened and actually showing it. The answer Jack knew was to blame Charlie . . . it made him feel better.

"Compton to Colonel Collins." Jack tried to return the call, but Niles jumped in too quickly, cutting him off. "Compton to Colonel Collins, come in."

At that very moment Charlie reached out and took Jack by the arm, tilting his head to their rear. Collins looked and saw nothing, but Ellenshaw pointed to his left ear and tapped it. Jack listened. He heard the sound of heavy breathing, and then something crashed far away but on the same level.

"Damn, we have company on this level, Doc," he said as he started walking faster toward the large curve and the stairwell beyond. As they moved away from the sound behind them, Jack reached down and made sure his volume was lowered since he didn't exactly know how sensitive the soldiers' hearing was. "Collins to Compton, come in. Over," he said softly into the microphone poised at the corner of his mouth. "Collins to Compton, over," he repeated.

Suddenly Ellenshaw saw the colonel jerk as the voice of Niles came screaming over his earpiece.

"Colonel, listen, I don't have a lot of time," Niles said while breathing hard and running. "I have one ugly son of a bitch chasing me. You have to get down to level eighty-four immediately. Those smartass bastards have shut down the oooling pumps for reactors one and two. Do you hear? Level eighty-four, Jack, eighty-four—gotta go!"

Charlie saw Collins freeze as he heard what Niles had to say. "What is it?" Ellenshaw whispered as he turned when another crashing noise was heard below them.

Collins reached back and grabbed Ellenshaw by the collar, forcing him along the hallway. As they approached the stairwell door, Jack cursed as he heard something back along the corridor start running after them.

"Oh, there's something coming, Colonel," Charlie said as his feet were flying down the hallway past Jack like a scared rabbit with the colonel dead on his heels.

The two men finally reached the nearest stairwell door and Jack threw it open. He took one step inside and started to fall. Ellenshaw reached out and caught Jack by his collar, reversing the roles from just moments before. Collins had stepped right off into space. Charlie dropped the M-14 and tried using both hands to pull Collins back from the abyss as he realized the creatures had torn out the landing and the stairs below it. Collins dangled as the three assault packages slipped from his grip and tumbled end over end into the darkness below. Charlie struggled to keep the colonel in check, but he was quickly losing the battle. Collins finally managed to reach out and take hold of a twisted piece of metal to arrest his fall and help Ellenshaw, who was far stronger than Jack had ever given him credit for, gain a better handhold on his shirt. Finally he found purchase for his foot on a partially ripped out stair and pushed himself backward. With a final heave both he and Ellenshaw fell backward through the open door. As they both tried to catch their breath, they heard the pounding of heavy footsteps stop and then the sound of breaking glass as whatever it was crashed through the window into the nuclear sciences labs.

"Thanks, Doc," Jack said as he gained his feet and pulled Ellenshaw to his. He quickly reached out and grabbed the three remaining assault packages strapped to Charlie's back. He immediately knew what their only escape could be. He pulled out several large coils of very thin black nylon rope.

It wasn't thick but had the tensile strength of a thousand pounds. Jack quickly brought out his rapelling ring and attached it to his pants at the waist. Then he repeated the same for Ellenshaw who was staring at him with wider-than-normal befuddled eyes.

"What is this?" Charlie asked with a small whine.

"Have you ever rapelled before, Doc?"

"Uh, no," he said shaking his head even though Jack had already started prying at the elevator doors next to the stairwell.

"Well, suck it up, Doc, because you're about to get a crash course," he said as he finally parted the two doors and looked down the black tube until it vanished forty-two levels below. The draft produced by the empty and powered-down shaft lifted the colonel's collar as he watched and listened.

"Suck it up?" Ellenshaw said with panic forcing his eyes now even wider than the thick lenses could account for.

Jack continued to stare into the deep, dark elevator tube. He looked back through the doors when the sounds of crashing and breaking stopped inside the distant laboratories.

"We're out of time here, Doc." Jack went to Charlie and quickly threaded the rope through the tungsten steel ring attached to Charlie's waist. He could feel Ellenshaw shaking almost uncontrollably as he made the connection. "You have to go first, Charlie. I hate to say it, but if for some reason you fall you won't take me with you. I have to get to the reactors and start the cooling pumps." Jack added this last little tidbit to take the sting off of Ellenshaw's possible, no imminent, death.

"Reactors?" he said as he watched Jack reach into the tube and find a good solid attach point for the rope. Then he pulled out another coil of black rope and double-knotted the two together, adding the last of the rope from Charlie's third assault package. "I hope this is enough," he said as he stood and patted Ellenshaw on the back.

"What do you mean, you *hope*? What if it isn't?"

Jack smiled. "Isn't being a soldier fun, Charlie?"

"If I get out of this I am never leaving my lab again."

Jack quickly reached into the bag and pulled out two pairs of leather gloves, slapping one of them into Ellenshaw's hand. "Put these on, that rope's going to get hot."

"Hot? What do you mean—"

"Okay, sling that weapon, no, no, sling it to your back. If it's in the front it'll take your head off when . . . when you land. Now, take your left hand and hold the rope here. Then bring your left to your back and take hold of it there just above your spine. You control the speed of your descent by tightening and loosening your grip at your spine. Do you understand?"

"Uh, no, not—"

"Good, now lean out backward with a firm grip . . . that's it, just lean out over the tube. Balance yourself, Charlie, and hold both rope points tightly," Jack said as he heard another crash of glass, this time outward into the hallway close by. "I hate to be a little wimp here, Doc, but something wicked this way comes. Hang on," he said as he kicked Ellenshaw's feet away from the edge of the elevator doors.

Jack was shocked when Charlie disappeared in a split-second. All he saw was the last of Charlie's white hair as it vanished into the darkness below just as the colonel's heart fell through his chest. He knew he had just basically murdered Ellenshaw. He quickly came to his senses.

"Tighten your grip damn it!" Jack screamed, fast realizing he had just alerted the thing in back of them to exactly where he was. He leaned into the tube and tried to see Ellenshaw's bent and broken body anywhere far below. "Doc!"

"Wahoo, that was a rush!" came Ellenshaw's voice from deep inside the tube. The statement echoed six times before it vanished.

"Damn!" Jack said as he attached his own rope. "Go ahead, Doc, get moving and make it fast. Bizzaro superman is coming." He had to smile when he heard Ellenshaw zip farther down the tube into the black hole where there was once nothing but good people, and now was filled with monsters. "Good boy, Charlie."

Collins slung three weapons, the shotgun, the Ingram,

and an M-14 carbine over his shoulder, and then positioned himself facing away from the tube just as the creature hunting them came around the bend in the corridor. Their eyes locked and the creature exposed its teeth, which were wide and long and were showing through a surprised but very pleased grinning mouth. The abnormal eyes shown in the semidark like those of a hunting cat. It shook its head at the easy prey ahead of it and charged.

"You'll excuse me if I don't wait around dickhead," Jack said as he pushed off into the great abyss of the tube just as the beast roared in anger and defeat.

As the six men and women scrambled down the stairs, it was Mendenhall who realized after half an hour that he was not hearing the sound of pursuit from the creature that had surprised him in the doorway. He held his hand up and the others stopped their descent. Sarah reached around Henri and felt the blood flowing pretty freely.

"Will, the colonel's wounds have opened up," she said, trying not to shout.

Denise Gilliam raised the Frenchman's lab coat and surgical blouse. She shook her head. "Damn it, it's like he wasn't stitched up at all." She looked up at Farbeaux and shook her head, knowing he would have a hard time seeing her disapproval in the darkness of the stairwell. "You stupid Frenchman; why didn't you say something?"

"Well, Doctor, I didn't really want to stop and receive any more wounds. That chap in the doorway up there didn't look like the type that would pause for a wounded man. I don't think mercy to the fallen is one of their strong suits."

"Good point," Sarah said, finally smiling up at him.

"Okay, if he dies, it may be a better death than what's waiting for us," Will said as he turned and faced his charges. "Dr. Pollock, we're on sixty-one. The first vault enclosures are here. Is there anything we can use on this level to help us?"

Virginia tried to bring up the inventory secured inside vaults 0001-1000 from memory to see if anything stood out.

She shook her head. "I don't know, Will. We just moved new artifacts in four days ago. Hell, my mind isn't working."

"Can't say as I blame you for that," Mendenhall said as he cracked the stairwell door and looked through into the darkened corridor. He saw the security arch leading to the vault section. He could see the dead laser grid and darkened arch, meaning they could enter that section without getting zapped by ten thousand volts of electricity.

"Lieutenant, I think locking ourselves inside one of your magnificent vaults is a very good idea at this point. I prefer it to running aimlessly in this dark stairwell," Henri said as he tightened his grip on Sarah, who returned the gesture. He was beginning to like being the helpless one in the group.

Mendenhall looked back at the five people behind and above him on the stairs. Gloria looked at him with the hope that he knew what to do. He was loath to disappoint the doctor, so he nodded his head.

"Okay, Colonel, I think you may have something. But the electricity is out, meaning that the vaults are all open. But maybe we can find one of the larger ones and barricade ourselves inside until the cavalry comes."

"Sounds like a plan," Virginia said.

"Let's do it. I have a real bad feeling our luck on this stairwell is fast running out," Denise offered, looking nervously up into the darkness.

Will again pushed the door open and stuck his head out. He waited for something to rip it off, but nothing came out of the dimly illuminated corridor. He cautiously pushed the door open all the way and at the same time waved the others forward.

As they exited the stairwell next to the elevator tube, Sarah stopped and hushed everyone. They all heard it immediately. It sounded just like the muffled voice and yell of Crazy Charlie Ellenshaw coming from inside the elevator tube. But they all knew there wasn't an elevator for Ellenshaw to ride. Then the sound vanished just as fast as it took for them all to stop and listen more closely.

"That was weird," Sarah said as she took a stronger hold of Henri and started to move again.

Mendenhall held out the nine millimeter before him as he made it to the security arch. He cautiously leaned over the desk where a guard would usually be stationed to cover that level. He looked at the screen and quickly saw that it was still blue. Europa was still down.

"Damn it," he said as the others approached.

"Has anyone checked the old girl's batteries," Henri said as he slumped a little further against Sarah.

"Good one, Colonel. I'll remember to tell Dr. Golding of your comment. I'm sure he'll make allowances for the next monster invasion," Will said as he took Gloria by the hand and moved off into the long and curving corridor that housed the vault area. Mendenhall thought he had made a good return quip when he realized that he and Gloria were the only ones going inside the security arch.

"Uh, Lieutenant, our company has arrived," Farbeaux said as all at once all four people turned and ran through the arch past Will and Gloria.

As Mendenhall peered into the darkness where they had all been just a second before, he saw it. The beast, the glow of its eyes visible, was just standing by the stairwell, or *floating* would be a better word as the beast dipped and rose as it continued looking at him and Gloria.

"As I was told earlier, there is now nowhere to run," said the deep and raspy voice. The creature started forward at an easy gait, knowing the six men and women had no place to go but farther back into darkness.

As Virginia led the way, she turned suddenly to the left into a vault she had most recently been inside of just three days before. She stood at the front of the twelve-inch-thick steel door and waved everyone inside. Sarah and Farbeaux tripped over the steel threshold and went down, causing Will, Gloria, and Virginia to crash into each other. Mendenhall made a quick decision and pushed everyone farther inside and then just as quickly stepped back out of the vault.

"What in the hell are you doing, Lieutenant?" Virginia shouted angrily as she pushed through the others to try to pull Mendenhall back inside.

"Giving this thing two targets instead of one. Seal this up as best you can," Will shouted as he pushed the two-ton steel door closed, effectively shutting out the cursing from those inside.

They heard the beast laughing as it reached the very threshold of the vault Will had just left, or at least they hoped he had left. Virginia knew the vault door wouldn't lock as she spun the security wheel in the center of the stainless-steel door. Just as the wheel locked, Virginia felt the beast outside start to turn it back to the open position. She looked around in a blind panic, and it was a shocked and stunned Gloria who came to their rescue. In the light of the single emergency bulb in the back of the steel-encased room Virginia quickly saw what the young scientist was carrying. Dr. Pollock nodded her head vigorously as Gloria, tears streaming over Mendenhall's sudden departure, placed the short-shafted spear through the wheel's spokes and then secured its bottom half against the metal framing criss-crossing the door. She made sure the sharpened point was secure against the steel bracing at the top just as the beast outside pulled heavily on the vault's door and tried to turn the wheel from the outside.

Gloria and Virginia stepped backward with a start when the door was hit, sending dirt and small rocks down from the ceiling. The thick shaft of the spear held even though it bowed to the left, almost to the breaking point. Just as the wheel was about to turn, snapping the small spear, Denise and Sarah were there with two more of the short throwing spears, copying what Gloria had just done. Now there were three of these small spear shafts holding the door's locking wheel closed against the onslaught from the other side.

"Where would I be without you guys?" Virginia asked as she backed away from the steel door, watching the spears rattle and bend and then become still.

* * *

Will regretted not having at least perused the list of new artifacts now being stored on the newly constructed vault level. From behind him in the dark corridor with gleaming but at the moment dull stainless-steel vaults running along both sides of the wide hall, Mendenhall heard the scream of the creature as it attacked the vault he had just left with all of the women and a wounded Farbeaux inside. He was relieved when he failed to hear the screams of his friends after the first assault on the steel vault.

"Hey, you ugly son of a bitch, I'm down here!" Will shouted back into the darkness. The move had caught even himself off-guard. He shook his head as the beast situated around the bend in the hallway ceased moving and attacking the vault. Will just knew it was now looking down the once-gleaming corridor trying to discern where his prey was situated and what trap could possibly be waiting for it.

Then Mendenhall heard what he feared most—the creature turned on its heels and started his way.

"Well, this is what you wanted," Will mumbled to himself as he turned into the largest vault on the brand-new level sixty-one and closed the giant door behind him, shutting out the running footsteps of the creature as it came on.

Inside vault number 0001, things had calmed when they felt that the beast had left the vault door. As they relaxed momentarily, everyone fought for breath and as they did they all noticed for the first time what vault Virginia had led them into.

"I'll be damned," Gloria said, wiping her eyes dry as she staggered over to assist Sarah in getting Henri to his feet.

Farbeaux whistled as he took in the artifacts he could see with the single light bulb at the back of the vault.

"You people never cease to amaze, I'll give you that."

Arranged around the large vault were riches and artifacts that had once belonged to a Zulu king known to the world as Cetshwayo—the man who brought down British forces in the largest defeat of a modern well-equipped army by native tribesmen in history. That battle brought on the legend of the Zulu Dawn, a historical fact that the trapped men and women inside vault number 0001-61890 had in common with the British Empire on January 22, 1879. They were in danger of being trapped and wiped out without mercy.

11

Niles ran so fast around the blind corner that his black shoes caught on the carpet and sent him flying to the floor within sight of the computer center. He cursed his own clumsiness as the radio flew from his hand and smashed against the far wall. He quickly tried to rise as he heard the creature slam into a wall as it negotiated its huge body around the bend in the hallway, taking the turn too fast. Compton hurriedly tried to raise himself from the floor, and as he collapsed back down he knew that he had broken his left ankle. He tried once more and finally made it to his knees and then to his right foot. He hopped three feet before he had to reach out and take hold of the plastic-lined wall. He shook his head in anger and realized he would never make it the thirty feet to the bulletproof computer center.

Suddenly and frighteningly hands were on him lifting him up, and for the life of him he couldn't help it—he screamed. It was a high-pitched sound that he couldn't believe had emanated from his own mouth.

"Oh, hang on, you sissy!"

Niles realized that the tall and lanky Pete Golding, who hadn't lifted anything heavier than a stapler in the past ten years, had actually picked him up and placed him over his slight shoulder in a fireman's carry. He was running down the carpeted hallway to the sanctuary he called home. Before Compton realized what was happening they were through the double six-inch glass doors and he was roughly thrown onto a large desk as Pete swung around and manually locked the doors. As Golding backed away he saw how close they had come to a bad end. In his efforts, through his grunting and his yelling, he hadn't realized how close Niles's pursuer had been to catching them from behind.

"Oh, shit!" Pete yelled as he backed away from the glass so fast that he crashed into the desk where Compton was fighting to rise. The desk tilted and Niles went flying off onto the risers above the computer center floor.

The beast hit the glass wall just to the left of the double doors. The impact into the bulletproof glass sent a wide, streaking crack snaking through the reinforced wall. The beast rebounded and then fell to the floor, surprised that it hadn't crashed through this glass like any other in the complex. Pete watched in stunned silence as the former mercenary shook its head and jumped back to its feet. Instead of backing away and gaining momentum for another charge, it took two steps to the left and started to examine the wall. Its head tilted right and then left as it studied the problem before it. The two men saw the wide swath of blood as it coursed down from the left ear of the giant.

"Jesus, Niles, it's using problem-solving skills," Pete said as he backed farther away from the glass. "It's that advanced even though the massive dose it ingested is at this moment killing its brain cells, the very ones the drug just activated. If these men had taken a normal dose, a dose intended in actual combat, they would have just been unafraid to die; still thinking, just a want of killing slicing through their expanding brains."

Niles looked up at Pete as if he were crazy.

"Perhaps it would be better if you filed your report on Perdition's Fire later, when we have more time?"

Pete knew he had started running on because he was so frightened at what was happening. Explaining something to Niles allowed Pete to slow his mind and get a better grasp of the situation. He cleared his throat and moved his weight away from the director.

The creature stopped examining the crack in the window for a moment as Pete's movement caught its glowing eyes. It watched the thin computer director for a moment and then like the others before it, it smiled. It slowly placed a hand near the spiderweb crack and ran one of its elongated, trunk-like fingers over it.

Pete turned to look at the computer center's main viewing screen and saw the ticking down of Europa's power system. She had forty-four seconds of life left to her.

"Europa," Pete called out loudly, hoping her internal systems could pick up his voice, "are you still with me, baby?"

After examining the glass and probing the crack, the beast closed its hand into a ham-sized fist and hit the broken glass precisely where the riverlike crack formed, sending small pieces of clear material onto the carpeted floor inside the computer center. The smile widened as it caught sight of Pete once more. Then its eyes moved to Compton as the director finally managed to stand on one leg and use the desks to hop away from where he thought the mercenary was going to crash through the wall.

"Yes, Dr. Golding," Europa finally answered.

"Tell me you came up with something while I was out?" Pete said as he reached out and helped Niles down the steps leading to the center's floor.

"If you are referencing our earlier discussion on power replacement, yes, I have a solution, but it involves a major shutdown of all civil systems."

"What in the hell does that mean?"

"Europa, commence implementing your plan immediately!" Niles called out loudly.

"Yes, Dr. Compton."

"For God's sake, hurry before you're dead in the water!" Pete added as the beast hit the wall again, this time with both hands, fingers entwined. A plate-sized hole appeared in the wall as glass cascaded into the center.

"Well, we gave it a hell of a shot, Peter," Niles said as he hopped in time with Pete's movement to the floor.

"Yeah, we did, boss," Golding said as he watched a third blow shatter ten feet of wall.

The creature smiled broadly as it stepped through the

hole it had just created, its bare feet crunching through the thick glass as it did so.

Niles Compton and Pete Golding watched as their fate stepped toward the large aisle leading down to their location on the center's floor.

It was over.

The New York, New York
Hotel and Casino, Las Vegas, Nevada

The fifty-five-year-old man who had worked all of his life in his family's dry cleaning business in Wheeling, West Virginia, one who had saved for this vacation for he and his wife for two years, watched as the smiling but sorrowful blackjack dealer pulled the last of his chips away. His last card was a queen of hearts, breaking him at twenty-two. His wife placed her arm around him as the last of their savings had disappeared in less than twenty-four hours. The man hung his head as a stranger patted him on the shoulder.

"Tough luck, buddy," he said with a less than genuine smile. "Think I can have that seat now that you're done?"

The dry cleaner could only nod as he finally looked over at his wife. He expected her to be angry, but instead she smiled and leaned into him placing her arm on his waist and making the man waiting for an empty seat roll his eyes at the sentiment being displayed.

Suddenly the lights in not only New York, New York but every building inside the Las Vegas city limits went out. The power was taken from lines all the way to the outskirts of Los Angeles as Europa had done the only thing she could do—she had hacked directly into the power grid streaming outward from Hoover Dam.

Women screamed and men jumped in the seconds just prior to the emergency lighting coming on. The dry cleaner was knocked to the swirling red carpet as he lost his wife of thirty-two years in the confusion. The blackjack table was knocked over on to him and was literally broken in two as men scrambled for the thousand chips that were loosed on the floor.

What everyone thought was mass panic was actually the largest robbery in the history of the United States, as every casino in Las Vegas attempted to fend off every man, woman, winner, and loser inside of their darkened establishments. The revenge for sixty years of casinos in Las Vegas separating people from their money had started.

The dry cleaner tried desperately to gain his feet as men and women rushed around him in the dim lights of the battery-powered system. The backup generators for New York, New York kicked in at thirty-one seconds, but not before mass chaos struck the strip.

Suddenly the dry cleaner felt hands on him and was helped to his feet. He was bleeding badly from a scalp wound as he realized it was his wife who had helped him escape the stampede. As they tried to traverse the gaming floor and make it to the front doors, security men came running in every direction. Then the backup generators kicked in. The bright lights illuminated a historic mess as men and women fought hand to hand for the spoils on the tables and floor. Security was doing its best to get the situation under control, making people drop their chips and warning them that all chips on the floor that night were accounted for and their surveillance systems knew exactly which players were winners and which ones were losers. The frenzied crowd didn't really care. They looted anyway.

As the couple made it to the front door, the two security men pushing people back into the main floor saw that the man being helped by the woman was cut badly on his head. Looking around to make sure they weren't being watched, the two large guards had a moment of sympathy and allowed the couple to get free of the mess inside the main casino.

As they hit the hot night air they saw that the situation outside wasn't any better than inside. Cars had rear-ended each other and there were massive jam-ups on Las Vegas Boulevard. The couple walked until they found a stone bench that had been placed in an area designed to look like

Central Park, another place they had always wanted to travel to. The woman used a handkerchief to wipe some of the blood away from her husband's head. She leaned over and kissed his cheek.

"I'm sorry, honey," the man stammered. "I should have known I wasn't a gambler. I'm an idiot."

The woman smiled and put her arm around the man who struggled to get by at their dry cleaners in Wheeling all of their married lives.

"Oh, you're not that bad," she said smiling. Then she reached over and showed him the inside of her purse. It was full of cash from the drop box located on the bottom of the blackjack table. When the locked steel top had been stepped on so hard that it was forced open, his wife had struck as fast as John Dillinger. While everyone was fighting for chips they would never be able to keep, she had grabbed the one thing that would never fail—cash. The man looked inside the purse and his eyes widened.

"What . . . how—"

"Look, I would say we came out of our little foray to Las Vegas about five thousand dollars ahead of the game. What do you say we go home?"

The man leaned over and kissed his wife deeply.

"Yeah, let's get while the gettin' is good."

Event Group Complex
Nellis AFB, Nevada

Suddenly the overhead fluorescent lighting came to full power, stunning the beast as it entered the computer center. It shielded its eyes as Europa came back to full life. Immediately alarms resumed sounding throughout the complex as Niles slapped Pete on the back.

"At least we gave those below a fighting chance!" Compton yelled happily.

The creature above them finally recovered its vision and shook its giant head once more. It took a moment to reacquire the two men, and when it did it smiled, once more exposing enlarged, crooked teeth. It was the most frightening grin either man had ever seen.

Before they realized what was happening, the beast stopped in its tracks and its body started to convulse as a cacophony of noise so loud it brought the men down accompanied by bullets teasing through the broken glass of the computer center. The beast roared and turned toward a threat it hadn't seen coming. It tried to shield its eyes and head from the onslaught, but there was just too much metal-jacketed lead flying. Bullet after bullet struck the former mercenary. Large-caliber rounds tore its upper body to pieces as it went to its knees. The eruption of gunfire continued until four very loud blasts echoed inside the center. The head of the beast, along with the hand and arm that had been covering its face, exploded in a spray of red mist. The firing ceased as the body of the mercenary fell forward out of view of Niles and Pete who managed to look up in time to see the creature's demise.

"Clear!" called out a voice from the hallway.

Niles looked over at a stunned Pete Golding who had covered his head with his arms after they had hit the floor.

"I said clear damn it!"

"C . . . c . . . clear!" Niles shouted.

As they looked up over the stair risers above them, a small man along with five others came through the hole in the glass wall. One of the men emptied a full magazine of nine-millimeter rounds into the twitching torso of the giant at his feet.

"Identify yourselves, please," the man in the lead wearing an old bush hat called down. He reached up and handed his ambient-light goggles to one of his men.

"Dr. Niles Compton, Dr. Pete Golding!" the director called out as Pete slowly helped him to his feet.

"Dr. Golding, answer a question for me, please," the small man with camouflaged black and gray greasepaint covering his features said as his five men came forward and aimed their weapons at the two stunned men.

Niles could now only shake his head as the events of the last minute finally zapped his remaining strength and the adrenalin rush started to ebb.

"What is your nickname that the president uses when speaking to you?" the man asked as he cradled the Barrett fifty-caliber rifle across his chest. At that moment their savior didn't look at all friendly, and neither did his men.

Niles looked from the six men above them to Pete. Then his eyes went down to examine his broken ankle.

"Baldy," he mumbled.

"Sorry, sir, I didn't hear your response," the man said as the five aimed weapons zeroed in a little tighter than before.

"Baldy, damn it!" Niles answered loudly enough for his voice to echo inside the computer center. He finally looked up, angry as hell his nickname had been exposed in front of Pete.

The man smiled and gestured for his five men to lower their weapons. He used hand gestures to order them to take up station out in the hallway. He stepped down the risers as agile as a man walking on cotton and came face to face with Niles and Pete.

"I'll have one of my men look at that ankle, Dr. Compton," the small man said as he took in the haggard men before him.

"Who are you and who sent you?" Niles asked as he leaned on Pete even more than before.

"Well, sir, I am a major in the United States Army. I cannot tell you my unit, but I can say that we were sent by the president. Now, is Colonel Collins here and is he alive?"

"Yes, he's here and was alive the last time I saw him."

"Excellent," Major Garcia said as he turned and started up the stairs. "Where is he located at the moment," he asked as he moved back up the risers.

Suddenly Europa came fully awake. "There are fifteen minutes and twenty-seven seconds left till core meltdown. Repeat, there are fifteen minutes, *twenty-five* seconds remaining till core meltdown."

Garcia pointed at the overhead speaker system. "I take it

the colonel's location has something to do with that?"
"Grateful Dead" Garcia asked as he came to a stop on the stairs and then half tuned to look down on the two men once again.

"Level eighty-four, the reactor section, and he probably has some very angry and insane company down there with him."

"Then that's where we have to be," Garcia said as he started back up the steps. "It was an honor to meet a friend of the president's, Dr. Compton, and a man this mission was codenamed for."

Niles looked from Garcia's back to Pete and then back at the army major again. "And what was the code name?" he asked as his anger started immediately to grow.

"Operation Nerdlinger, Doctor. My medic will be down to help you ASAP."

"Operation Nerdlinger, that bastard!"

Level Eighty-four

As Collins traveled down the length of the darkened elevator tube he heard the beast they had just escaped from fall silent. He thought for sure the altered mercenary would have done what he had noticed the giants had become adept at—following them. As he slowed three levels from the bottom, he adjusted his grip on the rope and managed to get a small flashlight out and examine the sides of the stainless-steel shaft. His hunch was correct as he examined the deep indentations from one of the creature's efforts to traverse the slippery sides. That confirmed in his mind that one of them was below on the reactor level waiting for them, and his soldier's instinct told him who that would be—Smith.

Jack pocketed the small light and slowly continued his descent toward the lowest level of the complex.

Before he reached level eighty-four, he saw the top of Charlie Ellenshaw's head. The white hair acted as a beacon to tell him where the bottom was. As he gently touched down he realized that Charlie wasn't on the bottom of the pneumatic tube, he was kneeling on the top of the disabled elevator rubbing his knees and rocking back and forth. When he heard the whine of Jack's hands on the rope, Ellenshaw nearly panicked and tried to grab the M-14 he had lain beside him. He fumbled it as Jack lightly landed on the elevator's torn top.

"You alright?" he whispered as he undid his rigging.

"I damn near broke both of my legs," Charlie said as he continued to rub his scraped-up knees.

"Are you going to live?" Jack asked as he examined exactly where they had landed.

The top of the air-assisted elevator had been wrenched open like a can of soup. Jack kneeled down and looked inside the dark interior. It was empty.

"I think I heard something a minute before you dropped in," Ellenshaw said as he finally reached for his fallen weapon. Charlie shook his head as he wiped blood from his chin.

"Damn, Doc, did you slow down at all before you hit?" Collins asked as he placed his legs over the edge of the hole.

"I slowed down just fine," he said and slapped the two weapons still slung in front of him. "Then these damn things came up and nearly coldcocked me when I hit." He looked over at Jack. "I made one hell of a lot of noise, Colonel. If one of those things is in there he had to have heard me yelp like a schoolgirl."

"Well, there's nothing we can do about it now, right?" Jack asked, feeling the stickiness of his gloves as he braced himself at the opening. He raised his hand and smelled the substance and knew immediately that it was blood—thick, rich, and still wet.

"Right," Charlie answered, sad that he had let Collins down.

Jack looked at Ellenshaw one last time and slowly lowered himself into the black hole of the elevator. He hit softly, making sure nothing on his person rattled or made a noise. As Charlie's foot came through the top, Collins reached up

and tapped his black shoe. He saw Ellenshaw look down and
Jack held his hand up and pointed. Charlie frowned as he
understood that the colonel wanted him to stay put for the
moment. Ellenshaw nodded his head, thinking that Jack was
condemning him to once more stay out of harm's way.

Jack hesitated as he leaned against the frame where the
doors of the elevator once were. He saw one of the doors
about ten feet away. In the dim lighting of the emergency
lamp near the far wall, he saw even more blood on the side-
walls of the car. He looked out and saw the rail lead off toward the reactor. He just hoped that whichever creature was
down here was too wounded to fight, or possibly even dead.
Collins took his first step out onto the concrete floor of the
reactor room.

Charlie watched as the colonel vanished. He knew he just
couldn't hang back like Collins wanted. He hated disobeying his order to stay, but as he was reminded time and time
again by the security men he admired, he wasn't a soldier.
So orders meant little to him. Charlie eased himself through
the hole, careful not to go crashing down and making him
look the fool again. When he eased his aching feet onto the
carpeted floor of the car, he quickly removed his glasses and
wiped them clean. With a deep breath that he was careful to
hold and expel silently, Ellenshaw stepped out into the open
to follow the colonel.

Collins saw the two reactor vessels and the steam lines
running out of them. Then he looked to the right and saw the
coolant lines. He took a breath, relieved that they hadn't
been smashed into oblivion. He allowed his eyes to adjust to
the near darkness and then took three quick steps over to a
large tank of distilled water. He saw fifteen of the 5,000-gallon
tanks and again was relieved to see that they were undamaged. He stopped at that point and listened. He thought he
heard a sound coming from a distant corner of level eighty-
four, but he wasn't sure. He knew he couldn't risk turning on
the pumps, which were located between the two reactor
cores, without ascertaining if one of the killers was in here
with them.

He eased himself along the stainless-steel tanks, careful to place his boots on nothing more than concrete. He brought the Ingram up close to his cheek so he wouldn't have to get off a snap shot at anything that came out of the dark. He came to a small separation between water tanks five and six and risked a look in between them. He saw a longer blood trail, but couldn't see where it led. He cursed the darkness as he continued to move forward. He finally came to the last tank, meaning that the next step he took would leave him fully exposed to anything in the large room. Before he did that he looked around the giant tank and examined what he could of reactor number one. He saw the view port in the sixteen-inch steel door. There was a soft-green hue emanating from the vessel. He realized that time was running out. The steam from inside, generated by the nuclear fuel rods not being cooled, looked as if it were starting to melt the rubber seal not only around the view port but the thick containment door as well. There were streaks of blackened rubber flowing down the front of the reactor. He didn't have to see number two as he suspected that it was also in a state of total meltdown. He looked down at his wristwatch and saw that according to his calculations he had about eighteen minutes to get the coolant flowing again. He had to risk exposure.

He stepped out from the protective cover of the last water tank.

The wounded beast struck Jack from the side. He was sent sliding along the polished concrete floor until his head slammed into the twenty-inch steel base of reactor number one. The stars flew bright as he came close to losing consciousness. As he shook his head to clear his vision, he was shocked to see the very same soldier he thought he had killed on level seven. The shots to the head, coupled with its fall down the elevator tube, should have smashed it to bits. Then he understood that the blood he found and the scratches and dents in the tube meant that the creature had somehow arrested its fall.

As he tried to sit up, he saw that the beast was staggering. It hit the water tank and came close to dislodging it from its

secured base. Then he saw the stumps at the end of its long
arms. Blood was pouring from the wounds where he had
shot free the massive appendages. Jack reached for his
fallen weapon, but the beast acted much faster than Collins
would have thought possible considering its state. It actually
leaped from fifteen feet away and landed in front of him. It
kicked out with its tree trunk–sized foot and smashed Jack
in the ribs, snapping two of them. With no air in his lungs
Collins tried to roll before he was kicked again. The beast
roared in anger as bullets started slamming into it from behind. As he rolled away, his eyes saw a sight he would never
forget: Charlie Ellenshaw was limping forward from the
spot he had just been. He was taking careful aim with the
M-14. There was one second between each perfect shot as
bullet after bullet struck the wounded soldier in the neck,
face, and head. It staggered as Charlie ejected the spent
magazine, and with a determined look he slammed home a
fresh one. Then as Jack took his first breath in thirty seconds,
he saw Ellenshaw stop and push his glasses back up his nose
and begin his deliberate firing at the beast once more.

The creature finally went down to one knee and then both.
Ellenshaw with a determined gait purposefully stepped as
close to the dying creature as he dared and placed the muzzle of the M-14 against the center of its forehead. As the
former mercenary meekly lifted its handless arm to protect
itself, Charlie quickly placed four 5.56-millimeter rounds
into its brain, making sure each side of that brain received
two bullets. The naked creature fell over onto its side and
died lying against nuclear reactor number one, right next to
the badly hurt Jack Collins.

Ellenshaw slowly lowered the weapon and took a breath
before he passed out from lack of oxygen. He felt his knees
weaken and caught himself as he saw Jack struggling to get
up. He quickly forgot about his own feeling of nausea at
what he had just done and rushed forward to assist the colonel. He knelt beside Collins and helped him to his feet,
where Jack took one and then another deep breath, each one
more agonizing than the one before it.

"Good thing I didn't stay put, huh? That fella was treating you like a football."

All Collins could do was nod his head.

"Well, let's get the water flowing again," Ellenshaw said. Jack nodded still in dire pain from the broken ribs.

Suddenly the overhead lights blared to life, filling the reactor room with such a bright luminescence that it stunned the two men. Charlie lowered his eyes, the light nearly blinding him as it shot through his glasses. Immediately after that the scram alarms started, and the warning bells began decrying the stoppage of distilled water to the cooling pumps. Then came the shock of their lives as Europa announced in her sexy voice, making the message sound trite and flippant, "There are fifteen minutes and twenty-seven seconds left till core meltdown. Repeat, there are now fifteen minutes, *five* seconds remaining till core meltdown."

"Oh, shit," Ellenshaw said as he held Collins upright. "We have plenty of time, right Colonel? I mean, we just have to switch on the cooling pumps right?"

He suddenly felt Jack move as he started struggling against Charlie's grip. As Ellenshaw looked down he saw the colonel's face go flush. He tried to see what it was Collins was seeing, and then he did.

Standing not thirty feet away with its huge arms at its side was the creature once known as Smith. In his right hand both men saw something in the bright light. As Smith smiled, the creature allowed the six large fuses to slip from its grasp and strike the floor at its feet.

"Uh, what are those?" Charlie asked staring at the six large tubular-shaped sticks.

Jack coughed up blood but managed to get the words out as he looked up at the gloating Smith, who stood with a large and sickening smile on his elongated face.

"They're . . . four . . . hundred. . . . amp fuses."

"And what are the fuses for?" Charlie asked slowly, getting a horrible, sinking feeling in the pit of his stomach.

"The . . . cooling . . . pumps."

"I take it that's bad?"

Jack again coughed up blood and then fell to his knees.

"Well, why the hell not?" Ellenshaw said, feeling all alone and not exactly ready to face the hulking giant before him.

All around him the sound of the alarms increased as Europa continued her countdown from five minutes.

Level Sixty-one

Will Mendenhall placed his weight against the giant steel door, knowing his body couldn't possibly fend off that much beef. The beast struck the door once more, and Mendenhall lost his footing when the space between the door and jamb widened by a foot. Will caught his balance and then pushed back, using the very weight of the door as leverage. But the beast pushed back before the door could seal itself. This time Mendenhall flew back as if tossed by an angry child. His back struck something in the dark and the impact sent a sharp jab of pain jolting through his entire body. After striking the large object, he slid down to the floor where his head came to rest next to something that smelled like an old worn-out tire. As he lifted his head from the tiled floor, he saw the large steel door standing ajar. Will in a panic raised his arm and tried to find a handhold to assist him to his feet. Instead of finding something solid, his hand wrapped around something that rattled with a metallic sound as something broke and he and his failed rescuer fell back to the floor.

"Damn it!" Will shouted as he just knew that the beast was coming straight through the door at him. He struggled to frame the open door in his vision and noticed that the door hadn't moved since he had been knocked down. The sound of the beast was gone. Mendenhall reached down and pulled up the object he had grabbed a hold of before it broke away and saw that it was a belt of large-caliber ammunition.

"Damn, these are fifty-caliber machine gun rounds," he said beneath his breath as he finally managed to pull himself to his feet. He checked the door once more and stepped forward. He slowly turned as his eyes finally adjusted to the near darkness of the vault. As his eyes widened he saw the giant torpedo bomber rising majestically above his head. There were more lined up on either side of the first. "Wow," was all he could say as he took in the doomed aircraft of Flight 19. The planes looked down with their empty canopies like they were cyclopian eyes angrily watching an invader to their cave.

Will examined the contents of the vault and saw that the ammunition belt he had grabbed was dangling from the loading port underneath the left wing. Then his eyes spied the three barrels of the Browning fifty-caliber machine guns protruding from the wing's edge. His eyes roamed to the right wing and he saw three more barrels sticking out there. He looked over and saw a large battery-powered cart. It was used for moving heavy loads. Then he glanced up at the magnificent-looking aircraft once more.

"Jesus, Ryan, where are you when I need you? This is just about right up your alley."

Mendenhall again looked from the Grumman TBF Avengers to the electric cart with the tracked drive system. A plan started to form.

Just as Will started moving on his idea, sharp, ear-shattering blows started coming from down the corridor. The beast was again at work on Virginia's vault and this time it was using tools.

Mendenhall was running out of time to help his friends survive the darkest night of their lives.

Sarah, Farbeaux, Denise Gilliam, Virginia, and Gloria Bannister liked the silence even less than the pounding or twisting of the locking wheel on the vault's door. The beast outside was roaming around the corridor and every once in a while it would slam its great fists into a wall in frustration at not being able to get at its enemy. Then its rage would move off farther along the corridor as if it were looking for something, or someone, else.

"I have a sneaking suspicion that our friend is out there doing that problem-solving thing we discussed earlier,"

Henri said as he allowed Denise to change the rough material covering his wounds. The doctor looked up and saw that Sarah was looking at her while she held Henri's head in her lap. Gilliam shook her head negatively. "Please, Doctor, you can tell her what it is you're thinking," Farbeaux said as he looked up into the bruised face of Sarah.

"Okay, Colonel. If we don't get you upstairs in the next half an hour, you're going to bleed out on us. You not only tore out your stitches on the outside, but you somehow managed to break open the three I had to put into your arterial artery in your hip."

"I can't imagine how that happened, Doctor," he said as he continued to look into Sarah's face. She again pulled his blonde hair out of his eyes and then smiled. "I guess the prospect of life in one of your federal prisons wouldn't look too bad about now."

"Knock it off, Henri; we'll get you out of here," Sarah said.

Henri decided to risk Sarah dropping his head onto the cold steel flooring. "I don't think Jack the giant killer is going to come this time, little Sarah."

McIntire looked away as the reality of losing Jack struck once more. She turned and with the smile still weakly planted on her lips looked down at the Frenchman.

"He's been late before."

"What in the hell is that noise?" Virginia asked as she placed her ear against the steel door. "Is that scratching?"

Gloria joined Virginia at the vault's barricaded door and also placed her ear against the cold steel.

"What could it be doing out there?" she asked.

Suddenly they heard hammering against the door. They realized immediately that it was not flesh against steel, but metal upon metal. It started at the upper corner of the door, paused, and then started again. Virginia stepped back and looked upward. She heard the banging stop and then begin once again. Her eyes widened when she saw the corner of the door nearest the solid steel threshold opposite the locking mechanism vibrate from the continued hammering.

Henri sat up in Sarah's arms, stilling the hand of Dr. Gilliam as she placed another makeshift bandage on his hip. Farbeaux cocked his head and listened.

Virginia walked up to face the door as the blows became louder.

"Shit," she said as she realized what the beast out in the hallway was attempting to do.

"The tungsten hinges for the vault door are on that side, aren't they?" Henri asked, already knowing the answer.

"Yes," Virginia confirmed just as they heard the almost muffled sound of something hitting the door with a ping and then a thump.

"It's taking the door off at the hinges," Virginia said as she pulled Gloria Bannister away from the door.

"If it would make you feel better, young Sarah, even I would welcome your Jack Collins at this particular point."

Sarah stood, easing the Frenchman's head down, and with strength she didn't know she had, started pulling Henri by the lab coat's collar toward the back of the vault.

"We're not catching a break here," Virginia said as she also started pulling Gloria in the same direction as the others. After they had reached the back of the vault, Virginia started examining what they had to fight with. She counted ten more of the small spears. There were also cowhide shields and slingshots, but no rocks.

"The instrument of death you're looking at, Dr. Pollock," Henri said motioning toward the small spears, "is far more dangerous than it looks. It's called an assegai. I had a few in my own collection at one time. I believe it's a very appropriate weapon for our circumstance."

"Why is that, Colonel?" Gloria asked as she pulled two of them off the wall.

"It's a brutal close-in stabbing weapon, which I believe is the sort of battle we are about to fight."

"Damn it, I hate it when he's right," Virginia said as she also removed two assegais from the wall and handed one to Denise who hefted it and tested the weight.

Sarah placed Henri against the rear wall, but he fought

against her in order to stand. She cursed and helped him do so.

"I think I would much rather go out standing my dear," he said as he reached down and took Sarah's small hand, bending with considerable pain and kissing it.

McIntire reached up and, not caring if the others saw her movement, kissed Farbeaux deeply on the lips. "There, we're even, you ass," she said smiling and stepping away to get the last two spears hanging from their steel holders.

Henri's shocked face registered his surprise as he watched the small woman hand him one of the assegais.

"I'm going to go down fighting. I have decided I very much want to live," Henri said as he looked at Sarah and winked, not knowing if she could see the gesture in the darkness. "If only to have you visit me in prison," Henri finished as he braced himself against the wall just as Virginia announced with a fear-laced voice that the second and middle set of hinges just fell to the floor outside the vault door.

As the five trapped people prepared to make their final stand, the beast outside threw them a curve as its animalistic impatience must have overwhelmed its intelligence. It started pulling on the eighteen-inch-thick vault door. At that very moment Europa got the power back on just as the thick steel was ripped away from the frame. They heard as well as saw the large locking rods slide out of the door, but they had nothing to slide into.

"If it weren't for bad luck, we wouldn't have any luck at all," Virginia said as the lights in the vault illuminated a sight they hadn't wished to see—the beast raising the two-ton steel door over its head and tossing it out into the corridor.

Brave Virginia, so scared she was furious, was the first to move as she charged the beast before it had a chance to recover from throwing the door. The nuclear sciences engineer stabbed outward with the four-foot-long assegai. The razor-sharp tip slid easily into the creature's abdomen and struck its liver. It howled in pain and reached down and snapped the Zulu spear off, leaving its tip imbedded in its stomach. The beast came into the vault. Denise Gilliam, forgetting Henri's advice, threw her spear and it struck the mercenary in the shoulder where it immediately ripped it free. The creature caught Virginia totally off-guard by swinging the shaft end, and it struck her across the chest, sending Virginia crashing into the steel wall of the vault.

Gloria stabbed next and hit the thing in the upper thigh. Again it cried out in pain, but it still kept coming. It swung at the CDC doctor, but she easily moved out of the way.

Sarah started forward, but Farbeaux grabbed her and threw her back, sending her crashing into the enclosure where Cetshwayo was laid out in his temperature-controlled sleep. Henri charged, moving slowly due to his loss of blood, but charge he did. He planted the spear deep into the giant's chest, pulled it free, and then struck at it again. The beast was so shocked at the sudden and vicious strikes that it half turned and kicked out with its leg. The giant's foot struck the Frenchman and sent him flying the length of the large vault where he hit the wall and bounced off, striking the floor and remaining still.

The once-upon-a-time soldier roared in triumph as it regained the initiative and came on. The defenders saw their fate moving toward them and would have liked to have continued the fight but knew they had nothing left to fight with.

Suddenly the vault erupted with bright flashes of light and the creature turned away from its intended victims only to be met by a withering wave of gunfire from outside the doorframe. At least a hundred and fifty rounds struck the future of soldiering, with the bullets that struck its head dropping the already wounded beast in the doorway. The next thing they saw was a large man in black Nomex battle dress jump atop the still moving creature and empty a full magazine into it.

Sarah held Farbeaux and Gloria roused Virginia from the floor. Denise Gilliam stepped forward and looked up at the man still standing atop the downed beast.

Captain Carl Everett winked at a still-reeling Virginia Pollock.

"You want to *really* apologize for that cheap shot you gave me in the football game, Doc?"

Virginia shook her aching head, trying to clear it further. "Okay, I did it on purpose."

"Uh huh," Everett said as he hopped down from the back of the dead mercenary. "You owe me and my men here dinner . . . no, a lobster dinner."

"I'm not that sorry," Virginia said as she hugged the blonde captain. The vault filled with the remnants of Everett's fire team who had finally made it to the armory on level forty-two and were now assisting with a wounded Farbeaux and the others.

"Okay, we have to get these people out of—"

Everett saw the giant shadow rise from behind him. He saw the reaction of every person still inside the vault when the beast they thought they had killed rose from the supposed land of everlasting peace they had sent him to.

"Oh, damn, the bastard's right behind me, isn't he?" Everett said just as the beast screamed in triumph and sprang at Carl's exposed back.

Suddenly a deafening roar filled every square inch of level sixty-one. The heavy popping noise pierced through the air and almost knocked everyone standing inside to the floor with its power. As Everett dove for cover he felt the heavy impact of metal against flesh. Before he hit the floor he heard the slap and thump of something hitting the beast. The creature was struck so hard that it didn't have time to react to the attack.

"Jesus!" Carl called out as he turned over on his back to see round after round strike the beast in the chest, legs, neck, and head, sending it reeling backward. The fifty-caliber bullets kept filling the air to the point that the echoes and the actual sounds of the rounds exploding became one and the same.

Silence filled the air and then they all heard the voice outside.

"Hah, got you! That looks like it hurt!"

Everett tried to stand on shaky legs. He looked over at

Sarah who was holding the head of Henri Farbeaux in her lap. Once standing, Carl walked to the doorway and looked out. He had to smile when he saw the face of Will Mendenhall as he leaned against the large electric cart that held the still-smoking Browning fifty-caliber machine gun.

"Nice gun," Everett said as he leaned against the sill of the vault.

"I've got a torpedo bomber that comes with it."

Will stepped inside and helped the others leave their small sanctuary. It was Gloria who came up and gave Will a deep, well-meaning kiss on the lips.

"What about the reactor?" Sarah asked.

"Europa says we have someone down there restarting the cooling pumps right now, but we still have to get the hell out of here," Everett said.

Sarah and Denise helped the unconscious Frenchman sit up.

"Carl, give us a hand," Sarah said as she struggled with Henri's weight.

"Do I have to?"

Level Eighty-four

"There is now three minutes, seventeen seconds until core meltdown," Europa announced just as Smith attacked the two men.

Collins quickly pushed Charlie Ellenshaw out of the way as Smith hit him full force, sending him flying once more across the reactor room. The creature laughed as it turned on Ellenshaw.

Crazy Charlie knew he had to get to Jack because he didn't know where the fuse box for the cooling pumps was located. He hurriedly scrambled back behind the water tanks, turned, and made his way toward the spot where the colonel had landed. Instead of coming after him, Smith went for the stunned Collins fifteen feet away.

Jack opened his eyes as he took short, painful gasps of

air into his damaged lungs. He felt the heavy steps of Smith as he came forward to finish the job. The drool hit Jack's back as the beast stood over his prone body. Jack tried desperately to get his hand under his body as he knew he only had seconds before Smith stomped him to death.

"I remember you now—Jack Collins, Fifth Special Forces Group, Afghanistan, 2004," came the horrid deep and booming voice. Smith chuckled. "You going to tell Congress about this, Collins?" the beast asked as it reached down and picked Jack up by the body armor collar and lifted him to face level.

Jack opened his eyes and spit blood into the distorted face of Smith who raised his free hand and wiped the blood away, licking his fingers as he made a yummy sound deep in his throat.

Charlie charged at the creature's back, not firing his weapon as before for fear of hitting the colonel. He jumped onto Smith's back and started pummeling the giant with his thin-fingered fists.

Smith shook his body vigorously until he dislodged Ellenshaw. Charlie hit the hard floor and lay still.

"He is irritating. Is that the best you can do, Collins?" The fetid breath struck Jack, helping to bring him around.

"You now have one minute, fifty-one seconds to reach safe distance. Core meltdown is imminent."

Jack heard Europa's calm voice and smiled, wondering why he had never been able to find the culprit who had altered her voice synthesizer to that of the deceased Hollywood sex goddess.

"Drop the colonel and back away," said a voice in back of Jack, "you ugly son of a bitch!"

Smith looked up and saw twenty men facing him. But still he smiled as he knew they would never kill him in time to stop his eventual suicide.

"Come and get him," boomed the unnatural voice as the beast raised Jack up closer to its head and almost unhinged its jaw as it opened its mouth wide with laughter, realizing that any rescue was now too late. It wouldn't be stopped.

Jack found his opening. He had what he had reached for in his hand as Smith opened his mouth with that irritating laugh of his. Jack had already pulled the pin on the grenade before he had been lifted free of the floor. He drew his arm back and then let the safety handle pop free. He slammed the round grenade as hard as he could into Smith's exposed mouth. He broke teeth off as the beast realized what had happened. Smith let Jack fall free and then tried desperately to dig the grenade from his large and deformed mouth.

As Jack hit the floor he rolled away, damaging his ribs even more. He finally stopped and managed to look up.

"Fuckhead," Jack whispered lowering his head and covering up just as the grenade detonated.

Smith's eyes widened when he realized what was in his mouth. His fingers finally managed to lock around the object and as he tried to pull it free, it went off, sending brain matter and skull bone out in an arc that covered the two reactor vessels.

Before Collins knew it, hands were on him, turning him over. He opened his eyes into the smiling face hovering over him.

"Hello, Jack."

"Grateful Dead, I'll be damned," Jack whispered.

"That you will my friend. It looks like we were a bit too late to save the day here, so I guess all us grunts are damned," Garcia said as he cocked an ear upward just as Europa sounded her final warning.

"Detonation of nuclear material will occur in one minute and forty-one seconds."

"The fuses," Jack said low in his throat.

"What's that, Jack?" Garcia asked.

Suddenly the warning alarms ceased. The red and yellow reactor lights started to slow their steady pulse and Europa made her last announcement as Collins tried raising his head.

"Core temperature has now been stabilized at six hundred fifty-two degrees. Coolant flow has been restored."

Garcia helped Collins sit up as Charlie Ellenshaw came

around the number ten water tank. He was waving his hands through the air as if to cool them. He grimaced as he saw the DELTA team and even Colonel Collins looking at his burnt hands.

"I couldn't find the damn fuse box for the pumps. And then I didn't know that you couldn't push the fuses back in with the switch handle in the *on* position. That freaking hurt!" Crazy Charlie said as he waved his charred hands through the air.

"Hmm," Major Garcia said as he looked down at the man who had trained him ten years before. "One minute and forty seconds to spare. You're getting old, Jack; you used to be exciting."

Collins closed his eyes and passed out.

Level Eight

Doctor Denise Gilliam had every bed and most desks filled with wounded men and women. Virginia, Sarah, and Gloria had volunteered to assist the doctor as she tried to bring things under some kind of control. Niles Compton was complaining more than anyone that he would like a real doctor to help him as Virginia did her best to place the temporary cast on his ankle.

Two men no one recognized stepped into the clinic. They stopped and noticed Denise Gilliam attending her patients.

"You got room for one more, Doctor?" a large man asked as he slung a weapon over his shoulder.

"Sure, the more the merrier," Denise said with weariness lacing her voice. "Who is it?"

"Well, he may be one of yours. We found him passed out on the loading dock about a half hour ago."

"What makes you think he's one of mine?" Denise asked as curiosity finally made her look up from one of Everett's security men.

The two strangers looked at each other and everyone could tell they wanted to laugh but held back.

"Well, ma'am, he's wearing what looks like a candy striper's outfit."

"He?" Denise asked.

"Bring him in," the first man called through the door.

As everyone inside the clinic waited, even the director stopped complaining long enough to watch. Two other men in black clothing brought a third man in and laid him down on one of the desks.

Will Mendenhall had to stand up and shake his head in wonder. Sarah's eyes widened, and Niles had to laugh at the escapee from a hospital in downtown Las Vegas.

Jason Ryan, still replete in his stolen candy striper's uniform, managed to look up to see where he was and then lay his head back down.

"Is this the best you can do for a bed, after all I went through to get back here?"

Denise walked over and shook her head at the naval aviator. Then she smiled.

"You know, that's not a bad look for you, Mr. Ryan."

"I know."

Sarah finally got her smile under control and stopped by to check on Henri. He was lying in bed sans handcuffs with his eyes closed. He had a whole pint of blood dripping into his veins from an IV line attached to his right arm. McIntire was about to turn away when she heard his voice whisper.

"Please tell me this is some of your blood, my dear," he said so low she had to bend over to hear him.

"Sorry to disappoint you, Henri, but I think you have some of Mendenhall's blood in you. The blood bank went bad because of no electricity."

Henri managed to look up and around until he saw Mendenhall sitting on a desk a few feet away getting his head bandaged by a highly attentive Gloria Bannister. Mendenhall saw the Frenchman looking his way and raised his right hand, extending his middle finger.

"I knew you liked me, Lieutenant."

Sarah smiled, but she knew she had to leave the clinic before the smell of blood and medicine did her in. She stepped into the hallway and Henri watched her as she leaned against the glass. He watched her and knew that he was in love with the woman and wanted to tell her. But he also knew he was going to prison, and he knew that she didn't love him. She loved Collins and would for a very long time, even if he was dead.

As he started to lie down he saw Sarah straighten from the wall. He watched as she frowned and then started crying. She stepped forward as two men carried a third man in between them and threw her arms around the man being assisted. Henri Farbeaux felt his heart sink when he saw the familiar face of Jack Collins as he allowed Sarah to hold him. The two men carrying Collins looked away as Sarah McIntire welcomed Jack Collins back to the Event Group.

Farbeaux turned away and closed his eyes against the harsh florescent lighting.

Baltimore, Maryland

The Baltimore state trooper watched as the two bodies were loaded into the ambulance. He shook his head at the senseless violence that happened on a daily basis along the Baltimore Beltway.

It was evident from the car that was still sitting on its jack stand and the spare tire lying nearby that the two women had stopped to fix a flat late at night. The two bodies had been found fifty feet from the car. Each had been shot once in the chest and left sprawled in the high grass close to the Beltway. This hadn't been the only occurrence of violence on this stretch of road. There had been seven other murders, some drive-bys, others like the one he just recorded in his notebook, a senseless killing, probably at random, of two people changing a tire after a night out.

The trooper was approached by his sergeant. "We ID the driver?" he asked, also shaking his head as the bodies were finally sealed inside the ambulance.

"Yeah, we found her identification in her car. The younger woman we haven't discovered anything about yet. The driver is Lynn Simpson. She has a company badge."

"Yeah, what company?" the sergeant asked as the ambulance drove away.

"That's why I called you out here, Sarge. She worked for the CIA."

"Oh, boy."

Event Group Complex
Nellis AFB, Nevada

Niles Compton listened to the president speak, but his words became almost unintelligible as he listened. With his ankle in a cast, Niles was forced to sit and listen to his old friend. After the president said his piece he waited for Compton to say something. He waited for a long time as his friend sat stunned at the news that had been delivered. He was so stunned he couldn't speak.

"Niles, would it help if I called and gave him the news?" the president asked.

Compton finally looked up and into his friend's eyes. "You know Jack is not going to buy this bullshit the Maryland State Police are telling you."

The president shook his head. "Why should he, I don't. I've ordered CIA Director Easterbrook and the FBI to give this investigation a full-court press. I want to know what happened. I'm not a believer in coincidence."

Niles sat and listened, maybe believing his old friend, maybe not. He was fast becoming a skeptic in such matters as governing a country.

"We have a detailed briefing by Pete Golding in two days. I think maybe you better be here to hear what he and Europa have to say," Niles said.

"I'll see what I can—"

"Mr. President, I never ask you for anything, yet you have

asked me for everything. I want you here to learn what in the hell we're dealing with. Then you can take your ball and go home."

The president saw that Niles Compton was in no mood to hear anything other than yes.

"Okay, Baldy, I'll be there in two days. Also I want Colonel Farbeaux transferred to FBI custody when he's able to travel."

Niles nodded his head without really answering and reached out and shut off the computer with the president's image still on it, breaking every rule of etiquette and protocol on the books. He didn't want to discuss the fate of the Frenchman and knew his friend the president just wanted to remind him he was still in charge. Compton reached over and hit his intercom switch to connect with the computer center.

"Golding," came the quick response.

"Pete, ask Europa the location of Lieutenant McIntire."

"Okay," he said and returned just a second later. "She's located in suite nine, level eight."

"Colonel Collins's room?"

"Yes."

Sarah watched Jack as he in turn looked at her. She reached out, took his hand, and smiled.

"You took your time leaving Alice's house," she said.

"You know me, I had to finish painting or Alice would have thrown a fit."

Sarah shook her head. Then she became serious. "Jack?"

"Yeah, short stuff?"

"Colonel Farbeaux, what's going to happen to him?"

"That's not up to me, but I imagine he's bound for trial for the murder of our people and possibly many others."

Sarah bit her lower lip. "Do you believe he killed people from our Group or murdered innocents from anywhere?" she asked watching him closely. "I mean, do you really think he's capable of cold-blooded murder?"

"Doesn't seem to be his style does it? But I wasn't here in the bad old days. I just don't know," he added. "But deep

down? Yes, I believe Henri has killed in the coldest blood
possible in the past."

Jack watched Sarah closely. He knew she was feeling in-
debted to the Frenchman for coming after her in Mexico.
But he also knew there was something else he couldn't quite
grasp. The why of it, he supposed. He saw the sadness in her
eyes when he had hinted at Henri's fate.

"Listen, I think—"

A knock sounded at Jack's door. Sarah stood and hesitated a moment and then looked down at Jack.

"I love you."

Collins didn't say anything; he just winked.

Sarah went to the door and opened it but not before noticing that Jack didn't respond when she had said she loved
him. She looked up when she opened the door. Niles Compton stood there with a pair of crutches supporting him.

"Lieutenant, may I come in?"

"Of course," she said as she stepped aside. "Would you
like Jack . . . ," Sarah caught herself a bit too late, "the colonel to yourself?"

"No, I think you better be here for this."

Sarah's brows rose as she closed the door and worriedly
looked at Collins who lay in bed bare-chested and bandaged
heavily across his broken ribs. He was silent as once more
he waited for the other shoe to drop on his head.

Niles nodded at Collins and leaned against his desk.

"Do you want a chair?" Sarah asked.

Niles just shook his head no.

"I'm no good at this, Colonel." Niles lowered his eyes.
"So I guess I better just say it before . . . before I lose the
courage."

"Just say it," Jack said, keeping his wary eyes on the director.

"Colonel, uh, Jack," he said turning to the familiar. "Your
sister Lynn was murdered in Baltimore last night—she and
a friend of hers from Langley."

Sarah was stunned as she looked from Compton to Jack's
frozen features. He seemed not to know what to do with his

eyes as he looked from the director back to Sarah and then
quickly away again. He cleared his throat and then again
swallowing several times.

"What . . . what happened?" he finally managed to ask,
avoiding Sarah's look of shock.

"The Maryland State Police say she and her companion
were killed randomly after they had a flat tire after midnight
two days ago."

Jack Collins went silent and remained that way for several minutes.

"Would you excuse me? I have to call my . . . our mother."

Niles nodded and limped to the door as Sarah opened it.
He didn't use the crutches as he felt they would fail him at
this, the worst possible moment.

Sarah remained by the door, but Jack never looked up as
he reached for the phone.

After Jack had informed his mother of the death of her
only daughter, he went silent for two days. Alice had volunteered to take Cally Collins back to D.C. to make arrange-
ments for the family. Then the colonel clammed up. Sarah
couldn't reach him, and even when Carl Everett came to
check on him and jokingly report on the progress of Lieutenant Ryan, the candy striper, Jack remained silent, only
nodding that he heard what was said. Even when the president of the United States came into his room just before the
debriefing Niles had ordered he remained almost totally
mute, nodding his head and mumbling at the appropriate
times in the conversation. He did that with everyone he
came in contact with.

The conference room was only half full as most of the departmental managers were busy cleaning up the mess in
their various departments from the recent attack on the
complex. Niles Compton had decided to keep all of the information to be explained to the people meeting that day
tightly controlled. The director had ordered a select few to
hear Pete Golding explain, in theory, what they had been
dealing with.

Jack sat in his customary place at the opposite end of the long table facing Dr. Compton. His eyes were dark and still haunted as Everett came in and sat beside him. Sarah was three seats down from the president and chanced a glance at Collins, but he never looked up until the meeting started.

Virginia sat next to Compton. He nodded his head, not making eye contact with anyone. The assistant director stood.

"Okay, we have a lot to cover, and the president can only fool the *Washington Post* for so long before they discover he's missing."

No one in the room laughed at her small joke except for the president. As he saw no one else, not even Charlie Ellenshaw, crack so much as a smile, he went as silent as the rest of the men and women present. Will Mendenhall, who was attending his first debriefing in the conference room, sat next to Gloria Bannister, whom Niles thought deserved to be in on the tale Pete had to relay because of her losing so much in the attack.

"Pete," Virginia said, "the floor's yours."

"Thank you," Golding said as he stood with pointer in hand. He strode to the main viewing screen and nodded his head at the navy signalman.

"Perdition's Fire," Pete began, "has been kept a well-guarded secret for over a hundred years, but has been in existence for over three thousand years." Everyone in the conference room exchanged glances at the claim Pete had just made. "The formula has been analyzed by Europa and our Event Group people at CDC and the Harvard School of Medicine. We also brought in the CSU School of Botany and the National Center for Genetic Research. The information is factual and indisputable."

The first slide provided by Europa appeared on the screen. It was of Lawrence Jackson Ambrose.

"Our friend here did something truly amazing and also a hundred years ahead of his time. But somehow the good professor Ambrose lost his way. The man was brilliant but quite possibly the most insane person of his time." Pete nodded and the next picture depicted confused those watching. "This is an official police report submitted and classified as top secret by the government of Great Britain. It concerns a series of murders that occurred in the year 1888 at a location in London called Whitechapel." Pete saw the recognition in the faces around the table. Even the president leaned forward in his chair to read the hazy report from 142 years ago.

Jack finally looked up and stared blankly at the screen. Everett and Sarah watched, but the colonel made no move to take part in the debriefing.

"The report was filed by the metropolitan police, in conjunction with the chief medical examiner's office in London. This document is part of the most unbelievable cover-up the world has ever seen. It all started with a writer of some renown doing research for a little book he was writing on aggressive behavior through the miracle of modern medicine. The name of the book researched was a novel we know today as *The Strange Case of Dr. Jekyll and Mr. Hyde* and that author was Robert Louis Stevenson."

This bit of information caused another round of talking and exclamations around the table. Still Jack Collins remained silent even though he heard every word spoken.

"It was Robert Louis Stevenson who originally tried to warn the metropolitan police about the true nature of just what they were dealing with."

"What is it we are looking at on the screen?" Virginia asked Pete.

"This slide lists the autopsy reports of six women murdered in Whitechapel in 1888. These reports are in direct conflict with the reports filed by the medical examiner in Whitechapel. The local medical examiner listed the horrendous wounds received by these women. They were bad enough that anyone reading them would never suspect the police, or the British government, of trying to hide anything. That is where these reports come in." Pete slapped the large screen with the pointer. "They were discovered buried in the archives of Scotland Yard and in the journal of Lawrence Ambrose himself, which the Event Group had in its possession for the past 120 years. But the real gold is the culpability of the British government in all of this that Europa uncovered through police sources directly."

"I take it you and your computer friend broke into their system to uncover these?" the president asked with a frown while gesturing to the reports on the large-screen monitor.

"Yes, sir, that's what Europa and I do."

Niles nodded his head, thankful that Pete stood up for himself and Europa against the snide remark of his friend the president.

"What is not listed in the professor's journal but can be found in the police archive reports is the fact that among the horrifying wounds received by these women in the tainted autopsy reports, each of the prostitutes listed as murdered had been pregnant at the time of her death. The real reports state that the two-to-three-month-old embryos had been cut from the wombs of these ladies. The massacre of the women that ensued afterword was to cover up the fact of the missing embryos."

"Wait Dr. Golding. Are you saying that Jack the Ripper was responsible for this?" asked the president.

"No, not the Jack the Ripper that has been presented to the world by the London constabulary, Mr. President, but Professor Lawrence Jackson Ambrose, the real Jack the Ripper or, if you like, the real Jekyll and Hyde. He murdered these women while under the influence of small doses of Perdition's Fire so he could break the laws of man and science with a clear conscience. He collected the fetuses to be used in an experiment that should not have been possible at the time, but one that Europa has uncovered evidence of— the stem cell research that led to gaining strength, growth, and intelligence, all to be used as an additive to the food eaten by members of the British armed forces. That is exactly what he was hired to do. Make supersoldiers for Her Majesty's government. Not crazed beasts as we saw here at the complex, but coldly calculating men with superior fighting strength and intelligence. That's with small doses."

Everyone was stunned to silence as Pete went through his

gathered evidence, from Queen Victoria's letters ordering the hiring of Ambrose and the purchase of his advanced theory, to the cover-up that ensued. Even the photo analysis of the advanced equipment used by Ambrose to create a genetic monster for the ages, as they themselves had recently been witness to, was fully documented. The experts say Ambrose was a genius and a hundred years ahead of his time.

"He was the first true geneticist," Virginia commented.

"Let's skip to the point, Dr. Golding. Do you and your outlaw computer know who sent in these mercenarys?" the president asked Pete, turning to Niles directly.

"No. But we will find out who assisted them over here; I damn well guarantee that," Niles said, almost challenging his old friend to deny his efforts in that regard. "I lost twenty-two men and women in this attack, and I will find the people responsible. Do you agree?"

The president nodded his head.

"Thank you."

With that the Event Group began in earnest to continue on with its work. Only now all 656 members of Department 5656 had the added incentive of finding out who the Americans were who assisted in the traitorous act of attacking their home.

San Antonio, Texas
Three Days Later

Jack stood next to his mother as the coffin was slowly lowered into the grave. The colonel was happy that Sarah and his mother Cally had hit it off so well and in such a trying time as this. Jack wondered if maybe one day his mother would have another daughter to help with her sorrow of losing Lynn.

As Jack watched, he knew that his sister's murder was not as random as the police made it out to be. Like the president, he never believed in coincidence. He had a gut feeling she had died because of him in some way. He felt responsible.

Cally Collins reached out and took Jack's arm, reaching over with her other hand to take Sarah's on the opposite side. Together they strode over to where a very sore and weak Jason Ryan, alongside Will Mendenhall, Gloria Bannister, Virginia Pollock, Alice Hamilton, and finally, Captain Carl Everett, stood waiting for them.

Jack saw Niles on his crutches with Pete Golding and Charlie Hindershot Ellenshaw III standing next to him. They were all dressed in their best black suits and looked as out of place as ever. Collins excused himself as Everett and Sarah joined him while Alice went to speak with Cally.

Jack faced the director of Department 5656 who only nodded his head and reached inside his jacket pocket, bringing out a piece of paper and handing it to Collins.

"Colonel, what would you like me to do with that?"

Jack looked down at the resignation letter and handed it back to Niles.

"Process it, I'm done," he said as Sarah placed her arm through his.

"Jack," Ellenshaw said, no longer the goof he was a few years back when Collins had joined the Group, "tear it up. You need us, and we sure as hell need you."

"Sorry, Doc, but—"

"Colonel, listen to what Niles has to say, will you?" Pete Golding asked.

Collins took a deep breath and dipped his chin in surrender. Niles was going to say what he wanted to say.

"The FBI recovered the vehicles used by the assault forces in Las Vegas. They found very little with the exception of these," Niles said handing over two sheets of paper to Collins.

"Recognize those, Colonel?" Pete asked for Niles as Jack studied the papers.

"They're privately generated satellite target tracking reports. No company name though."

"The tracking target, Jack, was you. Evidently that was

how this Smith character tracked you to Nellis. You must have been tagged by those maniacs in Mexico during the rescue that night," Niles finished.

Collins shook his head, barely controlling his anger over the fact that he had been bugged and hadn't even suspected it. He started to give the tracking reports back when Niles pushed them away and gestured for Collins to look at the reports again.

"Jack, the reports are time and security stamped by a government agency that accepted them. The code is listed as one belonging to the CIA."

Collins was stunned, but not quite as much as the others that were standing there listening.

"Someone at the CIA passed this information on to Smith and his assault team," Sarah said, her own anger at the obvious betrayal showing in her voice.

Compton watched Collins for the longest time as Jack continued to look at the two tracking reports with their computer-generated time stamps on their faces. Niles swallowed and got the colonel's attention.

"Jack, you have many duties at the Group, and if you would stay with the department and continue as the head of security, I swear to you that whenever you're free, I'll give you carte blanche to use any means at the Group's disposal to find your sister's killer. And I don't mean to bring whoever it is to justice. You do it your way, and I'll back you 100 percent. Everyone here will. Just use all of your skills and find them."

Collins swallowed hard. He looked at Jason, Will, Virginia, Niles, Pete, and finally Charlie Ellenshaw. He smiled and glanced at Everett, who just nodded his head. But it was Sarah who reached out and took the resignation form from Compton's hand and tore into two, allowing the pieces to fall to the grass.

"Alright," Jack said as he took in not just his colleagues but his friends. "But on one condition," Collins said with his jaw set firmly. "Because justice has to start somewhere, and I think I know just where it does."

* * *

On a small rise overlooking the cemetery, Hiram Vickers stood next to Director of Operations Samuel Peachtree.

"Imagine my stunned silence when I learned from the president himself that the brother of Lynn Simpson was a war hero and a favorite of the commander in chief?"

"I read his file, he's not that frightening," Vickers said.

Peachtree laughed, turned away from the gravesite, and started walking back to the limousine that was waiting for him.

"You find that funny?" Vickers asked.

"Tell me, Hiram," Peachtree said stopping and turning, "which file was it you read?"

"What do you mean?"

"You are an idiot, aren't you?"

"I am still not intimidated by a man who only achieved the rank of colonel in his time with the army. Not very motivated is he? The president's friend Collins is nothing but a once-upon-a-time tiger that has been declawed and placed out to pasture, buried at some desk where the army can keep track of him."

Peachtree smiled as he allowed his driver to open the rear door as he approached.

"You know, Hiram, the president explained to me in the Oval Office after he lamented on Ms. Simpson's passing that Jack Collins is probably the single best combat soldier this nation has ever produced." He smiled. "Maybe you should really try doing your homework sometimes on people who could bring us both down."

"Why is that?"

"Because if you did, you would know that Colonel Jack Collins won't rest until he kills you. And that dear Hiram is from the mouth of the president of the United States himself." Peachtree laughed as he sat down inside the limo. "Hell, he probably won't rest until he kills both of us."

Samuel Peachtree closed the door and the limousine left in a cloud of dust, leaving Hiram Vickers alone to contemplate his fate if Collins found out he was behind his sister's murder.

EPILOGUE

What is justice?
This unapparent fairness
supposed to combine rather than divide,
just a word that likes to hide,
this unapparent fairness,
what is justice?
—Aadil Malik

Washington, D.C.
The Justice Department
Five Weeks Later

The man known as Colonel Henri Farbeaux sat in a chair across from none other than the attorney general of the United States himself. He had been read his rights and informed that the president had taken a personal interest in his case.

Henri was read his rights for the third time under American law and the charges against him were read. Still feeling weak from his wounds received at the Event Group Complex deep beneath the Nevada desert, Henri really wasn't interested in how many charges of murder and theft they could come up with.

"Do you have anything to say at this time?" the attorney general asked, smiling that he was sitting across from the famous French thief and cold-blooded killer.

"The jail complex in which I am currently residing has absolutely the worst cuisine I have ever sampled. Can you do something about that?"

The attorney general smiled and then stood up with his two assistants.

"Oh, we'll get right on that, Colonel," the attorney general quipped. "The guards will take you back to city jail. Have fun getting acquainted with our local criminals. They don't have quite the discriminating taste you have, but they're a fun bunch of boys to spend a little quality time with."

Farbeaux watched as the three well-dressed men left the room. He reached up and scratched his nose, rattling the handcuffs on both wrists. He heard the door open and two guards walked in. One lifted him up by the arm and the other pulled out his chair—all done in a not-too-gentle manner.

"Okay, pal, time to go," said a voice behind him.

Henri was led out of the room, and instead of going straight to the elevator they made a detour to the stairwell on the fifth floor. One guard with dark hair opened the door and the other who stood behind Henri pushed him through the exit. There was a third man waiting in the shadows that he couldn't see. The large man cleared his throat. Then he tossed something to the man standing behind him. Suddenly the Frenchman felt the pressure of the cuffs as they fell free of his wrists. Rubbing them with his hands Farbeaux thought he understood. What was about to happen to him?

"Ah, shot while trying to escape. Very good. After all, you could have me spilling too much about deep, dark government agencies no one knows exists, right?"

The large man reached out from the shadows and opened the second exit door. As Henri looked out into the stairwell and the bright sunlight beyond, he glanced back at his two guards. He saw the larger man step out into the lighted doorway.

"As we say back home, Colonel, you better get while the gettin' is good."

Farbeaux saw the captain named Everett, resplendent in his blue guard's uniform, standing before him. Henri turned and saw Will Mendenhall and Jason Ryan as they peeled off their absconded uniform jackets and tossed them onto the handcuffed guards they had taken them from who were wiggling and cursing under taped mouths.

"Gentlemen, you have my thanks, so before someone changes his mind, I bid you adieu." Henri ran from the fourth floor and didn't stop until he was on the crowded street far below.

As Farbeaux crossed the street he saw a familiar form standing on the corner. He stopped short and smiled at the man staring at him. Henri then stood ramrod straight and saluted. Henri Farbeaux laughed and crossed the street, disappearing into the thick traffic of the capital.

On the corner watching the escape of one of the most wanted criminal minds on earth, Colonel Jack Collins nodded his head as he saw Henri escape from American justice.

Jack took a deep breath and turned as Sarah approached and took his hand.

"Satisfied?" he asked as he finally smiled and looked down at her healing face, seeing his own reflection in her sunglasses. Unlike Farbeaux a few weeks before, he was able to see his reflection and not turn away in shame.

Sarah McIntire smiled and went to her tiptoes to kiss Jack on the lips.

"Thank you, Jack."

As Sarah released Collins he continued to look at her and wondered how long it had been since Sarah had started falling for the Frenchman.

"Shall we go home?" Sarah said, smiling up at Jack Collins, who was caught with his darkest thoughts running through his mind. Finally, he smiled back.

"Yeah, let's go home."

in the face and numbly registered that it was all the crowd had time to follow.

As Parkman crossed Lexington he began to sway in other form hardly noticing it. He stopped short and stared at the man walking at him. Her figure stood forward a right and pale and empty, and almost fought to embrace the sharp the man watched the black center of the pistol.

On the corner watching the center of the sides almost wished for an instant in stared for an instant tighter. He defeat held in his pocket. Thee was a great Parkman taking her in a deep breath and moaned as Sarah almost and spoke to her hand.

"Sarah?" She asked as she slowly turned and looked down at her healed face, where the wax seal about her her husband. She turned Parkman slowly to look behind. He was the ever the weapon one he not have gone in either.

Parkman there mutely and went to her arms, in deep tears of relief.

"Thank You, God."

As Sarah returned Collin be turned to take her by and reluctantly let his arms fall, then give a Sarah and with her into the ambulance.

"Let me go home," Sarah said, smiling at her hand taking him, who she caught with his fingers through her hair. Then at the mind finally he would she.

"Let's go home."

Read on for an excerpt from
David L. Golemon's next book

CARPATHIAN

Coming soon in hardcover from
Thomas Dunne Books / St. Martin's Press

Prologue

Hong Kong Harbor,
April 1, 1949

The six-decked yacht sat anchored in the bay of Hong Kong, glistening in the illumination cast from a full moon and festive lights that had been strung from bow to stern. The largest yacht inside the harbor was hard to miss as it sat motionless at a minimum of two miles from any fishing or harbor patrol boat, creating an island unto itself in the great expanse of Hong Kong harbor. The only vessels allowed near the gleaming white *Golden Child* were the rented whaleboats that had been cleaned and lined with satin pillows for the invited guests as they traversed the busy waterway on their way to the largest auction of Palestinian and ancient Canaanite antiquities the world had ever seen.

Golden Child was owned by a man known as Charles Sentinel, a Canadian commodities broker of some ill repute. It boasted accommodation for forty overnight guests and had an interior salon that measured one hundred and eighty-two feet in length and could actually handle a party for hundreds. Tonight, however, the salon would only accommodate thirty. The remaining space would be taken by the items everyone on the *Golden Child* had come to see. The evening belonged to Lord Hartford Harrington who had agreed to the astronomical lease price of the ship for a flat two million dollars for the weekend. There could be no other secure location for the greatest antiquities sell-off in a hundred years.

As the third to the last whaleboat wound its way around the tied-up water taxis made famous in Hong Kong, the woman saw the *Golden Child* in the distance for the first time. As her green eyes roamed over the shape and silhouette of the ship, her mind raced. This was the first time she had assigned herself a field operation, and also the first time she had ever disobeyed an order from the director. If he knew she was four thousand miles from home with no field security team in place, she might as well find a home to live in inside the borders of China, because she could never go home again. *"Garrison would kill me,"* she mumbled to herself as the whaleboat slowly made its way to the large staircase-like gangway that had been set up on the starboard side of the three-hundred-foot-long *Golden Child*.

Twenty-one-year-old Alice Hamilton was outfitted in the finest dress her limited bank account could cover. She had to borrow the wide-brimmed white hat that matched the dress. The gown itself was a satin turquoise, one-strap item that made her feel a tad uncomfortable. It was almost embarrassing that her field equipment was listed as one party dress and one borrowed hat while the other field units in her department had to settle for desert camping gear and weapons hidden amongst their picks and shovels. If she were lucky, Alice thought she might be able to come up with a nail file for protection. She wondered once more for the hundredth time if she knew what she was doing.

Alice tried to hide a large intake of breath as a line was tossed to one of the deckhands waiting on the bottom platform of the yacht's gangway. Here she was getting ready to step into the den of some of the most ruthless dealers in ancient art and antiquities ever assembled, and she was going in with possibly a nail file and a knockout dress. Alice knew she had to chance it once word had reached her desk at the Event Group that something unusual in the antiquities world was about to take place so Alice had used every contact and informant, and had even called in favors owed to her by the FBI and the new CIA to get the location of the auction. This was her baby and not even General Garrison Lee could bully her into not taking this chance to end a portion of the theft of the ancient world.

Alice Hamilton was the widowed wife of one of Garrison Lee's men from his old Office of Strategic Services days during the war. After the surrender of Japan, the young widow had gone to work for the new director of Department 5656 in September of 1946. The man named Garrison Lee was a beast and by far the hardest man in the world to work for. The former senator from Maine was a thinker who covered every aspect of field operations, and one of his staunchest rules was that no office, lab, or academic personnel could go on field missions without a military escort. She smiled at the standing order. Alice knew she was none of those. She was the personal assistant to one of the most ingenious men she had ever known. And now she wished he were with her.

As she was assisted to her feet by the white-coated helmsman of the whaleboat, she thought about Lee and his reaction when he found out her little vacation to visit her mother back home in Virginia had turned into a weeklong trip to the South China Sea in search of stolen artifacts. She had fought for the assignment but Garrison Lee had said no—that it was not part of the Event Group charter to rescue stolen antiquities. She knew this to be the largest lie Lee had ever told her. He took chances time and time again to recover items from not only the past of the United States, but of the world.

Department 5656 of the National Archives, or better known to the scientists, archaeologists, teachers, professors, and military personnel as the Event Group, was a creation of President Abraham Lincoln in 1863. It became a chartered oeotion of the National Archives in 1916 and was signed into U.S. law (albeit secretly) in that same year. Their mission was to discover the true history of the world's past. Their job was to ensure that the United States avoided the pitfalls stumbled into by mankind throughout history by learning the truth about how we got to where we are, and to possibly learn where it was the world was going. The Event Group protected the United States from committing the same sins as our forefathers and their ancient European or Asian ancestors by learning from the mistakes of the world through science and discovery and avoiding those very same circumstances again.

Alice loved the concept but had found the actual work that had been chosen for her by her boss, Garrison Lee, too mundane and boring—more an academic investigator than actual team leader—and that was not Alice and Lee knew that. The general could not keep her caged up like he had the past four years; he was overprotective of her and that infuriated the twenty-one-year-old widow to no end. Thus this one chance to prove she could be a field operative and handle the very worst in people.

Alice adjusted the stole around her shoulders and the fishnet, large-brimmed white hat that half-covered her beautiful eyes. As she made her way up the gangway, she received her first real hint of nervousness as she spied the two men at the top of the gangway who were watching her move slowly up the steps. Their eyes saw the shapely body beneath the expensive dress and the subtle movement of her breasts that were hidden very badly in the French-designed fashion. Alice felt so humiliated knowing the dress was not anything like her. She was far more comfortable in men's pants and shorts and far happier traveling around with a shovel and pickax.

As she reached the top of the steps, she saw the two men were armed with weapons that were not hidden very well in their waistbands. She knew the men *wanted* her to see that they were armed.

The first man half-bowed and held out his hand. Alice

swallowed and then pulled the invitation from her handbag. The gilded, gold-embossed invitations were numbered, and a security code printed on the front ensured that no one uninvited would be allowed to leave this ship. Again Alice swallowed hard but managed a smile as she handed the forged invitation over to the large guard. The security man looked it over and without hesitation handed the invitation back to the young American.

"Welcome to the *Golden Child*, Mrs. Hamilton. Your host eagerly awaits your opinion on his collection. Please follow Mr. Chow into the salon."

Alice was about to speak but her words caught in her throat as she realized that she was far more frightened about what she was doing than she thought she would be. Instead Alice nodded her head just once and then followed the largest Chinese man she had ever seen onto the boat deck. As she did, she heard the engines of the *Golden Child* start and then the sound of the anchor being pulled up rattled the teak deck under her heels. She stopped momentarily as she felt the great yacht surge forward in the calm bay of Hong Kong.

"Don't worry, ma'am, the *Golden Child* will anchor ten miles out to sea for . . ." the Chinese brute smiled down at Alice, "security reasons."

Alice knew then that if she needed help of any kind, it wasn't to be found beyond the territorial limits of Hong Kong. That meant if for any reason her true intent was found out, she would find it hard swimming the ten miles back into the bay, especially with a few bullets in her back and sharks following her. She knew then that she might have made the biggest mistake of her young life.

The *Golden Child* put to sea.

Alice Hamilton, a girl of twenty-one from the town of Manassas, Virginia, who until this year had never been farther away from home than the state of Nevada, found herself being escorted to the fantail of the magnificent yacht. As she rounded the corner, she took a deep breath and told herself to relax. As she told herself this, she felt the giant ship give a small shudder and then she felt the slow movement as the *Golden Child* started for the open sea. The departure wasn't noticed by the many men and women on the fantail standing and sipping drinks as waiters and other servants wound their way through the expensively dressed guests.

Alice froze momentarily as she stood looking at the white dinner jackets and budget-breaking gowns worn by the men and women. As they stood with martinis and other beverages in their manicured fingers, she realized as soon as she opened her mouth to one of these people, they would know immediately that she didn't belong. They would eventually see right through the forged invitation that had been prepared for her by the intelligence department inside Department 5656, another little item Garrison would be furious about. She swallowed, wanting to jump off the fantail of the ship before it was too far out to sea.

"The water is extremely cold and you would more than likely get run over by a water taxi—that is if the sharks don't get to you first."

Alice felt her heart catch in her chest at the sound of the thick, even voice behind her. Masked beneath the dark veil of her hat, her eyes closed momentarily as she mentally tried to gather her courage. She opened her eyes and turned.

"And I hope that dress didn't come out of the petty cash drawer in your desk."

Alice looked up and into the face of Garrison Lee. He was dressed in a white dinner jacket, bow-tie, and, of all things horrid in the world, a bright red cummerbund. His eyepatch was placed over his right eye but that didn't stop Alice from seeing that the scarred brow itself was arched in that way Lee had of intimidating those who worked for him. The brown hair was perfectly combed and the small touch of grey at his temples made him look far more menacing than she had remembered seeing him.

"We don't have a petty cash box, and if we did, I would have told you to use it to buy another tuxedo—or at least a cummerbund that doesn't look like you're wearing a stop sign," she said with as much dignity as she could muster, trying to get the upper hand for the battle she knew was coming.

His brow furrowed even more as he self-consciously looked down at his waist as Alice walked past him and toward the group of high-stakes antiquities players. She deftly reached out and took a glass of champagne from a passing waiter without missing a step.

Lee watched her leave and then looked down at the bright red cummerbund once more. He was now actually confused as to how Alice had turned the tables on him before he could get her into a corner about vanishing like she had from her desk at the Event Group complex. He grimaced and then followed Alice into the milling crowd.

"Well, we're here so I suspect you have a plan?" Lee asked the retreating form of Alice. "Most field agents have a plan before going in. Or at the very minimum ask their director to assist in formulating that plan."

"Champagne?" Alice said as she suddenly turned and thrust a glass into Lee's hand. As he reached for it, she suddenly pulled it away. "Oh, I forgot you're a bourbon man," she said as she quickly turned for the bar near the far railing.

Lee smiled and nodded at those few guests that had heard the brief exchange. He nodded and embarrassingly made his way toward Alice who had her back to him while standing at the ornate bar. He stepped to her left and leaned against the bar, letting his cane dangle uselessly at his side, his anger spent for the moment. A few of the high-priced guests who were near the couple looked up and saw the scarred, very large, and very angry man leaning next to them and then they smiled uncomfortably over Lee's facial scars and ducked away.

"You know, Hamilton," Lee said as his eyes momentarily followed the three guests as they exited the bar area of the fantail, "I counted no less than four suspected murderers, two known antiquities thieves, and a well-known and respected British Lord who is suspected of raiding dig sites throughout the Middle East during the British occupation. And I noticed all of this in just the past few seconds walking over here. You, Mrs. Hamilton, are out of your element. And that gets people killed." Lee didn't turn to face her; he just reached out and took the offered drink from the bartender.

"How am I supposed to learn anything stuck in that underground hell you call a complex?" she hissed as she smiled at the bartender as he passed her another glass of champagne.

"Listen, I—"

"Ladies and gentlemen, welcome aboard the *Golden Child*. I believe we have a very special evening in store for your pleasure."

Lee and Alice turned at the sound of the announcement. The man was impeccably dressed in a white tuxedo with a black cummerbund.

"I told you, red is so tacky," Alice hissed through the side of her mouth.

"I apologize for not having the same taste as our host, Lord Hartford Benetton Harrington, the seventeenth Lord of Southington."

"Sounds made-up," Alice said as she looked the stately old gentleman host over from head to toe.

Lee glanced over quickly as he took in Alice for the first time without his anger blinding his one good eye. He saw her eyes beneath the black veil watching their host make his greeting. The perfect jawline coupled with her slightly turned-up nose usually calmed Lee down like no sight in the world, but this night was different. Her looks now had the opposite effect on him as he realized what a dangerous situation the girl had placed herself in.

"Tonight you will be witness to one of the great collections in the world. We will present to you, ladies and gentlemen, many items of history from the dawn of man and his understanding of not just himself, but that of his God, or Gods." Many of the guests nodded their heads appreciatively. Lee just watched with distaste. "These are not just mere antiquities that will thrill and enthrall you at each viewing, ladies and gentlemen, they will mesmerize you— and of course, checks will be acceptable."

The gathered guests chuckled at the humor displayed by the Englishman who smiled and nodded at the men and women as they passed him, heading for the salon belowdecks. Lee noticed that the man had the appearance of a smiling shark as his prey swam around him.

"Since we're here, do you think you could put my perceived shortcomings on the knowledge of field operations aside long enough to allow us to do our job?" Alice said as she pulled the stole around her shoulders and made ready to follow the others. She half-turned and her green eyes settled on Lee's blue one.

"I had already come to that conclusion and told you so before you stormed off half-cocked." He looked at her with an intense gaze. "Don't think this is over, Hamilton."

"Believe me, I know it's not over," she said as she extended her left arm. "Now, shall we see what all of the fuss is about, General?"

Lee smiled enough that his teeth blazed. "By all means, Mrs. Hamilton."

As they fell in line with the crowd walking through the gilded glass doors of the salon, Lee felt many sets of eyes on them. Thus far he had counted at least seven armed guests. At least five heavily armed guards, and of course that wasn't counting the crew. He now felt he and Alice were walking into the bowels of a pirate ship, and he knew also they were making this up on the fly. He leaned in close to Alice when he knew no one was in hearing distance.

"We observe and we take mental notes of the facts of what we see being auctioned. Then we report everything to the Hong Kong police. If we're real lucky, we can get the information on what's here and where in the hell it all came from. All our department is interested in is the history of the pieces involved, not their value, but their provenance. Our job is not recovery. Our job is to document the history of the pieces and discover if we have a historical precedent to alter the perceived historical reference to those items or the location in which they were discovered. Agreed?"

"I never intended anything different," was her short and curt reply.

As the guests walked down a wide carpeted stairway,

Alice was the first to see the black satin-covered objects set up in the massive salon of the *Golden Child*. Spotlights had been arranged for maximum effect after the black dust covers were removed. To Garrison Lee it was nothing more than antiquity thieves making thievery as legitimate-looking as possible.

Alice was the first to notice that some of the objects in the salon were massive in size, while others were small. She quickly counted eighty-seven objects. As the guests were again offered drinks and champagne, the satin covers were slowly pulled away from the items to be sold.

"Ladies and gentlemen, the items on sale here tonight have all been authenticated and a provenance has been established for the . . ." the British Lord smiled almost embarrassingly, ". . . the more controversial pieces." The seventeenth Lord of Southington raised a flute of champagne. "Please, peruse the collection and enjoy, the sale will commence as soon as everyone has viewed the items."

Lee turned slowly, taking in the faces of the buyers. Alice momentarily watched Garrison. She knew his mind was one of those rare things in the world that makes one afraid to know someone too closely. As Lee looked at the faces around them as the guests moved toward the illuminated objects, she knew he was mentally taking a picture of every face he saw. He had a photographic memory and never once forgot a name he had been given or the face that was attached to that name. The man had made Alice extremely uncomfortable before she got to know him in the years since she met him at Walter Reed Army Hospital in 1945 where he was recovering from his devastating wounds received at the end of the war.

"Well, are they all arch-criminals?" she asked as Lee accepted another drink from a waiter.

"While not arch-criminals, yes, there are some very seedy characters here," he said as he pretended to sip at his drink. "And a few others that don't belong here at all." His eyes wandered over to a man who stood in the far corner with a small plate in his hand. The man was slowly eating caviar on toast, and Lee saw that he wasn't that good on his surveillance techniques. "Like this gentleman in the far corner, he seems quite interested in you, far more than the antiquities at auction. I suspect the revealing dress is far more interesting to him than any old broken pottery."

Alice didn't look, she just raised her own eyebrows and then quickly realized Lee couldn't see the copied gesture of interest under her veil.

"Is there anyone else who doesn't belong in this den of thieves, General?"

"A few," he answered and then turned away. "I think we'd better split up; we seem to have attracted the attention of our host."

Alice smiled and then slowly turned and saw Lord Harrington was conferring with a uniformed crewman and two of the plain-clothed security men, and they were looking right at her. Alice turned slowly away and moved into the milling guests as they started to examine the artifacts.

Lee moved off to the far end of the lined exhibit, stopping in front of two urns that had been braced upon the tops of columned pedestals. The director of Department 5656 was just starting to look away when he decided that he needed a closer look at the two urns. His interest perked. The urns were faded, and both had several large cracks coursing through their surfaces where the artisans had taken painstaking time in their reconstruction. Lee saw designs and artwork he wasn't familiar with. He could see they were possibly Canaanite provenance in construct, but the images were unlike any he had ever seen before. The former OSS general leaned closer and read the placard that was attached to the pedestal.

THE BROTHER AND SISTER URNS
UNEARTHED AT TELL ES-SULTAN—THE ANCIENT CITY
   OF JERICHO
12/8/1943

"Son of a bitch," Lee hissed beneath his breath. The exclamation was loud enough that a French woman next to Lee gave him a distasteful look and quickly moved away to the next exhibit.

"Those were almost my exact words when these two beauties were unearthed."

Lee closed his one good eye and then quickly gathered himself as he straightened after reading the placard. He smiled and nodded at the smaller man standing next him. He had a pencil-thin moustache, and his cheeks were reddened, almost as if the man were wearing rouge.

"You must be Lord Harrington?" Garrison asked, placing his hands with his cane behind his back instead of offering the host his hand in greeting.

"The very same, uh, Mr. . . . ?"

"Kilroy, Addison Kilroy," Lee said as he held the man's eyes with his own. Neither man blinked at Lee's use of the infamous cartoon greeting used by a million American servicemen during World War Two—the famous *Kilroy Was Here* graffiti.

"Ah, I see. Many apologies, Mr. Kilroy, so many invitations were sent out I failed to recall sending yours."

Lee reached into his dinner jacket and produced the wax-sealed invitation forged by the same agent at the complex that created the fake documents for Alice.

"Sir, I have no need to see your invitation. I just wanted to greet my guests and offer any explanation of the items that I may."

"Well, I must say these are two very important pieces—if they're real of course. I mean the ruins at Tell es-Sultan are closed to archaeological study, ordered by your government in the forties, and the no-dig policy has been carried over by the new state of Israel."

Lord Harrington smiled and nodded his head. "Yes, the ruins at Tell es-Sultan have been closed, as you can see for very good reason. There are some unscrupulous people in the world today, Mr. Kilroy."

Lee nodded his head and then smiled crookedly. "There

are indeed, sir, very unscrupulous people. I mean the mystical city of Jericho? A lot of people would call that blasphemous to dig there." Lee leaned in close to Lord Harrington who stood his ground not too comfortably against the scarred and very much larger Garrison Lee. "I mean, the city was supposedly destroyed on the orders of God Himself. Frightening stuff," Lee said with his brow arched high above his eye patch, waiting for a reaction from his host.

"Fairy tales to scare the unenlightened, Mr. Kilory."

Lee smiled, broadly this time. "I've learned that fairy tales, when ignored as such, tend to be more truthful in the end than first thought, and that they also usually come back and bite you right in your hindquarters when taken too lightly, Lord Harrington."

The smile from the American was unsettling to the Englishman, enough so that he half-bowed and slowly backed away, nodding toward his security people that this man was to be watched. Lee lost his smile as he turned back to the stolen urns.

Alice nervously looked over her shoulder and saw that Lee was holding his own with their host. She closed her eyes and nearly walked into a woman who was standing in her path.

"Oh, excuse me," Alice said as she placed her empty champagne glass on the tray of a passing waiter. Then her eyes locked on the young girl she had nearly collided with. They were approximately the same age. As Alice looked closer at the raven-haired woman, she could see that dark-haired beauty had one brown eye and one green eye. She was a beautiful girl. Then Alice saw that she was also being examined, *or more to the point,* she thought, she was being sized up by the girl like she was a possible adversary.

"American?" the girl asked as her eyes roamed over the dress Alice was wearing. The young woman was wearing a plain black dress that was as gorgeous as Alice's expensive gown. Her equally black and shiny hair was straight, and she wore large but not ostentatious gold hoop earrings.

"Yes, I'm American," Alice answered as she watched the

young girl with the strange European accent and multi-colored eyes look over every inch of her.

"Yes, I can actually smell the difference," the girl said as she finally stopped examining Alice and then looked into her eyes under the veil.

"Excuse me?" Alice said with that tinge of anger that exposed itself at most times unbidden—Garrison was rubbing off on her—and to her horror she felt her defensive hackles rise.

"Well-fed—Americans smell well-fed," the gorgeous young woman answered as she turned to look at a large stone block. She crossed her arms and looked at the ancient section of wall that once stood at Tell es-Sultan—the ruins of the city of Jericho. "Interesting piece, don't you think. . . . Miss. . . . ?"

"Hamilton, and it's Mrs.," Alice said, looking from the girl to the giant block that looked as if it taxed the carpeted salon deck with its massive weight. Suddenly Alice's eyes widened when she realized what she was looking at. She didn't see that the girl beside her smiled as Alice leaned closer to look at the strange object embedded in the stone.

The block was eight feet high and as many feet thick. It had been rough-hewed and quarried many, many thousands of years before. Alice could see that the tool marks were still clearly visible on the blocks' leading edges, a surefire way of detailing the provenance of the piece as the tools themselves were identified to a certain province of the Middle East.

However, it was the relief of the carving in the dead center of the stone that froze the heart of the American girl from the farmlands of Virginia. The raised outline of the animal was clearly visible. The stone block looked as if the relief was carved around the depiction of something out of a nightmare. The muzzle of the beast could clearly be seen and even the claws of its hands were in stark contrast to the surrounding stone. Alice suddenly realized she wasn't looking at a carving of a deity of some kind from long-ago Jericho, she was looking at an animal that had been crushed between two massive stones. She could even see scorch marks from a long-ago fire. Her eyes went to the stone-colored, and now petrified, beast. It was massive, and as Alice examined the piece, others were drawn to the stone block. Many were crying hoax, and some were angry at an obvious attempt at humor by their host, Lord Harrington.

The young girl smiled as she watched the American woman, and then without another word, and with her eyes on the man Hamilton had been speaking with a moment ago, the strange but beautiful girl left the gathering crowd of skeptical bidders.

Alice never noticed that the woman had left her side as she couldn't remove her eyes from the block and the animal mysteriously encased there. Recognition sprang immediately to her memory.

"Vault 22871," she whispered to herself. Most of the gathered guests had already voiced their opinions on the stone block and its obvious defacement, or outright attempt at a hoax, and then moved on, leaving a stunned and shocked Alice who suddenly turned and knew she had to bring Garrison over to the stone block. The assistant to the director of Department 5656 knew she had stumbled onto something that even the great General Lee could not ignore. As she turned, Alice came face to face with a small and ancient-looking woman.

"You will have to excuse my great-granddaughter, things related to our distant past do not impress her the way that they should."

Alice heard what the old woman was saying but nothing was registering in her head. A well dressed and appointed lady in a light but elegant white gown with pink highlights. Alice placed her age at somewhere in the eighties. Her cane looked like an old wooden walking stick, complete with what on closer inspection looked like the Eye of Ra embossed in gold on the handle. Not an ordinary walking stick. Her clothes were beautiful. The dress was satiny and fine, and her gold jewelry sparkled in the salon spotlights. Alice looked closer and saw the beginnings of a tattoo that began at the woman's neck and then disappeared into her dress. The tattoo was that of a Pentangle, the five-pointed star, but she couldn't see what the rest of the tattoo beheld below the neckline.

"I am Madam Korvesky." She turned to look at the stone block and the animal that had been crushed to death by it more than three thousand years before. "We have come a great distance to denounce this . . . this abomination." The old woman smiled and then looked at Alice with her aged eyes. "But I can see that you have seen this sort of trickery before, my dear, am I correct?" The old woman stepped closer to the young American. "Yes, I see the recognition in your eyes, young one."

Alice didn't say anything at first; she just raised her white-gloved hand and slowly reached out and touched the petrified image of the beast.

"Don't do that." The old woman reached out and lightly took Alice's hand and pulled it away. "Bad things can come of it," she continued, but her next action betrayed her warning as a lie as she herself reached out and lightly ran her old and weathered hand over the stone-hardened fur and teeth of the beast. Then the old woman smiled and looked at Alice. "You seem to not belong among these people." She looked around with distaste etched on her wrinkled features. She tapped her cane on the carpeted deck once, and then a second time. She then smiled again at Alice, making her very uncomfortable.

"You don't seem to belong either," Alice finally managed to say.

"I belong nowhere, my lovely girl. *We* belong nowhere." She leaned close to the American woman and whispered in a deep, East European accent, "You seem kind, not like these . . ." She gestured around her at the men and women eating, laughing, and preparing to buy the stolen items taken from an illegal archaeological dig at Tell es-Sultan, ". . . people, these scavengers of our shared history." The old woman bowed her head and then looked up minus her warm smile. "Forget what you saw here tonight, and if I am correct and you have seen something like this before, tell no one and keep your secret buried. . . ." She hesitated only a moment as she looked deeply into the eyes of Alice Hamilton. "Wherever that may be." Her European accent vanished and her next words were spoken in unaccented English and were far deeper in bass than her voice had been a brief second before. "You have just twenty minutes to remove yourself and your one-eyed handsome escort from this ship, my dear. All of this," she gestured with her wooden cane, even going so far as to accidentally poke an English woman on her rather ample derrière which elicited a shocked yelp and angry look; "is going to be at the bottom of the South China Sea momentarily."

"What?" Alice asked, shocked at the slowness of her reaction.

The old woman had gone. She just melted into the milling buyers as if she had never been there at all.

Lee was getting close to the explosion factor that had made his early years in the Senate a legend, and one of the reasons it was suggested to him by his own party at the time that he was maybe just a little too high-strung for politics. The general always found his temper hard to control when sheer audacity of privilege and corrupt people at every walk of life threatened his keen sense of justice. He brooked no ill will directed at either the people under his command, or his country, and this entire ship was an abomination to the men and women who discovered their history without stealing it.

As his eyes counted the varying degrees of thievery, his eye fell on two small items on display that made his stomach roil. Lord Harrington had actually uncovered human remains at Tell es-Sultan. A cursed thing to do at any archaeological find was to openly display remains that had not been studied and guaranteed to be something from antiquity. It was also something that any well-bred museum curator would find hard to put in any exhibit. Lee shook his head and decided at that moment that this secret auction would remain so forever. These finds would not find their way to the private sector because he would destroy them all first if that need arose.

"I see anger in that one, beautiful eye."

Garrison looked down to see the young woman who had been talking with Alice a moment before. Lee had seen her spying him from across the salon and was uncomfortable with the look she was shooting his way.

"Then you should look closer, young lady, because what I see is sadness that this is happening. And if you're here to place your money on any of these artifacts, I would save it; I think it's going to be a bad investment."

"I was just speaking with your most beautiful companion. I see in her eyes that she adores you."

Garrison looked closer at the raven-haired beauty. Her gaze seemed to go right through him. "Again, you better go take a better look, and study my companion a little closer. Soon enough she will reveal her cloven hooves, horns, and vipercated tail."

The young girl looked confused for the briefest of moments and then smiled and laughed—a disarming and innocent sound that made Lee look twice at the girl standing with her arms crossed over her breasts. Her one brown and one green eye took Garrison in from head to toe. The eyes lingered momentarily on the bright red cummerbund.

"Ah, I see how the game is played with you Americans. Even though you are emphatically in love with someone, you deny it and show nothing but contempt at the mere suggestion of it, even in the face of something so obvious."

Garrison Lee was stunned for a moment. He wasn't used to dallying words with someone so young, but this girl had a way of getting into his thoughts that was just a little unnerving.

"If I may be so bold, you were a soldier, am I correct?" she asked as she watched Lee's lone eye for a lie.

"I and many others."

"Not many aboard this pirate ship, I think," she said as her eyes left Lee for the briefest of moments to study some of the human waste that were the bidders for the world's past. Her double-colored eyes turned back to the general, and this time she examined him like she was looking for a disease. She titled her head and that was when Lee saw the beginning of a tattoo at the base of her neck that wound its way down into the black dress. "You are a keeper of secrets."

"Excuse me?" Garrison said as his smile tried to cover up his consternation at the girl's prognosticative prowess. "I think your crystal ball may be a little cracked, my dear."

The woman placed her small hand on Lee's lapel. "Leave this ship—immediately," she said, and her smile was replaced with a seriousness that Lee found disturbing as he slowly pulled the girl's hand free of his jacket. Her smile slowly returned as Alice joined them, her eyes on the girl.

"I see you espouse cryptic things to complete strangers and then you go off and flirt with a man who is old enough to be your father," Alice looked from the girl and then back to Lee, "or your grandfather."

Lee's brow furrowed once again, only this time without much enthusiasm or threat behind it.

The young girl, who reminded Lee of the gypsies he had met while on assignment during the war, smiled even wider as she turned to look at Lee.

"My crystal ball isn't as cracked as you would like to believe." She bowed toward Alice and then to Lee. "Mrs. Hamilton, Senator Lee." The young woman turned and left without another glance.

Lee and Alice watched the young girl take her great-grandmother's arm, and with one last smile at the both of them, the two strange guests of Lord Harrington left the salon.

"Strange, I don't think I—"

"Told her you were a former senator," Alice finished for Lee.

"And I don't fancy being lectured to by a twenty-year-old girl on the politics of world history," Lee looked down at Alice, "or anything else for that matter."

Alice patted Lee's thick arm. "Calm down or your good

eye will pop out of your head." Alice smiled at some guests standing near them when she leaned into Lee. "I got a tip that we should leave this ship in no uncertain terms unless we want to see this boat turn into a submarine." Alice looked right at Lee. "And for some reason I believe my source."

"I saw you looking at the block of stone." He turned and faced his assistant. "Get it out of your head. There is no relationship to Vault 22871." He quickly held up his hand, his cane dangled as he stopped Alice from speaking. "That is a hoax—a forgery. I heard some genius in the peanut gallery say it was Anubis, the jackal-headed god that held sway over the dead, until old Anubis was ousted by Osiris, at least according to the Egyptian priests at the time. I don't think the god Anubis got slammed between two rocks during the actual historic siege of Jericho. This petrified monstrosity is as fake as that thing the Group has in Vault 22871."

"That is your opinion; everyone else thinks the animal remains in 22871 are viable. Our best people say there have been no post-mortem alterations to the bones—the same alterations that would have had to occur to this animal right here. The articulated hips can clearly be seen under the petrified fur. The fingers and claws, Garrison, look at the fingers and claws for God's sake; they are exactly the same as the remains the U.S. Army recovered in France after World War I!"

Lee looked around as other guests started to pay them unwanted attention.

"Calm yourself, Hamilton, I believe *you* believe it. But this is ridiculous, Anubis for crying out loud." Lee wanted to walk Alice to the ancient stone block and take a hammer and chisel to it and prove that this display was nothing more than a curiosity and no one would take it seriously. "There is one thing that really tears at my ass when it comes to our own science departments; that's the fact that there has never been one of these animals ever found in the fossil record the world over."

"After inventorying every item we have in the Event Group vaults, you have the guts to say that to me? No fossil record?

Just when does that prove the non-existence of an animal? You of all people should know there are things out there we know nothing of, even the great General Garrison Lee is capable of being wrong once in a few hundred damn years."

Lee saw the anger in Alice's eyes and her words were scathing, almost the same exact speech he had given, no, shouted at his people at the Group since he took directorship of Department 5656.

Garrison looked around and nodded as people were passing by with their secret bidding envelopes and giving them looks that were making Lee feel extremely uncomfortable.

"Okay, I'll give you that one, Hamilton, but—"

"Good evening, I couldn't help but overhear your conversation, as well as many other men and women here."

Lee and Alice simultaneously looked over at a small man wearing the traditional headdress of the Palestinian people of the Gaza Strip—the kuffiyeh, the checkered head scarf seen on every male of the region. That was where the similarities fell off sharply however. The tuxedo the small man wore was cut perfectly and fit the bearded man to a "t".

"Mr. Kilroy, I don't think I have had the honor," the man said as his eyes fell on Alice.

"Alice, this is Mr. Hakim Salaams Saldine, our resident Palestinian authority on ancient Jericho—Saldine, Mrs. Alice Hamilton, also an authority it seems on ancient Jericho and the animal life contained behind her ancient walls."

Alice ignored the small insult and held her gloved hand out as the man kissed it, making sure not to touch the hand itself.

"So, you are an authority on Jericho. What is your opinion on the talk of the auction?"

The man looked confused at first and then smiled. "I do not offer my opinion on things that are irrelevant, and believe me, my young friend, that is the most irrelevant piece I have ever examined—it is a hoax."

"You have been to Tell es-Sultan?" Alice asked as she looked at the newcomer's reaction.

"Yes, many times have I ventured to Jericho. I'm afraid it

has never held that much value to us as a people. It was, after all, a place of defeat for us."

Alice smiled and nodded at the man, and then she looked at Lee and the smile vanished. The man continued to insult her intelligence and she was getting seriously sick of it. It was time to put General Garrison Lee in his place.

"You do know where you made your mistake don't you, Mr. Saldine, if that is your name?"

"Excuse me?" the man said, trying to keep his features neutral.

"The ancient word Jericho is thought to derive from the Canaanite word Reah, which you obviously should know already, I mean, since you are an authority and all and obviously a Palestinian." Alice smiled again. "This little Virginia farm girl learned at an early age in continued Bible school taught by her uncle, that Reah in Palestinian, or Jericho if you will, is pronounced totally different. It's spelled with a 'Y,' not a 'J', which was clearly pronounced when you said the word very clearly," Alice smiled as she made a show of looking around the room. The man shuffled from one foot to the other. Lee rolled his good eye, knowing Alice was hanging them both out to dry.

"What is your point, madam?" the man with the head-dress asked, looking over at Lee who just grimaced, waiting for the other shoe to fall.

"Mr. Saldine, you are no more Palestinian than Garrison Lee here. You are Israeli intelligence, maybe Mossad, maybe just a policeman, but definitely no Palestinian. When you pose as another nationality, at least make sure you stick with their language, not your own," Alice dipped her head and moved away.

"Who in the bloody hell is that?" the man caught in the lie asked.

"She's a royal," Lee said as he started to go after Alice.

"A royal?" the Israeli asked.

"A royal pain in my ass; Hamilton, wait a minute."

Alice stopped on her way to the salon staircase. She turned to face her employer.

"When are you going to stop this unrelenting testing of my knowledge? It took me all of a minute to figure out who your buddy was. Trust, Garrison, that's what's missing in your soul, trust." She started to turn away but Lee grabbed her arm.

"Look, his name is Ally Ben-Nevin. He just took over the Gaza region for state security. He's here to keep the Palestinian people and his own from having their shared history vanish into rich European mansions."

"And you're telling me he knows who you are?" she asked, skeptical at the very least.

"Of course not, Truman would have me hung from the Washington Monument if that little secret got out. No, Hamilton, he thinks we work for the State Department."

"I'm shocked that you're competent enough to pull off that little deception without getting caught."

"Okay, that's about enough of—"

A tremendous explosion rocked the *Golden Child* from bow to stern.

Alice was thrown forward and Lee wasn't far behind. As the ship listed sharply to the starboard side, Garrison saw what was happening and quickly pulled Alice aside as the giant block from Jericho tilted crazily on its steel pedestal. Alice was able to pull her legs free at the last second as Garrison pulled on her for all he was worth. The stone block hit the carpeted deck, and then after a moment's hesitation, the massive weight of the block smashed through the teak wood and then crashed into the bowels of the ship. Lee was stunned as a giant geyser of water shot through the opening and slammed into the ornate chandelier on the ceiling. Water and glass cascaded onto the men and women trying to pick themselves up off the deck.

"I believe our host may have angered someone, I think this bloody ship is sinking," Ben-Nevin said as he helped both Lee and Alice to their feet.

With water already lapping at Lee's ankles, he quickly reached into his jacket and pulled an old Colt .45 automatic from the hidden place beneath his bright red cummerbund.

He turned and looked at Alice and just winked with his good eye.

"Now you know why the giant red cummerbund, Hamilton." Lee nodded his head at Mossad agent Ben-Nevin and then gestured toward the large staircase where people were finally making their way out of the salon. "May I suggest we see if there's another mode of transportation back to Hong Kong?"

Around them, horns and sirens were blaring and men and women were screaming. Lee just started pushing women and men toward the stairs. Alice turned and the last thing she saw of Lee was him disappearing into the panicked crowd of secret bidders. The lights flickered and then went out to the accompaniment of more screams and shouts. Somewhere in the darkness a gunshot sounded. Then was followed by another. Lee found a woman on the flooded floor and assisted her to her feet. It was the haughty English woman who had given Lee a most distasteful look earlier in the evening.

"This is unacceptable, unacceptable!" the woman screamed as she tried to push Lee's hands from her.

"Well, you're going to find out there's a hell of a lot more that's unacceptable in a minute if you don't get your fat ass up those stairs." He slapped her hard on her behind, sending the shocked socialite through the water. As Lee watched her leave, he saw a small statue float by in the churning and boiling waters. His eyes widened when he saw the wolf's head and the articulated hands depicted on the carved wood. Lee reached out and grabbed one of the surviving auction pieces and then shoved it into Ben-Nevin's jacket pocket. "Get this to your people and tell them they're hemorrhaging antiquities and the bloodsuckers are getting rich. Now go!" Lee pushed Ben-Nevin away even as his eyes didn't understand.

As the eighty-plus guests and crew fought their way through the jumble of tumbled and broken artifacts and buffet items, Lee saw that the water was rising far faster than the men and women were moving. The ship must have taken a shape charge directly to her waterline and possibly one to her keel. A professional job if he was correct.

The last twenty men and women were close to the top of the stairs when something blew. It knocked several people back and over the top of the darkened stairs. Lee saw Agent Ben-Nevin hurled into the far wall where he hit and then slid into the water. Garrison pulled the Mossad agent to his feet and pushed him toward the now bent and burning stairs.

The fire was spreading across the ceiling of the salon. Lee saw that his escape was blocked, both at the main salon entrance and the exit leading to the galley.

"Oh, this is good," he said as he quickly shoved the Colt back into his pants and then scanned the interior of the darkened and fire-lit salon for Alice, but she was nowhere to be seen. For the first time in many, many years, Garrison Lee was frightened. Frightened that he had lost someone he really cared about. He shook his head as the flames and the water were coming close to meeting in the middle, one from above, the other from below. Fire and water were to be his downfall. He knew he could deal with that, but not losing Alice before he had a chance to tell her that the strange little girl from this evening had been absolutely correct about his feelings for Hamilton. Now he would never be able to say anything to her, not even to apologize about the vault and the secret hidden there deep under the Nevada desert. Especially since he was not entirely a nonbeliever on the subject, he just hadn't wanted to cave in front of Alice and Ben-Nevin. He loved Alice, had from the very first moment he had laid his one good eye upon her in the hospital in Washington, D.C., in 1945 when she had come to enquire about the husband she had lost in South America during the war. Why he thought the most beautiful woman in the world would, or even could, love a man as scarred as physically and emotionally as Lee, he could never figure out. But Lee knew he had to try. As flames reached from above and water from below, Garrison Lee made a quick decision and then dove headfirst into the gaping hole where the wall block and its strange animal had vanished when it crashed through the deck to the spaces below.

"You!" The shout came from behind Lee as he examined

just how desperate the situation was becoming. As he turned, he saw their host, Lard Harrington, standing between two of his guards. They had guns pointed his way. The Englishman was soaked and his hairpiece looked as if it had hit an iceberg. "I don't know who you are, but you did this!"

Lee was beginning to wonder if his real identity and intentions were stenciled on him at some unseen location on his body. First the girl and now this antiquities thief seemed to be excellent guessers at his true vocation. Garrison felt the weight of the old Colt .45 in his cummerbund but knew he would never reach it.

"Who sent you?" the Englishman asked as another, even larger geyser of sea water shot through the massive hole in the deck. Garrison saw his opportunity as he was obscured at the last second by the eruption. He pulled the gun, ripping away the hated cummerbund, and dove for the water. He surfaced and with the biggest guess of his life Lee took a chance and started shooting as soon as he surfaced. The first two .45 caliber rounds missed. The third struck one of the armed men and sent him backward into the roiling waters. The Englishman's eyes widened as Lee took quick aim at the second man and fired. The bullet caught the man dead center in the forehead. He slowly eased himself back down into the water, not feeling anything in his now-dead brain. Garrison quickly moved the barrel toward Lord Harrington.

"No, no," he shouted, raising his arms up.

Normally Garrison would have had no compunction in shooting the thief, but he also realized that it wasn't his job. He lowered the .45 automatic. The look on Harrington's face was decidedly relieved. That was short-lived, however, when, as Lee looked on in stunned silence, a three-foot-long aluminum shaft slammed into Harrington. The small spear protruded from his chest as he stared down at the instrument that had killed him. He slowly looked up at Lee who grimaced as he realized the man had been murdered right in front of him and among the chaos of the sinking *Golden Child*. He watched Harrington also slide beneath the water.

As Garrison looked around, aiming the gun in the darkness and the flickering electrical shorts, he saw what he was searching for immediately. The girl smiled, lowered her diving mask, and then tossed the spear gun toward Lee. The young woman with the strange eyes waved at Lee and then vanished into the roiling waters. Garrison saw one of her fins swipe at the air as she kicked away beneath the shattered deck.

Lee quickly decided that the girl was showing him a way out. He dove after her, praying that Alice had made it to the main deck and over the side.

Alice watched as the panic-driven guests fought their way to the main deck. She angrily removed the fur stole and her white gloves as she reached down to assist an elderly man to his feet and then unceremoniously pushed him over the railing of the vastly listing *Golden Child*.

"Goddamn it, Garrison, where in the hell are you?" she shouted at the many frightened faces jumping over the side of the ship. She kicked off her high heels and furiously started back toward the salon opening.

Lee held his breath as he felt the shudder come from beneath the *Golden Child*. He knew then that another scuttling charge had gone off, sending a pressure wave through his eardrums that came near to stunning him. The blast was obviously meant to send the six-million-dollar yacht to the bottom of the South China Sea. The murder of the antiquities thieves and bidders had been meticulously planned out. The first charge was meant to send the guests scurrying off the ship. The second was intentionally meant to break the back of the *Golden Child* and send her to the bottom. A tactic Lee had used himself on numerous occasions during the war, both in Europe and South America.

As he swam though the darkness, a fresh rush of sea water struck him from beneath. The powerful explosion placed along the keel of the ship sent a torrent of heated water upward where it slammed Lee into the very block that Alice had been mesmerized with not fifteen minutes earlier and that now sat at the lowest portion on decking near the engines.

Garrison was starting to lose faith that he had enough air left in his lungs to escape through the bottom of the *Golden Child*. As his hands fought for purchase against the rush of incoming sea, his fingers tore loose a large section of the stone block from Jericho. He held on to the small piece of stone as his vision started to tunnel and his lungs were close to exploding.

He knew he would never see Alice again. And he found that was the only regret he had. Alice.

Suddenly his leg was tugged on and he felt himself being pulled farther down into the water. Whoever had his leg was not too gently pulling him to the bottom of the engine spaces where all hell was breaking loose. As Garrison fought to keep consciousness, he saw the floating bodies of many of the *Golden Child*'s crewmen. Most were burned and some had parts of their bodies missing from the two powerful explosions. He was pulled even farther along the hull. Then suddenly Lee and his savior were free of the *Golden Child*. The water was much cooler as he felt himself rising from the depths. When he broke the surface of the choppy sea, he didn't think he had enough strength to take a deep breath, then just before he did, he felt his face being slapped hard.

"Don't you know when you abandon ship you head to the deck, not the engine room?" the voice said as a life preserver was thrust into his hands.

Lee tried to catch his breath as he saw who his rescuer was—the young gypsy girl from the salon. She was treading water not inches from Lee's face. Her smile caught the senator off guard.

"Don't think us cruel," she said as her swim fins kept her easily above the choppy water. "I set the first charge to scare the guests, the second to sink the ship, but I'm afraid it went off too early. I'm really not that good with explosives."

"Who are you and who made you judge, jury, and executioner?" Lee said, spitting saltwater from his mouth.

"I am no one, Mister Lee, but the woman who gave the execution order is that Pig Harrington's judge, jury, and executioner, and also my queen." The girl smiled and lowered her dive mask. "Your woman is your equal, American, but don't allow her to follow us. It will only bring her grief. If we ever meet again, keeper of secrets, it will not go so well for you."

Lee started to say something, but the girl quickly turned and swam away. As she did, the tattoo along her neck and back was more exposed as the girl dove back into the water. The Eye of Ra was clearly discernible on her neck. Lee watched her swim away as sirens and patrol boats from the distant harbor were starting to get closer to the scene of the tragedy.

"Thank God!"

Lee quickly turned around in the water.

"Hamilton!" he said as he reached for her.

Alice placed her arms around Lee, and then they both just remained that way as the seas lifted them and then lowered their floating bodies back down. As Lee held her, he noticed that they were being carried away from the survivors and the arriving rescuers.

"We better start swimming or it may be a while before I can apologize for being such an ass."

Suddenly and before Alice could speak, a splash sounded next to them. As Lee looked up, he saw that an inflatable raft had been tossed into the sea.

"As I said, my crystal ball may be cracked, but it still shows a pretty clear picture of future events. Mrs. Hamilton, Mr. Lee, good luck, and swim that way."

Lee and Alice looked up onto an ancient-looking Chinese junk. Standing at the railing was the young raven-haired girl. She was still wearing a wetsuit and was wrapped in a blanket. Standing next to her and leaning on the old wooden railing, the girl's grandmother stood with her arm through that of the girl for support. The junk was slowly pulling out of the debris field left by the sinking *Golden Child*.

"Remember, Mrs. Hamilton, what you have seen here

tonight cannot be." She slowly waved her small hand as did her grandmother. "God doesn't have that kind of sense of humor, after all, animals like that cannot, should not exist, God wouldn't have it," the girl shouted. The junk slowly vanished into a fog bank and was gone.

"That has got to be the strangest girl I have ever met."

Lee didn't answer Alice, he just pulled the CO_2 cylinder, and the raft immediately inflated. He pulled himself in and then Alice after him. As the sirens and the screams slowly started to fade because of distance, Lee looked into the fog after the fleeing Chinese junk.

"What are you thinking?" Alice asked as she slowly pulled the expensive gown over her head and then tossed it into the boat. Her slip was soaked through and Lee could see that Alice was in no mood to care who could see her body underneath the thin material—especially Garrison Lee.

As the small boat bobbed in the water and searchlights started to poke through the mist, Lee reached into his jacket pocket and pulled out the piece of stone he had torn from the block after it had fallen through the deck. He looked it over and then pressed the large piece into his palm and closed his fingers around it.

"I'm thinking we had better take a closer look at what we have in Vault number 22871 when we get back to the complex."

Alice tilted her head as she also tossed the wide-brimmed hat into the sea. She shook out her long brunette hair and then quickly caught the item Lee tossed to her.

"Because I have never seen anyone go that far to create a hoax."

As Alice brought the chunk of block closer to her salt-encrusted vision, her heart froze. "Yes, I think we may have a little more something to investigate at Jericho than just the ancient ruins of the city, because something else was happening a few thousand years ago that isn't recorded in the Bible."

As the small piece rolled in Alice's hand, the bone was clearly seen underneath the petrified fur of that long-dead animal. What antiquities forger would think to do that, place bone under the petrified skin of a hoax?

Alice Hamilton and Garrison Lee of the Event Group had learned that night for the first time that things do go bump in the night and there is always the beast under the bed and in the closet. *So, yes, Mrs. Hamilton*, Lee thought, *there really may be monsters in the world.*